A Certain
Finkelmeyer

A CERTAIN FINKELMEYER

By

FELIX ROZINER

Translated by

MICHAEL HENRY HEIM

W · W · Norton & Company

New York   London

The text of this book is composed in Sabon,
with the display set in Trump Mediaeval Semi Bold Condensed.
Composition and manufacturing by
The Maple-Vail Book Manufacturing Group.
Book design by Margaret M. Wagner.

First Edition.

Library of Congress Cataloging-in-Publication Data
Roziner, Feliks, 1936–
[Nekto Finkel 'maĭer. English]
A certain Finkelmeyer / Felix Roziner ; translated by Michael
Henry Heim.
p.   cm.
Translation of: Nekto Finkel 'maĭer.
I. Title.
PG3485.6.Z55N4513   1991
891.73'44—dc20   90–49195

ISBN 0–393–02962–X

W.W. Norton & Company, Inc., 500 Fifth Avenue, New York, N.Y. 10110
W.W. Norton & Company, Ltd., 10 Coptic Street, London WC1A 1PU

1 2 3 4 5 6 7 8 9 0

People say a writer is destined to live the life of his hero. Whether or not that is so, I was once pushed over the line dividing me from that life. I still do not know what saved me. But I do know what saved the novel from almost inevitable disaster: many close friends and many friends I scarcely knew.

It is to them that I owe its publication and to them, inside and outside Russia, that I dedicate it.

FELIX ROZINER
January 1981

PART ONE

—Quel est cet homme?
—Ha, c'est un bien grand talent, il
fait de sa voix tout ce qu'il veut.
—Il devrait bien, madame, s'en
faire une culotte.

"What sort of man is he?"
"He is extremely talented. He can do
anything he desires with his voice."
"He'd best make a pair of breeches
with them, Madame."

ALEXANDER PUSHKIN,
Egyptian Nights
(Epigraph to Chapter One)

I

AFTER several hours in flight—the plane was far beyond the Urals—the clouds below grew dark, the windows went blank, and the lights came on in the cabin.

Nikolsky was at a loss to keep himself occupied. He had finished reading the newspapers and looking through the documents he had brought with him, made a list of things he would have to do after reaching his destination, and even arranged them in order of priority, though he knew perfectly well that circumstances would take no account of either himself or his list. Every town, every enterprise, had its own laws and, what was more important, its own way around them, and the success of his trip would depend on whether he was agile enough to turn the local customs to his advantage.

He drifted into a kind of lazy self-pity.

Here you are, off for the back of beyond again, about to pontificate to a bunch of strangers, listen to the stupid things they say, and respond with a show of earnest concern, sleep in a room with God knows who. . . . It's always worse when they pack you off to the ends of the earth saying "Emergency, no time to lose, immediate departure!" without even a hotel reservation. I wonder whether a dump like—what's the name of the place?—Zaalaisk even *has* a hotel. . . . The trips aren't all bad, of course; I couldn't get along without them, in fact.

But as usual the moment he felt tempted by a little soul-searching, he cut himself short.

"Enough, enough. The same old story," he said almost aloud. Then all at once his lips, obeying an involuntary and seemingly unmotivated impulse, whispered, "Go fleetly, do not stumble, hunted stag . . ."

The words took him by surprise. He repeated them over and over, trying to recall how and when they had become embedded in his memory. All he could remember was that "hunted stag" rhymed with "stunted day," a rhyme Nikolsky found especially appealing. A tired deer, running across the dreary tundra with its brief polar day, the boundary, never far, of night, death, nothingness—now that is poetry! And all at once his mind lit up with recognition: he had seen the lines in the magazine lying open before his neighbor—a strange-looking man with a gaunt, sickly face.

When requesting a window seat, Nikolsky had wondered who would end up next to him for the many long hours of the flight, the B to his A. Luckily, B had turned out to be of an intellectual bent and, more important, a nontalker. Despite the tedium of plane trips, to say nothing of endless journeys in train compartments, Nikolsky found travel chitchat highly distasteful. Not that he was particularly taciturn or a bad listener, but you had to be favorably disposed to an act of communication, you had to be in the mood for it, and on the road—good God, the people you were thrown together with. Whether you listened or not, they'd worm their way into your thoughts and turn theirs inside out for you—filth, degradation, misfortune, and all! Four people trapped in a compartment, each, like Tolstoy's Pozdnyshev, Pozdnyshev, with his "Kreutzer Sonata" to tell. . . . But that poor hunted stag still plagued Nikolsky, and in the end he turned his head to the right and put his neighbor through a careful examination.

What he saw was a clearly delineated profile: a long, conspicuously aquiline nose, expressive lips, a small chin, and that peculiar sort of small eyelid that makes the eyes seem fixed, unable to blink—in a word, birdlike. And in fact the man was staring fixedly, motionlessly, at the seat in front of him, very much self-absorbed. Nikolsky had no intention of launching into intimacies; he simply wanted to have a look at the magazine.

"Excuse me," he said, leaning over to the man. "May I!" He motioned to the thick magazine lying in the man's lap.

At first the man looked up at him uncomprehendingly, but then he nodded and reached for the magazine with thin, recalcitrant fingers. The magazine fell open and began to slip between his shaking knees. Nikolsky managed to catch it, though crumpling and nearly tearing out a page in the process. At that moment the man gave a nervous twitch, bumping into Nikolsky's elbow and dealing himself what appeared to be a painful blow just below the ribs.

"I'm so sorry!" Nikolsky muttered, embarrassed. His neighbor's case of nerves had now infected him, and he was furious with himself for having asked for the damn magazine in the first place.

"No, no! It's my fault! All mine!" the man objected, waving his arms and wiggling his long fingers. "I'm a regular cripple. Look at these prongs. They can't do a thing!" He laughed uneasily, opening a mouth full of teeth so close to one another they seemed to overlap. Nikolsky had the feeling the man was as used to bearing the blame as others were used to laying it elsewhere; he personally disliked both extremes, nor was he inclined to accept this pitiful creature's apologies.

"Stop it! Please! Thank you for the magazine. Sorry to have bothered you."

Nikolsky's delivery was so brusque that his neighbor instantly fell silent, turned away, and, letting his hands drop back into his lap, assumed his former detached pose.

The name of the magazine was *Friendship*. As was plain from the list of authors on the title page, it specialized in translations from literatures of the non-Russian nationalities. Since none of the fifteen or twenty names rang a bell, Nikolsky started thumbing through the pages, skimming those with poems on them. One after the other they proved to be silly, high-flown bouts of rhetoric coerced into a meter and surrounded with empty, unnecessary rhymes by the cold calculation of their translators. As a poetry lover Nikolsky felt something akin to revulsion. Then, close to the end of the issue, he found what he was after.

There were five of them in all, and together they took up only two facing pages. They were separated by asterisks; none had its own title. The only signs of identification were the heading—"Selected Poems by Aion Neprigen"—and a line of small italic print at the end that read "Authorized Translation from the Tongor." Nikolsky immediately delved into the poems.

They were magnificent. Each line had an unexpected something, childlike yet simple, embedded in it; each quatrain formed a unit of its own, yet flowed naturally into the next; and the poem as a whole—after the short pause the singer needs to take a deep breath and raise his voice higher, project it farther—the poem, barely ceasing, drew you into the following quatrain, which sounded both similar and slightly different. They reminded Nikolsky of a line from an A. K. Tolstoy poem, "in the field every stalk, in the sky every star"; they had a primordial feeling about them, a feeling of the world's perfection, overlaid by a mother-of-pearl-like reflection of the North and suffused with an inexplicable, all but ineffable yearning. And only in the final poem, the one about the hunted stag, did the nature of the yearning become clear. Everything dies, everything disappears in this world, even the splendid stag, for as soon as its strength fails, the hunter shoots it and sets his dogs on its still-warm carcass. When Nikolsky read the last line—"The sun awash with azure in the sky"—he suddenly thought, Yes, yes, the sun at its peak! It's like Dante: "In the middle of the journey of our life . . ." But in Dante the otherworldly plays a part, whereas here . . . Once the short summer is over, the polar night sets in—ice, eternity, nothingness. . . .

No, really, thought Nikolsky, he had to have a copy for himself. He glanced at the cover and made a mental note of the issue number, but what if it was no longer available? No, the only thing to do was copy them, all five of them.

He took out his notebook and pen, undid the latch of the tray-table in front of him, pulled it down, and began to write. He caught himself whispering the lines, savoring one or another of them, using his best penmanship. A feeling akin to bliss enveloped him, and he experienced a kind of spiritual epiphany: he still had it in him to feel, be moved by, take simple delight in, beauty. He even felt his face break into a smile, but sensing his neighbor's glance on him he quickly wiped it off. Annoyed, he turned to repay the glance and was amazed to see—at close range, indecently close range—two enormous shiny pupils brimming with tears. Nikolsky and the man sat motionless for several moments. Then suddenly the man let out a sob, twitched again, and, grabbing Nikolsky's hand, pressed his lips to it.

"What are you doing?" Nikolsky all but screeched, tearing his hand away from the man's prehensile, inhumanly long fingers.

Passengers began turning in their direction. The madman loosened his grip at last. Nikolsky released the afflicted hand, and the two men sat motionless again, embarrassed by what had gone on between them.

"Why did you . . . do that?" Nikolsky whispered. "It was disgusting."

"Yes, you're right! You're right," the man muttered in an overwrought, almost delirious voice. "But still . . . I was so grateful . . .

I didn't know how to thank you. You'll forgive me, I hope. I know it looked terrible, but I . . . I . . . ."

His voice broke off, his arms and legs started flailing, and his knees and pointy elbows underwent a series of complex maneuvers: he was preparing to extract a handkerchief from his inside pocket; he wanted to wipe his eyes.

"I'll be all right in no time at all," he said, already a good deal calmer. "No time at all. In a minute everything will be back to normal."

Before long he had in fact calmed down completely. His face even registered a hint of an ironic smile, and his words, or rather the way he intoned them, had a caustic ring. So abrupt a transition in his neighbor's mood rather perplexed Nikolsky.

"Let's see now: hysterics, neurasthenic behavior, a comic exterior, and to top it all—a slobbery kiss on the hand! What do you make of that, eh?" The man gave a little laugh and waved a hand in the air. "Yes, what must *you* think if *I* find myself so sickening! You really must believe me. A case of nerves—that's all. You understand, don't you? I can tell you're sensitive too. And here you pick up your pen and a slobbering idiot grabs your hand and—"

"Don't be ridiculous!" said Nikolsky sharply, to stem the man's tirade. "You know nothing about my sensitivity. The whole thing is too . . . Let's not talk about it anymore."

If Nikolsky sounded annoyed, it was because he was angry with himself for having tried to hide his repulsion and angry with his neighbor for not only sensing the kind of impression he had made but making a statement about it.

"Don't worry," said his neighbor with another of those little laughs.

"Worry! Who's worrying? You or me?"

"Now it's you," the man fired back at Nikolsky with aplomb. "And I was right, wasn't I?"

"Right about what?"

"About your sensitivity."

Nikolsky shrugged his shoulders.

"You didn't just read those poems; you devoured them. Not many people have it in them to read poetry like that. And then you started copying them into your notebook."

The man is clearly laughing in my face, Nikolsky thought as he felt that face blush red. Serves me right, copying out poems like a mawkish adolescent! What a thing to do! Stupid of me!

"Here's your magazine back," said Nikolsky in an almost hostile tone.

"No," said the man, shaking his head. "Keep it."

"Thank you," said Nikolsky sardonically, arching into as much of a bow as the seat permitted.

"Look at me." The man's voice was so even and composed that Nikolsky was obliged to look him in the eye, obliged to see the terrifying aloofness in his face, and the grief—deep, hopeless grief. "I want you to understand. I thank *you*. *Thank* you. You see, those are my poems you were reading. I watched you as you read them . . . watched the expression on your face. You can't imagine what it meant to me. . . ."

And he turned away.

II

DURING the thirty or forty minutes that remained before landing, the strange man said no more. Nikolsky too was silent, but his thoughts were in a state of turmoil. He tried to look calm, but found it impossible to sit motionless like his neighbor, and kept shifting in his seat or rummaging through his papers. When the plane began to lose altitude, Nikolsky played the curious passenger who is flying for the first time and keeps his eyes glued to the window the moment anything comes into sight. Watching the scattered lights below him, Nikolsky kept thinking how unreal the whole thing seemed: his ungainly neighbor, their silly tiff over the magazine, the poems he found so moving, the gratitude he found so outlandish, and then the man's confessing to having written them—what was going on, anyway? No, one of us must be a bit touched in the head, he thought. And even though he's the more likely candidate, I'm not much better. Why did I let myself get so wrought up? "Uncommonly agitated," as they used to put it. "Uncommonly agitated, the count proceeded to the boudoir with rapid steps. There he found Madame

de Grisot . . ." What is this nonsense? Come on, Count. We're landing. Make sure you haven't left any of your valuables in the over-
head compartment. . . .

As soon as the engine noise subsided, the passengers jumped up
and crowded the aisles. After any number of superfluous gestures
Nikolsky's neighbor managed to escape from his seat as well. He
proved to be a rail of a man, well over six feet tall. Advancing behind
him in fits and starts, Nikolsky observed a narrow back, jutting
shoulder blades, shaggy hair above the nape, and a deep, childlike
hollow in the middle of the head.

Having made their way down the steps and begun to cross the
dark airfield, where a snowstorm was in progress and their faces
immediately froze, the two men walked side by side. Nikolsky felt
it would be awkward to hasten his step or fall behind. Given the
poetry encounter and its aftermath they could no longer be considered utter strangers. His neighbor apparently felt the same: he
was clearly trying to adapt his stride to Nikolsky's and even turned
in Nikolsky's direction from time to time, losing his step, getting
caught in the folds of his coat, and gasping the burning-cold air
through his half-open mouth.

At last they came to the airport building, a small, filthy one-room
affair with gray-green water-stained walls and iron potbellied stoves
in the corners. It was overheated by the stoves and stuffy from the
many weary people dozing on the benches, crowding round the
refreshment counter, and besieging the single ticket window.

"Well, we're here," said Nikolsky, surveying the sickeningly
familiar scene. He surprised himself by adding, "What's your destination?"

In lieu of an answer his new acquaintance said confidently, "You
must have a room booked at the hotel."

Nikolsky shook his head.

"In that case . . . let's see, it's ten now, isn't it? The Moscow flight
doesn't leave until half past twelve. People won't be checking out
for another hour, hour and a half, and you'll have to wait until the
rooms are ready. . . . What would you say . . . what if we had something to eat?"

"But it's so revolting here," Nikolsky objected, glancing over at
the restaurant sign. It was decorated with paintings of blue roses.

"Here?" said the man, first clasping his hands, then burying his neck in his shoulders as if choking. "Why, you'd never get out of here alive! No, we'll go to the hotel. There at least . . . well, there you have a fifty-fifty chance of survival."

Nikolsky laughed. They left the building just in time to jump onto a departing bus.

So he's not staying at the hotel himself, thought Nikolsky. But he couldn't be a local. He's not the type.

They made it to the hotel without further incident. There a sprightly old man popped up from a stool and tossed aside a newspaper to help them off with their coats and scarves, which he skillfully draped over his arm like so many napkins, and their fur hats, which he placed reverently on top.

In the restaurant they took a window seat near a corner, as far as possible from the podium, where, encouraged by the twangings and poundings of four musicians, a heavy, aging woman in a close-fitting green taffeta dress was huskily crooning "Love Is a Planet All Its Own" while trying to have some kind of sex with the microphone. They ordered a small carafe of vodka, a plate of sprats, a salad, the only hot meat dish, and coffee. "Oh, and later, Nikolsky added, "when you serve the coffee, bring us a hundred grams of cognac." There were no lemons, of course. "Chocolates?" the waitress offered. Nikolsky gave a sluggish wave of the hand that translated as why not.

When the vodka came, Nikolsky filled their vodka glasses and raised his own. "Well, shall we drink to our acquaintance? My name is Nikolsky. Leonid Pavlovich."

"Glad to meet you," said his table companion, breaking into a broad smile. "As for my name—well, I'm warning you, it's quite a mouthful! Aaron-Chaim Mendelevich Finkelmeyer, at your service! Cheers!"

"Old Testament, eh?" said Nikolsky. "Cheers!"

They drank, passing the sprats back and forth and helping themselves to salad, discussing whether it was good or not, whether it needed salt, filling their vodka glasses again, going on about the insignificant but pleasant things that are in fact absolutely essential when two people sitting together know next to nothing about each other, but know that after the next vodka they'll suddenly feel a lot closer, almost intimate, and their tongues will loosen and they'll start learning things—well, not only about their drinking partner, they'll suddenly learn something astonishing about themselves.

Both of them felt pleasantly warm. The frost, the crowd on the bus, the commotion at the airport, the boring, nerve-racking hours in the sky had receded far into the distance. As for the morrow . . .

"I'd send the morrow packing, that's what I'd do," said Nikolsky, and Aaron-Chaim Mendelevich Finkelmeyer agreed.

"Right. But how do you want to send it? How do you want to pack it?"

"Airmail!" said Nikolsky after a moment's thought. "Airmail and wrapped in a white rag, no seams showing. Notification of delivery required."

"Wrong," said Finkelmeyer. "I know the post office inside out. Especially inside. You want to send it registered. Then you get to state the value of the contents."

" 'Value of the contents'? Why, it's a load of shit!"

"Sorry," Finkelmeyer protested, holding up a finger so long it seemed to have at least five phalanges, "we don't accept organic matter."

"Ah, but I'm sending it out of the country," said Nikolsky, leaning over to his sparring partner with a look both meaningful and confidential. "I export it. To the jungle."

"Well, that's another matter," said Aaron-Chaim Finkelmeyer. "Fertilizer for the jungles of Africa, is that it?"

"Exactly," Nikolsky nodded. "After all those years of colonialism the soil is exhausted."

"Dear me! Dear me!" Aaron-Chaim Finkelmeyer mourned, grabbing his head and groaning.

"But now that we send them our shit, they've started growing bananas again. We give them shit; they give us bananas." He grabbed a passing waitress and said, "Hey there, got any bananas?"

"None of your jokes, please," said the waitress mildly, pulling away and moving on.

"Looks like we're still short on bananas," Nikolsky sighed. "Shit galore, and not a banana in sight."

"See that guy over there?" asked Finkelmeyer, pointing to a man sitting at a table near the podium. "That's me. The ideal me. The way I'd like to be, like to live."

"And is that me sitting there next to you?"

"No. You're out of the picture. You don't need a double."

"What do you mean? Aren't we splitting everything fifty-fifty? Which reminds me: more vodka?"

"Let 'er rip! . . . And you see that hulk over there, the one in the striped blue suit?"

"A striped hulk. Sounds exotic. Tiger? Banana peel?" Nikolsky peered into the tobacco smoke and fumes from the nearby kitchen in an attempt to make out the person Finkelmeyer was pointing to.

"Holy Jehovah! He's spotted me. He's coming over. Why is it whenever I need to be seen I'm ignored and whenever I need to melt into the background I stand out like a sore thumb?"

"You have my sympathy," said Nikolsky agreeably, universal agreeability being one of vodka's great pleasures. "I'm always sympathetic when I drink—and when there are women involved."

By this time the blue-striped suit had lumbered into Nikolsky's line of sight. Pretty roomy togs he's got on there, he thought. Even for that paunch. Which comes with matching posterior, I see, though at least that's a close fit. And the lapels! Perfect right-angled triangles, bomber wings. The picture of brute force—two hundred and fifty pounds' worth.

"Come on over, Manakin!" Finkelmeyer called out to him, pulling a free chair up to their table. "Why so bashful? You're not a little girl anymore."

Manakin—a Yakut or Chukchi, thought Nikolsky—opened his mouth, narrowed his already slitlike eyes, and burst into a high-pitched giggle. Perhaps he had found Finkelmeyer's joke funny, but more likely he was simply playing along. Finkelmeyer laughed too, but the laugh was openly contemptuous, all rapaciously flashing teeth and dark eyes.

Pretty little scene, Nikolsky said to himself.

Manakin sat down with great delicacy, his posterior testing to make sure there was a seat waiting to greet it.

"Do break bread with us, kind sir," said Nikolsky, half-filling a large wineglass with vodka and pushing it over to him.

"Who is the comrade?" asked Manakin, smiling at Nikolsky.

"The comrade is Comrade Nikolsky," Nikolsky answered, holding out his hand.

"Comrade Manakin," said Manakin seriously, and carefully eased his plump fingers into Nikolsky's hand. "Danil Fedotych."

"Leonid Pavlovich," said Nikolsky, thereby drawing the introductions to a close. "Drink up, drink up."

Manakin gulped the vodka down like water, his face impassive. He did not partake of the customary bite of food afterwards.

"Good for you," Finkelmeyer exclaimed, "showing the comrade from Moscow here how Manakin appreciates our famous Moscow trademark! Yes, a fine way of saying 'Long live the inviolable friendship of our peoples and the monolithic unity of our society!' "

"Your profession, Comrade Nikossky?" Manakin asked, paying Finkelmeyer no heed. He had a marked accent (he confused or omitted r's and l's and lisped badly) and spoke in a hoarse, flat voice.

"Administration," Nikolsky answered. "I'm an inspector." Manakin was clearly impressed.

"And Manakin here is what you might call a Party boss," Finkelmeyer inserted. "He alerts the masses to the decisions made on high."

Manakin turned his hulk to Finkelmeyer and said in the same colorless voice, "Head of Cultural Affairs. Since the fifteenth of January, Comrade Finkelmeyer."

Aaron-Chaim froze. Then his jaw dropped, and he trained his birdlike eyes on Manakin. *"Vey iz mir!"* he whispered at last.

Meanwhile Nikolsky had been picking at the meat with his fork. Is this Finkelmeyer fellow clowning or is he really scared? he wondered. And what is his connection with that rack of beef? For connection there is—that's clear. Well, whatever it is, they can thrash it out between them. It's none of my business. I've got enough troubles of my own.

"May I be excused?" Nikolsky asked with great pomp, and moved off in search of a toilet. He found one off the lobby, and before leaving it spent a long time washing his hands. Peering into the mirror above the sink, he saw the face of a man who had something in common with Nikolsky, though Nikolsky was hard put to say what. It was a rather long face, and the corners of the mouth curved down, giving it a nasty, scornful expression. The eyes were insolent with big bags under them, the eyelids red and swollen from cigarettes and insomnia. True, somewhere behind it all lurked regular features and a classical profile, and the temples were dashingly peppered with gray, but that merely made the rest look all the more seedy. "You old fart," he muttered through his teeth. "You old wolf." The brash face in the mirror stuck its tongue out at him.

Out in the lobby again Nikolsky watched the still-raging storm through the dark window. The wind was playing havoc with the streetlamps, and there was not a soul in the street. "Do not stumble, hunted stag" flashed back into his mind. He turned and reentered the restaurant.

Finkelmeyer was gesticulating wildly, his arms raised high above his head. "But can't you see, you stupid oaf, it won't cost you a thing!"

Manakin's face showed no sign of emotion.

"Not a thing! What's your job got to do with it?"

Manakin said not a word.

At that point Finkelmeyer caught sight of Nikolsky and said with a sigh, "All right, we'll talk it over tomorrow. You can go. Comrade Nikolsky and I still have our coffee to drink."

"Tomorrow is bad," Manakin said in his hoarse voice. "Tomorrow I am flying back."

Fixing Manakin with venomous eyes and struggling to keep himself under control, Finkelmeyer said softly, "I've had enough of this, Manakin. Tell them the plane's been held up and I won't get in until tomorrow afternoon."

"Why afternoon?" Manakin countered quickly. "Why not morning?"

"I said afternoon and I mean afternoon!"

Manakin thought a moment, then stood with great dignity, said, "Goodbye, Comrade Finkelmeyer. Goodbye, Comrade Nikossky," and left the room as if nothing had happened

Nikolsky sat down and finished his meat. Next to the coffee, now cold, stood their two cognacs. The vodka carafe was empty. Finkelmeyer swallowed his cognac in one gulp and washed it down with the coffee. "On the one hand and on the other," he began thoughtfully. "On the one hand, it would be nice to sit here a bit longer; on the other, it's time to find you a room. Besides, the restaurant's closing."

"Let's get a bottle for the room, and the three of us—you, me, and the bottle—we'll go up to the room and sit there a bit longer. That is, if we can find a room free of snoring bodies."

"Leave that to me," said Finkelmeyer with great confidence. He seemed suddenly in the best of moods.

They ordered a bottle from the waitress, paid the bill, and went out into the empty lobby. The old man, now dozing, jumped up immediately and was soon fluttering all over them, handing them their coats, giving them a once-over with his clothes brush, tugging at the cuffs, and babbling, "Had a good time, a good meal, young people? It's always nice to take a rest and warm up after a long trip. Thank you kindly. Thank you. Have a good stay now. Have a good stay."

They picked up their suitcases, and Nikolsky followed Finkelmeyer down the dark hotel corridor.

III

THEY stopped at the end of the corridor in front of a door that was not quite shut. There was faint light shining through the crack. Finkelmeyer gave a soft knock; they heard a chair move back and someone stand. Then the door opened and out of the tiny room— or, rather, out of the cubicle, because there was space for no more than a chair and a small table—stepped a pleasant-looking woman in an old-fashioned blue suit, the hotel uniform by the looks of it. The moment she saw Finkelmeyer, she was all smiles.

Turning to the side and stepping back to observe them without staring, Nikolsky was both amused and bemused to see Finkelmeyer bend over and put down his suitcase (upsetting his overcoat from its perch in the crook of his elbow and just managing to keep it from falling on the floor) while the woman waited patiently for him to straighten up, whereupon she went over to him and, standing on tiptoe, touched her lips to his unshaven cheek and put her arms around him.

"Hello, Dana," said Finkelmeyer. "You see? I *have* come."

"Hello," she said, disengaging herself gently. "Hello," she said to Nikolsky as well.

"Good evening," said Nikolsky, bowing his head. His only thought was to make himself scarce.

"Introduce yourselves," said Finkelmeyer informally, in no position to introduce them himself as he was still fussing with his sleeves, of which there seemed to be an extraordinary number.

"My name is Leonid."

"And mine Danuta." She held out her hand.

Then Finkelmeyer and Dana fell into a dialogue that gave Nikolsky the opportunity to take out his cigarettes, light up, inhale a few times, and feel the effects of the alcohol diffuse. He both listened in and tried not to, but most of all he watched. Very pretty, actually, very feminine. . . . Can't quite place the accent. Polish? Estonian? . . . An odd couple they make. If he's sleeping with her, he's a lucky man, bumbler or not. . . .

". . . only just come on duty. It's twelve."

"I know. That's why I waited. There was no point in going to your place when I knew you'd be leaving so soon."

"I got your letter. Did you get mine? I wrote I had night duty all week."

"Yes, yes, I got it. Don't you see? I've worked things out perfectly."

"You're tired. You've been drinking. You've got problems."

"Problems, problems . . . *mit kompot!*"

"Will you be staying long?"

"How should I know? I want to. I want a lot of things." He burst out laughing.

How does that Balmont poem put it? Nikolsky thought. "I want to be strong, I want to be bold, I want to tear off your clothes . . ."

"What are you laughing at?"

"Sorry, Dana. I've had a lot to drink. I'm in a good mood. . . . A week or so. I don't know."

"Fine. I'm just glad you're here."

"So am I. I'm sick and tired of what's going on there."

"At least you'll have a rest."

"I may, I may not. But I'm glad to see you."

I'm glad, you're glad, he, she, or it is glad, and so on and so forth, thought Nikolsky in a melancholy vein. The meaningless words meant to conceal the lovers' true feelings drove Nikolsky to distraction and a nearby window. Dammit! They'll find a place to sleep, all right, but what about me? I bet there's not a room left in this whole bloody fleabag.

The weather had changed, he noticed. It must be warmer: the snow had turned to sleet; it was blasting against the panes. How long would the two of them stand there together? He could see their reflection in the glass. They were completely gaga, on the brink of foreplay. It made his stomach turn. He felt sorry for himself as only the recently drunk know how.

"Leonid!" It was the first time Finkelmeyer had called him by his first name. "Come on. Let's go. Dana will take care of everything."

The three of them went up to the second floor. Dana produced a ring of keys, one of which she used to unlock a door to a room with an entry hall of its own. "Come in, please," she said.

The room was unexpectedly luxurious. Though what recently built hotel had anything to offer in the way of *real* luxury? Only the grand old places dating back to czarist days, hotels like the Astoria or National in the historic centers of the country, had the necessary style. All the Sputniks and Tourists that had sprouted here and there— and few enough there were even of them for a country that was constantly shifting, flying, and crawling, gallivanting off to Moscow on some mission and hurrying back with rugs and children's clothes— all the new hotels had no use whatever for gilt sofas or bentwood chairs. You could consider yourself lucky if your room had a wardrobe with a broken hanger for your coat. And luxury? Luxury was a sink and shower and—yes—toilet to yourself, a bedside table with a lamp and a lampshade left unslashed by your drunken predecessors, a bed that nearly accommodated your full length, and a mattress with springs that didn't squeak through the night at the slightest provocation.

The room Danuta took them to had it all. It had more: a separate sitting room (a sitting room!) with a couch, a coffee table, and two armchairs; then—in addition to the shiny, scratch-free wardrobe— a glass-doored cupboard stocked with dishes that would be the pride of the most self-respecting housewife; next, a refrigerator; and finally, a telephone and an up-to-date telephone book! For once in his life he would be spared the ignominy of wheedling telephone time out of the hotel manager.

"Well done, Dana, well done," said Finkelmeyer, while Nikolsky surveyed the royal suite. "Leonid and I will sit around and chat for an hour or two. He seems duly impressed."

"I'm impressed, all right, but a room like this could really break me. Four rubles a night? And then the moment a big shot shows up I'm out in the street."

"Don't worry," said Danuta, shaking her head. "It's reserved for local officials, and they're all off on a campaign, away for another four days. Oh, and it's free."

"Sure you won't get into trouble?" Nikolsky asked for the sake of decency, but Danuta shook her head again.

"Make yourself at home! Make yourself at home!" Finkelmeyer commanded grandly, taking Nikolsky's suitcase, tugging at the wardrobe door, and bumping into a chair and the bed as he bustled about.

Luxuries free of charge! Four days guaranteed! When he put the bottle down on the coffee table, Nikolsky had the feeling he was staking out his territory, making the room his own. Yes, he chuckled to himself, this time he'd hit the jackpot!

Danuta had slipped out unnoticed. The men took off their jackets and put away their things. Then they took two vodka glasses out of the cupboard. Nikolsky rinsed them off, and Finkelmeyer dried them with a bath towel he found hanging in the shower. They blew out as much lint as they could and picked the rest out with their fingers.

"Shall we rinse them off again? What do you think?" Finkelmeyer asked.

"Don't be ridiculous!" Nikolsky answered, collapsing into a chair and pouring out the vodka.

Each of them pulled out a sausage, and Finkelmeyer, who had brought Dana a few pounds of oranges from Moscow, decided to sacrifice one for the occasion. They peeled it neatly and separated it into sections, then set the sections out on a saucer.

They drank slowly, making small talk—whether they'd had trouble booking their plane tickets, how revolting a town with nothing to offer but a factory club and a movie theater could be—but in point of fact the leisurely, on-again-off-again conversation was unimportant; what they really enjoyed was simply sitting around after midnight, sitting at a table without anyone, be it wife or maître d'hôtel, to chase them away.

Nikolsky smoked nonstop, and Finkelmeyer lit up now and then as well. The yellow shade covering the ceiling lamp was soon awash with blue-gray smoke.

" 'The sun awash with azure in the sky,' " Nikolsky recited, savoring each sound, elongating each word. "The poem about the hunted stag is the most successful of the five."

"Thank you, Lyonya," Finkelmeyer muttered with a nod. "You're right. You understand it all so well. It is the best."

"*Understand,* you say? Tell me, Aaron, why the note about the poems being translated from that language—whatever it is—if they're your poems?"

"Oh, they're my poems, all right," said Finkelmeyer with a sigh.

"Well?"

"Well what?"

"Well, why isn't your name on them?"

"You think I know why?"

Nikolsky realized he was close to losing his temper. "Look, Aaron," he said in as even a voice as he could muster, "I really liked your poems—"

"Oh, I know you did, Lyonya!"

"Hold on a minute. First listen to what I have to say. I keep up with what comes out, and—how shall I put it? Well, I can tell when there's something shining in the manure pile. And since in the plane you went so far as to tell me the truth and since we're sitting here and drinking together, how about telling me your story? I mean, poets don't grow on trees, and here I've stumbled across one in the person of Aaron-Chaim Mendelevich Finkelmeyer—I did get it right, didn't I?—and I want to know who he is, what makes him tick."

Finkelmeyer took a long time to respond. The chair was too low for him—his knees were almost on a level with his chin—but he sat there motionless, hunching his already stooping shoulders, staring down at the floor. It was in this pose that he finally began to speak.

"If all I do is tell you why the poems are called a translation, you won't have learned very much. And if I tell you the whole story . . ."

"I've got all night ahead of me, and we've only just opened the bottle. Though it's up to you."

Nikolsky filled the glasses, clinked his gently against Finkelmeyer's, tossed it down, and, biting into his sausage, settled in to wait.

Finkelmeyer emptied his glass too and leaned back in the chair, digging his fingers into the arms. Suddenly, his eyes, enlarged by the black circles around them, then his whole face, rumpled from lack of sleep, broke into a radiant childlike smile. "I know what! I'll tell you about Cherkizovo!"

IV

YOU'RE a Muscovite; you know there's a section of the city called Cherkizovo. But you may be surprised to learn that Cherkizovo is a shtetl. That's right, in the middle of Moscow. Oh, it's got its share of high-rise monstrosities and prefab boxes now; the metro even goes there: "Our capital is growing in leaps and bounds, upward and outward." Far be it from me to question a slogan. But a while back I was in the neighborhood—I'd gone to see a composer who had a commission to write a song cycle, a cycle of Soviet romances, and wanted me to do the words—and I thought I might venture farther, into the heart of the place.

In the end I thought better of it. You know why? I was scared stiff. Look at me: tall and slim, getting on in years, gainfully employed, perfectly respectable in other words, and respectably dressed (I particularly remember a hat I wore at the time, a soft German number that made me look like an intellectual; I've lost it since)—anyway, supposing I, Aaron Finkelmeyer, made a sudden appearance in the heart of old Cherkizovo. I had a nightmarish vision of being spied on from behind every crooked fence, every doorway, every window. Disheveled old crones, yarmulked graybeard in worn quilted jackets, snot-nosed children nibbling on crackers, pudgy women hauling bags of produce from markets on the other side of town— stopping, staring: "*Vos?* The son of old man Finkelmeyer who ended up in jail? Aaron Finkelmeyer, is that who it is? A regular big shot he looks like! Hey, Aaronele, don't you even recognize your Aunt Channah?"

No, Aaronele didn't venture into Cherkizovo; he went no farther than the composer's new cooperative flat. He went there to pick up his sure thing: the romances. And you know what? It wasn't so sure after all. Instead of romances I wrote a cycle about Cherkizovo and its philistines, and after the absolute final deadline had passed, the composer gave me hell over the phone and found a non-Cherkizovian to take my place.

You've caught on by now, haven't you, Lyonya? I was born in Cherkizovo, born and bred there, spent—let me see—yes, half my life there, sucked my mother's dug there, pissed my pants there. When I was older, I ran down to the courtyard, but the courtyard toilet wasn't for kids and we weren't the potty kind, so as a child I would stand on the porch, aim as high as I could, and marvel at the golden stream sparkling in the sun.

The toilet was in the courtyard, the water pump in the street. There was gas in the kitchen—it was installed after the war—though it took some time for the women to get over their fear of it. In other words, it was a house like any other: part barn, part shed; the first floor brick, the second floor boards; and a crooked porch always about to crumble.

What made it different was that the perpetual puddle at the pump would leak its way under the fence—its own little stream, its own little rill—to the porch, where even in the hottest weather it made the kind of voluptuous, muddy mess so beloved by barefoot urchins. The courtyard was a bit below street level, which is why the puddle formed down at the porch, and people were constantly slipping and making classic pratfalls in front of the steps. We called them "Russian reverences" because they affected only outsiders. *We* knew where to step.

One day my friend Fimka Krul—we were ten or eleven at the time—ran up to our place yelling, "Quick! Quick! The colonel's here in his Opel! Quick!"

Let me tell you about the colonel. Fimka had a sister named Adina, Adka. Men went wild over her. She had an exquisite figure, exquisite face, hair down to her knees, and a milky-white complexion— the picture of the Shulamite bride in the Song of Songs. True, she was as brainless as she was beautiful, but it didn't matter. Everybody from kids to geezers was in love with her; even women liked her in their way.

Well, she'd just turned eighteen and found work as a lab assistant in a clinic somewhere. I remember her coming to see us in her white smock. "Could I look at myself in your full-length mirror, Aunt Golda?" she asked my mother, laughing and swirling, admiring herself.

We couldn't take our eyes off her either.

"You're a good-looking girl, and you're grown up now," my mother said. "Time for you to watch your step."

"Time for me to fall in love!"

And fall in love she did.

A young man began seeing her home on his motorcycle. He would drop her off two streets away, but we kids didn't take long to catch on to them. They would kiss goodbye and he would wait until she reached the corner. Then he waved, turned, and roared off. Once or twice we hurled a piece of brick after him, but just as a matter of form—we actually quite liked him, first, because he'd fought at the front and wore an officer's uniform under his leather coat, and second, because he'd brought back that nifty BMW motorcycle as his part of the spoils.

And what happened? What happened was that she got pregnant. Shouts, moans, tears—just what you'd expect—with all eight apartments of neighbors intimately involved: worrying, arguing, giving advice. After things had calmed down a little, the following details came out: his name was Vasily, he had been just old enough to fight in the final months of the war, he was a student at the prestigious Bauman Engineering Institute, and his father was a colonel in the secret police.

Anyway, Adka told Vasya she was pregnant, and he didn't blink an eye; he said his father had brought back all kinds of junk from Germany and could keep them in style. She told her parents; he told his.

Her parents didn't know how to react. On the one hand, the girl was pregnant; on the other, the boy was a goy, a Russian! The disgrace! What have we done to deserve this, o Lord?

His parents, in the person of the colonel, immediately bristled.

"Marry a Cherkizovo kike? And ruin your life? You must be out of your mind!"

The upshot of it all? Our side wasn't long in coming round. Vasya roared into the courtyard with a bottle of sweet wine and a selection of delicacies available only to high officials, and started kissing Adka's parents and calling them Mama and Papa. A few minutes later Fimka ran over to our place brandishing a shiny German pistol. A gift from Vasya. It had a holster, too. And everything worked. Except the trigger.

Once things were settled in Cherkizovo, the groom helped the bride into his new sidecar—she was expecting, wasn't she; he had to take care of her—and off they roared to his parents. There too everything went well. The moment the colonel laid eyes on Adka he was done for. She was in her third or fourth month, and her femininity was even more marked than usual: the creamy face showed a touch of rose; the gait, normally quite awkward (I now see she had a certain vulgarity to her), was smooth and serene. Vasya's mother had no say in family matters; she always looked to her husband. And what she saw was that he couldn't take his eyes off the girl. But Vasya had yet another trump: he'd coached her to ask about the war. She started things off brilliantly with: "Look at all the medals you have! Vasya's only got one!" The colonel beamed.

By the next day he'd had a chance to think things over—pretty as she was, *he* wasn't going to sleep with her—but it was too late: Vasya not only acknowledged paternity, he claimed it; Papa would have to support them. "All right, damn you, if that's what you want, but at least let me have a look at her family." So they jumped in the Opel and off they flew to Cherkizovo.

All of us—Fimka, me, the whole gang—stood and watched as the driver, a young sergeant, ran—cursing the road for giving his colonel such a jolty ride—to open the door for the colonel. Out came the colonel's shiny-booted feet, testing the perimeter of the puddle for dry ground and proceeding with measured steps along its edge. We ran on ahead to the porch. Soon the whole house was staring out of the windows and the future relatives—Mama, Papa, and Adka—were racing, pushing, tripping down the stairs. Such a guest we're having!

But suddenly the colonel's neck stretched out like a gander's, his eyes bulged, his face turned purple. We looked down and saw his feet sliding slowly, ever so slowly, through the mud. All he had to do was pick one up and move it ever so slightly to the left, but how could he know? We froze. Just lift your boot, the left one. It's only another foot or two. No, no, the *left* one! . . .

Splash! A more perfect Russian reverence we had never seen.

The sergeant ran and helped his colonel to his feet. Uniform, medals, and face—they were all one brown blob; he looked as if he'd been—sorry, there's no other way of putting it—shat on by a gigantic cow. He took out a white handkerchief, shook it open, wiped his eyes, nose, and mouth and—left face!—lumbered back to the fence. "Home!" he roared bearlike at the sergeant, and bearlike he scrambled into the car. Before we knew it, he was gone.

But why am I going on like this? I'll be brief.

"Look, you got her pregnant," said the colonel to his son. "Marry her if you want. But don't think you're living with Papa. No, go back to your mud hole. Oh, don't worry. I'll give you money. Not for you, for my grandson. He's not to blame."

The grandson turned out to be a girl, a perfect little wide-eyed gypsy, the kind that falls to the floor with a thud and lets out peals of laughter. Vasya moved to Cherkizovo.

For two or three years Vasya ran across the courtyard to the toilet. He took little Rozochka to her grandfather for regular visits, and her grandmother, who turned out to be a fine, kind-hearted woman, made secret visits to her granddaughter. Little Rozochka wanted for nothing.

But then the inevitable began to happen: Vasya would stay over at his father's—and stay on. After all, in Cherkizovo he and Adka shared a room with her father and mother and my friend Fimka and when the lights went out he was afraid to hold her close, what with the squeaky mattress and the sleepless relatives snorting and twisting and turning, while in his father's place there were four rooms—not counting kitchen and bath—which meant a room of his own with a desk of his own for his work.

Apparently he didn't spend the night alone either, and apparently she was a fellow student, and as soon as Adka had the facts—pow! She laid into him but good. "Out! Go home to Papa for all I care! You think I have no admirers of my own?"

It was spring and Vasya's exams were coming up, so he did move back to Papa's for a month. Well, Adka went wild and stayed out late every night, leaving Rozochka with her mother. When her mother broke her leg, the whole house got together and gave up on her: she didn't care about the baby, she'd go crazy without a man, the baby would be better off with her other grandma. So the Opel returned, this time laden with toys and a crib.

Then something else came to distract us. The doctor Adka worked for at the institute was arrested. It was a year or two before the Doctors' Plot, but Jews were already being picked up here and there, and the head of Adka's lab was one of the first. They closed the lab and fired Adka, but her admirer at the time, a civilian pilot (Adka was a pushover for men in uniform), encouraged her to file for divorce. He would take the baby too, he had his own flat, and she wouldn't need to work—his pay was ten times hers.

So she went and told Vasya she wanted a divorce, they'd never mend things anyway. Well, he began to bawl, as she tells it, and, well, so did she, and Papa called her into the study and told her in no uncertain terms, "Do what you want, get your divorce, but you won't get Rozochka. You're no mother and Vasya's not much of a father, and since I'm about to retire, the old woman and I, *we're* going to adopt her and bring her up, is that clear? Now tell me, this new flame of yours—who is he and what does he do?"

And Adka—can you imagine?—gave the colonel the pilot's name and the name of the airport he worked at; she even told him he was a Party member.

'Well, you know where *I* work, and if you don't give your consent, I'll have lover boy thrown out on his ear for moral turpitude, is that clear? Now go and talk it over with him. What difference does it make, anyway? You can make a baby for him if he wants one so badly."

End of story. Adka moved out, and though she visited from time to time I never did learn what her life with the pilot was like. I didn't mean to talk about her in the first place; I meant to talk about the house. But I got sidetracked. I suddenly wondered whether Vasya would have moved back to Papa's if the toilet had been inside. Maybe not. Or whether the colonel would have taken the newlyweds in if he hadn't had his pratfall. What do our lives depend on? Where we

live and how we grow. A weed among gravel, a flower among stones.
When the time comes to cast away stones, they are cast away. But
will anyone gather them together? And if so, what about the flower?
Will it be torn out by the roots? Trampled, flattened, left to die? Or
can it somehow pick itself up, recuperate, bloom again, the seeds in
its dry pod beating a victorious drumroll?

V

IT WAS a house like any other: eight families in four one- and
two-room apartments. We had only one room, but I can't say we
had it particularly bad. There were only four of us, Father, Mother,
Grandma, and me; some families were six or eight to a room.

Our life was, well . . . we did count kopecks, but to say we were
poor, no, that would be going too far. My father sold knitted wear,
and with a little snippet here and a little snippet there he managed
to make ends meet. Who didn't steal? People who could manage
without it, I suppose, but nobody in my father's line came under
that heading.

What? I don't believe it! He wants to know what the factories
were like! Look, fill my glass and I'll tell you all about it. You make
me laugh, you know that? Factories! Really!

If you try hard, you can still count up a hundred or so tumbledown stalls around Moscow sporting a sign that in the finest Franco-
Russian tradition says *TRICOTAGE*. You'll find them at markets,
near railway stations, in working-class districts, at factory entrances,
at tobacco stands and beer stands. Nowadays the policy is to build
proper shops instead, but then one day you're out taking the air,
you look up, and you see one of these signs. Back then, fifteen years
ago, they were everywhere. They got their stock from the cooperatives, which were also pretty big at the time. And in that jungle of a
world, in that dog-eat-dog world, my father was a rabbit.

Which is why he was arrested.

The long string of people implicated in the less than lily-white
undertaking ended with my father. All day long he would sit in his
stall selling everything from beads and razor blades to women's

woolen undies. The latter, like all women's knitted goods, were in chronic short supply. When an unclaimed batch of wool turned up— and heaven only knows where it came from—the little local cooperatives would knit underwear on the side—you know, in addition to fulfilling the Plan. The Five-Year Plan for the Development of the Soviet Economy had not only decided what they were required to do, it had decided that women who were cold in winter should spend their hard-earned money on—say, beads rather than warm underwear—because it had increased the production of beads and postponed a three-and-a-half-percent increase in the production of knitted goods until the next Five-Year-Plan. Anyway, my father and a large number of people over him—the list went as high as the Assistant Minister of Trade, though *he* only got shunted off to another ministry—were all convicted of helping a small number of women to buy warm underwear on the basis of the weather rather than the Five-Year Plan. The state couldn't accept the idea of a Plan disregarded or of profits that went into the pockets of little Cherkizovo *gesheftmakhers* like my father and big public officials like the Assistant Minister. As luck would have it, he was down with something when the scandal broke, and even though he'd been tipped off about the crackdown he was unable to get rid of the evidence in time. The officials in charge demanded an ungodly bribe to sweep his profits under the rug, and my father scurried all over town trying to raise it. He failed. Some managed to wriggle out of the mess, others bought their way out, and, as I say, the bigwigs were too dangerous to touch. My father and three or four other men were thrown in jail.

Looking back, I have no idea how we survived. True, we had a little money at first, because when Father realized he was done for and confiscation was imminent he managed to scatter a few things among relatives, but they were soon gone. Before long the walls were bare and we had nothing left to sell. People did what they could, but people are people. As long as our plight was fresh in their minds, they were helpful, but eventually they stopped thinking about it and the help stopped coming.

Mother sewed all day; Grandma knitted and sold their wares at the nearby market. I hadn't finished school yet, and Mother wouldn't hear of my going to work. "You want to end up a know-nothing? Sitting all day selling junk like your father? Over my dead body!

Pity your poor, stupid mama, Aaronele. You're all she's got! Go to school, Aaronele. I'll kiss your feet. Be an engineer, Aaronele. When you're an engineer, Aaronele, you won't have to do a thing your poor old mama says." Mother was barely middle-aged, but she looked like an old woman.

I can't say I was brilliant, but I did have something up there. A good memory at least. I could remember anything I set my mind to. Only I was terribly lazy. All I did was read—read and go to the pictures (one of our neighbors was an usher, so I never needed a ticket). Oh, and I pitched a lot of kopecks too, though I wasn't very good at it—as you've noticed, my coordination leaves something to be desired—and besides, where was I to get the kopecks? The only time I won anything was when we scattered a pile of coins and claimed them by stretching our fingers from one to the next. Since I had the longest reach, I could rake in a nice little fortune.

But to get back to my memory. In the end I decided my mother was right. Once I'd seen somebody solve a problem, I could solve any problem like it. The longest formulas were child's play. And in subjects where you merely spouted back what was in the book— you know: history, geography, literature—I was a regular machine gun. It's a funny thing. My speech was anything but pure—full of Yiddish turns and intonations—and as you can hear, even today I'm no Cicero, but I always *wrote* a literate Russian. My notebooks may have been filthy, my handwriting wild, but my Russian was correct.

To cut a long story short, my grades started improving. After a year or so I was up near the top of my class. And when I heard that the principal had been known to say at a staff meeting that Finkelmeyer was on his way to a medal, I pulled out all the stops. Medals were a sure ticket to engineering school! During the last semester I worked like a dog through exams. "Good work, Finkelmeyer! We're giving you an 'outstanding' on the writtens."

I did fine on the orals too, and after sailing through and out of the last one I walked straight into the arms of a weeping mother, who hugged and kissed me in front of everyone—"Thank you, Aaronele, thank you"—though she barely came up to my neck on tiptoe. Well, I started bawling too. A gold medal, after all!

I planned to recuperate by spending the whole next day in bed, but suddenly there was Fimka pushing our door open a crack and motioning me out so Mother couldn't hear. When I asked him on the stairs what was up, all he said was "Get to school, on the double!"

I flew. And what did I find out? The Regional Board had overridden the school's recommendation and revoked my 'outstanding' on the writtens.

It turned out the school had five medalists, three of whom were Jews. The board called in the principal and said, "What's going on here, Ivan Nikolaevich? Gromov gets a gold, fine, and Bezuglov a silver by the skin of his teeth, and the other three—all gold—go to Stern, Pevsner, and this fellow—what's his name?—Finkelmeyer?"

Almost half our class were Jews, but statistics or no, one thing was clear: "We can't let them have so many medals. One must go. Your choice."

What could Ivan Nikolaevich do? He looked over our exams again. Mine were messy, splotchy, hard to read. When he thought about it, I hadn't been "outstanding" for long, I'd only just taken myself in hand. Besides, my father was in jail, as the board must have known. Stern and Pevsner had ten years of "outstandings" behind them; they had earned their medals by the sweat of their brow and the fortitude of their backs and backsides. "I'll give you Finkelmeyer." I got a "good" on my composition and mathematics writtens.

In other words, I got neither a gold nor a silver. What could I do? All form of protest was out of the question. My mother's blood pressure shot up. As for me, I was upset, of course, but I recovered soon enough. I've seen it over and over in myself. If I get into trouble, I rant and rave and call myself every name in the book. I can't sleep. I start spinning long nocturnal monologues addressed to my rational faculties or common sense; I keep telling myself I have to take the bull by the horns, create my own destiny, be practical and—how do I put it?—*above it all*, that's it! By this time I *am* a Cicero, and since no Cicero can deliver an oration on his back, I leap up and start pacing the room, mumbling and gesticulating madly. But when someone else does *me* in, I retreat. Why suffer needlessly? It's not my fault people are bastards. Is it even their fault? All I'll do is add to the *tsores* others make for me, and before long I'll go off the deep end. No, nerves need rest, and I can't stay up all night every night.

So what did I do? I took my diploma with its two "goods" to the

Bauman Institute. The admissions committee took one long, eloquent, pitiful look at me, hoping to make me understand my plight
and leave without further ado. But I didn't; even after everything
that had happened I didn't quite understand. I was only eighteen.
"I've come to apply for admission," I said. Well, they gave me the
application form.

Remember those forms? They were to today's forms what *War
and Peace* is to a comic strip. Seventy or eighty questions, many of
which were divided into subquestions with special boxes and dotted
lines. You had to list the names of all family members of your former wives, let alone the current one; you had to provide the maiden
names of both grandmothers, let alone your mother. And worst of
all, you were forbidden to leave any space blank. In each of the
myriad spaces allotted to wives and their families, for example, I
had to write "unmarried." But I managed to work my way through
that section.

Then came the question about relatives who had spent the war
in areas occupied by the Nazis. Large numbers of my aunts, uncles,
and cousins had perished in Minsk, Bobruisk, and Kovno—that I
knew—but had they *all* perished? What if one or two had survived
by some miracle? Then the Germans would have barred my way to
higher education by failing to do away with one of my aunts or
uncles. And what about those who perished? The exact wording in
the form was: "Did you or any of your relatives spend time in occupied territory? List all family members, indicating degree of relationship." In other words, I would have to list Lazar Finkelmeyer,
uncle (whom I had never seen and who died in Bobruisk), Sara Finkelmeyer, aunt (his wife, who died with him), and so on—about
twenty in all. And because the form didn't ask whether they had
died there or not, because there was no provision for qualifying any
of the responses, and because the assumption was clearly that anyone in such close proximity to the enemy was a potential traitor,
those twenty shades cast an enormous shadow on my reliability.

Then there was the issue of relatives abroad. In 1918 my grandmother's brother ran away from either the Cossacks or the Poles—
I can't remember which. If he'd gone east, to the Bolsheviks, he'd
have had a long, hard journey across the front. The trip west was
short and comparatively sweet. So now his family—and maybe the

family of one of my grandmother's sisters as well—lived somewhere in America.

In short, not a pretty picture for someone in my position. I won't go so far as to say that a very clever person sat down to compose a set of questions specifically designed to do me in—me and my kind—but it certainly looked that way at the time. I had the feeling that while filling in the questionnaire I was parading naked before the icy stare of the all-female admissions committee and that with every answer my long, bony body revealed a new spot, boil, or abscess, heretofore hidden from view and now congealing in a single, enormous festering sore—my father in jail for robbery of state property.

I broke out into a sweat. "May I finish it at home?" I asked one of the women.

"If you like," she said, turning away. "It won't change a thing." But behind the show of indifference I sensed a kind of frustration: Didn't you know what to make of the pity in my eyes when you came in? Can't you see it's hopeless? No, you want to go through with the exams, waste your time and energy. Well, go ahead, if that's what you want. I wash my hands of the matter.

After thinking things over carefully at home, I decided I'd had no relatives in the occupied zone. And none abroad for that matter. They could look into it if they felt like it. But I did write the truth about my father. And not because it was easy to verify. No matter what traps the questionnaire forced me into, I was not going to betray my father. He might have been a festering sore to the outside world, but I'd known nothing but kindness from him.

I handed in the questionnaire a good six weeks before the exams were scheduled, and because there was no point in studying—I knew the material cold—I decided to earn a little money in the interim and buy a pair of shoes and some trousers or even, if I was lucky, a cheap suit. For several years, winter and summer, I had been wearing the same down-at-heel shoes, the same pair of repeatedly patched—especially in the more private regions—trousers. For a sports jacket I wore a reddish ski jacket with a zipper down the front and enormous pockets. People said it did a lot for me: the padding made me look plumper.

Maybe leaving school had given me a semblance of male pride—

now that I was going on to college, I needed to put on an independent front and hold my own, stop letting people push me around—and a new wardrobe seemed an essential element of my new, more self-confident image. But where could I find work? I had no skills. And who would take me for so short a period? Well, I was lucky. One day as I was passing the post office I saw an announcement for summer employment. I went in.

The woman in charge stared at me as if I were an escaped giraffe or camel. "Delivering telegrams is a job for women who can barely read or girls just in from the provinces. Why waste your education?"

"It's like this . . ." I began, dreading the long, involved explanation ahead. But suddenly I stopped and simply lifted my battered shoe to her line of sight. "I need the money."

She was a kind woman. She took my papers, copied out some information, and handed them back. "You start tomorrow. The pay is four hundred and one rubles. Not much, I grant you. But we work in three shifts, and if you're willing to do time and a half you can earn six hundred and one fifty. What do you say?"

I was deliriously happy, and after a few days' work I considered myself the luckiest man on earth.

The routine was not particularly strenuous; I even enjoyed it. Every morning they gave me a bundle of telegrams. I'd race through street after street, house after house, then back for the next bundle, and out again. The girls I worked with took a liking to me, and we had a grand old time together. They showed me the ropes, that is, the shortcuts and side doors. For example, when delivering telegrams to a certain establishment protected by an armed guard, you normally waited half an hour before someone came down and gave you a pass, but if you were in the know you could slip in through the boiler room and make your way up to the third-floor office on your own.

They had all kinds of tricks but only one goal: saving time, wresting an hour or two—or three—from the working day for their own needs. I had to cross half of Moscow to get to work; they lived in the neighborhood, practically next door, so they were constantly running home, looking in on their children, cooking a meal. Why else would they work there and for such low wages?

Well, there was another reason. They could do their shopping while on rounds. After work the lines were long and the affordable food was gone; during the day they might run across some cheap sausage or pork scraps or lard. Even if there were three hundred people ahead of you, you'd have them write a number on your hand and off you'd go, and by the time you'd made your deliveries and come back it was your turn. Nearly every day one of them ran in with a triumphant "Pigs' feet at the butcher's today! I've got a number!"

Of all the ways to save time the most popular was skimming the telegrams to see how long they'd keep. If you got one that said "HAPPY BIRTHDAY MANY HAPPY RETURNS YOUR LOVING SISTER NADYA," there'd be no harm done if you stopped off at a shop on the way. But there were others, the kind that said "YOUR MOTHER ANASTASIA BERYOZKINA DIED UNEXPECTEDLY COME IMMEDIATELY SIGNED CHIEF PHYSICIAN ZARECHENSKAYA DISTRICT," the kind you put on top and ran off to deliver without a second thought, and you'd find the Beryozkin family at supper, drinking tea and eating bread and butter, while Papa, a mechanic at the local motor-transport garage, went on about how his nagging had paid off and the foreman had come up with a new lathe. "Things wear out, after all. That's life." And little did he think that life, in the person of a lean and shabby figure, was on its way up the stairs, seeking out his door, and knocking with a bony finger, nor did he know how right he was when he looked at the figure and said to himself, "Pale as death." Yes, Beryozkin, death. Sign here. Date, hour, and minute. "Oh, no! Marusya! Come quickly! It's Mama! It's Grandma! Oh, no!"

The moment he signed, I took the pencil and fled, raced down the stairs, five flights of stairs to the peaceful courtyard with its linden-tree fragrance and girls playing hopscotch. "Go away! Go away! We don't want another player!" But I wouldn't go—not until I'd hopped, skipped, and jumped through their game.

Short as they are, telegrams contain the substance, the essence of life: births, deaths, diseases, dire straits, celebrations, transgressions, first loves, last hopes. The tape they come on is fairly burning with passions. But even passions can be sorted, and sort them we did, our goal being to set up a great-circle route, one that after taking us farther and farther out would lead back to a point near the post office.

Because we worked two or three to a shift, we had to map each sally collectively. I soon introduced a reform. I drew a map of the district and cut out squares to represent telegrams: red squares meant government offices, blue ones emergencies, yellow ones serious but less pressing matters, and white ones ordinary greetings. Very much the commanding officer on the eve of battle, I surveyed the field, shuffled the squares, and barked, "You go here, here, and here with this batch; you take this route; and this one's mine." The girls were thrilled—they had less walking to do and all kinds of extra time—and told the head of the post office, who, believe it or not, gave me a promotion and upped my salary fifty rubles.

After two weeks I got my first pay packet, but I decided not to breathe a word about the job until I'd passed my exams, and stashed the money away. My mother never guessed a thing. I told her I was in the library all day, and when I had night duty I told her I was staying overnight at a friend's.

In any case, for the first time in my life I had two hundred rubles of my own. No, two hundred and seventy-five. Where did the extra sum come from, you ask? Well, I'll tell you.

Early on my second day out, an elderly woman answered the door. "Telegram," I said. "Sign here, please." But instead of taking my pencil, she began to rummage in the pocket of an overcoat that was hanging in the entrance hall and came up with a ruble. When I tried to hand her the pencil again, the ruble fell and I bent down and picked it up. I wanted to give it back, but she said, "No, it's for you, it's for you," and we both felt we'd been caught in a vaguely obscene act. In the end, I dropped the ruble on a stool and ran out.

Before long I was having similar experiences several times a day. The girls asked how much I made in tips, and when I told them I didn't accept anything they couldn't believe their ears. "What's the matter with you?" they cried. "Don't you need the money? 'Cause if you don't, give it to us!"

"But I'd be embarrassed to take their money."

"What do you expect?" they whooped, making me feel an idiot. "Aaron here's got brains. He's going to engineering school." As far as they were concerned, my plan to go on with my education was just as crazy as refusing tips. "Look, we're just ordinary people. We don't care two hoots who gives us our money—the State or whoever comes to the door."

In the end I realized it was silly to hold out. It embarrassed me and irritated the people who tried to tip me, and their thank-you's often turned into "You're a proud one, aren't you!" or "You think a bit too much of yourself, young man."

Every three days I delivered a telegram to an elderly man whose daughter and small grandson had gone on holiday to the Crimea. Doting Grandpa had obviously asked for a biweekly report on the boy. The boy was always fine, and the old man was so pleased that he always tried to give me—guess how much—a ten-ruble note!

Once he asked me in, and I followed him into a luxuriously furnished room with pictures in heavy gold frames covering the walls, magnificent porcelain vases standing on pedestals that looked like miniature black marble columns, and a breakfront filled with china. When he saw in my eyes that his museum had had the desired effect, he smiled and said, "I knew you would appreciate it. You have a feeling for beauty; it is to your credit. But listen to what I have to say." He went up to one of the paintings and began examining it pensively. "My father was a civil engineer. He had a fine collection of paintings. Only this Flemish oil remains. The rest were stripped and sawn to pieces because the stretchers and frames could be used as firewood in the days when firewood was a matter of life and death. By the way—and not many people realize this—though the oils and the canvas they're painted on burn well, they give off no heat. . . . But the point I want to make is that for many years, that is, until I recently retired, I worked as a waiter at the restaurant of the Hotel National"—he pronounced it as if it were French— "although I have a degree from Moscow University, the old Moscow University—it was back in 1915—located, as you know, on Manège Square, near the National, as chance would have it. You, young man, if I may be allowed to repeat myself, have a feeling for beauty. As have I, you will have noticed. But there is a difference between us: I never refused a tip. My salary was five hundred rubles a month, but I had a daughter to bring up and my old age to look out for." He picked up a slip of paper from his desk and handed it to me together with a twenty-five-ruble note. "May I ask a favor of you? When you return to the post office, send off this telegram for me. My legs have been giving me trouble lately, and I go out as little as possible. Don't bother to return the change, and . . . think over what I've told you."

From that day on I accepted all tips.

It was an extremely hot July. There was talk of a drought in the Kuban region and in the Ukraine. Moscow was thirsting for rain, and in spite of occasional claps of thunder in the distance the sun continued to rise in a suffocating gauze and plant itself among the dusty roofs, enormous and scarlet, like a piece of glowing pig iron. Then on the twentieth, as night was coming on, the storm finally broke, a storm that flooded the streets and covered the post-office windows with a matte film. I turned off the light and flattened my nose against the glass, and even now I can remember how good it felt to stand there looking into the darkness, into the rain, and feel the stuffy heat dissolve.

My shift was over at midnight, and I was trying to decide whether to get soaked or wait it out when in came one of the operators with a piece of ticker tape and said, "From abroad. What do you say? If you don't want it, your replacement will be here by the time I paste it on the blank."

Well, why not? I thought. Might as well take a walk in the rain after all this heat. "Hand it over," I said. "I'll drop it off on my way home."

It wasn't far, and I ran the two blocks to a building everyone knew. The Ambassador, they called it, a name it must have earned before the war, when it was turned into a residence for employees of the Commissariat for Foreign Affairs. Whenever we got telegrams with addresses written in the Latin alphabet—they always made us laugh—we automatically took them to The Ambassador. It could easily have waited until morning, but we always treated anything written in those funny Latin letters as urgent. You never knew what might happen if you held it up—another war or something!

Even after running up to the fourth floor, I was dripping like a dead crow picked up by its tail from a puddle. I rang the bell. Rang again. And again. The people must have been sleeping, but I didn't

feel like taking the telegram back to the post office. At last I heard
a distant voice calling, "Who is it?"

"Telegram!" I shouted back. "Foreign telegram!"

"Coming!" the voice said, closer now, a woman's voice, all yawny
and cozy and warm. "Heavens! In this downpour!" she added sym-
pathetically as she opened the door.

And what do you think I saw, Nikolsky my friend? A robe that
opened wider with the door, and under the robe—she'd been in bed,
after all, even asleep, and when I rang the bell she threw on the robe
and ran out—under the robe two deep shadows, the shadows of
two breasts. I must have uttered a cry, because she looked up at me
and said "Oh!" and languorously, ever so languorously, reached for
the flaps of her robe and pulled them together.

"I thought it was a girl," she said. "It's always a girl." She meant
it as a kind of self-justification, but she just stood there smiling,
obviously enjoying the sight of a young man turned to stone by her
charms.

"Just look at you! Soaking wet! It must be pouring out! Well,
come in. You're letting in a draft." She shivered and wrapped the
robe tighter around herself.

Well, there was no draft at all, but I let myself be led in and she
pushed the door shut. It was pitch-dark, and I stood there a moment
or two, afraid to move. Then I heard a soft, cooing laugh coming
from where I had seen her last.

"It's like blind man's buff," she said. "I can't see a thing. Wait a
second. There's a light in the alcove. The switch is down here."

She took a few steps, and I felt a rush of breath on my hand,
sensed something soft sliding along my sleeve, and heard a soft meow-
like "Ooh! Cold! Brr!" Then on flashed the light, and once I was
over my blindness I saw a young woman with her hands pressed to
her cheeks standing near a wall and laughing gales of laughter at
the sight of me.

"Telegram," I mumbled helplessly. "Foreign telegram."

Stunned though I was, I knew very well what I must have looked
like. But between the waves of laughter I noticed her looking me
over with nothing like the disdain I felt I deserved, not even with
irony—no, with clear interest. For my part, I couldn't help staring
at her. My head was reeling, and I was so busy licking my suddenly

parched lips that I didn't hear the laughing stop; all I heard was "You really ought to go into the bathroom and wring out your clothes."

In a daze I went and undressed in the sparkling tiled bathroom, took the elegant terry-cloth robe she passed me through a chink in the door, and draped it over my shoulders. I still don't know whether I realized what it all meant at the time. Probably not. And I imagine my hostess took special, secret pleasure in plying the beanpole guest with her attentions and paving the way for his first sweet seduction.

I emerged from the bathroom timidly, my bare knees protruding conspicuously from under the robe. "Go into the room with the open door and have a seat," she called from the kitchen. "I'll be right in with some hot coffee." Then, to make things sound more domestic, she added, "We wouldn't want you to catch cold now, would we?" or something of the sort.

Oddly enough, the room where I was to drink my coffee turned out to be neither a dining nor a sitting room but a bedroom. It was dominated by a large bed with a beautiful heavy wooden backboard of a type I had seen only in foreign films. The sheets were rumpled, the blanket in disarray—I could just picture her lying there when I rang the bell. And on the far side of the bed I spied a swell of pink-and-white foam, all lace and silk and air. . . .

"Still standing? Oh yes, everything's a mess. I was in bed. . . . Now let's see what the telegram has to say. . . . No, do start. There's the sugar. And have one of the cream puffs. Do you like cream puffs? I just adore them, though they're not what they used to be. . . . 'DETAINED TWO MONTHS URGENT BUSINESS SALARY BY PROXY SMOLENSKAYA.' Oh là là! You like getting your pay packet, don't you? Well, so do I. Only you get your own, and I . . . Why, you're famished, poor thing. Look, we're both cultured people, aren't we? Then let's forget about etiquette. That makes you uncomfortable? No, sitting on a porcupine is uncomfortable. And standing through a diplomatic reception."

She brought in bread and butter, cheese, and some spicy sausage. I must confess I stuffed myself with sandwiches and gulped down the coffee as if it were tea, two cups in a row. And soon I felt better than I'd ever felt in my life. Where else could I have sat in an elegant robe at a groaning board surrounded by every comfort imaginable? Not in Cherkizovo (of less than sainted memory)!

Then there was the beautiful young woman, gazing at me with sleepy, half-shut eyes (she was slightly nearsighted) and smiling out of the corner of her full, shapely lips. Yes, her lips were full, her body round, pleasantly plump. You know the type: a short redhead with white skin that doesn't tan, the Titian woman, if I'm not mistaken. Well, that was Emma. Slightly pretentious for a Russian name, I grant you, but it suited her perfectly: her clothing was pretentious, her furniture, her extravagant behavior—inviting me in in the middle of the night, for instance, sitting me down at her table, and . . .

Much later she told me that lying in her spacious double bed and listening to the thunder, she had had a terrible attack of anguish, an inexplicable animal fear of loneliness such as healthy young women deprived of male companionship are wont to feel. There she lay, biting her pillow to keep from screaming, begging fate to come and change her life. When she heard my first ring, she thought she'd dreamed it, and when she opened the door and saw how I almost fainted when I saw her breasts, she could scarcely keep from pressing me to them, wet and cold and awkward as I was. She knew straight off that I had never slept with a woman, and—yes, these were her words—her heart went out to me. Now I can laugh about it, but then—then it was love. And I wish every innocent a love like that.

Tolstoy's advice to the virginal young man to find a virginal young maid and bind his body and soul to her is just so much decorous rot. Nothing will come of it but woe or, in the best instance, mutual boredom—if it lasts long enough, that is, to produce either. Love needs experience. At least one of the two must have lived. What's so bad about an eighteen-year-old boy and a woman of twenty-five who has no intention of tying him down or catching him in her web?

The only shadow over our idyll, Emma's and mine, was the existence of her husband. For me he was never more than an abstraction, a comma in the flow of our conversation; for her he had more substance. But a husband who lived in another world—he worked at the United Nations and was constantly hopping back and forth between Paris and New York—was more like a god, a pagan god providing bountiful food and clothing and asking nothing, not even fidelity, in return. Once in a while he showed up in Moscow for a briefing and took Emma to a reception or on an unofficial visit; he had even sent for her three or four times from "beyond the curtain" when ordered to. But that was all. He needed a wife because one needed a wife. Otherwise he was a confirmed bachelor, an intelligent and on the face of it perfectly decent man who married Emma when he saw that personal freedom could prove a liability to his career, that a man in his forties simply had to have a family. It all came to a head when his superiors discovered he was having an affair—an affair that meant a lot to him—with his secretary, and marriage seemed the only way to hide and preserve it. Marriage is an important step, particularly for a diplomat, and he took it seriously: Emma was the only daughter of a highly placed Party official who had recently died of a heart attack. In other words, her credentials was as pure as her body.

She realized where she stood before she had time to fall in love with him, but never felt she had been tricked or used. "I'm actually grateful," she said to me once. "I was a silly goose before him, and without him I'd never have been anything else. As it was, I caught on quickly, and now I know what I want out of life."

I didn't ask whether she'd had many men before me, but she certainly had enough love in her to take my mind off the rain for that night and everything else for several nights thereafter. Everything but the entrance exams, that is. Towards the end of the week I had to tell her.

"Well, well. And not a word all this time. What school?"

"Bauman."

Emma gave a whistle and shook her head. Then she went to the phone and had a long talk with a friend who had connections. She explained the situation and asked about the admissions policy at the school, adding, "By the way, his name is Aaron Finkelmeyer."

"You know what, darling?" she said, hanging up almost immediately. "Forget about Bauman. It would take a miracle to get you in. Try an agricultural college. Or the College of Transport Economics, which I went to until I got married. What do you say?"

But I preferred to go for the miracle. Youth is vain, after all. I had no idea what it meant to be an engineer, yet I rejected Emma's offer of her friend's pull at other schools. No, it was the prestigious Bauman or nothing.

On the first of August I took the Russian composition exam. I chose to write on Pushkin, "The Image of Onegin" to be exact. I was so inspired I covered fifteen sheets, and I was so sure I'd passed that when I reported for the mathematics exam a few days later I didn't bother to find my name on the list. Even after waiting in vain to be called into the exam room, I trusted that the error could be rectified in five or ten minutes—I'd just have to work a little faster to get all the problems done in time—and ran to my old friends the secretaries and demanded to know why I wasn't on the list.

They didn't need to glance down at a paper; they remembered both me and my name—a bad sign. "What's the fuss about, Finkel-meyer? You failed the exam. Here, take your application and go."

Suddenly the state of nervous excitation I'd been in gave way to resentment and despair, and I made a terrible scene. "Impossible! Impossible!" I yelled and stormed the tables piled with papers, files, and looseleaf binders in the hope of finding the list of examination results and convincing them I couldn't have failed. The girls got scared and tried to drag me away, but I kept at it until one of them cried out, "Here it is! Here it is! Read it yourself!"

But the letters "unsat" next to my name only infuriated me more. Now I had to find the composition itself and prove I couldn't possibly have deserved the "unsat." I decided the exams were in the cabinets lining the walls, and I was about to lunge at one and smash its glass doors when the girls screamed, "No! No! Go to the dean! He's in. He'll see you."

I raced up the stairs and along the corridors, bursting into a wrong room or two before I found him. He turned out to be a courteous gentleman who earnestly urged me to calm down and even poured me a glass of water. I drank it and said "Thank you" and sat down in a large leather armchair, but I didn't forget what I'd come for.

Why was I so certain I had made no errors in my work and we— that is, they, one of the finest institutions of higher learning in the Soviet Union—had made an error in ours? Why did I, a young man, blame them and refuse to blame myself?

"I know the curriculum well and I know Russian well. I want to see my composition."

In the end he told me he would need special permission from the Ministry of Education to show me my paper, but if I insisted he would phone the teacher who had read it. He then dialed a number, greeted the person on the other end of the line, and said he had an examinee in his office by the name of—excuse me, but what did you say your name was?—Finkelmeyer, who was upset because . . .

The dean did not need to go into detail. It was clear that neither I nor my composition had been forgotten. "Then I'll let you speak to him yourself," said the dean and handed me the receiver.

"You know very well you copied every word of it," said a cold, brusque voice.

"What?" I shouted. "Copied? I copied it? Where from?"

"Why, from Pushkin," the voice replied sarcastically. "From Pushkin himself. You gave abundant quotations, letter-perfect quotations, down to the orthographical idiosyncrasies of the author. You had the book in your lap, young man."

"That's a lie!" I cried. "That's a lie! I know *Onegin* by heart. Including the fragments from the unfinished tenth chapter!"

"You're wasting my time."

"Test me then! Any chapter, any line! Any one you feel like!"

"First learn to speak Russian correctly, Finkelmeyer," my most worthy interlocutor said to me in a combination of animosity and glee. "We say 'any one you please' or 'any one you wish.' You must speak correctly before you can write correctly." And he hung up.

I picked myself up out of the armchair and stood before the dean, a shriveled, gray Soviet professor and administrator who had completed all his studies under the czarist regime. "What chapter would you like to hear?" I said to him. His only response was a raised eyebrow. "Well, if you don't care, I'll start with the second—lots of people memorize the first—and go on till I come to the very end, the tenth. This is the middle of the second chapter:

" 'But friendship, as between our heroes,
can't really be: for we've outgrown
old prejudice; all men are zeros,
the units are ourselves alone.
Napoleon's our sole inspiration;
the millions of two-legged creation
for us are instruments and tools;
feeling is quaint, and fit for fools . . .' "

Ten minutes later two graduate students were poking their elbows into my stomach and shoving me into the corridor, but I twisted my body in such a way that I faced the dean and could continue my recitation at the unexpectedly ironic point:

> " 'To save the honour of our land
> I must translate—there's no presuming—
> the letter from Tatyana's hand:
> her Russian was as thin as vapour,
> she never read a Russian paper.' "

By this time I was choking with laughter, but just as they were about to jerk me out of the office once and for all I grabbed hold of the doorpost and managed to proclaim:

> " 'Our native speech had never sprung
> unhesitating from her tongue!' "

Because of the time it took to lodge complaints first with the Central Admissions Committee, then with the Ministry of Higher Education, I was too late to apply to any school at all. But more important, I had been lying for weeks to my mother. I told her nothing about the job at the post office, nothing about the exam fiasco, assuring myself it was for her own good—the truth would kill her. And naturally I never dreamed of telling her about my relationship with Emma (I was living with a strange woman and eating not her bread but her husband's)—I simply lied. Yet Emma's caresses—which I returned like an Adam exploring his Eve with a combination of ardor, wonder, and fear—were the antidote that kept me going through all those tortures.

Then one night the poison took its toll: I woke up in bed deathly ill, feeling Emma staring down at my face. Even now, more than ten years later, I can see the suffering and compassion in her eyes. I'm no expert when it comes to women's feelings; I'm no expert when it comes to my own, for that matter. But just before I sank back into delirium I realized that Emma loved me, loved me deeply and sincerely, even madly. "You've been tossing and turning, darling," she whispered, feeling me all over, "and your forehead's on fire."

As it turned out, I had managed to catch double pneumonia and was terribly run-down to boot. I was delirious over long stretches of time, often crying out scraps of mathematical formulas. In fact, it was the delirium that kept the doctors from making the correct diagnosis: they thought I had infectious meningitis.

The day after it began, Emma left me in the care of a close friend and took a taxi first to the post office, where she reported my illness and found out where I lived, then to Cherkizovo.

"Are you Aaron's mother?" she asked, walking into the house.

"Oh my God, what's happened to him?" my mother moaned.

Emma wept and went on about what an evil woman she was and how it was all her fault, not mine, and my illness was her punishment. When she reached the point of saying she would kill herself if she couldn't nurse me back to health, the two of them started weeping together. Then they climbed into the taxi and raced back to my bedside, which Mother left only for short intervals to visit her mother, who had been left in the care of neighbors. My darling Emma had managed to call in a team of doctors from the Kremlin Hospital (she told them I was a relative who had come from Minsk to take the university entrance exams). They were the ones who made the correct diagnosis. Emma moved heaven and earth to come up with the new wonder drug they recommended, and when even the Kremlin couldn't supply it, she sent an express telegram to her husband in Paris, begging him to find and dispatch it posthaste no matter what the cost. Apparently he had to go all the way to the top, but he did manage to get it into the diplomatic pouch on the next plane for Moscow.

By late autumn the crisis was over and I was able to put foot to floor. My head pounded, my eyes were dim, and I had to grab each piece of furniture so as not to fall, but I managed to reach the window and lower myself into the armchair. There I covered my legs with the blanket Emma liked to wrap around herself and peered outside.

Apparently while I was delirious the cerebral mechanism that regulates the way we perceive time reverted to its earliest, infantile stage, when everything is just strips of feeling. We don't know who we are in the first months of life. By the time we have recourse to memory, we are part of a world that has taken definite shape in our consciousness, even though we can understand little and name less. By the time we are two or three, for example, we look at a tree and know it to be *a tree;* we know a dog is *a dog,* the sun is *the sun,* and what hurts *hurts* and makes you cry. I saw a falling leaf, and it was a shattering event, one I couldn't put into words. It was a miracle, an inexplicable yellow flutter, a quivering yellow, a shivering circle. Look at all the yellow flutters, the slowly floating shivering circles! A cloud hovering above a roof was a broadening of light, a vanishing whiteness, a growing blueness, a cold, sharp outline melting up into the distance and down into the breast. . . .

Mother and Emma were rattling some dishes in the kitchen, and it took some time before they heard my cough. I was coughing because I was crying, and I was crying because I was alive. They ran in and saw me crying, crying and smiling. "It's moving on," I said to myself as the tears ran down my cheeks. "It's almost over." What was moving on? Time? Life? And what was almost over? The pneumonia? My childhood?

It's moving on, Lyonya, still moving on. Hear it there outside the window? The cold flutter, the white darkness, the shivering circle. The storm, the blizzard, the wild wench called winter.

VI

THAT WINTER Emma got me into a sanatorium in a snow-covered pine forest. I took long walks and read, and Emma visited me often. When my days at the sanatorium ran out, she found me a room in the house of a retired nurse. I spent another six or eight weeks there. By the time I returned to Moscow in March I was my old self again.

I was still on record as a post office employee, so I reported back to my branch. The girls were overjoyed to see me. They immediately ran out to the shops and regaled me with sweet Kagor wine and sprats. The post office was as understaffed as ever, and the branch head looked over my record quickly and said, "You've got experience now. I can promote you to head of delivery, and higher rank means higher pay." I accepted.

There was some money due me from before my illness, and adding it to what I'd salted away I had a considerable sum. I divided it in three; one third I gave to Mother so she could take a break from her sewing and buy something for the house, one third I used to fill out my wardrobe, and with the last third I went to see my friend Leopold Mikhailovich, the former historian and waiter with the china and oils collection.

I had been to see him several times before my illness. He invited me to come whether I had telegrams or not; he liked the way I studied the art and asked about the artists, and he liked to give me lectures on them. Soon I had a clear idea of Dutch and Flemish painting and of the Barbizon school.

I told him I wished to find a gift for a woman who had done a great deal for me, and as I had no experience I needed his advice. My red face clearly gave me away, yet he still felt called upon to inquire—with all due respect, of course—whether I might not be in love with the woman in question. I nodded. "An essential point, don't you think?" he asked, and added, "And now a second question: How much can you spend?"

With this equally essential point out of the way he picked up his walking stick and we set off for the Arbat. The moment we entered the antique shop, a salesman ran up to him and the two of them went off on their own. Before long Leopold came back with a pleased look on his face and took me over to the counter, where the salesman held out a small oval locket depicting Apollo surrounded by the Muses. The locket—Leopold said it was French and "of the finest period for that sort of work"—had no chain, but was otherwise in mint condition. "Note that it opens in the back, young man, and has space for a memento." The only reason I could afford it was that the setting was of nickel silver. I bought it and gave it to her that very evening.

Of course I'd hoped Emma would like it, but I didn't expect so ecstatic a reaction. Damn, she was a fine woman! She immediately started rummaging in her jewel box and came up with a matching chain, then rushed to the wardrobe, hid behind the open door, and reappeared wearing a light-blue low-cut evening gown with the locket between her breasts.

She asked me for a picture. We tore the photograph from the public transport pass the post office had given me. Then, deaf to my protests, she grabbed a pair of scissors, snipped off a curl from the back of my neck, and placed it and the picture in the locket as "mementos."

The locket turned out to be a farewell gift. The next morning we awoke to Mother pounding on the door. She had brought my conscription notice. Again the two women wept together over their luckless Aaron.

I was in a terrible state: I was leaving behind my mother, who had her own mother to look after; I was leaving behind Emma, my beloved Emma; and I was leaving behind all my plans for the future. I remember being plagued by the idiotic thought that I was wrong to have spent all that money on clothes I wouldn't be able to wear.

From then on, military routine took over. Soon I was standing naked before the medical board, trying to shield my circumcised pride and joy from the nurses' quizzical looks. Then I had my head shaved so I would look like an utter imbecile, and then—"Farewell, O Mother! Farewell, my bride!!"—all aboard! Two hundred muddled head of cattle. Lurch. Here we go now, here we go now, *zait gezund* now, *Yoshke fort avek!*

Not only did I look like an imbecile, I acted like one—in everything that had to do with the military at least. Until the incident I'm going to tell you about, my life in the army was one long string of jokes, and I deserved my nickname, Aaron Švejk; I earned it in spades: kitchen patrol, leaves denied, the lockup (from which I was released on the intervention of the medical authorities).

The sergeant at the head of my platoon was one of those soldiers who'd stayed on in the army after the war. He hadn't much education, but was quick on the uptake, quick in general, and not a bad man; it was just that he had no idea there was a world outside military training or brains that worked differently from his. And, well, I couldn't help picking on him for picking on me, in other words, I enjoyed making him stop and wonder who was getting the best of whom.

His greatest tragedy was that Finkelmeyer refused to be buried in any formation; he would always stick out a head and a half above the others. So when Sarge bellowed "Left face!" Aaron Švejk would jiggle in place a few seconds as if lame and finally turn in the wrong direction, somehow managing to trip over himself, bump into the fellow in front of him, and drop his rifle with a bang.

Sarge would run over and lift his face to mine and roar, "Finkel-meyer! What kind of turn is that? Well?"

"I suppose you might call it less than perfect, Comrade Sergeant."

"Well, why do you keep getting it wrong, you fucking bastard?"

"You don't give me enough time to think."

"Think?" he would bray, turning redder than his decorations. "What's there to think about, shithead?"

"Which is my left shoulder and which is my right."

Once after an exchange such as this the Sarge tried to give me a punch in the teeth, but I instinctively ducked and our dear guide and master landed facedown in the dirt. I'll say this for the old campaigner, though: he didn't have it in for me. According to our captain, who happened to be in the vicinity and had been attracted by the commotion, I, a common soldier, had raised my hand against a noncommissioned officer. After I was out of the jug, to which I was consigned while they conducted their investigation, I heard that at great risk to himself he'd admitted to the captain that *he* had raised his hand against *me*. At the first opportunity I went up and thanked him for saving me from the court-martial's bench, but all he did was sigh and say, "Look, I went through the whole war an honest soldier. You think I'm gonna turn whore for some wiseass kike, even if he is the lousiest fucking soldier I ever saw?"

I tried to explain why I was such a lousy soldier and not the stalwart he might hope for. I told him I must have been missing the wire that carried a military command to the brain and set the body—arms, legs, torso—in proper motion. I told him I envied the country boys with little education who had no trouble taking apart or putting together a breech block and doing the manual of arms and all the drills out on the parade ground.

"You must be some kind of nut," he said, moving away from me as if I had the plague. "What about in bed? You have trouble knowing what goes where with a woman?"

"No," I said. "No problem."

"Oh, you Yids!" He spit in fury. "You and your damn brains."

From then on he was more lenient with me.

Six months into our term of duty the lieutenant colonel in charge of our regiment came to inspect his troops. He was accompanied by the assistant chief political officer, who had come to put us through our ideological paces, that is, test our familiarity with the international situation and the biography of our genius of a generalissimo.

We were marching four abreast past the lieutenant colonel when he called out, "Left face!" I had gone a good ten steps before I realized with horror that I should have made the turn slowly, almost in place, to give the other three a chance to turn around my axis. By the time I looked back, I was ten feet away from the column, which was in such a mess—everyone treading on everyone else's heels—it could scarcely be called a column anymore. Just as I started back, the lieutenant colonel shouted, "Halt! One, two!"

I froze.

While the soldiers resumed their original formation, the lieutenant colonel, his political officer, and Sarge, who had just come on the scene, strode over to me.

On the far side of the wasteland they called a camp there was a beautiful little grove, and I gazed over at it for my last look, certain that they would stand me against the wall then and there.

"What's going on in your head?" I heard the lieutenant colonel bark. "Writing poetry or something?"

What could I say? Either "Yes, Comrade Lieutenant Colonel" or "No, Comrade Lieutenant Colonel." I had no other choice.

"Yes, Comrade Lieutenant Colonel."

The sergeant sighed and shook his head. Finkelmeyer was at it again, and this time in front of the brass.

"What do you mean?" he sneered. "You mean you do write poetry?"

And suddenly—it was like a kick in the pants—I knew exactly how to proceed.

"Yes, Comrade Lieutenant Colonel, I do. Would you care to hear some?"

I stared straight at him, my smile all teeth, broad and idiotic, but the ratchet wheel inside my head was spinning, the words starting to take shape. The lieutenant colonel turned in amazement to the political officer, who, trying to dismiss the whole thing with a laugh and a shrug (he considered himself an intellectual), suggested, "Why not ask for a sample of his . . . poetry."

"Well?" said the lieutenant colonel, in a less than imperious, in fact, rather fearful tone of voice.

And taking as much air as I could into my lungs, I shouted:

> "Lo! the regiment's flag before us
> Bids us all to sing in chorus . . ."

Then I was stuck, and to make matters worse one of the soldiers belched loudly behind me.

"Well? Well?" the lieutenant colonel said, moving closer. "What comes next?"

Round went the ratchet and I roared:

> "Bravely wave in rain and sun
> Till the final battle's won!"

Grotesque, isn't it? Well, wait till you hear what happened next.

The lieutenant colonel paused and said, "You're not putting me on, are you? You really wrote that?"

"Yes, Comrade Lieutenant Colonel! All by myself."

"Here and now? On the spot?"

"Yes, Comrade Lieutenant Colonel! Here and now, Comrade Lieutenant Colonel. On the spot."

"Well, don't do it again!" he barked, realizing he'd slipped out of character. "No more poetry in formation, is that clear?" But then he backed down and said to me (in what military correspondents are wont to call "a paternal tone"), "You see what happens? You throw off the whole column."

"Sorry, Comrade Lieutenant Colonel!"

But even as he stood there looking sternly at me, I saw an idea come into his head. He took the political officer off to the side, and while they had a little talk, I wondered feverishly, Jug or no jug?

"Keep your pecker up, Švejk!" I heard one of the soldiers behind me whisper. "You're free and clear!"

And sure enough at that moment the lieutenant colonel turned and waved. "You there, soldier. On the double!" I ran over to them. "Think you could turn that poem of yours into a song for the regiment?"

I lifted my eyes to the heavens and started reciting softly:

> "Lo! the regiment's flag before us
> Bids us all to sing in chorus
> Bravely wave in rain and sun
> Till the final battle's won.
> We'll march with you into the fray . . ."

I hesitated and, none too confident, added, "And save the Motherland, hooray!"

"What do you think?" said the political officer. "Not bad, eh?"

The lieutenant colonel called to Sarge to carry on by himself, took me over to his jeep, and told the driver to rush us to the officers' compound. And there, as Pushkin might have put it, my fate was sealed.

Within two hours at the political officer's desk I had finished the song, and by the end of the next day our local composer—and band director—had come up with an appropriately bravura melody and was teaching it to the regiment. A district-wide review had been announced, and the officers didn't want to fall on their faces. They were expecting some really top brass, including a deputy to the Minister of Defense, if you please.

On the day of the review the band began to play and the boys and I marched forth singing "The Regiment's Flag" at the top of our lungs. Even then I did more harm than good: my ear is fine, but my voice is horrendous.

That evening we put on a talent show for our guests, and again "Lo! the regiment's flag before us" resounded in a mighty roar. During the break I was introduced to the Deputy Minister, who shook my hand and said, "Fine, I agree," which meant he agreed with Private Finkelmeyer's detachment to the staff of the regiment newspaper.

To bring this account of my poetic debut to an end, I should point out that "The Regiment's Flag" actually became part of the Red Army Chorus's official repertory and was performed regularly for a year until suddenly it was heard no more. One of the stanzas celebrated the "force of iron, lead, and steel,/Stalin's wisdom, soldiers' zeal," and when Stalin died the song died with him. May they both stay dead and buried.

Anyway, I began to work on the regiment's newspaper. As you have doubtless guessed, it was a pretty cushy post. Hard as it is to believe, I had a room to myself. I was a poet and needed privacy for my rendezvous with the Muses, my bouts with Inspiration. My main job was to grind out verse of the required length (a quarter of a column, a full column) and subject matter (army life, the Motherland, the Kremlin bigwigs, the struggle for peace against the imperialist warmonger), but there were special assignments too—a veritable epic about the Colorado beetle, for instance. Remember the Colorado beetle? America's secret weapon to devour our crops so when the imperialists invaded we'd be too weak to resist. Well, I wrote a long narrative poem to give the regiment the moral fiber to meet the beetles head-on. It was either us or them, after all.

What I learned from the experience was that I could fire off rhymed iambs and trochees with the speed of an automatic. They'd call me in, sit me down, and say, "Artillery Day, twelve lines, and step on it, will you? We're about to go to press." With nary a peep I'd clear my desk, whip out a clean sheet of paper, and the performance would begin. "Hey, come quick, everybody!" someone would shout into the corridor. "Aaron's at it again." And out of the doors they came. By the time they'd gathered round I was on line three, and by the time they'd read one and two, three and four were ready, waiting, and rhymed.

I never understood what made them ooh and aah so over the rhymes. Rhymes came automatically to me; they still do. But my colleagues, all officers and all quite a bit older than I was, considered me a real find: an ever-ready source of instant material—local, political, or humorous—and in verse!

We rarely signed our articles, of course, but when I did something major the byline read "A. Yefimov." The name came from the editor-in-chief.

"What's your first name, Finkelmeyer?" he asked me when we met.

"Aaron-Chaim," I said, and added, "Chaim is like Yefim."

The editor lowered his voice and said, "You're telling me? My name is Goldberg, and I sign my articles Zolotaryov. How about A. Yefimov? Sounds good, actually."

I had to admit it was a lot easier to get a Russian tongue around than Finkelmeyer.

In any case, from a walking joke I became a walking legend. My song was sung, my verses filled the columns of the newspaper, my slogans adorned the byways of our military backwater. The brass not only greeted me but excused or rather overlooked my various eccentricities. They overlooked some less than innocent capers as well. Once I made up a nasty little fable about a roly-poly piggy-wiggy that could only have been our general's wife, the terror of everyone in the district, the general included. It fell into her hands while making the rounds, but she was clever enough not to blow it up into a scandal. The general apparently had a good laugh over it and was rumored to have said, "A real card, our Jew poet!" The fable was anonymous.

I had a steady stream of letters from Emma, a trickle from Mother. My answers to both were long and playful. No letter can possibly convey the boredom, the melancholy, the depression of military life. Besides, every letter a soldier writes is read before it goes out. So I joked and clowned my way from one to the next. I never did take the military seriously anyway: parade-ground exercises, target shooting, "halt" "fire" and "double-time march," heavy, dream-less, reveille-punctuated sleep, inane political indoctrination ses-sions, and finally, when I started working on the newspaper, the absurd poetastering to order—it all flew past as if something had turned my brain into a phantasmagorical comic strip, a series of visions with only the most tenuous connection to reality and a most pitiful likeness of myself smack in the middle.

Letters were my only link with real life, which, while I was in the army, boiled down to concepts like "freedom," "love," and "moth-erhood." Could I be certain that a woman like Emma was true to my love? What right had I to hers? I never broached the matter in our correspondence; she was rather reticent herself. Then one day— I'd been in the service for more than a year at the time—she turned downright apathetic and mentioned "by the way" that she was leaving her apartment. That could mean only one thing: she was going abroad; I was losing her! I went through the rest of the letter in shock. One sentence stood out, though, and I read it twice: "No matter what anyone says, don't worry—your mother is well. Mother herself had added a line that said, "Now Aaronele, I don't want you worrying about your mother Golda. Everything is fine, believe me."

I didn't know what to think. Mother had a bad heart, a bad liver, and high blood pressure, so I always asked about her health. But why the admonitions not to worry? And why in a letter hinting of Emma's imminent departure? And what was "no matter what anyone says" supposed to mean?

It all became clear in a few days, when I received a telegram signed by a doctor informing me that my mother was seriously ill. After a moment of shock I caught on. Of course, it was all a hoax: the illness, the telegram, the doctor. Emma had made the whole thing up so we could have a few days together before she left. My shock turned first to joy, then to the distressing realization that she was in fact going away.

I spent ten days in Moscow. Ten days, nine nights. I embraced her knowing that someone else would soon embrace her and trying to believe her assurances that nothing could ever detract from our love. Even after our bodies gave out, desire remained; we were one insatiable whole.

At twilight we would wander along the banks of the river, the Ring, back streets, kissing under trees, in entries, behind the gates of small, tumbledown houses. It was July again; our love had a two-year past. But it had no future: Emma's husband had been named ambassador to one of the smaller Latin American countries, where embassy staffs remained stable for years. I was insanely jealous of the man who had only to extend an invisible hand to pluck her from me and of the men who might have been with her during the year I'd been away.

On one of our last days together we were drawn to an outlying corner of Gorky Park, one where attendants and policemen never strayed. Emma threw her coat on the ground, we fell on it, and at a point when the mind would seem to be blank, the voice capable only of moans, she whispered, "Thank you, darling, thank you for never asking. And now I'll tell you. No, there's been no one, nobody.

You're my only love, have been and always will be. I want to take you with me. For always. I want a child, your child! I want to take your child with me!"

Then she left. I went to the airport, but couldn't get near her. She was surrounded by ministry underlings, their wives, and a few friends. Forcing a smile, she pecked cheeks, nodded here and there, and threw me furtive glances of puppylike suffering. After the final boarding announcement she gave me one last smile and, the tears rolling down her cheeks, disappeared.

How stupid people are to number their conquests! If a woman is your first or your eighth or your thirtieth, give her a number, use whatever system you please. But when that woman is your love . . .

Forget what I said before about the experienced older woman and the virgin boy. Love can shatter if it so desires—raise you up and smash you to bits; love is God the All-Merciful and God the Almighty. Ours is not to reason why when it summons, and as long as it lives on in us, it is the alpha and omega, the beginning and end of everything. . . .

VII

THERE'S a saying in the army: while the soldier sleeps, his tour of duty shortens. Well, I slept my way through the summer and had nothing to show for it than that much less service time. What's more, my poems lost their former buoyancy and started sounding bilious. One day my editor, Goldberg-Zolotaryov, a limited and none too courageous soul, leaned on me a bit too hard.

"What kind of language is this, Private Finkelmeyer?"

You rat, I thought. The room was empty. "It's good, lean Russian, and if you don't like it . . ." And I let out a stream of Yiddish curses that even Russian would have been hard put to match. Oh, he had a go at me too, but pro forma, so to speak—he couldn't very well complain to the brass that a private had cursed him out in choice Yiddish. From then on he let me alone.

That winter a group of five or six Moscow writers paid the camp a visit in connection with Army Day. Though only one or two of them had written anything worth mentioning, the word "writer," to use Gorky's formulation, has a proud ring to it, and they were given the red-carpet treatment. In return they gave readings and hobnobbed with the soldiers, even joked a little, and in general acquitted themselves honorably.

On Army Day itself we put on another talent show. It goes without saying that the opening number was a rip-roaring full-chorus, drum-and-bugle-corps rendition of "The Regiment's Flag." And while the stage was being cleared of chairs and music stands, a tow-headed soldier in parade dress stood up in front of the curtain, a piece of purple plush that had seen better days, and in a tight tenor voice declaimed the "latest military poems of our own Private Yefimov."

After the performance my editor started bowing and scraping and wondering whether the comrades weren't tired after their long day; creative work consumes enormous amounts of energy, after all, and . . .

"Anyone for wetting the old whistle?" the most famous of the writers broke in with a laugh. "Well, boys, what do you say?"

So all of us—the writers, a general or two and other assorted brass, plus a select group from the newspaper staff—set off for the officers' mess. As the poet I was seated next to the oldest—and, to my mind, most likable—of the writers, a man who had published his first works before the Revolution, at about the same time as Mayakovsky, and thought of himself as a Constructivist. After a long silence he was allowed to publish translations from the French, but not until the war broke out did his own work see print again. Then another long silence. In recent years a few slim volumes have appeared, but by now he is a walking relic, surrounded by young admirers (when I see him I call him Master) yet despondent. He's faltering, in poor health, and completely dependent on the whims of his sister—they share an apartment—though I should add he's as paradoxical as ever, his tongue is still sharp, and he even writes a decent line now and again.

Anyway, back then, I'd never heard of him, or, rather, I'd heard his name and his poems for the first time the night before, from the stage. He didn't read like the others; his voice was simple, dignified, and—though the poems were serious—ever so slightly ironic. Maybe

I was so happy to be sitting next to him because from the start I felt he wasn't an empty shell or stuffed shirt like the others. As the host I kept his glass full and his plate well stocked with herring and mushrooms. When he complained of liver trouble, I could sympathize with stories of my mother's ailment.

There were a number of toasts. The officers started unbuttoning their uniforms, talk merged into a drunken din, and soon the Master was pretty far gone himself. At one point I looked up to see a greasy fork waving in front of my nose.

"They're a pile of shit," the Master said, his eyes flashing.

"What's a pile of shit?"

"Those poems of yours."

"Oh, them," I said. "Of course! But what about the stuff your colleague over there?" I nodded at one of the poets. "What about the stuff he writes? Isn't *that* a pile of shit?"

"Good for you, my boy," said the Master. "A rare talent, telling shit from shit."

"I've got another talent too," I said. "I can tell shit from something better."

"Oh ho! And what do you call better?"

"This, for instance."

I recited his own poems back to him, keeping as close as I could to his own style of recitation. The Master was amazed I had remembered them, amazed and, obviously, flattered. He started asking me who I was, where I was from, how I'd come to work on the newspaper. He asked whether I read a lot. Actually I hadn't gone beyond the school curriculum: Pushkin, Lermontov, and Nekrasov—the three nineteenth-century giants—and Stalin's favorite, Mayakovsky.

"What about Baratynsky. And Fet. Polonsky. Tyutchev. Blok. You mean you don't know Blok?"

Suddenly, knocking over his chair, he forced himself to his feet and, face beet-red from the rush of blood, bellowed, "Listen here, you hussars! Shut your mouths and listen while I tell you the bitter story of Russian poetry!"

The din around the table died down, and everyone stared up at us. Only the famous writer made believe nothing had happened and went on gobbling down his food like a wolf. The Master poked a finger in his direction, rocking so hard he nearly fell. "You there," he yelled, his voice full of hatred. "Stop that. Look at him, eating away . . ."

"Aren't we in a tizzy, now," said the writer in his oily tenor.

Of course there's nothing less Russian than goading a drunk, making a fool of him, but the famous writer was famous enough to overlook even the unwritten laws of his country; all he cared about was poking fun at his more talented but less fortunate colleague.

"Know what he did?" the Master persisted. "He and his kind? Burned all my books while I was away at the front. Three thousand volumes of poetry. Burned them to keep their asses warm in Moscow. *That*'s the bitter story of Russian poetry!"

"Look at the man," the famous writer appealed to the rest of the table. "Look at him. Stinking drunk!" But everyone tried hard not to look.

Meanwhile I propped him up from behind and with the help of a newspaper colleague steered him outside. The night air was brisk, and I asked my colleague to bring out the master's coat from the rack. The moment the door slammed shut, the Master gave a little laugh and freed himself from my grasp. He had sobered up instantly.

"Forget about the coat," he said. "Where do you live? In the barracks?"

"A private room. Across the road."

"Let's go. The vodka won't let us catch cold."

He sped off like a young man and was completely himself by the time we reached my room. The incident didn't seem to have fazed him. "He'll find a way to get back at me, the potbellied bastard. But he gets a kick out of our cat-and-mouse game. Otherwise he'd have had me put away long ago."

"Put away?"

"He'd drop a word at the right place and the right time, and they'd come for me, as they came for so many others, in the middle of the night—it scares you out of your wits and lets fewer people in on what's happening—ship me off to the wastes of Vorkuta or Kolyma and hard labor."

"But . . . writers ratting on writers? How can that be? My father was sent to jail to keep a whole ring from being implicated in some dirty business, but that was business. What kind of business can poets get messed up in?"

The Master laughed, then stared at me in silence. He was lying on my bed; I was sitting opposite him. And all at once he began telling me about how several years before the war he'd been terribly down and out—starving, in fact. Nobody would publish him or even find him a job in literature; they were all afraid of him. He had translated two or three poems by Georgian friends who turned into "enemies of the people" and were arrested. In desperation he went to the Moscow Town Council and inquired about employment possibilities in factory clubs or Young Pioneer groups, in libraries or even bookshops. There he came to the attention of a man who remembered him. "Why, of course, of course! One of the great names in Soviet poetry. I saw you at the Writers Congress, on the podium, next to Gorky." No, he hadn't read any of his poems, because he'd been "unable to devote the necessary time to a systematic study of both our poetry and the poetry of the bourgeois period," but he hoped to make up for it in the near future. He'd grown up in a poor village, finally seen the light and joined the local Party cell, whereupon he quickly and efficiently did away with the "bloodsucking kulaks," half of whom were related to him, organized the rest of the peasants into a collective, and set to ruling them with an iron hand. When Moscow began cracking down on the overzealous, he'd been transferred first to the local town, then to the provincial capital, and so on and so forth. Everywhere he went, he was praised to the skies. Who had a purer class background? Who knew better how to lead the peasants? And lead them he did, until somewhere along the line he realized that first, workers had a lot more to say about running things than peasants, and second, besides a Party card you needed an education. So, even though he was a high-ranking official by then, off he went to a gigantic foundry under construction in the Urals, heading a concrete-mixing crew by day and going to school at night. His rise was meteoric, from Party Committee to District Committee to Town Council to—Moscow.

Now he was in charge of the Moscow cultural scene. He was even writing a novel. It was about the class struggle in the countryside, which he knew well. Would the poet care to look at the first draft while he tried to find a position for him?

The Master wasn't born yesterday. He took the manuscript. Muddled and illiterate as it was, it had been accepted for publication. And sure enough its author just happened to find an opening for the Master at the publishing house that had accepted it. The Master was saved. He rewrote the novel sentence by sentence, altering plot line, developing characters. The novel was a hit. The man wrote another, this time about a gigantic foundry under construction in the Urals. During the war he'd written patriotic essays and stories, and now he was a big shot in the Writers Union.

"So you see why he wants me out of the way, why he wants even my name to vanish. And all I did was edit his first book."

"You mean he's the one! A wolf in sheep's clothing."

"Of course he's the one, though he's no wolf. A wolf has an eye for the ladies; he prefers little boys."

That night reminds me of this one, Lyonya. We stayed up till all hours. The only difference is that this time *I'm* doing the talking, and I have gone on, haven't I? You'll stop me when you've had enough, all right? Not yet? Well, I could give you a word-for-word account of what the Master told me, but it would take half the night and there's really no need. It all boiled down to "the bitter story of Russian poetry."

You see, I asked if I could hear more of his work, and he recited a group of his earliest pieces, then pieces from his Constructivist period, and finally one or two long, sad pieces from the thirties, works that have remained unpublished to this day. Then he remembered I hadn't read the classics. "We'll start with Baratynsky," he said, and recited two or three poems, then named another poet and recited a few of his works, and another and another until he'd put together a whole anthology. It was from him I first heard names like Polonsky, Apollon Grigoryev, and Annensky, to say nothing of Balmont, Bely, and Tsvetaeva. He recited Pasternak, Akhmatova, Khlebnikov—my mind was awash in beautiful, no, sublime poetry. I had brought with me from school the idea that between Nekrasov and Mayakovsky there was a great, yawning abyss like the one stretching between classical antiquity and the Renaissance. Suddenly it was filled in, and I sensed an ocean and lush new lands beckoning.

The next evening, standing at the bus that would take the writers back to Moscow, the poet gave me his address and told me to write and include poems in my letters.

"Poems!" I cried in disbelief. "You can't expect me to keep churning out drivel after what I've heard. I'm going to resign from the newspaper. See the soldiers putting up those barracks over there? I'd be better off carting bricks."

But the Master shook his head, grabbed the lapels of my coat, and pulled me close enough to talk into my ear. "Don't be a fool, you hear? Give the paper all the rhymed nonsense it needs, but use your time wisely. You've got a gift for literature. I can tell. Use your time to study, to prepare for the Literary Institute. Read poetry, and write the real stuff—from the heart. I can't promise anything will come of it, of course, but I do promise to read anything you send. Remember. I'll be waiting."

For days I walked around in a stupor. I would wake up in the middle of the night and hear poems reeling through my mind—strange, wonderful poems. It was as if I'd taken them down from the Master and stored them in my memory. It was spring, and the blood was coursing through my veins. I needed love, there was no one, and when a poet can love only a shadow, he mortifies the flesh with verse. I began to write.

Long ago—I was still a child, I think—I heard a radio program about Dante. It may have been in connection with an anniversary of his birth or death or it may have had something to do with Tchaikovsky's *Francesca di Rimini*—yes, that's it! Nobody would ever just do a program on Dante; there had to be a reason. This time it was the "great Russian composer." But oddly enough, the commentator didn't stop with Francesca's plight; he went on to talk about the *Inferno* and the whole *Divine Comedy;* he brought in the *Vita nuova,* quoted sonnets and examples of *terza rima,* and told the story of Dante's love for Beatrice. It was thanks to that anonymous commentator that at the age of twenty I caught a glimpse of Dante and Beatrice.

My first genuine poem began with the words "The *Vita nuova* has come to an end." It was a mixture of self-pity and self-irony, the latter taking the form of an admonition to "console yourself with another." There were rosebuds to be gathered, a new life to live. It was spring.

I sent off the poem to the Master and received a long letter in return. "I am happy," he wrote. "I have had many discoveries.

Few have persevered. Some were destroyed; others destroyed themselves. Still, there has to be someone to tell a poet, 'You are you—a poet by the will of God, by birth,' someone to brand him with the stigma of his slavery forever. Persevere, my boy. Persevere."

Well, he branded me, all right, and I bear the stigma like a curse. Many's the time I've tried to tear it out, but all I get for my pains is skin and bloody flesh. . . . But tell me, why am I so bloody sober? And is this what you wanted to hear?

"It is. I wanted to hear anything you wanted to tell," Nikolsky replied.

"It's a crossroads."

"What was that?"

"Nothing. Look! Danuta's back."

"I'm very sorry. I didn't mean to disturb you. I've just brought Aaron the key to my sister's house. She'll be glad to see you, only . . . it's so far, and you're so . . ."

"Drunk? Not in the least. How long does your shift last?"

"Twenty-four hours. And the couch down there is too short for you. You need a good sleep."

"Aaron can stay here," said Leonid. "I'll sleep next door, puffed up on pillows like a sultan."

"A noble proposition."

"But he's our guest."

"Leonid's above such conventions, can't you see? You think the doorman has any vodka?"

"I'll ask when I go for your sheets."

"Thanks. Here's something for his pains. . . . Now tell me, Lyonya, what's your schedule for tomorrow?"

"Oh, I'm my own man. I'll sleep late, have something to eat—then decide."

"I assume you're going to one of the hush-hush institutes. Well, if it's the green box you're after, the entrance is only a short walk from here."

" 'Green box'?"

"The town has two institutes. One's got a green fence around it, the other a blue one. People say, 'Where does your husband work?'

'The green box.' 'And yours?' 'The blue box' Or, 'Have you heard? The blue box is getting in a shipment of yeast'—they're making believe they don't know that the blue box is really Post Office Box 43 and the green box Post Office Box 28. See? I don't know either. And here's something else I don't know: that in all likelihood you're going to 28."

"Right you are."

"Elementary, my dear Nikolsky. Everyone who comes to this godforsaken hole from Moscow goes to the green box, and everyone who comes from Novosibirsk goes to the blue box."

"Which means that you too are—"

"Oh no, I don't count. I just happen to be here. True, I do happen to be here a lot, though actually I'm on my way to the ocean. I'm with the Ministry of Fish Production."

"Fish Production, eh? Everybody I know is either a physicist or an engineer. Even my bed partners."

"He meant to say 'even my closest lady friends,' Danuta. He didn't see you come in."

"I apologize, Danuta, I had no—"

"Sorry, I didn't hear what you were saying. Really."

"Thanks for the bottle, Danuta. And don't worry. Leonid here and I—we'll just have a glass or two and leave the rest for tomorrow."

"I'd be very happy if you joined us, Danuta."

"Sorry, I'm on duty. Good night."

"Good night."

"I'll be in soon, Danya. All right?"

"All right."

"She's never touched a drop in my presence. Not even the most innocent stuff. . . . So you're an engineer."

"And a graduate of the Bauman Institute. I must have applied in the same year as you. Under very different circumstances, of course. Got through by the skin of my teeth. . . . Anyway, let's drink to your Danuta."

"And to . . . is there anybody?"

"How shall I put it? A peach gone sour."

"So you're married."

"No. But let's drink to women in general."

"I find that more attractive myself, actually. And now a little something to go with the vodka."

"Caviar. Well, well."

"Why so surprised? Remember my job. And if I find your toast attractive, it's that there are quite a few women in my life. A wife and two daughters, to begin with."

"Ah, paradise. By the way, what was that crossroads you were talking about?"

"Crossroads? Oh, that. My life, your life. Coming together here on this stormy night. By the way, it's warming up. All the snow will be gone by morning. Everything will be naked clay, clay and cracks. Old Mother Earth."

"One more and we'll call it a night, agreed? Vodka's a joy, but sleep has its place."

Finkelmeyer emptied his glass and tottered in to Danuta, his shirt hanging out of his trousers, his step uncertain, his long arms dangling.

He's going to sleep with her in my bed, thought Nikolsky. I'm all but tucking them in. I wouldn't mind changing places with him. I feel so sorry for myself. And for him. For her, too, because she's with him. And for myself for being sorry for her. No, wait, you're all mixed up, you drunk.

When Danuta came in with a pile of sheets, Nikolsky jumped up from the table to let her past. Danuta didn't go over to the bed, however; she left the sheets on the table and started cleaning up the mess the two men had made. Danuta smiled at Nikolsky's meek protest. Finkelmeyer gazed on absentmindedly from the doorway; he looked as though he would crumple to the floor if there were no wall to lean on.

Nikolsky made sure the door was securely shut after them, then climbed into bed. He could see the light under the door and hear Danuta's springy footsteps and muffled laughter. Soon they too will be getting into bed, he thought, but you won't catch me listening for the squeaking bedsprings, the moans and cries—I'm not sixteen anymore. I'll drift right off. I've got to be up early tomorrow anyway. . . .

An invisible mask descended over his face, and after a convulsive sigh he began to breathe deeply and evenly.

VIII

WHEN he woke up, the pounding in his head made it hard for him to unstick his eyelids. He brought his watch all the way up to his eyes. There was something strange about the dial. It was a while before he realized that both hands were standing straight up. He had slept through to noon.

The first thing he did was have a drink of cold water. Then he gulped down a glass of vodka, sent a little mound of red caviar on the tip of a knife riding into his mouth, and crushed it against his palate. Only then did he feel himself coming back to life.

There was no one in the room next door. The bed was perfectly made up, without a crease. It looked so staid, so austere, that it could have been exhibited in the house of a long-dead writer or revolutionary.

Nikolsky took a shower, got dressed, and sat down to make his calls. None of the people he needed to speak to was in. Only then did he realize that Siberian time had left his watch far behind: everyone was out for the all-important late-afternoon meal. Moreover, the vodka he downed on an empty stomach had whetted his own appetite. He gave himself a perfunctory shave and left the room.

On his way downstairs he noticed a heavyset man pop up from one of the chairs in the small lounge near his room. Since no one but Danuta and Aaron could possibly have known his room number, he paid him no heed. As he rounded the landing, however, he saw the man running down the stairs with mincing steps, and although the man looked somehow familiar, Nikolsky made straight for the restaurant. A girl wearing an apron and a little white-lace crown in her hair flew up to him and asked, "Which menu do you want, lunch or dinner? I can bring both, if you like."

"You strike me as someone who knows what's what, my girl. Well, you have before you a healthy, hungry man who, as I hope you've noticed, is in the prime of life." The girl giggled. "Bring me whatever you think best suited to my condition, but first a cup of coffee. No, two. And strong."

"How about our house special? Chef's Beef. That's beef stewed and served in its own little pot. The chef's in today; he's making it himself. And a good dry Georgian red to go with it."

"Fine. I see I was right about you. You serve by the glass, don't you?"

"Yes, we do," she said, all apple-tree pink and virginal. Or maybe not so virginal, he thought, watching her walk away.

"Hello, Comrade Nikossky."

It was the man from the stairs, pancake face beaming and hand, protruding beyond rotund stomach, begging to be shaken.

"Everyone seems thrilled to see me today," Nikolsky thought philosophically, squeezing the man's plump appendage and trying hard to recall where he had seen him and heard his "Comrade Nikossky."

"Good morning, Comrade . . ."

"Comrade Manakin," the man prompted. "Danil Fedotych."

Of course. Last night here in the restaurant. The man who'd come over to see Finkelmeyer. Why had Aaron started bickering with him?

Manakin eased into a chair, bumping the table with his stomach and making the silverware clink.

"You slept late. Didn't want to disturb you, Leonid Pavlovich." His words implied that he needed Nikolsky for some reason: he had let him sleep and he had remembered his name and patronymic.

"How did you know where my room was?"

His only response was to crook a finger at the approaching waitress and say to her, "Bring me what the comrade here ordered."

The bastard! Tailing us last night! Well, let's see what he's after.

"So you're in cultural affairs, are you?" Nikolsky asked, trying to recall what Manakin had said about himself? "Have you been at it long?"

"Just started," Manakin responded willingly, his beady eyes showing a sudden sign of life. "Used to be in agriculture. Party instructor on the district level. Two years."

"Well, well!" said Nikolsky, duly impressed. He even looked up from his salad to ask, "But why switch from *agri*culture to *culture* culture? There was a promotion involved, of course. Department head—isn't that what you said last night? But agriculture! Agriculture is the country's number-one priority. You've read Comrade

Khrushchev's latest speech, haven't you? What was it he said? 'We must place all our energy into boosting production.' " And up went Nikolsky's fork to show how high production was to be boosted. "Besides, what is culture? Mere superstructure!"

Nikolsky's tirade and his position on matters of state had the desired impact.

"Yes, I read the speech. I read it," Manakin responded quickly in his high monotone, while unloading Nikolsky's soup plate from the tray that had just floated up to them. "And culture—yes, you're right, Comrade Nikossky—culture is superstructure. . . . Are you, I mean, do you work in culture?"

"I'm on ministerial business," said Nikolsky mysteriously.

Nikolsky could almost see the workings in Manakin's black box crank into motion and come to a halt in a new alignment.

"Not Party business?" he asked with patent relief.

"I'm with the ministry," Nikolsky confirmed with great dignity. The whole thing was so ridiculous he would have laughed and told Manakin where to go if it hadn't been clear that Finkelmeyer was somehow involved. Damn the man for ruining my meal, he thought, but I'm going to get to the bottom of this.

"You say you spent two years as a Party instructor," he said, adopting the tone of a suspicious official. "What did you do before that?"

"Chairman of the Fur Collective, Leonid Pavlovich. Won many prizes. Yes. Letters of commendation. Yes. Promotions. Began as a common hunter. Yes."

The memory of his hunting days seemed to upset him. Was it the loss of freedom? The half-forgotten sense of reality? Or was it that the most tangible result of exchanging the taiga for an armchair was a paunch?

"The cultural front is important now," said Manakin slowly and clearly. "We are a small nationality. The Party says we need national forms of socialist culture to . . . so we can . . . ."

". . . take your place in the multinational socialist state, isn't that it?"

Manakin wiped his forehead with a handkerchief.

"Well, if that's what the Party says, then of course it's impor-tant," said Nikolsky with as much conviction as he could muster, but then wondered whether he wasn't going too far. Manakin was probably smarter than he looked. There had to be some reason why he avoided a frontal attack. Trying to win me over first, Nikolsky thought. We'll see.

"Tell me, Danil Fedotych," he said, using Manakin's name and patronymic for the first time to get in his good graces, "even if culture—culture and ideology—can in fact be considered a matter of top priority these days, why entrust it to you, a man of the woods, of the land?"

Manakin broke into a smile and even blushed, but immediately regained his composure and said with dignity, "I am also a man of culture. I write poetry. Four years."

Afraid the half-chewed piece of meat in his mouth would come flying out, Nikolsky pulled a handkerchief from his pocket, pressed it to his lips, and forced himself to cough. Even after he had washed down the meat with wine, folded up the handkerchief, put it away, and coughed again, he could come up with nothing better than "How interesting." Well, at least he'd kept from roaring with laughter in the man's face. "I'm in charge of publications, by the way," he added after regaining composure, and watched Manakin prick up his ears. "I'm glad to see you've taken the advice of our great Mayakovsky to heart: 'Till the country's soil; write the country's verse.' Have you tried to publish anything? Locally, I mean."

"Tried? Locally? I am no amateur! I did not say amateur!"

Nikolsky stared at him in amazement.

"I am a member of the Writers Union! Four years. I publish in Moscow too!"

"I don't know," said Nikolsky, shaking his head and pausing to light a cigarette. "I don't know. . . . I read a lot of poetry—it's one of my responsibilities—and I can't say I've run across your name. I'm sorry, Danil Fedotych, but . . ." He shrugged to avoid putting the bad news into words.

Manakin stared into space for a while, then broke the silence by asking as nonchalantly as he could whether Nikolsky had known Finkelmeyer for a long time. The question was so unexpected and so slurred that Nikolsky had to ask him to repeat it twice.

"You known Aronmendelch for long?"

"Excuse me?"

"Aronmendelch."

"I'm sorry. I still don't understand."

"Finkelmeyer," he finally said, and added, "You known him long?"

"It's not the easiest name to pronounce, is it?" said Nikolsky, back in his role again. "How long have we known each other? Let's see now. We met on the plane—we had adjoining seats." He looked at his watch. "Just under twenty-four hours. Why do you want to know? What's it to you?"

"Twenty-four hours! You ate together! Shared the room!"

"If a man starts a conversation with me on the plane, shows me how to get to my hotel, and recommends the restaurant, what's wrong with inviting him to eat? And if the only room he can find is with four other people and I have the best room in the hotel all to myself, what's wrong with offering him a bed? No, I'm sorry, Comrade Manakin. . . ." Nikolsky pulled back his sleeve and looked down at his watch again. "Time to go. I've got a meeting."

"So you're *not* together," he said, his face radiant. "Then just one minute, Comrade Nikossky. Very important. One minute!"

So that's it, you dirty bastard! Nikolsky said to himself. As long as you thought I was with Aaron, you were scared stiff of me. Now you want to turn me to your advantage. Not on your life!

"No, impossible," he said with a shake of the head. "I'm late as it is."

Just then the waitress ran up, and as he handed her a generous tip he said that if he weren't in such a hurry he'd ask for the comments book and write a paean of praise to—what was her name? Galina?—to Galya so she could show all her boyfriends what a good girl she was. Galya couldn't help smiling, but she did her best to cover the gold tooth that was stylish here but a definite minus in Moscow.

"I told you the truth," Manakin droned on. "I am a poet. Member of the Writers Union. Publish in Moscow. But I have a pen name. Neprigen. Aion Neprigen."

"What?" Nikolsky's heart began to race. "What was that you said? Aion Neprigen?"

Night is falling, the clouds are growing dark, and a stag soars across the dusky tundra. Suddenly a man in deerskin raises a rifle to his shoulder. . . .

"Those poems in *Friendship*—they're yours?"

"That's right, Comrade Nikossky. Five poems. Mine."

I've got to find Aaron, Nikolsky thought, ditch Manakin and get hold of Aaron. This is turning into a nightmare.

He held out his hand with a great show of pomp. "Very pleased to have met you, Comrade Manakin. Very pleased. . . . Aion Neprigen! Of course! Fine verse. And from a small nationality whose language had no alphabet before the Revolution, isn't that right? The Tongors, if I remember correctly?"

"That is right. 'Hunter' in Russian. Only one thousand seven hundred left. Down to six hundred once. No alphabet, no houses, no radio. Now we have everything. But still behind. Many Tongor still prefer no house. But we make them see. That is why I say: culture is important."

Nikolsky found himself warming up to this representative of a dying people. Maybe he shouldn't have been so hard on him.

"I'm sorry I can't talk to you now, Danil Fedotych, and I'm busy till late this evening. Would tomorrow morning suit you?"

"Tomorrow morning is good. Bad weather. No plane."

"Then it's settled. Tomorrow at, say, twelve. My room."

They shook hands again, and Nikolsky went back upstairs to the telephone to take care of all the boring formalities—making appointments, having the necessary files made ready, ordering passes—formalities that anyone who travels on official business learns to accept. Yet through it all he never stopped thinking about his conversation with Manakin. "God only knows what that was all about," he said once or twice aloud. It was the only way he could put his impression of their talk into words.

On his way out of the hotel he paid a visit to Danuta. She met him with a smile so sweet and placid that he wondered whether she smiled that way all the time. No, she must have been thinking of last night. She really must love Aaron. And when her shift was over, she'd be taking him home for all to see. Because in a small place like this there were no secrets. Of course she loved him. A worthy Dulcinea to his still-youthful Don Quixote.

"Please ask Aaron to come and see me before he leaves. It's very important."

"I'll tell him," she said with another radiant smile.

It didn't feel like Siberia outside. Spring had arrived in Moscow. Could it be on its way here too? Now that the wind had died down and the sun was out, the frost was refreshing. Still, Nikolsky huddled into his overcoat when he looked down and saw the frozen earth in the cracks beneath his feet. So that was what Finkelmeyer had been talking about last night.

Yesterday's blizzard had stripped the blanket from the ulcerous, scabby body of the steppe, and there it was, a house or two away, all flat and white and never-ending. Here in town it was traveled, trampled, and worn. What could it care for spring? Not a tree, not a bush, not a clump of anything, as desolate as a parade grounds this shapeless square, a bulge in the main street with a three-story brick building, a windowless shed, a garage, and a childlike, naive reminder of times known as czarist—a portal with four nearly vertical columns—giving way to Khrushchev's cement-block prefabs, our new reality, fruit of our dreams, from each his labor, to each his box.

And here is the fence. Eye-dazzling green. No perfidious foe, no nosy rubberneck could dream of penetrating this fortress of finely meshed concrete slabs. Here is the double gate. Wrought-iron, but painted the same dazzling green and decorated with red stars in the center of both flaps as if to say, "Do not tarry here. This is no ordinary industrial plant with open-hearth furnaces or blooming mills; no, this is a hush-hush post office box! See the stars? Well, do you? Actually, you'd better forget you did. Mum's the word." All these "post office boxes" are top-secret. True, half the town passes through the gate twice a day and the other half passes through a blue gate with the same red stars, but the secret remains. In fact, it remains so secret that the entire population of the town might just as well not exist.

But Nikolsky knew a thing or two. More than the people who worked there perhaps. He knew the plant manufactured all kinds of electronic . . . knickknacks. None of the workers knew—or cared to know—whether what they produced would be used by the most powerful and most peaceful army on earth or go into their wives' irons—though they did seem to know where to put the parts they stole, into the motor for the children's fish-tank pump or the still for making moonshine.

Nikolsky knew something else. He knew that some of the products manufactured there were destined for export—that is, the poor things would have to compete on the open market under the cutthroat conditions known as capitalism. If we had to play according to the inhuman rules of capitalism, so foreign to our nature, we would have to keep up with world standards, no, exceed them, come up with something new, something deserving of—that awful word—a *patent!* And Nikolsky knew three foreign languages and was a specialist in international patents.

After graduating from the Bauman Institute ten years before, he had been assigned to the engineering department of a large factory, where he immediately developed an aversion to gates and passes with all kinds of mysterious stamps and armed amazons at every turn, in other words, to "procedure," realizing that it has less to do with discipline than with a ritual that admits only the initiated. Even so, the bright, young, energetic engineer quickly made his way up the ladder, and by the time he had worked off the three-year stint required in return for his education he was taken on as a section head in another factory. There too he made quick progress, and when the department head died unexpectedly he took over as acting head. For months he performed his duties piously, staying late at the office, drafting plans and reports, calling meetings, consulting with the sacred "triangle" of management, union, and Party, dealing with personnel problems like retirement, alcoholism, maternity leaves, and replacements, and sitting through the flattery of his subordinates and contumely of his superior. As time passed, however, he felt the engineer in him giving way to an administrator who worked and lived according to the principles of "those are my orders" and "that's the way it has to be." Once he had even caught himself thinking about plans and reports just after orgasm.

When the time came for his title to be changed from "acting" to "official," the intimate talks he had been waiting for—"Haven't you ever thought of joining the Party, Comrade Nikolsky?"—began in earnest. He dodged the motives behind his refusal as best he could, most often claiming he felt "unworthy of the honor," but in the end the head of the Party Committee, a retired colonel with a chestful of medals, lost his temper. "Just you wait, Nikolsky!" he screamed in front of the assembled dignitaries. "The Party offers you membership and you turn your fucking back!"

The colonel had really put his foot in it, poor chap. Couldn't keep up with the times. "So I've 'turned my fucking back on the Party,' have I? Just whose Party did you have in mind, you Stalinist bastard?"

An old school friend took him into his laboratory, which thereby became a three-man operation: the two of them and a young lab technician. Their ostensible goal was to produce electronic gadgets—"mice" that could find their way through labyrinths, jumping "frogs," and the like—but what they were really after was an answer to the question gripping all progressive mankind at the time, namely, Can a machine think? Since all three were positive it could, they applied their Edisonian energies accordingly, and although the truth eluded them they did acquire an intimate knowledge of the field. Nikolsky, assuming the role of prospector, sifted through the nuggets in the few foreign journals available to them and was soon at home with scientific jargon on both sides of the Atlantic.

People began taking notice. First the laboratory was made a department, then (after Nikolsky's friend defended two dissertations) an institute surrounded by its very own fence and protected by an armed guard and first—that is, secret-service—division. And together they served science and science served the people and the plans were fulfilled.

But by that time Nikolsky was far away. Whenever he pondered over which of the "last of the scientific cottage-industry Mohicans" (as they proudly called themselves) had profited most from the venture, he couldn't help thinking it was the technician. Nikolsky's friend was certainly out, because the duties and salaries and titles had gobbled him up whole, him and his wife, who had once, in the good old days, been a fine companion, well, actually, one of Nikolsky's women, who had either thrown him over for his friend or whom he, Leonid, had thrown over *to* his friend—it had never been quite clear which. In other words, his friend had got a raw deal in every respect. As for the technician, he was fed up with science and the measly eight hundred a month he was taking home in its name when his former drinking and wenching companion, now demoted to his boss, told him that like it or not, he was going back to school. So he said to himself, Five years of torture to boost my salary to a still measly twelve hundred? Whereupon he climbed into a taxi and had been driving it ever since. Whenever Nikolsky had the former technician take him to the airport for old time's sake, the man would say, "Work is fine, money's better, but earning a decent salary with no boss on your back—that's paradise."

Nikolsky understood him perfectly, because he had been lured away from his friend's operation with a position that paid a decent salary and involved minimal interference from the bosses, mostly because the bosses had precious little understanding of what he was doing. For the first time Nikolsky felt his personal interests and the interests of society coincide. It was a feeling so invigorating that to call it the result of material stimulation plus normal work conditions seemed a gross oversimplification.

The reason Nikolsky was so urgently needed was that the state had decided to open its own patent office. Someone somewhere had decreed that the disagreeable, unnatural, and—when you get down to it—un-Soviet institution of the patent office was in fact as safe, sound, and convenient as a savings bank. The only trouble was that no one seemed to know how to go about setting one up. No one but Nikolsky, as it turned out. In the course of studying all those foreign inventions, he had come into contact with the major patent systems of the industrialized countries. In other words, he was just what the doctor ordered.

So Nikolsky became a patent expert, consultant, etc. etc. It gave him an inordinate amount of freedom: his time was his own, his office was his own. The higher-ups treated him with respect, even reverence. All they could do was offer him a project and hope he would accept it and finish it in time.

Some of the projects were interesting, others less so. He had been sent to the green box, for instance, to straighten out a rather complex affair that no one had been able to make head or tail of. The bosses had begged and pleaded with him, assured him he was the only one who could get to the bottom of things, and he felt obliged to take it on, especially as it involved a major American company that had registered a protest against a Soviet product. It was an affair of state.

Poring over a pile of technical drawings and descriptions, Nikolsky could see he would be stuck there for more than a day or two and have plenty to keep him busy back in Moscow as well. The green box was only one of the product's purveyors, and the issue at stake had many sides to it. The day was nearly over, and he'd only scratched the surface. He felt himself sinking into a familiar state of self-pity—par for the course after a night of hard drinking—but while he usually managed to sidestep meditations on the meaning of life and such, today he had no luck. He knew why, of course: Finkelmeyer and the midnight monologue. He began running *The Rise and Fall of Leonid Nikolsky* through his mental projector, cutting all sex and violence and emphasizing the moral. Suitable for children. Newsreel prices. Finkelmeyer's would have been a full-length feature. He was a real poet, he really had it. Aion Neprigen. What a joke!

Finkelmeyer must have gone back to the hotel and would be waiting for him there.

IX

AARON-CHAIM MENDELEVICH FINKELMEYER lay sleeping peacefully, though he seemed surprised by something in his dreams: his eyebrows were raised, his lips rounded in what looked like an imminent "Oh!" Last night's bottle rested on a piece of paper on the bedside table. The message scrawled on the paper read, "What did you want to see me about? Wake me up if you want a drink."

Nikolsky was touched by Aaron's temperance and told him as much while shaking him awake. "But let me go straight to the point," he said when they were sitting at the table attacking sandwiches after their first round of vodka. "I want you to tell me about Aion Neprigen, Aion Neprigen the poet."

"Aion Neprigen?" said Finkelmeyer, staring at Nikolsky. "What in heaven's name for?"

"Well, I met a poet the other day, a real oddball. 'I'm a Jew,' he said, 'but I compose my verse in Taymyr and write it down in Russian. My name is José-Aaron-Maria-Chaim-Don-Quixote-de-la-Aion-Neprigen.' Just then up came a roly-poly little chap and the poet said to me, 'Lyonya'—my name is Lyonya—'Lyonya," he said, 'I want you to meet Sancho.' Well, this Sancho was a real character himself. Another poet. Not Jewish. Though he wrote in Taymyr as well. Taymyr or Yamal. And his name was Diego-Salvador-Sancho-Panza-ibn-Aion-Neprigen. Funny coincidence, eh?"

"A real scream," said Finkelmeyer grimly. "I see you've had a little chat with Manakin. What did he want from you?"

Nikolsky picked up his copy of *Friendship* and waved it in the air. "Who wrote these poems?"

Finkelmeyer's eyes flashed with such fury that Nikolsky immediately dropped the journal and said, "All right, Aaron, all right. I know. I understand. Then why does it say they're a translation? And what does Manakin have to do with them?"

"Nothing," said Finkelmeyer with a crooked smile, "though according to our agreement he gets half the royalties."

"All I ask for is a clue now and then, Aaron. Just a clue. I can see you don't like talking about it, but I need to know. I have a feeling Manakin is trying to use me somehow."

"What makes you think so?"

"Hard to say."

Finkelmeyer hesitated a while longer, but finally gave in.

"It's the kind of story you'll wish you'd never heard. The only other person who knows about it is the Master. In fact, it was basically his doing. He was if not the father of the idea, then its midwife. He officiated at its birth, when it was still a naked little thing, and we gave it its first bath together. It all began because nobody much wanted to publish Aaron Finkelmeyer. There's no such poet, really. You'll find one poem of his in a collection of new voices, another in an obscure journal, and that's it. Whenever the Master introduced me as 'Aaron Finkelmeyer the poet,' he might as well have been a radio announcer announcing that the next aria would be sung by a People's Artist or winner of the Stalin Prize. Besides, I wasn't so sure I needed to sing in public—or that I was good enough to. I lived the life we all lived at the time; my poetry was merely an intimate detail. When you have an indigestion problem or shoes that pinch, you don't go trumpeting it to the world.

"The Master did a lot of translating. Sometimes he was so busy he would pass assignments on to me—Caucasian or Central Asian poems that came with literal prose translations. I had no trouble putting them into verse, but I was no good at the other half of the job: 'elevating' them from what tended to be a rather modest level. All the Master had to do was make a twist here, a turn there, and suddenly the poem would work. The poets he thus rendered into Russian wrote articles about problems of translation, naively admitting that the Russian version surpassed the original and thanking him for guiding their 'mountain streams into the ocean of Russian poetry.'

"One day when the Master was either ill or malingering, I delivered some translations of his to an editor. 'Yes, he phoned,' the editor said, 'and he told me you sometimes help him. Are you a writer?' I mumbled something like 'Isn't everybody?' and said I had a full-time job that left me little time for such things. But she was curious and asked me where I worked, and instead of going on about crabs, shrimps, and mussels, I made some vague references to the Far North and Far East. 'How about bringing us back a poet the next time you go? A deerslayer or whaler—something exotic. An Udmurt or an Evenki.' I remember laughing and asking her whether I shouldn't myself return as an Aleut, but my joke fell flat. She was perfectly serious. So was the Master when he heard my story. 'Why *not* bring back a Siberian Homer?'

"I found my Siberian Homer at an outpost of the Siberian Hunting Cooperative. I was frozen stiff and hoping to buy a pair of socks, but there was a lock on the door and the only person in sight was a man rocking back and forth against a railing, his eyes glued to the ground. He was drunk and singing a mournful song.

" 'Hello,' he said, finally noticing me. 'Vodka?'

" 'Hello. No, sorry.'

" 'Cigarettes?'

"I had a pack and gave it to him. It quickly disappeared into his furs.

" 'We go to the canteen. The shop man does not come. The canteen is warm.'

"I had no objection to getting warm, and as we sat by the stove my new acquaintance began to thaw out as well.

" 'What was that you were singing?'

" 'How can you ask?' he replied, clearly amazed by my question. 'What I sing, I sing; what I say, I say. I can't say what I sing.'

"His words bowled me over. They taught me one of the best

lessons I ever learned about poetry. Clearly I had a poet in front of me.

" 'Well, sing it again then.'

" 'No good the second time. One poem goes; another comes.'

"I could have hugged him.

" 'You speak the truth,' I said. 'But can you sing me the song that is to come?'

"He half-shut his eyes, started rocking again, and sang. Would you like to hear what it sounded like?

Finkelmeyer looked down at the ground and, rocking back and forth in his chair, began intoning in a high, monotonous voice:

"Aion neprigen!
O-o-o! A!
Aion neprigen!"

Nikolsky recognized Manakin's voice immediately. The mournful sound sent shivers down his spine and made him distinctly uncomfortable.

"He was very surprised when I started repeating what he had just sung. I may not have reproduced the melody accurately, but I came pretty close with the words. He gazed at me as if I were a divine being and asked me almost fearfully how and why I had done it. After a while I was able to drag out of him that *aion neprigen* was a kind of incantation to conjure up good fortune. What kind of good fortune? Any kind: good hunting, good health, the end to a blizzard, a house with food, drink, and a woman—the only things a Tongor needs, he explained. The song was about how fur will fly from sunset to sunrise and lead will fly up to where the bright winter star shines at night, and when the fur and the lead meet and cease to fly, then 'O-o-o! *Aion neprigen!*' 'Fur' meant 'fur, furs, any fur-bearing animal, white, red, or brown.' 'Skin' or 'pelt' meant 'a large animal.' A deer, for instance, was a 'pelt with horns.'

"For a while I couldn't get the complicated, skipping rhythm out of my head, but gradually it yielded to lines of my own. I jotted them down. They were a poem.

"My new acquaintance watched me as I wrote. He asked why I was writing. I shrugged, but he kept after me, genuinely curious about why anyone would write words down on a piece of paper without an ulterior motive; he even asked whether it wouldn't do him some harm. Only then did I realize that he was the exotic poet I had been asked to bring back alive.

" 'Actually, what I'm going to do is try and sell this piece of paper. And if I do sell it, I'll send you half the money.'

" 'You are smart,' he said to me with great respect in his voice. 'You did not want to tell the Tongor; you wanted to take all the money yourself. But the Tongor is smart too. Write on a new piece of paper: Danil Fedotych Manakin, Free Tongoria Hunting Collective.'

"That was his receipt.

"I returned to Moscow. The Master was delighted with the poem, but said I would need more than one if I had publication in mind.

" 'But all he sang was one.'

" 'What difference does that make? You've caught the spirit, the style, the rhythm, even the alliteration. Why not write a few on your own? The Russian classics imitated Byron, borrowed from Heine; you're in good company. All you need to bring across your view of the world is a form and a system of images. Couplets, tercets, quatrains—they each have their rules. The same holds for longer forms like the sonnet or ballad. The same holds for imagery: the sun, the morning stand for joy; the night, the moon for longing, melancholy. And so on. Put yourself in the saddle, dig in your spurs, and let it run away with you. Feel your inner freedom. Something very original could come of it.'

"The Master was highly persuasive. That night I twisted and turned a lot before falling asleep, but I dreamed some unusually effective lines. What remained of them the next morning became the basis for my next few poems. I had written quite a bit of poetry by then and was well acquainted with the Russian and European traditions, but only after meeting Manakin did I realize how little it took to make poetry what it is. I don't mean 'a poem is like a beautiful woman who needs no fancy clothes or cosmetics to look ravishing'; what I mean is black and white and a splotch of blue or yellow, the simplicity of practically nothing—that's all an artist needs. My poetry begins where the boundless *everything* joins the equally boundless *nothing*.

"The Master let out a whoop when he read the poems. 'Your Manakin has given you the chance of a lifetime. No Finkelmeyer could publish these poems. No Ivanov for that matter. They're too removed from reality—asocial, idealistic, pantheistic. That's what any editor would tell you in his rejection note. But poets from national minority groups have a certain leeway. They don't need to satisfy rigorous socialist standards. So long live Danil Manakin!'

" 'Wait a second!' I said. Whose poems were they, anyway? Either they came out under my name or they would damn well stay where they were.

"Well, the Master flew off the handle. So I wanted to commit a crime against literature. The pure, the sacred, the eternal muse! It wasn't enough what those illiterate sons of bitches were doing; no, we had to go and help them—was that it? 'I only pray you'll agree to a compromise: publish the poems under an exotic pseudonym and call them a translation from the Tongor.'

" 'And what shall we call the poet?'

" 'I only pray again that—'

" 'Stop!' I interrupted. 'I only pray again—sounds like *aion neprigen,* doesn't it? Well, why not call him that? Remember? The Tongor expression for good fortune!"

"When the Master got the point of my Tongor-Russian linguistic acrobatics, he joined in my laughter and declared it a capital piece of literary mystification.

"The poems were published word for word, preceded by a short note reminding the readers of the great cultural strides made by national minorities during the Soviet period and rejoicing in the discovery of the first Tongor national poet. The response to the editors' indiscreet note was felt far and wide.

"Before long a Siberian newspaper inquired of the journal who this Aion Neprigen was and how they could locate him. They wanted to reprint the poems and do a proper article on him. The journal passed the letter on to me, and I told the editors about Manakin and showed them the receipt for the money I had sent him. After long deliberation they gave the Siberian paper the right to reprint the poems, but pointed out that as good Siberians they ought to know that Aion Neprigen means 'good fortune' in Tongor and that if the poet had chosen to publish under a pseudonym they certainly weren't going to reveal his identity."

"Meanwhile I kept writing. I'd never had such an easy time of it. Every poem the genuine article: Aion Neprigen. The Master wanted me to publish another cycle using the same ruse. He said I wasn't the first 'translator' to use it. I refused. But then the Writers Union began showing an interest. It seems there was a movement afoot in the Khabarovsk branch to further Siberian literature, and the first Tongor poet was just what they needed to start the ball rolling. After a good deal of soul-searching I offered to find Manakin and take him to Khabarovsk. I armed myself with documents from the District Council and the Free Tongor State Farm.

"Arranging the trip was no problem, because few of my colleagues were willing to go on extended Siberian inspection tours in the dead of winter. We met here, in this town, on this spot. Only instead of the hotel there was a wooden hut for transients—and for bedbugs as large and juicy as cherries. But to get back to my story, Manakin's head was reeling not so much from the plane trip as from the manhunt they'd staged to find him. He could scarcely speak. Later I learned that after two or three telephone calls from on high they had sent a posse out for him as if he were a major criminal. Nobody stopped to ask what they were after him for. If they were after him, he was a criminal. He himself told me he would have run away, hid in the taiga—some friends had come and told him he was a wanted man—but as it happened he was blotto, smashed, incapable of thought. To give him his due, he was a good Tongor in those days: either out in the tundra hunting or at home dead drunk. Anyway they grabbed him and shoved him on a plane, and only then did he sober up enough to realize he'd done something to offend the bosses. The District Council official they sent with him couldn't tell him anything—he didn't know what was up either. They delivered him to me at the airport more dead than alive.

"The moment he grasped who I was he begged me to believe he was completely broke but could make up the amount of the royalties in furs if I would just . . .

" 'Listen, Manakin,' I said to him. 'Can you read Russian?'

" 'Some,' he said.

" 'Well, try and read this.'

"I showed him the passage in the journal about how the Tongors had been illiterate until recently and had now produced their first poet.

" 'That's you,' I told him. 'Aion Neprigen is you.'

"He had no idea what I was talking about. It took me a good hour to get it through his head that Aion Neprigen really *was* him and that I had translated the song he sang for me in the canteen, but when at last he pieced things together, his reaction was positive: 'Two names is good. I will live long.'

"From then on I had an easier time of it, though I met with some opposition when I told him he would have to go to a public meeting and sing his song there.

" 'Will there be important people?' he asked, still afraid of being hauled over the coals.

" 'Very important people, Manakin. Very important. But you're an important person now too.'

"And in fact I saw him become an important person before my eyes. I watched him pull himself up to his full height, stiffen his neck, even wrinkle his forehead."

" 'Manakin will go,' he said regally, and pointing to the poems: 'Read what you wrote.'

"I had clearly been reduced to his amanuensis.

" 'The first poem is the song you sang in the canteen. I added the others to round it out. But they're similar to what you sang."

" 'Manakin approves,' he said. 'Now read what you wrote.'

"When I'd read them all, he stunned me by saying coldly, 'Manakin sings better songs.'

" 'What do you mean?' I shouted. 'All you sang for me was that one.'

" 'I sing everything,' he said disdainfully. 'Beasts, guns, fire, snow, night, sun, roads, children, trees, women. You have not heard. I sing more than you. I sing everything.'

"He cared nothing for form, that is, how concepts find their way into lines, what gives a text the right to be called poetry. What he meant by literature—though he did not of course call it that—was the 'singing' of words that designated phenomena, events, and activities in the world as he knew it. He wasn't trying to lord it over me or advocate the superior nature of Tongor poetry; he'd simply 'sung' about the same things as I had, and liked the way he did it better. As is often the case when people argue over art, our argument had very little to do with art.

" 'What do I say to the important people?' he asked.

" 'You can tell them about your people, about the taiga, about what it's like to go hunting . . .'

"The meeting of Siberian writers was Manakin's first triumph. As one speaker after another repeated the only thing known about him—that he had single-handedly founded Tongor literature—Manakin listened attentively and applauded with the audience.

" 'And now we give the floor to Aion Neprigen, Tongor poet.'

"Manakin waked majestically to the podium.

" 'Taiga all around me. Taiga and Tongor.' He paused, not quite knowing how to proceed, though knowing enough to look thoughtfully into the distance. The writers were impressed. Here was a real folk poet. No cliché-ridden preambles for him.

"Suddenly Manakin twisted his torso, flung up his arms, and went, *'Shoosh!'* It was so fine an imitation of a gunshot that everyone jumped.

" 'Bull's-eye,' he said, calm again. 'When the Tongor sells his fur, he is happy: he has money, he has vodka.'

"For a moment the Siberian writers were uncertain how to react; then they burst out laughing and clapped wildly. 'A joke only Sholokhov would dare pull off! How little we know the people, the *real* people!'

"Manakin waited with dignity for the ovation to die down. *'Aion Neprigen* means *good fortune,*' he said at last. 'Now the road goes. A song comes.' He closed his eyes, began stomping his feet behind the lectern, as if tramping home from a hard day in the tundra, gave his head a shake, rocked back and forth a few times, and launched into his song.

"I often had occasion to watch him perform, and after a while he had it down to an art. But that first time it was unrehearsed, spontaneous; he *was* in a state of ecstasy. After a few minutes he broke off abruptly—stopped singing, stopped rocking—opened his eyes, and said, 'The Tongor has come home.'

"Manakin's career took off with a *shoosh,* so to speak. He returned to the state farm a member of the Writers Union, immediately joined the Party, and was called to District Party Headquarters for special training. He went back to the farm as deputy chairman, but was soon recalled to District Headquarters and made a high-ranking official.

"Whether he still hunts I don't know. I know he still drinks, but cautiously, so as not to ruin his reputation. As far as literature is concerned, he keeps to the tacit agreement we made at the start: I publish what I please under the name of Aion Neprigen, and we share the royalties equally. We meet from time to time—when he comes to Moscow for a Writers Congress or meeting or plenum of some kind, and when I happen to be passing through here—but that's the extent of our contact."

Nikolsky filled their glasses. "You had a good thing going there, the two of you. Now it seems a bit rocky."

"Right. He's begun to balk. He told you he was head of Cultural Affairs, didn't he? Well, take it from me, he's a sly old fox, not at all the fool he makes himself out to be."

"I've noticed."

"And now he realizes he's on thin ice. He's scared of everything and everybody, my poems and me most of all. He's never written a line in Tongor, and anyone who so desires can find that out and use it against him. The song and the gunshot imitation may have worked for the hunter-poet, but the head of Cultural Affairs will have to come up with something else.

"I enjoyed my 'Neprigen poems,' enjoyed turning the severely circumscribed devices into simple, limpid verse. In fact, they were the only things of mine I could still read. And basically the only ones that had seen print. Still, I hated needing *his* presence to prove *my* existence, and in a strange way I'd grown wildly jealous of him. It was as if he were sleeping with my daughter. The time had come to put an end to it.

"And then what do I learn but that Manakin's been asked to do a book. The publisher sends him a contract, promises him they'll publish it within the year, and the idiot never even answers. The first I heard of it was when the Master told me the publisher had asked him how to get in touch with me. I was thrilled: a book! The Neprigen poems were a cycle, a unified series of variations; they belonged together. Go through them and you'll find the sun, the moon, the heavenly bodies making their rounds, you'll find birth, growth, decay, and death—the natural, the eternal cycle.

"Anyway Manakin categorically refused. It was all I could do to get him here. I threatened to raise a stink in Moscow if he didn't come, but I'm not making any headway with him. He knows the publicity won't do him any good—he's a big shot as it is. For him, Aion Neprigen is as dead as the Danil Manakin who sang those endless songs whenever he got enough alcohol in him. I phoned the Master today and told him to have the publishing house remove the book from its list."

"To which the Master responded . . ."

". . . by calling me every name in the book. What kind of diplomat was I? he wanted to know. I shouldn't have screamed at Manakin; I should have given him a nice, polite scare and then tricked him into it."

"Why not let me have a crack at him?"

Finkelmeyer shrugged.

"He's coming to see me tomorrow morning. Do you think the Master's delivered the message?"

"The message?"

"To the publisher."

"Probably not. It was late in Moscow by the time I got through. What do you have in mind, anyway?"

"Give me his number. No, give me the number of the publishing house."

"I don't know the number! Motherland Publishers—that's all I know. Look, don't go sticking your Aryan nose into this dirty business. What can you tell them, anyway? And who do you think will listen?"

"Nobody," said Nikolsky, picking up the telephone, "because I'm not going to talk. . . . Good evening, operator, I'd like to place a call to Moscow tomorrow. . . . *All* the lines? . . . Well then, make it an emergency call, all right? At one o'clock in the afternoon local time. I want to speak to Motherland Publishers, head of the poetry division. I'm at the hotel, and I want the call billed to me—Nikolsky's the name—but the party to ask for here is Manakin: Ma-na-kin. Got it? Thank you very much. Oh, and tell me, operator, *you* wouldn't happen to be on duty then, would you? . . . Oh, wonder-

ful! . . . What do you mean? It will give me another chance to hear
your beautiful voice. Good-bye for now. One o'clock tomorrow—
don't forget!"

"Well, well, well," said Finkelmeyer without much enthusiasm.
"He's got talent, that Nikolsky. Ilya Naumovich, my Cherkizovo
neighbor, used to say that a man who can sweet-talk a woman can
do anything. We'll see."

X

MANAKIN entered Nikolsky's room with a certain formality, his
smile and gestures subdued. This time it was Nikolsky who beamed,
running up to Manakin with his arms outstretched, like a good-
natured superior supposedly putting you at ease, ready either to
pump your hand or place a paternal arm around your shoulders
and pace up and down the office with you, then plump you and
himself into armchairs, where, after smiling at you for a minute or
two, he comes out with, "Well now, what was it you wanted to talk
to me about? I'm all ears!" And you start telling him and he starts
frowning, and out comes a cigarette and a genuine agate lighter,
and flash goes the flame in your eyes, poof goes the smoke in your
face, and nary a thought on his part of inviting you to join him.
You've got to watch out for them, those bigshots; first they roll out
the carpet for you, and when you're not looking it rolls up again,
and *smack!*—right in the back—*smack!*—once more for good measure—*smack!*—never two without three, and damned if you know
where that cloud of dust came from, the carpet or your head.

"I'm all ears, Comrade Manakin."

"A matter of . . . vital importance. You must . . . put in a good
word for me." Though clearly in a state of agitation, he was careful
to use the expressions he had acquired at Party headquarters. "I will
now lead Cultural Affairs. It will be much work. Much time. You
need much . . ." He pointed to his head.

"Oh, you can handle it, Danil Fedotych!" Nikolsky fired back,
very much in command. Then, lowering his voice to add a note of
complicity, he added, "When the Party calls, you have no choice."

Nikolsky felt a lump in his throat as he spoke. He recalled some actor friends telling him he had everything it took to go on the stage, and experienced another rush of self-pity.

"Yes, yes!" Manakin replied enthusiastically. "Great responsibility. But free from other responsibility."

"I'm afraid I don't understand."

"Other responsibility. You are right. No choice when the Party calls. No choice."

"But what other responsibility?" Nikolsky asked, lowering his eyes to hid their rapacious gleam. He was on the brink of cracking the case. "Could you be more specific? How can I help if I don't know what you want of me?"

"I have a letter. A letter to the Writers Union. You have influence. You are a boss at the Ministry of Culture. You can put in a good word."

"Now I see! You want me to make sure your letter gets into the right hands, is that it?"

"Yes, yes! You understand!"

"Let me see it."

With unwonted alacrity Manakin produced a piece of paper from his breast pocket. He unfolded it carefully and handed it to Nikolsky. It was typed, but there were a number of corrections penciled in.

From: Danil Fedotych Manakin/Aion Neprigen (pseudonym), Poet
To: Writer's union

I request my membership in the Writer's union be revoked as I am currently involved in important Party work that prevents me from working as a Poet for lack of time and poor health.

"Really now, Danil Fedotych, resigning from the Writers Union! Who do you expect to act on it?"

"That is why I ask you to help." Clearly he had been apprised of how unusual his request was. "Too much responsibility: Party work, cultural front . . ."

"True, true, but can your membership in the Writers Union really be so burdensome as to—"

"Great burden! Yes. I am the first Tongor poet. They always call. Need a delegate, need a speech. Represent small nationalities. I have no time. Poor health . . ."

Nikolsky's eyes were riveted to the paper and remained there while he spoke.

"All I can tell you," he said, modulating his voice from Party bass-baritone to World Historical bass, "is that you're on the wrong track. In our country, Comrade Manakin, the writer is a figure of great respect."

"Oh yes, yes," Manakin tried to insert, but Nikolsky broke in with a cool, overly courteous, "Just a moment, please. Just a moment. Let me finish."

Manakin froze.

"We," he began again after a pause, "and those above us do everything we can to promote art and culture, especially among the smaller nationalities. You have indicated that you understand the rationale behind our policy. And now you wish to reject the honor the Party has bestowed upon you, the chance to serve your nation and nationality? What will the people think? What will the leaders think? First the Writers Union, then the . . . Party?"

This time the pause was so dramatic that Nikolsky himself felt a certain chill.

"You made a strong impression on me last night. I was ready to help you. I even put in a call to Moscow on your behalf. But after this letter . . ." He tossed the paper on the desk as if it were a playing card.

"Comrade Nikossky talked to Moscow?"

"That's right. I wanted to consolidate your position. As I told you, I keep up with these matters, and I know that Aion Neprigen was admitted to the Writers Union *conditionally.*"

"Conditionally?"

"Yes. Since you'd published no more than a few poems—you see, I *do* keep up with things—you were admitted on *condition* that you continue to produce. So after our little talk last night I thought, The best way to help Manakin is to arrange for a whole *book* of his poems to be published!"

Nikolsky looked over at Manakin as pleased as punch.

"But . . . but a whole book?" Manakin asked hoarsely after recovering from the initial shock.

At this point Nikolsky reverted to the intimate mode, the voice of experience setting a naive friend straight.

"Once you have a book under your belt, you can do as you please. No one can say, 'Who is this Manakin? What does he write?' Because you can say, 'Here is my book. And now that I've justified your trust in me, I must ask you to leave me in peace. I have important Party projects to attend to.' Moscow will be returning my call any minute now, Comrade Manakin, and I want you to talk. Not a word about me, of course. One doesn't come straight out and say, 'Comrade Nikolsky promised to put in a good word for me,' does one now? The people who need to know know, if you get my meaning. So take the receiver when I give it to you and tell the editor who you are and that you're willing to let him publish a volume of your verse."

Just then the phone rang. Nikolsky picked it up with the smile of a successful medium and said, "Is that you, operator? . . . And how are you today? . . . Yes, yes. Thank you. . . . The poetry editor, you say. Good. Put him through, please."

He handed the receiver to Manakin.

"Hello?" said Manakin. "Hello? . . . Yes. Manakin. . . . Hello. . . . Yes, I agree. . . . Yes, that's right. . . . Thank you, comrade. . . . Contract, yes. . . . Yes, with Finkelmeyer. Yes, I understand. Sign together, yes. Today, yes. Fine."

He had no time to take out his handkerchief. He wiped the sweat away with his hand. It looked like tears.

After Manakin had left—saying, "Thank you, Comrade Nikossky, thank you, Comrade Nikossky"—Comrade Nikolsky noticed eight sable furs on the chair nearest the door. That evening he gave four of them to Finkelmeyer—for Danuta or his wife, as he saw fit. The other four went into his briefcase.

XI

THE NEXT DAY Finkelmeyer disappeared. Nikolsky assumed he had gone to stay with Danuta, who was no longer at her post. Then early one morning he knocked on Nikolsky's door, bade him a hasty farewell, and was off to the ocean and his fishermen. Manakin had left on the day when Nikolsky's incantations raised Aion Neprigen from the dead. As for Nikolsky, he stayed on for a week—long enough to show the engineers at the green box how to dodge the Americans—then decided it was time to go home.

Waiting at the airport ticket counter, who should he see towering over a crowd of arriving passengers but Finkelmeyer. Nikolsky called out to him, and Finkelmeyer stopped, peering around helplessly, pummeled right and left by passing suitcases, until Nikolsky went up and pulled his sleeve. Nikolsky immediately suggested they should fly back to Moscow together, but Finkelmeyer objected to leaving immediately: they'd have a better plane the next day and a Moscow crew, and besides, he was dog-tired.

"Who do you think you're fooling, Finkelmeyer? You just want another night with Danuta."

"Can't pull the wool over Mr. Patent's eyes, can I?"

The next day the airport was snowed in and they were stuck at the hotel for an indefinite period. Nikolsky spent most of the time sleeping; Finkelmeyer would withdraw for two and three hours at a time to Danuta's cubbyhole and peck away on a typewriter borrowed from the main office. When Danuta was on night duty, Finkelmeyer would sit up with Nikolsky, chatting over a game of chess and eventually bedding down in the adjoining room as on the first night.

"Why I don't kick you onto the couch I'll never know," Nikolsky would grumble each time, their friendship having reached the stage where they could say just about anything to each other. "What I wouldn't give to invite that little waitress up from downstairs and—"

"Galya of the Golden Tooth? It wouldn't be her first night in this bed!"

"Why you dirty old man, you! That girl's the picture of innocence!"

"*Vey iz mir!* A bona fide *mishugener!* No more jokes or we'll be up all night laughing."

One night Nikolsky was awakened by a terrible racket. Noticing the light on next door, he leaped out of bed and ran into the room in his T-shirt and shorts to find Aaron desperately trying to assume Chaliapin's pose in the role of Mephistopheles in the 1908 production of Boito's opera at the Opéra de Monte-Carlo (that is, *mutatis mutandis*, trying to wrap a blanket around his naked torso while various items of the hotel's inventory flew past him), Danuta standing by the bed, hurriedly buttoning up her uniform, and a great Siberian bear of a man, all sheepskin coat and fur hat, stomping in the doorway and shouting, "You're the Muscovites, aren't you? Well, the weather's still the weather, but there's a break in the clouds for a couple of hours, and it'll let us through, I know it will. Are you with me?" And when the sleep-dazed Muscovites held their peace, he added, "Two passengers is all I need—they won't let me up otherwise—and I've got to get to Moscow. Oh, I know what you're thinking: tiny plane, night flight, stops galore. Well, so what if it's tiny, so what if it's night? Four short stops and you're in Moscow. What do you say?"

An hour later a decrepit little Ilyushin was whining through the dark skies, its lights blinking like the eyes of a night-blind animal. While Nikolsky rearranged the clothes he had stuffed into his bag, Finkelmeyer tried making piles of the pages he had typed.

"Here, let me help," said Nikolsky, laughing at Finkelmeyer's distress when the piles kept slipping off his knees and getting mixed up. "How many copies did you make?"

"Three. The problem is, I forgot to number the pages, and—"

"What is this, Aaron? Have you switched to prose?"

"It's all your doing, actually," said Aaron, not without a touch of rancor.

"What do you mean?"

"You're the one who . . . wound me up, opened the floodgates. I can't stop now. Besides, writing things down helps me get them off my chest."

"Would you mind if I read it?"

"What a question! Of course not. It's only the continuation of what I told you."

Yet it was clearly a sore point, a shameful weakness, a repellent disease, and Finkelmeyer was so relieved when Nikolsky took charge of the papers that he fell immediately into a dreamless sleep. Nikolsky turned sheet after sheet, making neat piles and reading as he went. Glancing over at Finkelmeyer, he could all but hear his voice.

XII

IN THE ARMY (Continued)

THE NEWSPAPER offices were in the same building as the library.
The librarian was respectfully referred to by her name and patronymic, Olga Andreevna, though she was still a young girl. She rarely
uttered anything more than the formalities necessary to check out
books, and lived not so much by herself as in active isolation from
the rest of us. As soon as she had locked up the library for the day,
she effectively vanished, never appearing at a film or even the grocery. The reason for her self-imposed exile was not hard to guess:
she was terribly misshapen; it was as if a gigantic iron fist had
squeezed her hips out of joint.

To hide her deformity she wore an old-fashioned floor-length shawl
with fringes—in summer over her dress or smock, in winter over
her coat—but she couldn't take a step without jerking back and to
the side, and always seemed on the verge of toppling over. Her features, despite their customary deliberate look of indifference, were
regular and appealing, the cool expression attractive in the way the
chiseled face of an Egyptian empress attracts. In Olga Andreevna,
however, it merely served to intensify the pity people felt for her,
and she was both intelligent and sensitive enough to feel, without
even raising her eyes, the compassion with which the soldiers who
came to use the library viewed her.

As a librarian she was highly conscientious, keeping up with the
latest books and doing what she could to acquire the best of them
for the collection. Unfortunately, the country was going through a
double famine at the time: it was as low on books as it was on meat,
milk, and bread. Oh, there was plenty of trash; they published hymns
to Stalin's construction sites, they published dithyrambs in honor of
his plan for transforming nature. But they published virtually none
of the sort of poetry the Master had encouraged me to read.

The only things Olga Andreevna could come up with were a small volume of Blok and a smaller one of Pasternak, the latter having made its way into the library because it included a few war poems. I also reread the classic Russian poets and plunged into an eight-volume edition of Shakespeare.

One day I was checking out a book when Olga Andreevna handed me a copy of our newspaper featuring the latest in A. Yefimov's potboilers.

"That's really you?" she half told, half asked me in her beautiful, rich, yet distant voice.

"It is. Why do you ask?"

She looked up at me, her deep, dark eyes flashing with disdain. It was the first time I had actually seen them.

"Because you read Blok," she said, carefully delineating every syllable. Then she handed me my Shakespeare.

I could feel my face burning. I rushed out of the library filled with hatred, grabbed the folder where I kept my "real" poems hidden (they numbered about thirty by then), and raced back.

"Here, read these if you're such an expert!" I said, tossing them on her desk. "Only they're by Finkelmeyer, not Yefimov."

Not even deigning to look up at me, she opened a drawer, dropped the folder into it, and immediately started rummaging through her checkout slips.

I stopped going to the library.

A month later I received a card with the following message:

Comrade A. M. Finkelmeyer:

The book listed below is overdue. Please return it immediately. Appropriate measures will be taken in the event of noncompliance.

I complied.

Olga Andreevna gave a triumphant smile upon seeing me, but instantly turned serious again. "You remember I have your folder," she said in her melancholy half-question, half-statement manner. There was a long, awkward pause, which she herself broke by saying, "You need to read more poets. Which do you want to read?"

I shrugged and named ten or fifteen. "But what's the point? They're none of them available."

Her only answer was the slip for the next Shakespeare volume. I left without taking back my folder, and although I started going to the library again, there always seemed to be another patron around to keep us from taking up where we had left off.

Then one day she spoke up anyway. "Tomorrow's Sunday. You have the day off. You can help me."

By now I knew enough to interpret the last statement as a request, nor could I help noticing that the effort it had required showed in her face as pure agony.

"Why, of course," I answered, as nonchalantly as I could. "At your service." I even bowed.

And then she laughed. I must have looked terribly funny. She laughed! "Straighten up! Straighten up or you'll snap!"

But as I did, I saw her face change back to its passive, stony mask, and I realized why: the words "straighten up or you'll snap" had ricocheted back to her, the cripple who would never straighten up.

The next day we took a perilous journey along the muddy April roads in a rickety officers' bus. The driver was up to it, though, and after about two hours of spattered brown views we pulled up at a godforsaken whistle-stop. Out came a doddering stationmaster with a greasy register for Olga Andreevna to sign, and the driver and I loaded three enormous crates into the bus. After a number of adventures—we kept getting stuck—we arrived back at the base and lugged the crates up to her modest room. Just as we were ready to retire, she turned to the driver and said, "That will be all, thank you. And you"—by which she meant me—"can stay and help."

As soon as the driver roared off, Olga Andreevna disappeared into her room to change. I waited out in the dark entrance hall, leaning against the crates and feeling suddenly serene. Was it the light shining behind the door, the warm, feminine fragrance of clean linen, of perfume in little bottles? Or was it simply the return to human habitation, an atmosphere free of barracks noise and sweat and carbolic acid?

She must have opened the door a crack and, hidden by the light, stood there watching me take in deep breaths of her room with my ridiculously long nose, because when she finally said, "Come in, Aaron, come in," I gave a start.

"I'm afraid my boots are caked with mud."

"Then take them off."

"But the foot cloths . . ."

"You'll have to keep them on. Not even your *toes* will fit into my slippers."

"Foot cloths are not only unaesthetic"—there was so much she didn't understand—"they unwind when you take your boots off."

"I see," she said, and slipping back into the room, she opened and closed a few drawers and reappeared with two elastic bands that could only have belonged to that intimate item of apparel called panties, which, by the way did not embarrass her in the least. When I had pulled off my boots and secured my foot cloths—the institution of the Saturday bath ensured that they were not too smelly— she invited me to take off my coat and make myself comfortable. Somehow I couldn't bring myself to, and waited outside the door until she returned. Her arms were filled with platters of food.

"Don't be shy," she said with a smile.

"A maiden's chamber . . ." I replied—and immediately cursed myself for making so stupid and vulgar a remark. But all she did was open the door wide and walk in.

The room was oddly furnished, or rather only half of it—the far half near the window—was furnished at all. The first piece of furniture I came to was a couch that pretty well divided the room in two. Olga had sat down in an armchair in the middle of the furnished part. It had one arm removed so she could slide in and out easily. Next to it there was a small card table with sawed-down legs and a revolving set of shelves filled partly with books and partly with feminine accessories—jars, boxes, a variety of small bottles, a tiny mirror—and a chest of drawers, from which, without leaving her chair, she took a tablecloth, two plates, a knife, and forks. Sitting opposite her on the couch, the only place left to sit (the room was clearly not designed with visitors in mind), I admired the grace with which she laid the table, using only her beautiful, agile hands, and in general the skill with which she had arranged her life. Later I realized that the armchair was more than a comfortable seat; it was a kind of shell, a coat of mail, a snail's house, in sum, a refuge, which, once she withdrew into it, offered her security, protection. Outside it, all she had was her mask, her brusque manner.

The teapot on the electric hot plate at her feet was bubbling, the platters overflowing with delicious-looking sandwiches, and Olga Andreevna asked me how long I could stay.

"All night," I blurted out, instantly realizing I'd put my foot in it again. "That's not what I meant, really . . ."

"I won't keep you," she said, cutting me off and retreating behind her mask.

"No, no, you don't understand!" I cried. "All I meant was I don't need to report back at any given time. I have a room of my own. I didn't mean I wanted to stay the night. I only . . . I just . . ."

Oddly enough, the more tangled I got in my explanations, the more Olga Andreevna's face melted. Soon it even showed traces of a slightly ironic, self-satisfied smile. What a victory, after all! For once it was she—so well versed in the fear of being misunderstood, the difficulty of making contact, the desire to vanish into thin air— for once it was she who had made someone self-conscious.

Then and there I knew we were going to be friends. I broke into a smile and said, "You know, Olga, I'm starving!"

"You know, Aaron," she said softly, starting to laugh, "so am I."

Half an hour later the teapot was bubbling again. My collar was open, and Olga Andreevna's shawl lay folded in her lap. Looking at her now, no one would guess she had a physical defect. Her body was lissome, the line of her neck and shoulders appealing, her breasts modest yet inviting—a winning combination of features womanly and boyish.

We talked and talked. Almost from the outset we settled on school memories—what our teachers were like, how we made fun of them in my boys' school and how they made fun of them in her girls' school. I couldn't get over how much like boys the girls were in their malice.

"Girls are basically stupid little brats," she said. "All my friends were boys. And I bet you ran after the girls."

"Me?" I laughed.

"What are you laughing for?" she said, looking at me in a critical, very feminine way. "The girls must have liked you."

"Because they're so stupid, is that it?"

"*Touché,*" she said. "You really take a girl at her word. But enough banter and enough tea. Time to unload the crates."

The first one gave me quite a bit of trouble: there was nothing to open it with—no hammer, ax, chisel, or even corkscrew in the place, and the knife I slid under the admirably sturdy boards threatened to snap under the pressure of my twistings and turnings. Dripping blood from a multitude of splinters, I scoured the kitchen for a better tool and lit upon a dustpan. I forced it under a board and squiggled it up and down a few times. The nails cracked; the board gave.

"The first one's yours," said Olga Andreevna, coming out of the room.

My hand told me that what I had suspected was true. The first object I touched was a small, thick book. Before I could see the title, Olga Andreevna shouted, "Heine! The Academia edition! You certainly are lucky! It'll be hard to part with."

"You don't think I'm going to take you at your word this time, do you? . . . Are they really all yours?"

She just smiled.

I took out one volume after the other, glancing at the title and opening to the first page, the middle, then leafing back and reading, reading, reading, until I felt a sudden cramp from standing in one position for so long and glanced up to see Olga Andreevna riffling through a volume, looking for her favorite lines. I changed my position and went back to unloading, but every once in a while I snatched a glimpse of her observing me, watching jealously which of her books I was reading, *hers* not so much because they were her physical property as because she had made them her own spiritual property when she first read and then reread them. She had left something more significant between the covers than an *ex libris;* she had left the stamp of her mood, the stamp of her memories, the stamp of her past.

She started looking at me with a sad, condescending smile. I pounced hungrily on the books, picking up a new one before I had finished with the one in my hands, going through more and more. At one point I heard a muffled wheeze, a moan in the background; it turned out to emanate from me in my ecstasy, in the pain of my all but erotic bliss. Only a poet could empathize with a poet's outpourings!

Those three crates contained the most carefully selected, the most complete poetry collection I have ever seen. Russian poetry, beginning with Kheraskov and an exquisite hundred-year-old edition of Derzhavin's odes, and moving on to Zhukovsky and the entire nineteenth-century pantheon, to say nothing of lesser lights like Mei and Fofanov and Baron Rosenheim in a thick morocco-bound edition. It had the wonderful poets who straddled the turn of the century, starting with Annensky and including the Symbolists and Blok—slim little volumes or several unbound booklets of the same poet carefully grouped together in a folder that was then enclosed in a soft ash-gray cloth cover; it had all the Futurists—including the young Mayakovsky and a collection of Khlebnikov (from the early thirties?)—and of course all the Poet's Library editions, Large Series and Small; it had everything: the Greeks and Romans in several anthologies, the French in the original and translation (Musset and Hugo, Lamartine, Prudhomme, Baudelaire, Verlaine, and many others too numerous to mention—I had had some French in school, and went back to it so as to make my way through at least some of the originals), the Germans (Goethe, Schiller, Heine), the English (Shelley and an enormous volume of Byron), and one American (Walt Whitman—and in the Chukovsky translation!).

When Olga Andreevna told me it was past midnight, I failed to grasp what she was getting at. She had to add, "Thank you for your help, but I'm falling asleep on my feet," before I let her see me to the door. By then we were old friends and no longer needed to handle each other with kid gloves. So when she told me to take something back to the base with me, I could ask, "Something?" and she could answer, "As much as you like, and you can come back for more when you're ready."

I chose five or six, wrapped them in newspaper, said goodbye, and off I ran. Back in my room I threw my coat at its peg, pulled my boots off—they had been cleaned and shined—flung myself on the bed fully dressed, and began to read.

From that day on I was a frequent visitor at Olga Andreevna's. She couldn't hide how much she enjoyed the visits, but would chide me for gulping down the poetry so fast: "Really, Aaron, how can you? They're not adventure stories, you know."

At first I tried to argue my way out of it—anything to avoid parading my phenomenal memory, of which I was more embarrassed than proud. Then one day I had enough of Olga Andreevna's contempt for my superficial approach and said, "No more lectures, please. See those books? Well, take any one and pick any poem in it—only make sure it's a good one; I don't bother with second-rate ones. Then read the first line, and I'll recite the rest."

People never really get close to each other until they stop trying to control their relationship. Until that movement I couldn't let myself forget that Olga Andreevna was a cripple. I always gave her a hand, did things for her. And suddenly we were nothing but rivals. She must have felt it too, because for the first time she moved impulsively, not caring what her deformed hip looked like or how her disobedient legs got her to the desk. And I, rejoicing in my imminent victory, looked on with a self-satisfied smile and suddenly thought, Here I am, watching her struggle, and I feel no compulsion to run to her aid. All that mattered to both of us was the poem.

"Ready, Aroshka?" It was the first time she'd called me by a pet name. "Here's one of my favorites. Just try to tell me it's second-rate!

> 'No, do not reason, rage, or weep
> Though folly govern, madness glitter.' "

"Tyutchev!" I cried, triumphant, and nearly shouted the rest:

> " 'Your daily wounds assuage with sleep
> And let the morrow do its bidding.
> Learn how to feel the full of life,
> Its joy, its woe, its trepidation.
> Why court desire? Why beckon strife?
> A day is done. Thank your Creator.'

"So there!" I said and very nearly stuck out my tongue. "Now will you stop hounding me?"

"Oh, Aroshka!" she laughed, standing in front of me by the couch. "WIll you ever forgive me?"

"Oh, Oleshka! Only if you kiss me on the cheek!"

"Oh, Aroshka! I just might!"

And she stuck her neck out and gave me a noisy kiss.

The last, thin wall between us had tumbled down. I dropped the formal "Olga Andreevna" once and for all and called her Olga, Olya, even Olyushka when we were both in high spirits. Not that Olga was always in so playful a mood. Although I always felt a warmth in the depths of her eyes, the veil she wore over them, like the shawl she wore over her shoulders, was impossible to lift.

Then one evening I felt a special reticence in her. We had been discussing what makes the *vers libre* so magic a verse form, and all at once, pouring me some tea, she stared out into space and recited a nursery rhyme about "poor little Olga run over by a cart." When she noticed what a fright she'd given me, she smiled and said mournfully, "I'm terribly depressed today. I do apologize! May is an awful month for me. Everything blossoming. . . . I swore to myself I wouldn't burden you with it, but I seem to be doing it anyway. Open the window, will you? Do you want to hear about it?"

She had just turned eighteen. She was in her first year in Russian literature at the University of Leningrad and in love with a merchant seaman more than ten years her senior. Her father, a professor of social science at the university, was very upset by the relationship. As a Marxist and personal friend of the great Lunacharsky, Professor Karev was proud his daughter had fallen in love with a proletarian who had fought bravely for his country and was now serving her on the open seas, but as a doting father and widower of long standing he could not reconcile himself to the idea of being left alone. Besides, what kind of life would she have, married at nineteen or twenty to a man who spent half the year at sea? For a while her studies would distract her, but later, when her real life began?

As for the seaman, he was no child; he had no interest in drawing things out. A thirty-year-old sailor can find even a week too long to wait if he is about to go off on a long voyage and knows that the wonderful creature he is in love with wants nothing more than to marry him.

It was May. She was in the middle of exams; he was busy with his crew at Gatchina. They snatched meetings on the run. Then one day she ran out of her house to find him waiting at the entrance.

"What's wrong?"

"We're weighing anchor tomorrow."

She didn't think twice.

"Wait here. I'll be right back."

She raced upstairs, told her father she would be spending the night at a friend's, studying, and raced down again to tell her lover she was his. He was beside himself. He immediately phoned an old wartime friend and current first mate and asked to borrow the Opel he had brought back from the war.

"Look, you haven't got a license," the friend objected, and good friend that he was, he offered to act as chauffeur.

"Don't be crazy. You and your wife have only one night left yourselves."

"We've been married for five years."

"But I want her and Olya to be good friends."

Olga couldn't remember exactly how it happened. All she knew was that he was driving very fast—the truck ran into them on their way into Gatchina—and that they were laughing at the time. She was told they found him with a broad grin on his face. Her hips were crushed between the bashed-in door and his body. A major artery had burst, and she would surely have died from loss of blood long before the forty minutes it took to summon the ambulance from Gatchina had her dead fiancé's hand not lodged itself just above the gaping wound. The moment they moved his body a jet of blood spurted out of her. Fortunately, the doctor in charge was able to stop it.

Fortunately? For Olga the dead man's guilt consisted entirely in leaving her behind.

The courts hauled in the first mate for lending his car to a party without a license, but when Olga regained consciousness she made a statement to the effect that they had taken the car without the owner's permission. The judge couldn't have asked for an easier way out.

Professor Karev was in a terrible state. He reproached himself constantly for being too lax, failing to watch over his daughter, letting the relationship go on when it was clear from the outset it would lead to no good. Olga was at her wit's end with his moanings and tears. The resentment she felt at the thought of the long and burdensome years ahead with her father—although he probably hadn't admitted it to himself, he must have realized at some level that his beloved daughter would never leave him now and that becoming her slave was the best fate he could have wished for in his old age—drove her to distraction. Yet she had to face up to it: she would be an invalid all her life, always pitied as "the cripple." What should she do, then? Go back to her studies, to the world of her peers? They were healthy and foolish; they spent their days in cinemas or on playing fields, their nights worrying about exams or the burden of virginity.

A student would bring her lecture notes. She would keep them for a day or two just to be polite and return them unread. The girl, who had been appointed by the Komsomol, reminded her of Maupassant's Boule-de-suif; she had big, round, blue eyes that were incapable of hiding the horror she felt at the sight of Olga's legs, yet she felt it her duty to remind Olga of how Nikolai Ostrovsky wrote his classic *How the Steel Was Tempered* in straits more dire than hers. One day the girl blurted out that by refusing to work Olga was spoiling their Komsomol record. Olga hurled a crutch at her and closed her doors entirely on the outside world.

She made one exception: her seaman's first mate. He was the only person who had the slightest notion of what was going on inside her. It was to him she went for help with her plan—to find a job in a place far removed both physically and intellectually from the life she had known—and it was he who came up with the idea of the military base. It seems that during the evacuation of Sevastopol in 1942 the two friends had saved the life of a man who was now a general in the infantry, and the first mate promised to look him up and see whether he could do anything for her. He not only offered her a job, he sent one of his men to accompany her to the base and then looked after her like a child.

Olga decided not to tell her father about the move until just before it was to take place. The old Marxist fell to his knees and begged her to have pity on him; he even had what appeared to be a minor heart attack. He quickly recovered, however, once assured that Olga would not be deprived of her Leningrad residence permit—in other words, that she could come back at any time.

"And you will come back, Olga darling, I know you will," he said, his hands trembling as he passed her the items she was packing. "You won't be able to stick it out there, Olga. You'll see."

"I'll be back, Papa," she replied patiently, firm in the knowledge that nothing would induce her to return. "I'll be back."

"It's been three years now," she told me, "and in every letter Father asks about my plans for the future. But I refuse to think about the future. About the past too, for that matter. The past is gone, and there is no future. Nothing was, nothing will be."

"But there *was* something!" I said passionately. "There was *love!* And I know what it's like to have love ripped out of you from one day to the next. You can't forget it."

"You're lying! You're lying!" she shouted, her voice cracking, her eyes flashing. "You say you were in love. Then you know the joys of love. You were together, you spent nights together! Well, didn't you?"

"We did."

"Well, we didn't! It was the night before, not the morning after!" She bit her lip to keep from crying. "Don't you see? There wasn't anything to remember! And all I have to look forward to is the life of crabby old spinster, a scarecrow, a witch!"

"Don't be silly."

"I'm *not* silly, and I've given it a good deal of thought. Tell me, do you think I ought to sign up for a correspondence course?"

"That's just what I was going to suggest!" I said, overjoyed she had brought up the idea herself. But the way she laughed at me—it was a mocking, deadly laugh, as if she took me for a ridiculous-looking insect—made it clear it was just a trap. She must have sat through that kind of advice—study hard, work hard, do your bit for society—a hundred times over. The best I could do was admit defeat and change the subject.

"The books—are they your father's?"

"Yes. He has a huge library. Rare editions galore. Some came from my grandfather; others he bought when he was a student. The non-Russian books—philosophy, economics, history—he brought back from abroad—he was a political émigré for a few years before the Revolutioin. Right after he came back, Lunacharsky appointed him as what you might call head censor of Leningrad, which meant he automatically received a copy of every book published—a total of several thousand. You can imagine how devastated he was when he got my letter asking him to break up his beloved collection—the books mean a lot to him. But evidently I mean more."

She drew the shawl around her shoulders, glancing at the window. I walked over to it and pulled it to. It was dark out, and the air was cold. The sweet, sticky fragrance of sprouting leaves came from a bush near the wall. I was about to turn back when I heard her muttering, as if unaware of my presence, ". . . everything blossoming only to die. Year in, year out. The third anniversary of my . . . my botched departure. Though I might as well be dead. . . ."

I went and stood behind her chair. By the dim light of the table lamp I could see only the silhouette of her bent head, a few lockets of shiny hair, and the folds and fringes of the shroud she had buried herself in, buried herself alive. I carefully laid my hand on her head. She remained immobile for several moments, then took it and brushed it slowly across her cheek. But regarding my hand as too coarse an object to bring consolation to a woman, I bent over and kissed her cheek and hair.

"Thank you," she said. "Now go. Please. I think I'll be able to sleep."

The next time I went to see her she jokingly, flirtatiously offered her cheek, and an innocent kiss became our little tradition.

Although I never gave much thought to why we came to set such store by our soon almost daily visits—we were simply relieved to find release in each other's presence from the idiocy of military officialdom—Olga clearly felt a need for more than spiritual friendship. One evening when I was about to get up from the couch and leave, she came over and said, "May I?" and kissed me at the corner of the mouth, nearly on the lips. I could feel the curve of her small breasts as they brushed against my shoulder. Our eyes met. She looked so agitated that I lost my composure and was forced to replace it with a strained smile. The source of her agitation was clear, but the idea of physical intimacy between us was impossible. Once the stone walls in which she had enclosed herself came tumbling down, there would be no end to her agony; her feelings would rise and fall with no outlet, like dough leavening in a cramped space.

The best course of action, we decided, was to stop seeing each other, at least in private. We continued to meet in the library, but we both felt bereft, and one day, when after a few weeks of misery we happened to be alone in her office, she sighed, "Oh, Aroshka!"

"Oh, Oleshka!" I said. "What fools these mortals be."

"What fools," she replied without raising her eyes from the slip she was filling in.

" 'No, do not reason, rage, or weep . . .' "

"How right he was," she said with a smile. "Scared of our own shadows."

"See you tonight then."

"Minus the endearments."

Our evening visits took up where they had left off. Olga began delivering long monologues on, say, a German poet she had read in the original under her father's tutelage. She prepared short surveys of the major periods of European literature. I was a diligent pupil, deluging her with questions, but also drawing her into arguments. The view she had taken over from her father and from the books he had given her—namely, that literature was the "product" of the social forces of a given period of history, a mirror of the conditions in which the author lived—clashed head-on with my intuitive approach, which led me to regard a work of art as something all but inexplicable, the most personal, individual means of expression one could imagine. I had no interest in the class conflicts racking Germany at the time when Heine's *Harzreise* appeared. No, I argued, I was more interested in whether Heine was fat or thin, whether he drank hard and slept with whores or sipped boiled milk and was chaste as a monk. She would laugh, I'd explode, and neither of us would budge an inch. It invariably ended with her asking me to recite a new poem; I invariably had something ready. I would begin with the one or two I had written that day and then move back in time. It wasn't long before I could go on for an hour or so, and that hour was the most dangerous period for us: as I recited, as the rhythm of the verse filled the half-dark silence of her room, I could see the familiar agitation returning to her face, see her fidgeting in her chair, winding the shawl around her, chewing her lips behind a hand vainly poised to hide them.

Back in my room I pondered what made her react as she did, why she fell apart only when I recited my verse. Would she be indifferent to me if I didn't write poetry? I rejected that hypothesis out of hand. I was simply the only man with whom she was in regular contact. And then I saw it clearly: with me she was distressed less by her deformity than by her virginity. She had fallen in love and was on the brink of becoming a woman, and an hour or two before the great event—"it was the night before, not the morning after"—everything had fallen apart.

Much as I brooded over Olga's psyche, I avoided looking into my own. One reason was that watching her lower her eyes and chew her lips I felt something akin to pride. But more important, watching her face turn thoughtful and her cheeks lose their pallor, redden with excitement, I was ready to acknowledge that I could find her attractive, did find her attractive, though . . .

It always passed, leaving me horrified at my temporary loss of equilibrium. Then two or three days later it would happen again, and each time the "though" was longer in coming. Soon I found myself having dreams about our "fornication," as I thought of it, recalling Tolstoy's quotation from Matthew.

We decided to stop seeing each other altogether.

Everyone—everyone on the base and in town—knew about my visits to the library (everyone knew everything about everybody, whether it was true or not), but Olga and I, separately and together, seemed to enjoy a kind of immunity from gossip—she because of her deformity and I because of my reputation as a joker who might be a whiz at rhymes but when it came to women—and the town had an abundance of them in all shapes and sizes—had a long way to go. Once I was given to understand that a plump little cook was ready to jump into bed with me, and when I paid no attention one of my colleagues on the paper said to me, "Maybe they snipped off a little more than they meant to, eh, Aaron?" To which I replied, "Actually they lopped it off altogether. Want to see?" From then on all the cooks would blush and giggle each time I went into the mess hall.

Everyone pitied Olga, the men as well as the women, the men even more—at the thought of a fine body gone to waste, perhaps, or because they felt guilty for ignoring her. In any case, they were relieved when I started visiting her. If an editor asked for me and learned I was with Olga Andreevna, he would make do with somebody else.

And suddenly I had stopped seeing her. For a while people simply looked at me a little strangely, but then public opinion, in the person of the base's Komsomol leader, couldn't stand it any longer. "Tell me, Aaron," he said to me one day, "you haven't had a falling-out with Olga Andreevna, have you?"

"Why yes, I have, actually."

What else could I say to public opinion?

"Really, Aaron, I'm surprised at you," he said with a frown that did less than wonders for his browless face. "Oh, she's got that way about her, I know, but think what she's been through. . . . We've been talking, and well, we feel you ought to . . . you know . . . make peace with her. I'll tell you what. I'll make it clear to her you have something you want to get off your chest, all right? The general asked me to look out for her when she first came here—he's got a real soft spot in his heart for her—but I was never good at it. You know how to talk to her, with your books and poems and all. What do you say, Aaron? What do you say?"

There was nothing I'd have liked more than to punch him in the nose and send him sprawling into the narrow aisle between the desks. What stopped me was not so much the base's punishment cell as the rumors that would start circulating even before Comrade Komsomol had picked himself up off the floor, the lewd looks she would get from the soldiers who came to check out books. So I tried to keep calm and said, "Fine. Whatever the collective thinks is right."

General's orders! So it wasn't only pity or the discomfort the healthy feel at the sight of the lame that made them all feel guilty. The general had ordered them to be kind to her, and they were none too good at it.

Then a repulsive thought crossed my mind. What about her? Spending all that time with me. And her desire to . . . cross the threshold. Could she want me to . . .

I pushed the nightmarish thought out of my mind. I refused to allow myself to think of Olga in those terms. Yet somewhere deep inside me, far from logic, far even from words, the suspicion festered and seemed to poison the very air I breathed.

I didn't go. I wanted to, but was afraid. I tried to force myself, but was ashamed. I was nervous, I stalled, I didn't go.

For some time a longish piece in verse had been running through my mind—a narrative poem, a play, a dialogue, or, rather, a string of monologues with two main characters: He and She. I wasn't certain where it was going: I composed it large chunks at a time, in a kind of fever, and I was afraid it was disjointed, but I didn't touch it, didn't change a thing, I never even reread the mounting pile of manuscript pages. Now it had all come to a halt, and for two or three weeks I hadn't written a line.

The summer—misty, rainy, humid—had drawn to an abrupt close. Cold winds began blowing from one day to the next. The rains continued, and the leaves disappeared before they could turn yellow.

One morning I returned to my room from night duty more tired and dispirited than usual. Without even turning on the light, I sank onto the bed in my wet clothes. The moment before I dropped into nothingness, however, I became acutely aware of the necessity to go and see Olga. I knew for a fact she was standing at her front door waiting to open it before I rang the bell. I felt I was in for a terrible misfortune. I had to run. From it? To it?

I leaped out of bed and rushed to the door, tugging at it, hurling myself at it; it refused to open. When at last I tried turning the key—in my confusion I'd forgotten I'd locked the door myself—my fingers would not obey. But then the door flew open by itself, and I found two men standing on the threshold, looking me up and down. I was so rattled that I cried out, "Let me go!" though they hadn't touched me. The moment I tried to slip past them, however, they caught me and led me off, the lieutenant on one side repeating, "Don't worry, it's nothing" in an agitated mutter, the middle-aged sergeant on the other sighing, shaking his head, and cursing.

They piled me into a jeep that was waiting outside, and off we sped. All I could hear was puddles being slashed like scraps of old material. After one or two sharp turns we slowed down, and I saw the gate of what looked like a warehouse loom up in front of us. The gate opened and we drove into a gigantic, barnlike area that immediately reverberated deafeningly with the motor's roar. The air was cold, damp, and stagnant; the place had no windows. The driver switched on the headlights. Their dead rays drew the opposite wall closer, illuminating each of the unnaturally rectangular bricks and their endless progression—up and down, left and right. Then the lights went out, and I stumbled ahead with my guards. All at once I heard a scraping sound, the sound of a door moving on its hinges. I was led past it. Then I heard the scraping sound again, a voice telling me, "Don't try anything funny now," and a key turning in a lock.

My apathy and lassitude immediately gave way to rage. I stamped on the floor, banged on the door, positively reveling in the chance to roar and scream to my heart's content. There was no response, of course. If I'd had my wits about me, I'd have realized that they had dumped me into this double-bottomed brick sack to make certain my protests would go unheard. In the end I either calmed down or lost my stamina and fell sound asleep.

How long I slept I do not know, but when I awoke I noticed first that my watch had stopped running, and second that there was some bread and three portions of cold, crusty kasha sitting by the door. I took a few bites, then fell asleep again. It was the last sleep I had in the cell. The insomnia was pure torture; I thought I would lose my mind. The soldier who brought me my food certainly treated me as if I were crazy. Later I learned I had been there for five days.

At last the lieutenant who had locked me up came and let me out.

As we walked along, he mumbled something to himself, something like "It's over."

I struggled to regain the gift of speech.

"What?"

"You mean you don't know?"

He stopped in his tracks, shook his head, and whistled under his breath. Then he started walking again without a word.

He took me to the infirmary, where the doctors milled around me like a swarm of white midges. They seemed less eager to treat me than to demonstrate how ill I was. Since my previous experience with the infirmary had taught me to expect a man with no temperature to be sent back to the barracks even if half dead, I realized something fishy was going on. The doctors perked up when they heard I'd had pneumonia, and one of them began muttering, "Asthenia . . . dysfunction . . . vegetative neurosis . . . emphysema . . ."

"Emphysema?!" a nervous, middle-aged, Jewish-looking doctor interposed. "I don't see a thing that—"

They practically gagged him. All I could catch was "General's orders . . ."

"I've served in the medical corps for twenty years!" the Jewish doctor fumed. And he hadn't learned to hold his tongue. I noticed he was only a captain.

Within a half hour I was sitting opposite the general. Since I knew that the best thing to do in the presence of brass was to play the fool, I decided to return his probing gaze. I must say he didn't flinch. Rumor had it he'd done time in the thirties and been in some pretty fixes during the war—he was wounded three times and had a deep gouge above his right eye—and although he wasn't known for his humanity and his officers went in fear of him, he never took his ire out on the enlisted men.

"Don't think you can stare your way out of this, Finkelmeyer. I want to know how it happened."

Playing the fool was one thing, being the fool something else.

"I'm afraid I . . . I mean I . . . I don't know what you mean, Comrade General."

His hand came down so hard on the table I thought my heart would stop.

"None of your fucking double-talk, you hear? On your feet!

I scrambled to my feet.

"Why did she take that poison?"

I grabbed my head; I thought my brain would burst. I started swaying; I was back in my seat. I had to ask, but didn't know how. All I could muster was, "Is it all over with her?"

"No, no. They found her in time."

The general poured me a glass of water, then asked whether I wouldn't prefer cognac. I nodded, and he managed to drain a shot through my chattering teeth. I relaxed slightly. The general poured another shot for me, then one for himself. Still trembling, I was at least able to talk. Though once the general saw I wasn't faking, he did most of the talking.

At the beginning of the summer Olga had come to ask him for a favor. He said he would be glad to do anything in his power. "One of your soldiers, a certain Finkelmeyer, has it in him to be a real poet," she said, "but he needs a different kind of basic training. If you discharge him now, he'll be able to enter the Literary Institute this year."

The general refused.

"She gave me a strange smile when she left," he said, "and told me to expect to hear from her again. Women. Sometimes you wonder if they're worth the effort. Anyway, I had the matter looked into, and my report said that a soldier who worked on the newspaper used to visit her regularly in the library and read her his poems and all, and that now he'd stopped seeing her. I never had her pegged for one of those, you know, lovey-dovey types, and then—bam!"

She was saved by a fluke. The morning after it happened, her neighbor, a nurse, ran out of matches and decided to peek through the keyhole before asking for some—she wanted to make sure Olga was up. Well, not only was a light on, there was a strong odor of morphine coming from the keyhole, and when no one answered her knock she ran for the nearest doctor.

The first thing the general did when he heard the news was to whisk me out of sight. "If she'd died, there'd have been an investigation and you'd have been thrown in jail anyway." That was clearly by way of apology. "Now tell me, was it because of you? You can be honest with me. I feel a lot for her. So do you, I see."

"I suppose it was. She was so lonely, Comrade General."

"I realize that." He paused. "Now here's what you do. Go straight to District Headquarters. Straight from here. Our doctors have found all kinds of things wrong with you. I'll give the head physician a call. Maybe you'll be discharged; maybe you'll be transferred to another unit. I just don't want you here. And if you dare to go and see her, I'll skin you alive, understand? Goodbye."

He stopped me at the door.

"One more thing. About your . . . poems. I'll have the editor write up a certificate saying you were the Regiment Poet. It might come in handy. Now go."

A month later I was discharged for reasons of poor health. Late on the night of the first snow I stole through the base and ducked into Olga's dark corridor. I knocked.

"Who's there?"

"It's me."

There was a long silence. Then I heard, "No."

"Wait! Listen! I've been discharged. I know it was your doing. I'm an idiot to come back, but I absolutely must read you some poems."

"Poems?"

"Well, it's one long poem, actually. Or, rather, I don't really know what it is. And I can't seem to finish it. I thought that if I read it to you . . ."

The door opened.

It was just as it had been. She sat in her chair, I sat on the couch. I called the poem "The Shore," because the first line was "Together they sat on the shore," and the image of the shore returned before each new section.

Together they sat on the shore, looking out at the sea, and he said how fine it would be if they could sail away, just the two of them, on and on, over the waves, all alone. And she said, yes, wouldn't it be fine. But what if I should drown? Together they sat on the shore, and he said he knew how he would save her: he would hoist her up on his shoulders and lift her high above the waves, and she would look up at the sky and breathe in good fresh air and soon be strong again. But what if *I* should drown? he asked. And she put her arms around him and said she knew how she would save him: she would put her arms around him just like this and carry him up, away from the depths, and he would look up at the sky and breathe in good fresh air and soon be strong again. Together they sat on the shore. But what if they *both* should drown? Then there'd be only the sky, the roar of the surf, and an empty shore.

It took a long time to recite and even longer to discuss. Somewhere along the way she slipped "I'm cured" into the conversation. I understood immediately, of course, and was grateful for the way she'd communicated it.

"It's late," she said. "Midnight. Just like old times."

"I can stay all night," I said, and we both laughed. In fact, I *had* to stay all night. When I gave the couch up to Olga, I tried falling asleep in her chair, but tired as I was and much as I twisted my legs and torso, I was unsuccessful.

"Neither of us will get any sleep at this rate," I heard her voice from the couch. "Come and lie down next to me. There's plenty of room."

I did. Her body was so small and thin we fit easily. She took my hand and tucked it together with hers under one cheek.

"Together they sat on the shore," she whispered.

And we fell asleep.

XIII

MOSCOW

I RETURNED to Moscow just in time to see my grandmother die. Mother hadn't written about her condition, of course, but the last few months had been pure hell: Grandma no longer knew where she was, she was incontinent, she howled with pain all night. Mother looked after her by herself, and I could tell she was having a hard time breathing. When I tried to get her to see a doctor, she said, "All that matters is that you're back safe and sound, Aaronele, and as soon as we bury Grandma I promise I won't be any trouble."

I called her an alarmist, the voice of doom, a scaremonger, but in fact I was nearly in tears. "You'll dance at my wedding!" I shouted.

"Not such a bad idea, a wedding. Just don't wait too long. What's a wedding without Mama Golda?"

"Alarmist!"

I finally did get her to a specialist. He took me aside and told me she hadn't long to live. He said she seemed to have had a coronary, maybe several, and he was later proved correct. The only hope was to hospitalize her. As if we could even think of it. I managed to make her lie down whenever Grandma dozed off, but that happened less and less often.

When Grandma died at last, a flock of old women arrived out of nowhere, tore the last rubles out of my hand, wound her in a shroud, and carted her off for a ritual burial to the Jewish cemetery, where a host of professional beggars, mourners, and gravediggers tugged at my coattails, screaming, pleading, and threatening God but thinking money, a *danse macabre* of gray beards, feverish eyes, filthy snow, and untended gravestones. "Don't bury me here, Aaronele! The Preobrazhensky's good enough for me. Where they burn the bodies. And so close to the house."

Mother calmed down a bit once the funeral was over, but she still refused to hear the word "hospital." How could she leave her little boy alone? Meanwhile, her little boy would run out shopping early in the morning, return with his meager pickings, and disappear for the rest of the day.

The first person I looked up was Leopold Mikhailovich. I was in for a surprise.

When I rang at his door, it was opened, opened a crack, by a woman of cold demeanor made up to appear younger than her age. She peered at me across the chain until I asked whether Leopold Mikhailovich was home, at which point she slammed the door shut. Immediately I rang again, intending to give her a piece of my mind, and immediately I heard the patter of light footsteps. But just as the lock began to turn, a strident voice called out, "Don't you dare! You hear me?" and all activity ceased. As I was standing outside wondering what to do next, a boy eight or nine years old burst out of the entrance, his coat, scarf, and hat all awry. "Are you the man who rang at our door?" he asked, gasping for breath. "The one who wanted to talk to Grandpa?"

"That's right."

"Well," and he dropped to a whisper, though there was no one in sight, "Grandpa doesn't live here anymore. He lives by himself. And he told me, he said, 'If anyone comes asking for me, you tell them I'm at the CEWA.' "

"The CEWA?"

"You mean you don't know the CEWA?" he said reproachfully. "C and E for Center, W for Working, and A for . . . A for . . . Artists!"

That evening I paid my first visit to the Center for Working Artists. When I asked for Leopold Mikhailovich, I was told he was not only in but giving a lecture. Knowing that my army coat and perpetually suspicious face would make it all but impossible for me to gain entrance, I told the man I was Leopold Mikhailovich's nephew and had only a few hours in Moscow between trains—I had just completed my military service and was on my way to Siberia. "You can see him after the lecture," said the man reasonably enough. I finally got in with a quavering, "But I've never heard him lecture."

It was a meeting of the Friends of Classical Painting. The only light in the large room came from a projector and its reflection on the pendants of a huge chandelier. The screen showed a portrait of the young Napoleon astride a fine courser crossing the Great Saint Bernard Pass. Leopold's shadow flickered up and down to Napoleon's right as he spoke. Hearing the ironic scrape of his voice brought back the slightly contemptuous way he would pronounce the names of expensive wines, hors d'oeuvres, and main courses when waiting on his exclusive clientele at the restaurant. I could tell he gave his lectures as he gave his recommendations, that is, always implying, "You can be certain it will be good, but only I know what makes it good."

"You can't help liking him, can you?" he said, tapping his pointer over Napoleon's anatomy. "The diagonal of the horse rearing up from the left trains your eye upon the horseman. And his face twisted in the opposite direction, his glance fixed on an object behind him, all but hypnotizes you. A canvas worthy of study by anyone who deems himself a Leader of Nations."

The stir the remark aroused in the audience showed that its relevance to the recent past had been duly appreciated.

"It is one of David's finest works, a *chef-d'oeuvre,* but it is also noteworthy for certain extra-aesthetic reasons. Look at this sumptuous representation of Napoleon and think of David, the former enemy of the former Académie, the former friend of the former Robespierre, the former tribune of the former Convention, the former prisoner of the former revolutionaries—all former, former, former. Here he has completely accepted the new regime, accepted the title of artist laureate from the future emperor, just as later, under the Restoration, he was forced to accept exile and the title of terrorist. And although he died a broken man, he did outlive his model"—at this point he gave Napoleon's leg a rather unceremonious tap—"and all that remains are the Saint Bernard and this painting in the Louvre."

After a short pause he moved off into realms even more abstract.

"Arthur Schopenhauer in his treatise *The World as Will and Representation* set forth the view that history is an incoherent stream of events and that only the individual, the individual who consciously manifests his will by guiding his actions, has any degree of reality, of inherent significance. He maintained, moreover, that suffering is much more an integral part of life than happiness, though of course one would never know it looking at so magnificent a canvas."

Leaving his audience to puzzle out this rather unexpected peroration, he disappeared into a corner and turned on the light. While their eyes adjusted to the brilliance of the chandelier, he added, as a parting shot, "Especially as *Bonaparte at Saint Bernard* was painted in 1800, at the end of one century and the beginning of the next. Next time, by the way, we too begin the nineteenth century. Any questions? . . . If not, thank you for your attention."

Immediately a group of energetic young women began plowing through the chairs in the direction of Leopold Mikhailovich, but he had caught sight of me before they got to him, and he smiled at me so broadly I felt tears come to my eyes.

It turned out that his daughter had recently remarried, and she and her new husband had squeezed out the old "parasite" (which is what they called him on account of his miserable pension). Clearly she intended to take advantage of her father's collection, which as far as she was concerned served no conceivable purpose until she could live high off the hog on it. So Leopold had moved to the tiny room they got in exchange for her husband's former room, leaving the newlyweds the apartment and its contents.

"You mean the oils and porcelains and bronzes? Why didn't you at least take them with you?"

"Don't be naive. They'd have had no trouble proving I acquired them with 'funds derived from outside sources'—in other words, that I hadn't bought them on my waiter's salary. Which means they'd have been confiscated and I'd have been put behind bars. Besides, I didn't like the idea of being blackmailed."

"By your own daughter?"

"If she is my daughter," he said rather mysteriously. "Now the boy—he's definitely my grandson. And he's going to have a hard time of it. I just hope they don't succeed in undoing our seven years together."

"They?"

"His parents and everyone else around us, under us, over us . . ."

By then we had crossed Pushkin Square and were proceeding through a tangle of narrow streets glistening with snow. For the first time since my return to Moscow I felt I was starting to live, and the past months, days, and hours came peeling off like so much dead skin.

Leonid told me how a friend with good connections had taken his old czarist diploma to the Center for Working Artists and talked them into giving him a lectureship. As a result he had a little more to live on, "and well, I still have a few canvases and pieces of bric-a-brac—things my daughter doesn't know about—stored away with friends I can trust."

We passed Nikitsky Gate, then Arbat Square, and finally made a right turn from Kropotkinskaya into the tiny street where he now lived. "I'm on the ground floor," he said, pointing his cane at a house with shiny white tiles around the entrance and colorful tiles between the windows. When they got close enough, he tapped one of the windows and added, "Knock like this whenever you see a light on, and I'll come and let you in."

I often took him up on his offer, spending many days—and many nights—in his "pencil box," as he liked to call his impossibly long, narrow space. I soon learned that an independent, solitary old age was better than an old age shared with a crowd of whippersnappers who look upon the elderly as an inferior branch of humanity or with somebody one's own age one had grown away from. I'd have fully concurred with his idea that suffering is a more integral part of life than happiness if I hadn't observed that his old age was in fact happy, at least in comparison with the Master's.

The Master, who was only a few years older than Leopold Mikhailovich, had a luxurious flat (compliments of the Writers Union) and was revered not only for the poetry of his youth but for a number of recent poems I found both more pungent and more mellifluous than the early work, and yet the Master lived in utter bondage to his sister, with whom he shared the flat and who never stopped reminding him how she had sacrificed her life for him. In her youth she had written a slim volume of verse under a pseudonym, one of those bittersweet concoctions budding poetesses managed to publish in the second decade of our century, and this sad fact in the history of Russian poetry gave her the authority to repeat endlessly to all and sundry that if it weren't for the "impossible conditions I've had to put with—you can imagine how difficult it was for an attractive and well-educated woman like myself, and I was highly attractive, I assure you, why Vyacheslav Ivanov paid court to me, how difficult it was to put up with all the scrubbing and cooking and queues—I'd be writing to this day. And it's all for my brother, so *he* can go on writing. Oh, I know, it's my own fault, I taught him to expect pampering, but he's always been so helpless, can't do a thing for himself. Why, if I didn't get the barber in here, he'd go out into the street unshaven. And the crowds he invites home! I'm always entertaining. Do have another cup. Yes, here's the sugar. I'm sorry, only lumps, but do take another. I hope you don't smoke. My brother has asthma, and his allergies have been acting up lately. . . ."

Then again, he couldn't live without her. As I'd found out on the day we met, he was capable of running around in February without a hat or scarf.

The best time to visit the Master was in the morning when his sister was out shopping or busy in the kitchen. True, he was usually sour in the morning, a hopeless combination of hypochondriac and misanthrope, but I could always bring him round with a freshly written poem. His dull eyes, all but hidden behind unhealthy folds of flesh, would start to sparkle; the sallow skin hanging on his cheeks would turn pink. He would leap up from the couch he had been wallowing on and start to tell me, gesticulating wildly, what made the poem work.

For all his ineptitude in everyday affairs he was amazingly astute when it came to publishers and editors. When I first returned to Moscow, he had his own typist prepare a fair copy of the poems I recited to him and kept one set for himself and "one to circulate among friends." Then he asked to see all the work I'd done under the name of A. Yefimov and, after sorting it out according to a system only he could discern, announced it would soon appear as a separate volume.

"You can't be serious!" I cried.

"Of course not," he replied. "Nobody in his right mind would take this stuff seriously. I'm thinking of our Military Press."

"But surely there's a difference between a military publishing house and a military newspaper."

"Of course there is: the difference between a pinhead general and a pinhead lieutenant. Look, Aaron, why are you arguing with me? Are you afraid you won't know what to do with the royalties? I'll teach you. It's as easy as pie. Now tell me. Did you win any awards while you were in the service? Anything we might use in your favor?"

"Awards, Master? Me?"

"Well, maybe a certificate to the effect that you had some part or other in the Komsomol, that you paid your dues on time—I don't know."

"I'm not even a member . . . But wait! There *is* something. The general sent me a letter—you'll scream when you see it—naming me the Regiment Poet and calling my poems a perfect example of the marriage of art and ideology. He said they filled a major gap in the political education of both soldiers and officers."

"God, you're naive!" the Master roared. "Where is that letter? Bring it to me immediately! But first tell me—do Jews light candles for people?"

"I don't know. There are candles on the Sabbath. But they're only for God, I think."

"All right, then. *I'll* light a candle for your general."

The book created a sensation at the press, but its author's first appearance there created a veritable furor. The Master had warned the editors that A. Yefimov was a pseudonym, but they were more likely to have pictured him a pirate with an eyepatch and a dagger or a wise man with a turban wound round his head than a long-nosed scarecrow of a Jew; they were more likely to have replaced Yefimov with Rasputin or Tolstoy than with Shapiro or Epstein. A Jew a poet of the Soviet Army?

"Have you . . . uh, completed our questionnaire?" one of them finally dared to ask. "I mean, we need to have your real name along with the . . . Tell me, what *is* your real name?"

Since I was being addressed by a man sporting an epaulette with a large star on it, I barked out, "Private Finkelmeyer, Comrade Major!"

The ensuing silence went on for so long that the secretary turned back to pecking at her typewriter.

"Well, here it is," said the major, handing me the form with as much aplomb as he could muster.

"They're just a bunch of whores," the Master said as soon as the door closed behind us. "You're their man, foreskin or no. All they care about is 'filling a major gap in the political education of both

soldiers and officers' and making sure the name on the cover will
raise no eyebrows. You know, I have a feeling they'll pass when it
comes to an author's photograph."

"But what if I'm the whore?" I mused out loud.

"There's no shame in being turned onto the streets by poverty.
Especially after being debauched by an old roué like me. By the
way, when women of the night give up their profession and marry
decent men, they make fine wives and remain experienced bed partners. So fill in the questionnaire. Meanwhile, I'll have a little chat
with the editor-in-chief. Don't worry. He's an old friend. It's in the
bag."

The Master was as good as his word. I soon had a contract. The
editors got busy cutting, padding, and pasting, and to their great
relief I let them do as they pleased. My head was spinning from the
exorbitant sum I'd been promised. I never quite believed it would
come.

It came at the end of spring—the first half, at least. I immediately
went out and bought Mother a large bouquet of roses and (because
with her heart trouble she was always cold) a large Orenburg shawl.
She burst into tears. Then I went to the Master's and drank and
drank, and when his sister started in with her "I hope you're not
planning to stay too late—my brother needs his sleep," I went off
to Leopold Mikhailovich's, who couldn't quite get out of me what
I was celebrating. I was too ashamed to tell him—or too drunk. The
closest I could come was to say I had received some money for
decorating toilet paper. Because, of course, my army poems ended
up in the latrines. For all I know they may be lying there still: not
all recruits were used to wiping themselves. There may even have
been some who left the service without a sufficiently developed
political awareness to have profited from one of the commandments
that, once I started the ball rolling, appeared on the walls of every
latrine on the post:

> Soldier! While you sit there shitting,
> Read the *Army News*. It's fitting.

Leopold Mikhailovich, hearing this, recalled the folklore of the
First World War, when the soldiers were really backward and graf-
fiti lacked the slightest hint of ideology:

If you climb up on the seat,
Sunday duty is your beat.

When I came to in Leopold Mikhailovich's flat the next morning, my first thought was of Mama, but my host immediately put me at ease. Apparently after tucking me in at one in the morning he had found my papers in a pocket and taken a taxi all the way to Cherkizovo to tell her not to worry about her son.

"He's not sick, is he?" was all she wanted to know. When Leopold Mikhailovich assured her I wasn't, she said, "The reason I ask is that once he came down with something terrible, and a girl came to see me, a girl he really loved, may God grant her a long and happy life. He's a fine son. Look at these roses. I never had roses like that, not even at my wedding. But it's a sin to complain. Everybody's got *tsores*—that's our way of saying troubles—don't you think?"

Leopold Mikhailovich agreed. He told me his own experience supported her point of view. Mama must have sensed his admiration, because she paid Leopold a great compliment: "You're a decent man. Are you a scholar? No? Well, that's all right. The main thing is that you should have something here"—she pointed to her head—"and here"—to her heart—"don't you think?"

As that was exactly what Leopold Mikhailovich thought, they parted very happy with each other.

Then from one day to the next everything changed. I came home to find a young girl sitting at Mother's bed. When I said hello, she turned and—still engrossed in her conversation with Mother—gave me a mechanical nod.

"So Basihes lived across the road?" I heard Mother ask.

"*Yo*, Basihes."

"But that means Hirshel Zaskin—you know, the one whose cow drowned—lived on the corner and you're a Zaldman, right?"

"*Neyn, neyn.*"

"*Neyn? Drey mir nit keyn kop!* The Zaldmans lived opposite Basihes Rubinchik."

"Not Basihes Rubinchik. Basihes Maizelis!"

"You mean the one whose husband sang in the street?"

"*Yo, yo.*"

"I remember now! He was a shoemaker, wasn't he?"

"*Neyn, neyn.* That was Leizer Maizelis. Their son Nonka was in kindergarten with me. We were evacuated safely, but the Germans caught up with them in Minsk. Them and Uncle Sholom and Aunt Basihes."

"Now I remember! Sholom Maizelis! So he's your uncle?"

"*Neyn, neyn.* They were our neighbors. I told you. My uncle's Moishe Kantor."

"*A naer nays!* Well, well! You hear that, Aaronele? Her uncle's Moishe Kantor! Why didn't you say so in the first place! And if Moishe Kantor's your uncle, Rohka must be your aunt."

"*Yo, yo.*"

"Well, her sister Tsilya met my cousin Mendel at our wedding, and they got married two months after us, which makes me your aunt! Aroshenka, Aroshenka! Come over and meet your cousin Fridochka. She's come to Moscow to study at the university."

It was a miracle she'd managed to locate us, though during their ten years at the orphanage she and her friend and neighbor Nonka Maizelis had repeated the names of far-off relatives and former shtetlmates almost daily. They had even tried, in secret, to keep up their Yiddish, hoping it would serve as a bond should they meet up with any of them, but all that remained was a few stock phrases.

The orphanage did what it could to find surviving relatives, but not until Frida wrote a letter on her own was there a lead to go on. The response came from a man she did not know, a Belorussian, who wrote that all the local Jews had perished and the shtetl no longer existed. The only thing he could think of that might help was that about ten years before the war the daughter of the local rabbi— he knew the family well—had run away to Moscow with a man her father disapproved of. The woman's name was Golda and the man had a close relative in the shtetl whose name was Finkelmeyer. He remembered the name because the man had been the head of the village soviet and the Germans put him in front of the firing squad on the day they marched in. Golda's husband's name might be Finkelmeyer too, and since they'd gone to Moscow they might still be alive and able to tell her more.

Frida graduated from secondary school with distinction, and the orphanage sent her off to Moscow and the university. Her first stop in Moscow, however, was not the university but a public information booth, where after only an hour's wait she was given a piece of paper with our address and a list of trams going to Cherkizovo.

"Nonka didn't think I'd find you," said Frida, smiling through her tears that evening. She wrote to him, but he wisely decided against Moscow in favor of a polytechnic institute in Tomsk, I think. Frida stayed on with us. "Until September, when lectures start."

Those first few evenings I would notice the bed shaking, then the curtain, and I'd ask, "Crying again?"

"Yes, Arosha. Sorry."

But they were tears of joy, tears of peace and quiet, of newfound freedom, and of something else that causes perfectly healthy seventeen-year-old girls to cry.

She filed the application late and, instead of taking her papers elsewhere, stuck stubbornly to the orphanage teachers' vision of her. The gigantic new university building fascinated her and flattered her ego. Yet never once did she open a book.

Instead, she took over our long-neglected household tasks with such vigor that she seemed to have two or three pairs of hands. Unlike Shiva, however, who, if I remember correctly, turned her extra hands to artistic advantage, Frida cleaned and cooked and washed, knitted, mended. She would work barefoot in the house and slip into a pair of terribly run-down shoes when she went out to shop or have Mother's prescriptions filled. One day I brought her home a pair of perfectly ordinary sandals, and she could hardly speak for joy. She placed them on the table beside her bed and kept running behind the curtain to ogle them. When she went out the next morning, she was wearing her old clodhoppers again.

The neighbors soon accepted her into the fold. "That Frida's a blessing from heaven," they would say to Mother, to which Mother would reply, "I'm not the one who needs the blessing." The women would give her knowing nods and me—whenever we met on the stairs or in the courtyard—knowing glances.

Mother was fading fast, and Frida's care and attentions comforted her, made her last days more bearable. How vicious life was, I thought: pushing this woman to the brink of the grave before giving her a taste of what it distributed so freely to so many. All it took was a little more money, a little less drudgery, and a sympathetic voice ready to twitter about something that might be less than earthshaking but was perfectly human—a pretty dress in the street, the length of the meat line, and if you're tired of potatoes I can always make dumplings, the way *you* taught me, Aunt Golda, just tell me how much flour it takes. No need to worry about poor Aaronele. He'll have somebody to look after him, cook for him, wash his clothes.

One stifling August night Frida woke me; she was in tears. Mother had passed away in her sleep.

A doctor came and auscultated, scribbled something, and left, while I simply sat next to her and talked to her, told her about what I was writing at the time or maybe about something else, I don't know, and I saw myself stretched out there beside her, and I didn't feel the least bit afraid or alone or even cold.

Then Frida pulled up a chair and started bawling away. I felt like slapping her.

The whole house came to the crematorium—a hoarse organ accompanied by a few feeble instruments, a hoist that worked without a hitch, a steady crackling from below, and the scrape scrape scrape of a wire brush against a metal griddle.

They would not let me bury her in Preobrazhensky Cemetery: they had run out of space "until further notice," perhaps for good. But I had a stroke of luck. An elderly man happened to have heard my supplications in the office and called me aside. I followed him into the depths of the cemetery, answering his questions about my mother.

"I can see you're really suffering," he said. "That's good."

We stopped at a grave with a large wooden cross. It was simple and peaceful, as Russian graves tend to be, and it had clearly been well cared for. My companion quickly crossed himself and said with an embarrassed smile, "I'm an atheist really, but somehow whenever I come here . . ."

He stood there silent for a long while.

"Is it an urn, comrade?" he said at last.

When I told him it was, he said, "Nice spot, isn't it? Makes you want to stretch out yourself. . . . How old was your mother?"

"Barely fifty."

"Just like my wife, may she rest in peace." He began to sniffle, crossed himself quickly again, then blew his nose. "Now listen carefully. I'm leaving Moscow to live with my son, and there's nobody to take care of the grave. Oh, I could pay the office to do it, but they're the biggest ghouls going." The curse he came out with shocked even me. "In ten years, maybe five, they'll dig her up—I'm sure of it—but I can gain some time for her by signing it over to you. What do you say, son? There's plenty of room for the two of them."

I was so touched by the man and so charmed by the place that I put my arm around his shoulders and said, "Thank you! Thank you!" He beamed and began telling me how to look after the grave. On our way to the office we argued over who would buy the drinks.

Suddenly something occurred to me. "Tell me," I said, "was your wife a believer?"

"Anastasia? Why, of course. *I'm* the one who—"

"My mother was Jewish."

The man stopped in his tracks and turned back and stared at the grave. But as no sign was forthcoming, he simply shrugged, sighed, and said, "The Church probably won't be too happy about it, but the way I look at it, either God exists or He doesn't, and if He does, then He's the same for everybody. Don't you agree?"

I did. So I buried my Jewish mother, Golda, under an Orthodox cross next to Anastasia, slave of God. They are lying there peaceful still. . . .

With Frida things more or less happened by themselves. One evening I came home late from Leopold Mikhailovich's, certain she was in bed. But just as I lay down I heard a neighbor's door close and Frida say good night. Then our door opened. The head of my bed rested against the back of our wardrobe, and the shadow of the wardrobe hid me from her when she came in. I heard her preparing for bed behind her curtain. Suddenly out she came to take the napkin off the food she had left me. She was completely naked.

I called to her in a whisper. She gasped and shrank back, but I held out my hand and drew her to my bed. Trembling, she dived under the blanket and pressed her body to mine.

For propriety's sake we left the curtain hanging, but one day the house manager stopped me in the courtyard and told me in the garbled jargon of the powerful that I was breaking several laws, to wit, I occupied more space than I was entitled to after the death of my mother, I was harboring a person without an official Moscow residence permit, and my "relations with said person, both financial and otherwise," were "in need of clarification." The nature of those relations was in fact painfully evident: Frida got pregnant almost immediately. The woman presiding at the marriage ceremony—she lived across the street, I believe—blessed our union with the words "It's about time."

We had enough to live on for the moment—I gave Frida everything that was left from the advance, and she managed it with admirable thrift—and since the second installment still loomed in the distance, I had no need to think about the future. Besides, how can you think about the future when you're writing poetry?

The Master, however, had some very definite ideas about the future. As soon as I received the galleys for the Yefimov volume, he instructed me to send them to the Literary Institutes. Within a month I received notification that A. Yefimov had passed the first stage of the application process and was requested to report to the institute for further information.

The secretary who took out my file handed me a piece of paper from it, saying, "Ordinarily we're not supposed to tell the candidates who reviewed their dossier, but Alexander Emmanuilovich expressly asked me to."

"Tell A. Yefimov," the note read, "to get in touch with me by phone. I want to talk to him about a collection of new poetry I am putting together." The signature was followed by *Ph.D.* in clear print, which was followed by a row of sticks with curly shoots sprouting out of them.

The secretary gave me his number, and I called him immediately from a public telephone.

"What did you say your name was?" he asked before I had a chance to tell him.

"It's about poetry."

"It's always about poetry, son. Just tell me who told you to get in touch with me."

"Nobody. My name is Finkelmeyer."

"I said, 'Who told you to get in touch with me?' "

"Well, you did, actually," I said, irritated. "It's about *The Regiment Flag.*"

"*The Regiment Flag!* So you're Yefimov! Where have you been, my boy? I've been waiting for you to bring me your poems!"

"But all you did was write a note in my—"

"What difference does it make, my boy? I must see them. I must see them today. And remember—new work only! Nothing published. Is that clear?"

When I failed to respond immediately, he repeated, "Is that clear?"

"Where shall I take them?" I asked uneasily.

"Why, to my flat, to my flat!" he said with a cluck and a gurgle.

"Could you give me the address?"

"It's in the directory, my boy. Of the Writers Union. . . . You haven't got it? Well, you have got a pencil, I hope."

A heavyset man of indeterminate age, he sported a magnificent mane, but the most striking thing about him was that even sitting in his armchair he managed to create a whole repertory of noises. In fact, noise seemed almost a way of life for him; he was incapable of operating without a constant accompaniment of crackles, wheezes, grunts, and throat-clearings.

"Hm, let me see now, son," he said, as I handed him the rather tattered sheaf of papers. "Phew! I'll never make it through all these!"

He glanced at the first poem, skimmed through the second, looked up at me questioningly, and, lifting the piece of paper with two fingers at the bottom and two fingers at the top, held it up as if it were a portrait, and asked me softly, even ceasing to wheeze for a moment, "Is this yours?"

"It is," I replied, feeling like a schoolboy caught by the teacher with a love note.

"I don't quite understand. You *are* Yefimov, aren't you?"

"Not really, though *The Regiment Flag* you read is . . ."

The pot had been bubbling beneath the surface, but now the top flew off. "Just a second! Just a second! What's going on here?"

The moment he heard about the army and the pseudonym, he knew exactly what was what; he stopped listening to my explanations and started poring over the pile of poems I had given him. For a long time I saw only the gray swirls atop his head, heard only his huffing and puffing and rumbling. After he had read them all, he turned to the window and carried on an agonizing dialogue with himself made up primarily of "Mmm!" "Psssh!" "Ha!" "Tsk!" and

"Bah!" Then he turned to me and asked me my name. The ensuing dialogue, again with himself, was much shorter than the first and gradually merged into a monologue, which was addressed to me and boiled down to the following:

As a man who has spent his life in literary pursuits, as a poet, critic, and scholar, I fail to understand how someone with your background—a first-rate Soviet education and the every bit as valuable experience afforded by the Soviet Army (capital S, capital A)—can lead a double spiritual existence. At a time when every youngster receives everything (everything, exclamation mark) necessary to develop a harmonious and well-rounded personality, you have embarked upon a road fraught with ideological deviations. As I read the galleys of your army book, I saw you as a red-blooded youth (I suddenly felt all skin and bones) full of patriotic spirit; here I see an organism poisoned by decadence and pessimism—yes, yes, the pre-Revolutionary attributes you have borrowed from bourgeois poetry (poetry in quotation marks) for your own individualistic verse (verse in quotation marks). As a result, I'm afraid I must reconsider my initial impression of your book and withdraw my recommendation.

At this point a sudden cluck caused him to twitch so violently that his arms flew off the armrests. "How could you, son? How could you dream of publishing such poems? How could you bring them to me in the first place?"

For all his fervor he reminded me of a balloon slowly losing its air. It made me want to pull out the valve and watch him subside into nothing in his giant chair. I did do something of the sort, in fact: I stopped at the door, turned to him, and said, "You leech! You old leech!" I swear I heard his inner tube deflate with a whoosh.

From there I went straight to the Master's. "Alexander Emmanuilovich!" he cried, grabbing his head. "Steinman! Steinman! The dirty, lowdown wordmonger! Why, he's an asslicker from the word go! A demagogue waiting for the highest bidder! The most pusillanimous piece of shit on the literary scene!" The Master was known for his invective, but I'd never heard him go quite so far. "You think he didn't know how good your poems are? He knew as well as I do. Oh, he's a clever one, he is! And when a Jew that clever goes and sells his soul, you keep out of his way—let me tell you! Why didn't you talk to me first? No, you had to run and show off your poems!"

When he had calmed down enough to think straight, the Master put in a call to Military Press. He began by asking whether the book would be out soon and then added, "By the way, I hear Steinman's got his hands on it. You know what that means. . . . Right. The minute he smells talent he sees red."

Then he turned to me and said, "Well, at least they hate him as much as I do. We wouldn't want the *book* to fall through. But you can kiss goodbye to the Institute." He was so upset I felt guilty.

A. Yefimov's *Regiment Flag* (including the title work but minus its lines about Stalin) came out in a printing of fifty thousand copies. I am certain that even the small number of them that made it into bookshops ended up like all the rest—in the pulper. And I imagine the fresh, clean stock that comes out of the pulper as providing the paper for yet another potboiler, which then goes through the same metamorphosis, and so on and so forth, like a literary—if that is the word—variation on reincarnation.

That summer Anna was born. She was named for Frida's mother Hannah, but Frida had had enough of what she called "national names." In any case, with a baby to provide for and the institute out of the picture, I had to find a job. When Leopold Mikhailovich's old restaurant connections came up with a post in the Ministry of Fish Production, I grabbed it, though at the time it seemed the height of absurdity. And when the Institute attached to the Ministry offered me a correspondence course leading to a degree in the economics of fish technology, Frida gave me no peace until I enrolled. It was her way of getting even with me for the sky-scraping, star-steepled citadel of learning known as Moscow University.

Nothing could have been simpler than the life I led: inhale, exhale; eat, drink; pay packets twice a month, nuptial favors twice a week. No sooner did Anna turn two than along came a sister. Frida insisted on naming her Nonka, after Nonka Maizelis, whom she loved more than a brother. By then I was past caring.

"Life is oh so simple," as my grandmother used to say, "when you tell it to an outsider."

PART TWO

A poet can have nothing more
distressing, more unbearable than his
calling and his name, for they brand
him with an indelible seal.

ALEXANDER PUSHKIN,
Egyptian Nights.

I

THERE are people who are born to be happy, who turn everything to their advantage. Fate may deal them a hard blow, but they land on their feet smiling, as if they had simply spun a cartwheel. If fate has even nastier blows in store, they may reel a bit, but they always recover, always regain their balance. Indeed, no matter how fate batters them, they stand firm, drink hard, smoke the strongest cigarettes; their wives keep having babies and abortions, and they flit from one mistress to the next. They even die easily, in their sleep, without a groan. Theirs is a truly enviable existence.

Then there are people who would seem to have everything they need—health, wealth, friends, lovers—yet are always depressed. Something is always wrong, or rather nothing is ever right. Their natural state is turmoil.

Nikolsky knew which category he belonged to. Even at the best of times—when he was excited about a new project or madly in love or speeding along the Georgian coast or carousing with friends for days on end—even then he could sense an ever vigilant, ever mournful eye deep inside him taking it all in and even taking a certain bitter pleasure in the melancholy of it all. Where did it come from? "It's just the way you're fucking put together," he was forced to conclude each time he felt the ultimately futile need to "know himself." But whenever he felt an unbearable attack of self-pity coming on, he would explain it away by saying that there was something he hadn't yet found—or somebody—and that life all around him was foul, that it never seemed to give him a break, that there were no breaks to be had, in fact.

One day he was walking along thinking a recurring thought—that all he needed was the proper chance—when something suddenly stirred in him, something so unfamiliar that he stopped in his tracks and tried to connect it with a sound or sight in the vicinity. He happened to be on the outskirts of Moscow, near the two Peschanye Streets. After coming out of the metro, he had walked past the church fence, the setting sun shining in his eyes, and turned back to see the tall crosses gleaming gold and, scattered among the large new concrete buildings, an occasional squat, four-windowed peasant hut or dandified steep-roofed dacha. He stopped at a birch tree that had pushed its way up through the concrete, and as he stood there staring at a shiny white stretch of birch bark, he recalled how during the war when he was a child—he hadn't thought about it for years—his grandfather, a former priest, would make an incision in a birch tree with his penknife and out would come drops of sap and he would lick them up and feel happy and sated.

Far from the center of town, spring seemed less gray and gloomy. No dirty-rag snowdrifts here: the bushes and grass retained their puffy white cover until the last thaw, and puddle ice remained transparent. When Leonid saw tiny streams forming out of the snow and ice, he suddenly felt a surge of hope. *Hope*—that was what had stirred in him. Yes, but hope in what? For a while he couldn't put his finger on it, but then *hope* began to take shape, take the form of a *name*. No, he said, shaking his head clear, and immediately pursed his lips into an ironic smile. No, the streams could trickle from here to kingdom come. He was not about to give in to *that*. And off he went in his usual resolute stride.

II

A TEN-MINUTE WALK from the metro station, off a wide street that had been a bus route for less than ten years, there was a house that stood out from a row of similar old "private" houses. With its steps, veranda, and little mezzanine balcony, it should have been the picture of a country house, yet it also had the feeling of the art nouveau townhouse so popular in Moscow at the beginning of the century. Art nouveau welcomed, even celebrated, cement and glass, which made it possible to decorate façades with intricate arches and curves and broad ornate openings for doors and windows; bricks and wood were thought of as "artistic" materials, for buildings in the "old Russian"—or what was soon called "pseudo-Russian"—style with its turrets, half crowns, and fancy fretwork. Accurate or not, this analysis provided the point of departure for the mistress of the Refuge (as she called the house) when explaining to her frequent and frequently puzzled visitors what she felt made for its originality: using traditional materials—brick and, even more, wood—to produce an Art Nouveau effect. Her father had liked to say that it was all in the beams, that "even-loaded" beams, the term he coined for them, made possible the kind of curve that was otherwise the domain of concrete. Of course it was all on a modest scale, which had its positive side: the authorities had not yet tried to move anyone in on its current—and sole—mistress, nor had they tried to move her out.

Actually, except for a tiny kitchen and a few windowless storage areas, the house was nothing more than a single large room with three archlike windows running along its length. In a Moscow townhouse of the nineteenth century it would have been the kind of room where the gentry gathered to make music, play cards, or read aloud, or a dining room built around that long, broad stronghold of leisurely living: the dinner table. But this house had been started about fifteen years after the indolent, half-urbanized landowner had given way to the rapacious businessman, a new breed that sent its sons to engineering school. One such fledgling seems to have taken it into his head to build a house of his own. An engineer by training but an artist by temperament, he set about erecting a sanctuary for the arts, a haven for lofty fantasies, a refuge for beauty. He longed to start life anew in a house that would place aesthetic values over physical comfort. The current mistress of the house still displayed the plans he drew up and published, to great acclaim, in the *Yearbook of the Architectural Society*.

Construction got under way just before the First World War and continued through ten years of chaos. It got bogged down in the twenties with the New Economic Policy and was never completed. Both inside and out there were numerous details needing work. The main room, which the author of the house conceived of as a combination studio (he dabbled in painting and had even exhibited a canvas or two), concert hall, and theater (a stretch of floor along one of the walls was a step higher than the rest of the floor and gave the feeling of a stage), went through a series of metamorphoses. First, an entresol (which meant nothing more than a jerry-built platform of rough boards) was built along the three back walls; later, planking was added to the wall with the windows at the level where they began to arch; then, part of the "stage" was blocked off to form an "alcove." Soon all sense of proportion had gone down the drain.

The changes came about piecemeal, on an ad hoc basis, because life did not quite pan out as the young man had expected; in fact, it had not panned out at all. Though a highly qualified engineer, he had received his qualifications before the Revolution, so for twenty years he wandered from construction site to construction site, always watched, always doubted, always hounded. He traveled alone, not wishing to subject his wife to the atrocious conditions he himself was forced to endure, but also hoping to save the house. His wife had clout: even before she fell in love with the idealistic young engineer-painter, she had been active in Social Democratic politics, and when the Revolution broke out she turned Bolshevik and was awarded a teaching position at the prestigious Institute of the Red Professoriat.

Then came 1937 and the purges. The engineer was arrested on a construction site in the Urals; his wife was picked up a few months later at the house. She was unusually fortunate, however: she was one of the few released as a consequence of the Yezhov trial.

While husband and wife were busy tearing down their old world and putting up our new one, they seemed to communicate mostly by notes. "Sorry I missed you! Off to a lecture. Love and kisses." "Leaving on the night train. Have the manager look at the tap. Much love." Thus read the scraps of paper collected during the house search. Yet somehow nature took its course, and this woman who was getting on in years by now and who had always thought of herself as a political being—this woman suddenly discovered she was pregnant.

It was the child that saved her. They let her go because it was nearly due. The father died never knowing he was a father.

She named her daughter Vera, Faith—not the faith of faith, hope, and charity, however; no, faith, unbending faith in the Wisdom of the Party and its Leader, but also faith in the innocence of her husband, who, she was certain, would return to his wife and daughter as soon as there was time to "sort things out."

Now, twenty-five years later, not only Vera's father was gone, her mother's Leader was gone, and even her mother had died a few years ago. The house was still very much alive, however, and its owner, like her father before her, saw it as a refuge for beauty. Ergo the old upright, its yellow keyboard permanently exposed; the wax-stained candleholders; the miniature marble and plaster sculptures (from the copy of a Canova to a bust of Nefertiti); a collection of fifteen or twenty oils and prints, the gifts of clearly talented artists; a sketch by Korovin and a watercolor by Benois; and great quantities of art books, scrolls of spotted engravings, piles of architecture journals lying everywhere—on tables and shelves, in corners, along the entresol, even in the kitchen.

If Vera had no desire to put her house in order, it was because order would have deprived it of whatever makes a house one with its inhabitants. And Vera had a disorderly flow of visitors dropping in on her at all times of the day and night. Most of them had something to do with art, and, engaging or not, they all contributed to the Refuge atmosphere.

Like many people who found their way there, Nikolsky found his way there by chance: he had been brought by an acquaintance who had been told by a friend that there was always something interesting going on at the place. That was three years ago, and Nikolsky could not remember what the something interesting had been.

He had been going through a hard patch at the time and naturally diagnosed it as the absence of a woman in his life. Which was also how he diagnosed his fast and furious attachment to Vera. But explaining a fling was one thing; explaining a relationship that had gone on all this time was something else. Nikolsky was not one to have trouble ending a relationship, but he always played fair when it was over—no running back for more when memories of love games began to taunt him.

Again and again he resolved to break up with Vera, but he could never quite bring himself to do it. She was the type of woman he was especially attracted to, a type not hard to find in the cities nowadays: bright, brassy, and completely independent. By the age of twenty-five or thirty, they had a salary and a flat that no man their age would turn his nose up at; they were sure of themselves and not at all interested in marriage. Nikolsky was astute enough to realize that what attracted him most was their self-reliance: an involvement was more pleasurable when it involved nothing more than pleasure. As for brains, he found he was perfectly happy with a giggling lightweight as long as everything in his life was going fine, but the moment the going got rough he would look for a woman he could have serious conversations with, a woman who had a receptive mind as well as a receptive body and would spur him on to truer confessions and greater eloquence. If few women managed to attain his ideal, it was not so much a matter of intelligence as of tact, the ability to listen and the ability to know when to agree and when to contradict.

Vera was always up to the situation. More than once he had stopped short in the middle of an argument and grinned sardonically to himself, storing away the perfect squelch for Vera, unwilling to throw the pearl before his swine of an opponent. He looked forward to her knowing smile, her clever assessment of the situation, her confirmation of his judgment. The only trouble was, it reminded him of how unsure of himself he could be.

Still, he thought, chasing that disturbing word *hope* from his mind, every time you go to the Refuge and pull back the curtain to the alcove, things are somehow right again. Besides, three years isn't so long. Your marriage—may it rest in peace—lasted only a year and a half, maybe less, but there are men who stay *five* years with the same woman—and without cheating on her. Besides, your sex life could use some toning down. Let's face it, you're not getting any younger. You might as well start preparing yourself for the worst.

Nikolsky had a key but rang the bell. After so long an absence he didn't want to barge in on her as if he owned the place.

"Oh, it's you," she said. "Why did you ring?"

"You never can tell," he said with a smile.

"Don't be ridiculous. Come on in."

A perfect demonstration of nobility on both sides: "I don't consider you my property." "Oh, but I belong to you."

Then Vera drew him close with a hand on the back of his neck, and while they kissed she took off his hat. "You might have shaved," she said after a few pecks, and added, "I'm with a pupil. Fend for yourself in the kitchen if you're hungry, or wait a half hour and I'll make lunch."

He climbed to the entresol and lay down on the sunken leather couch. He was about to reach for a pile of journals lying near the railing when a wave of fatigue came over him. He could hear Vera's clear voice, a bit higher than usual, all but singing the Italian, and the pupil trying to imitate her. All these would-be Galli-Curcis studying the language for a few scores of Verdi and Rossini. Why didn't Vera teach French or English? Could she ever have wanted to be a singer? She really was quite musical. Why not ask her about it sometime? Or about what she'd done when she was young, at school. But soon the journals' acrid smell of dust and yellowed paper and the languid flow of the Italian overpowered him, and he felt parched and thought how nice it would be to take a dip and swim out to that red buoy, but he couldn't bring himself to stand, and the sun was so bright that it hurt his eyes to look at the blond woman— what was her name again?—lying next to him on the sand, the one who kept trying to pull off her sweater but couldn't because she wasn't wearing one, she was wearing only a bathing suit, so he had to cover his eyes and turn away—he didn't want to embarrass her— but he couldn't turn away, he couldn't. . . .

When Nikolsky awoke, Vera was rocking in a cane rocking chair, smiling at him with a mischievous look in her eye.

"Has she gone?"

"Gone? Your lunch is sitting there getting cold."

"I've got a stiff neck, damn it!" Nikolsky moaned, rubbing a spot between his shoulders. Vera got up and sat next to him, and with the same smile started massaging the spot with her cool hands. Suddenly Nikolsky grabbed her by the waist and twisted her into the pose he had just been in himself. The embrace much more passionate than the one at the door.

"This is all well . . . and good," she said between kisses, "but could you . . . get me a pillow?"

"You didn't bring *me* one! Now you'll have a stiff neck too!"

"Sadist!" she said without much conviction, as Leonid turned from word to deed. . . .

The rays of the sun sent thick orange stripes through the semicircular windows and decorated the reddish wall opposite them with the silhouette of a railing and two reclining figures. The only motion in the shadowgraph came from the smoke of the figures' cigarettes as it rose along the wall, bounced off the ceiling, and descended again, a sacrifice deemed unworthy by the gods.

Nikolsky was annoyed with himself. Why the rush? But he knew that if he waited he would have to fume through an evening of guests and—when by ones or twos they had dispersed—a session with Vera about the reason for his bleak mood.

"If you think you're going to get out of feeding me," Nikolsky began, but Vera jumped in with, "I've got another think coming, right? Well, I'm starved too, so let's climb out of this bruiser—I'm back and blue all over—and get the show on the road."

While they ate, Nikolsky asked whether she was expecting a big crowd that evening. Vera shrugged. She knew that her guests tended to get on Leonid's nerves, though he never said as much—or interfered in her affairs at all, for that matter.

"I was thinking of inviting a friend, though I don't know if he'll come. He's a little . . . shy."

"Do I know him?" she asked, almost jealous. She introduced him to all her friends, male or female.

"Uh-uh," he said, swallowing a piece of roast. "I met him on this last trip. He's a poet."

"A poet? What's his name? Maybe I do know him. Maybe we have friends in common."

"No, impossible," he said, slightly riled by her reaction. But he reined himself in and thought, I refuse to let anything get to me today. "He's practically unknown. He doesn't belong to the Writers Union, of course, but his poems! . . ."

"Oh, Lyonya, I have an idea! Remember those scholar types who show up every so often? Well, they keep going on about this poet they know—I think he's their neighbor—and saying how much I'd like him. Why not see if they can bring him tonight?"

"But I don't even know whether my friend can come."

"What difference does it make? These things take care of themselves."

Given her experience he saw no reason to argue, and though he did wonder whether he should tell Aaron there might be another poet present he finally decided Vera was right: these things take care of themselves.

It was not yet six, so he phoned Finkelmeyer at work.

"Is that you, Aaron Mendelevich?"

"Yes," said a tentative voice.

"It's Nikolsky!"

"Who? Oh, hello!" said the voice, still tentative, even a bit reticent.

"You don't sound happy to hear from me."

"Really? No. It's just . . ."

"What?"

"Well, you know. You meet all kinds of people on the road, and you never know whether . . . I didn't expect you to call. At least, not so soon."

"You're an idiot, you know that?" he said in the rough-but-tender style they had fallen into at the hotel. There was a pause during which all kinds of parapsychological particles or telepathic fluids passed back and forth between them. "Look, let's get together. This evening. And don't try to tell me you're busy."

"But I am. I told a friend I might drop in."

"Well, take down this address and bring him with you."

"It's Leopold Mikhailovich. The one I told you about."

"Perfect. Tell your Leopold Mikhailovich that the house you've been invited to has a fine collection of art and sculpture, that it's a veritable refuge for the arts. Oh, and by the way, I'm looking forward to having you meet my lady friend. Got a pencil?"

Finkelmeyer mumbled something Nikolsky couldn't quite make out, but he did take the address and telephone number and promise to talk things over with Leopold Mikhailovich.

"Leopold Mikhailovich . . . Leopold Mikhailovich . . ." Vera muttered to herself. "Leopold Mikhailovich who?"

"An art historian or something."

"Leopold Mikhailovich?" she cried, beaming. "The CEWA lecturer! Why, he's marvelous, fantastic! They had to turn away people left and right! And you told him I had a *collection!* God, I'll die!"

III

AT ABOUT eight the doorbell and the telephone started ringing and Vera was soon running back and forth, making only occasional stops at the kitchen to tend the aromatic coffee. Nikolsky remained aloof from the action, firm in his decision not to play the host.

Although the regulars were well aware of his relationship with Vera, the independence the couple paraded in public enabled them to flirt a little on the side and even feel a pang or two of jealousy.

He sat down next to a friend of Vera's, the sweet, the kind Zhenya, who according to every indication was entering her thirties a hopeless virgin. When he asked about the material of her new skirt, which came high above her knees, her cheeks flushed, her eyes sparkled, and her voice grew throaty. The attentions of a man were a potent tonic to her organism.

"What are you staring at?" she asked.

"Suede, isn't it?" he went on, ignoring the question. "Is suede in?" He stuck his cigarette between his teeth and started fingering the material, tightly stretched over her ample thighs, as if trying to determine whether it was synthetic or real. Zhenya twitched and clamped her legs shut.

"Welcome! Welcome!" Vera called, and in came the "scholars," as the regulars referred to them. They were accompanied by a stocky young man with high cheekbones, a triangular forelock, and a small mouth. Though the picture of health, he seemed tense and highstrung; just standing there he gave the impression of pushing his way forward with his elbows, sweeping aside everything and everyone in his path.

"So you write poetry," Vera said uncertainly.

"Poetry *and* prose, actually," he said, pursing his lips. "Two books of poetry, one of prose. My name is Sergei Prebylov." And he held out his hand first to Vera, then to Nikolsky.

"Pre?" Nikolsky ejaculated.

"Come again?" said Prebylov with a shake of the forelock.

"How do you spell it? Pre or Pri?"

"Oh. Pre."

"Pre, eh? Can't say I've heard of Pre." And off he marched to the kitchen.

A moment later Vera came in to find him lighting his cigarette from the stove. She was choking with laughter.

"You're impossible, you know that?"

"What a *pri*-tentious, *pri*-sumptuous prig!"

"Look, how do you know? Maybe he writes good verse."

"*Pri*-posterous!"

Vera's laughter bubbled over as she ran off, and Nikolsky turned
his attention to the bottles of Stolichnaya and wine the guests had
left on the kitchen table. He twisted the top off one of the vodka
bottles, poured some into a coffee cup, and looked around for
something to eat with it. He decided he didn't need anything after
so recent a meal, gulped it down, and filled the cup with water for
a chaser.

Just then he heard voices through the open fanlight and squinted
out of the window to see two men stamping the snow off their feet.

"Aaron!" he shouted. "Don't bother to ring. Just open the door."

Aaron made his entrance by tripping over a pair of women's boots.
He was accompanied by a middle-sized, middle-aged gentleman
wearing a beret and a tattered coat much too light for the weather.
Nikolsky went up to him and shook his hand, saying, "Good evening. You must be Leopold Mikhailovich. My name is Leonid."

"Pleased to meet you, Leonid. Thank you, thank you. I can manage by myself."

Under the coat Leopold Mikhailovich had on a flimsy grayish
cardigan. He took a comb from the pocket to smooth back his few
gray hairs and remove the snow from his mustache, then adjusted
his rather crumpled bow tie, all with the slow and apathetic gestures
of a man resigned to looking after himself. The bow tie was especially characteristic of his psychology. He had probably worn it during
his years as a waiter, yet what was a somewhat extravagant accent
to the wardrobe of the contemporary male looked completely natural on the art historian.

Once Finkelmeyer had struggled out of his coat, Nikolsky gave
them a conspiratorial wink and led them to the kitchen, where he
filled three coffee cups from the open bottle.

"To your health!"

"Thank you. And to our friendship," said Leopold Mikhailovich.
"To you and Aaron."

They drank, and Nikolsky put a plate of cheese in front of them.

"A curious structure, this house," Leopold Mikhailovich opined
after a short silence. "Even at night one can tell there's an original
mind behind it."

"Right you are," said Nikolsky with a smile, "and you can look
forward to a comprehensive lecture from your hostess."

Before Nikolsky could explain, in came Vera, saying, "I knew I'd find you guzzling all by your . . . Oh, I'm sorry!"

"As you can see, I'm not all by my. Leopold Mikhailovich and Aaron . . . this is our hostess."

"My name is Vera."

Leopold Mikhailovich took Vera's hand and kissed it elegantly. "I hope you do not mind our boarding-school manners, my dear lady," he said, feigning the perfect combination of adolescent guilt and bravado. "At least we have no cigarettes up our sleeves."

Vera laughed, and Aaron, who still had not said a word, gazed at Leopold Mikhailovich with great devotion.

"We're old friends, actually, or, rather, I've known you for a long time," she said, beaming. "I went to your lectures."

"Not really!" Leopold Mikhailovich said half seriously.

"No, no, I did! I missed only one or two at most."

"But how can that be?" Leopold Mikhailovich asked, now playing his part to the hilt. "A pretty girl like you giving up evening trysts to sit through a series of boring lectures?"

"But, I can prove it to you!"

"And how, may I ask?"

"With my notes. I took all the lectures down in shorthand, then transcribed them, typed them up, and even had them bound. Now do you believe me?"

Nikolsky noticed how bright Leopold Mikhailovich's eyes were.

"Thank you," Leopold Mikhailovich said, taking both her hands and kissing them. "I never thought anyone would even . . . I am truly touched."

They filed into the main room, which was now occupied by fifteen or twenty people, not a crowd, but enough to assure the requisite level of noise and cigarette smoke. Nikolsky spotted only two new faces: Lilia, a striking brunette and former pupil of Vera's, had brought a balding runt of a man, a bland tenor José to her sultry mezzo Carmen, and Slavik, who worked in television (and had either once had an affair with Vera or now had designs on her—Nikolsky couldn't quite tell which), had brought a baby-doll type just smart enough to cross her bare legs as high as possible and smoke instead of talk. As for the most regular of the regulars, there was Tolik—a putative student, who spent most of the time off in a corner sketching and was known and loved for the reply he gave whenever asked what he wanted to drink: "A drop of anything dry"—and two real old-timers who had spent the last half hour arguing over the best way to revamp the collective farm: Borya Khavkin, a translator and classmate of Vera's, and Konstantin Vasilyevich, or "Uncle Kostya the recluse," as he often introduced himself, who lived nearby and had been a friend of Vera's parents.

Food and drink were slow in making the rounds that evening. Vera was engrossed in showing the house to Leopold Mikhailovich, who not only proved a most appreciative audience but often expanded on what she had to say. When Zhenya at last put things out, everyone set to—and with the great informal gusto the Refuge prided itself on.

Only Prebylov, the newcomer, made any pretense at order. "Discipline, everybody, discipline!" he called out like a policeman. "If you don't finish your first course, you don't get a second." To set a good example he attacked his own plate mercilessly. The first few minutes of the meal were accompanied by the usual nervous settling in, when the hungry are completely absorbed in their plates, the thirsty in their glasses, and the talkers know enough to hold off. But before long Slavik was giving everybody the lowdown on a film that a famous director had finally been allowed to shoot but that would obviously never make it to the screen, and when Lilia asked if it was true what she'd heard about such-and-such a cosmonaut and such-and-such an actress, he confirmed it at once, because a friend of his worked in the same theater as the actress, and if they wanted to know the details . . .

"You know what he can do with his cosmonaut," Nikolsky muttered at the far end of the table, where he was sitting with Finkelmeyer, Tolik, and Uncle Kostya, in other words, people he could trust. "You're an artist, Tolik. What do you think? Is our friend Slavik the informer type?"

"What has being an artist got to do with it?" Tolik asked timidly.

"What has being an artist got to do with it! The artist paints the inner man, Tolik! The inner man!" He turned to Konstantin Vasilyevich. "What do you think, Uncle Kostya? What does your experience tell you?"

Uncle Kostya peered over his spectacles to the other end of the table and said after due consideration, "A *potential* informer."

"Well put! Bravo! Did you hear that, Tolik? 'A *po-ten-tial* informer.' Hey, Vera! Why do you invite potentials?"

Vera, who was deeply involved in a tête-à-tête with Leopold Mikhailovich, looked up, disoriented, and when they all laughed she stuck out her tongue and went back to her conversation partner.

From the absentminded smile on Finkelmeyer's face Nikolsky could tell he was in another world. He ate and drank mechanically, like an ill or excessively obedient child. At first, Nikolsky hovered over him, then he left him in peace for a while, but in the end he lost his patience. "Aaron! Hey, Aaron! Wake up! If you're sick of the place, we can split any time you like."

"No, no," said Finkelmeyer, slowly coming out of it. "I'm perfectly happy to be here."

"And would another vodka make you even happier?"

"It wouldn't hurt."

"Well, this time let's drink to Danuta. A fine woman."

"Funny, Lyonya. I was just thinking about her."

They emptied their glasses.

"I'm not surprised, though I don't know why you looked so glum."

"You think I know? A person never knows what makes him tick."

"I'll drink to that."

By then the noise had reached the stage where each person can talk only to his neighbor, and no one tried to establish a general topic of conversation until Vera tapped a knife against an empty bottle and announced, "Quiet, everybody! You too, Borya! Good. . . . I propose that three of our guests, three newcomers, be subjected to . . . uh, what you might call a rite of initiation."

There was an immediate hum from the floor and a cry of "Horrors!"

"Just a second! Hear me out! All I ask is for Sergei and Aaron to recite a few of their poems and for Leopold Mikhailovich to tell us about . . . well, to tell us anything he pleases. I hope they consent. It would be in the best tradition of the Refuge."

The "scholars" applauded wildly and Zhenya, Lilia, and José joined in with whoops of enthusiasm.

"It's a new tradition to me!" Nikolsky muttered. He was annoyed with himself for getting Aaron mixed up in this.

"Traditions have to start somewhere!" said Borya Khavkin. "People used to get married in church, and now the tradition is for the groom to go out and buy himself a pair of trousers and the bride—"

"That's enough out of you, Borya!" Vera cried.

"—a nightie."

"Well then, who's in favor of my new tradition?" Vera went on, undaunted, and although scarcely half the guests raised their hands she announced, exultant, "It's unanimous!"

"Socialist democracy in action," said Nikolsky. "Ever thought of joining the Party?"

"Who wants to go first?" she asked, ignoring him completely. It was clear from her voice that she really wanted to make things interesting. "How about you, Leopold Mikhailovich? No? Then Aaron?"

Finkelmeyer looked this way and that like an animal at bay; Leopold Mikhailovich spread his arms in a gesture of helplessness.

"Well then, Sergei," she said, teetering on the brink of a fiasco, "perhaps you'll do us the honors."

"Me?" said Prebylov. "I'm no prima donna. Who do we write for, anyway? The people! I've got nothing to hide. I'm proud of what I write. I just don't want to go first."

"Then we'll draw straws," Uncle Kostya decided, "or matches. The one who gets the shortest match goes first."

Finkelmeyer seemed less than certain what was required of him, but, with a little prompting his spindly fingers extricated one of the matches. It immediately fell to the floor.

"The middle one," said Uncle Kostya. "You go second." He held out the remaining two to Leopold Mikhailovich, who drew the short one. "It's settled, then. You go first, Prebylov last."

There was no longer any need to silence the guests. They all looked expectantly at Leopold Mikhailovich. After weighing down their stomachs and lightening their heads with food and drink, they were both curious and uneasy at the prospect of the three men baring their souls in public. Everyone, from baby doll to hard-boiled skeptic, had succumbed to the evening's sudden new mood.

"Very well," said Leopold Mikhailovich, and with a weary wave at the leftovers he added, "but let's put all this behind us, shall we?" Oh, the battles he had witnessed—regiments in full dress storming fortresses of foodstuffs to the rumble of champagne corks, slicing, hacking, mashing, grinding, and then crawling away on all fours— and oh, the scorn he had heaped upon them! But that was as a waiter. Now the courteous, ever so slightly removed lecturer took over.

IV

"THIS WAY, PLEASE. And take your chairs with you."

They all obeyed, noiselessly forming a semicircle around him.

He was standing next to one of the Refuge's prize sculptures. It rested on a column of dark-gray marble and represented the upper part of a female figure, though most of the left breast and arm and the entire right arm below the elbow were lost. A large iron bracket ran along an S-shaped crack in the lower half of the statue. The head was on a level with the head of a woman of average height, and Leopold Mikhailovich placed his hand on the shoulder as if he were about to introduce the work as a new guest.

"I hope our kind hostess will forgive me if my taste does not entirely coincide with hers," he began and made a formal bow to Vera, "but I find this sculpture the most interesting piece in the house. It is unusual in many respects. I should even go so far as to call it mysterious. Let me show you what I mean. I didn't argue with you when you told me the figure was from the Hellenic period, Vera, but now I must admit I have my doubts."

"All I know is what my mother told me," said Vera, "and she got it from my father."

"I can't be certain, of course, but here's our first hint. You see where the hand breaks off? Well, there's an inscription there. Some-one—an archaeologist, perhaps, or the first person to own the statue—painted *Pantikapaion* in Greek letters and the number thirty-seven or eighty-seven. The number is doubtless a date and need not concern us. But what about Pantikapaion? Well, Pantikapaion is

modern-day Kerch, in the Crimea, and many statues found on Bosporan territory trace their origins to Greece; indeed, the local sculpture is rather simple, conventional, abstract in comparison with the
realistic human forms the Greeks were so skilled at creating. Besides,
most Bosporan sculptors worked in sandstone, and what you see
before you is the finest marble; the Bosporans covered their models
with tunics, and our model is naked; the Bosporans preferred figurines and busts, and our figure's proportions indicate it to be life-
size.

"In other words, the arguments in favor of Greek origin would
seem overwhelming. Yet who is she, this woman? A Greek goddess?
Diana? No. Aphrodite? No. Demeter? Cybele? No."

Leopold Mikhailovich examined the statue throughtfully for a
moment, then turned and said, "I wonder whether . . ." He paused,
and the corners of his mouth turned up into a barely perceptible
smile. "Vera, you wouldn't mind standing next to it, would you?"

Vera stood up and walked over to the point Leopold Mikhailovich had indicated, between him and the statue.

Nikolsky suddenly found himself on the edge of his chair. Could
he be the only one, or had they all been struck by it? No, *stupefied*
was the word. Apparently they had been, because Vera herself sensed
the general bewilderment and glanced over uneasily at Leopold
Mikhailovich. Catching the gleam in his eye, following it over to
the statue, she too understood and muttered, "Oh, my God!"

Nikolsky could not believe that after all the days and nights he
had spent in the Refuge he had never noticed the astonishing simi-
larity between the two ladies of the house. The outline of the head,
the contours of the neck and shoulders, the roundness of the breasts
(which Nikolsky could judge without the constraint of under-
clothes)—they all matched! But more important was the general
image, the impression that our brain sculpts from nature and causes
us years later to remember vaguely that we "know that woman
from somewhere."

"And now, if you would . . ." Leopold Mikhailovich said to Vera,
ignoring the impression he had made and turning into an exacting
ballet master, adjusting the position of her arms and asking her to
imitate the curve of his torso. In the end, Vera came to rest in a
graceful pose, the weight of her body concentrated on the left leg,

the right leg slightly flexed and off to the side, the right arm hanging freely, the left at shoulder height. "You have before you an ideal classical—that is, Greek—pose, by which I mean the position of the legs and slight twist of the body. To be precise, what you have is Diana the Hunter. Our charming model"—and here Leopold Mikhailovich bowed gallantly in Vera's direction—"could demonstrate any number of poses in which you would recognize the goddesses and generals' wives who grace Greek sculpture. But each time you would detect a difference between the pose struck by our model here and the pose in which the artist sculpted his statue. . . . Thank you, Vera."

But when Vera started off to her seat, Leopold Mikhailovich held her back and delivered the next part of his lecture holding her hand.

"So I don't think it's Greek, though neither is it Bosporan. The Bosporans, as I have pointed out, were in the habit of making miniature figurines and busts for crypts, burial vaults, coffin lids. Moreover, as far as we know—and this is of capital importance—their figurines were never naked. They always wore tunics or tunics and cloaks. To recapitulate: marble, not sandstone; nudes, not clothed figures; and life-size proportions, which we can easily extrapolate from the fragment we have here—all this contradicts local tradition. And last but not least, the pose."

Nodding to Vera, he gently but firmly tilted her head forward and to the left, then asked her to let her arms hang alongside her body but to turn them palms out.

"More, a little more," he prompted softly. "Arms at your side to the elbows, then out from the thighs below the waist. That's it. Very good. Legs straight, feet fairly wide apart, for balance. Perfect. Can you hold the pose for a while?"

"Yes, yes," Vera said, "it's perfectly comfortable." But her lips had begun to quiver, her breast to heave.

Is she beautiful? Nikolsky asked himself, and responded in the negative. For the first time he realized he had never thought her beautiful. Seeing her in this extraordinary situation, he realized that what attracted him most was her complete and utter defenselessness, the way she seemed to open up and say, Take my body, take my soul, and I shall accept whatever you give in return.

"Now let me tell you the tale of who she was, this statue that is so clearly neither Greek nor Bosporan."

A charged silence suffused the room. Placing a hand on Vera's shoulder, Leopold Mikhailovich began his tale.

"Once there was a stonecutter who did nothing but carve gravestones, and each was as much like the other as death is like death. But the stonecutter never thought about his own death, because Death fed and clothed him: the more often Death visited his neighbors, the more he and his wife and his children had to eat and wear.

"One day a woman came to see him in his workshop. She took off her cloak and her tunic and ordered him to make a statue of her body.

" 'If I grow old and my body grows infirm,' said the woman, 'my husband will gaze upon my statue and will love me. And if I die before my husband, he will gaze upon my statue and will love me. And if my husband dies before me, I shall place my statue in his crypt, and I shall be with him in the kingdom of the dead and he will love me.'

"And the stonecutter took a slab of pink marble and began to chip away at it, stroke by stroke. And while he worked, he was overcome by passion.

"When the statue was ready, he turned to the woman and said, 'How much wilt thou pay me?'

"And the woman said, 'Thy stone is more beautiful than my body. Thou shalt have this piece of silver, and this one; thou shalt have all the silver I own.'

" 'No,' said the stonecutter, 'for I cannot give you the stone. My passion for thee is so great that I constantly burn to touch it. And if I cannot slake my passion, my sweet love will go bitter, my mind take fire, my hands and eyes cease to obey me. When that time comes, thou hadst best fear me, for I know not what I shall do with the stone.'

" 'Then love me,' said the woman. 'Slake thy passion for me, and give me thy stone.'

"And he loved her on that day and the next and many more, for he was unable to slake his passion. And because on none of those days did Death visit the village, his wife feared lest her children should starve.

"But the day came when the stonecutter's reason returned to him and his hands obeyed him and his eyes saw clearly. And he said, 'Woman, take thou thy stone.' And she took it and gave him the silver for it.

"And the stonecutter took the silver home to his wife. And when she had counted it, she said, 'How camest thou by this wealth?' But the stonecutter did not answer, for he was sick unto death. And verily, Death, which had long awaited his return, came for him in the morning."

V

LEOPOLD MIKHAILOVICH fell silent, but the silence was almost immediately broken by an outburst of sobbing. It was Vera. The effect was that of a bomb: chairs toppled, glasses crashed underfoot, and a hysterical voice cried out, "Water! Get her some water!"

Nikolsky elbowed his way through the chaos, trying to reach her—she simply stood there, her face buried in Leopold Mikhailovich's chest—and he was annoyed to find that Aaron had beat him to it. But as both Aaron's thumps on the back and Leopold Mikhailovich's comforting words had proved ineffectual—she was still racked with sobs—Nikolsky shoved both of them away with a cursory "Sorry," and, biting down hard on his lower lip, planted a rapid pair of slaps on her face. She screamed. He whisked a glass of vodka to her lips.

"Here! Drink this down," he ordered roughly. "Drink it, I say!" He tipped the glass more and more, even spilling some vodka on her sweater, until he saw she had begun to choke.

"Now try and breathe. Easy does it! You'll be fine in no time."

"Oh, God," she said, exhaling unevenly, pressing her fingers to her temples, then beginning to breathe more or less normally. "I think . . . yes, it's over." She gave a weak smile. "How could I have let it happen? Please excuse me, everybody."

"Don't be so hard on yourself!" said Borya Khavkin, coming to the rescue. "And what are you goggling at, all of you? Isn't it time for another round?"

Borya's suggestion sent everyone scurrying to the table, and Vera was able to make a quick exit.

Nikolsky caught up with her, but she said, "That's all right. Really. I'm only going to wash my face. Though if you want to come in with me, that's fine too. Just hook the door, will you?"

She pulled off her sweater and began inspecting her puffy cheeks, still wet with tears and trickles of mascara. "What a nightmare." She spent a long time washing her face, brushing her hair, and redoing her eyes. From time to time Nikolsky held up a cigarette for her to drag on, and the combination of cold water, the cosmetics ritual, and the cigarette reestablished a kind of equilibrium.

"It was like being hypnotized. I just stood there. I didn't feel a thing. I became the statue. I wouldn't have been the least bit surprised if the statue had come to life. And you know, I visualized the whole story as he told it: the workshop, the monuments, the stonecutter himself. He had red hair. How did I know that? But then something snapped. Have you ever had the feeling? It was like all that matters in life was over, there was nothing left, and I suddenly felt terribly sorry for myself. Something similar happened to me when I was sixteen. I wept for hours. I bit my pillow to pieces. Then I washed it and sewed it together again. I'm a real case, I know. You're the only one who can handle me."

"Think of the slap as a kind of surgery. Painful, but necessary."

"I understand. What else could you do with a fool like me?"

"Don't think I liked doing it. It's disgusting."

"I must have looked disgusting too. My face wet with tears like a slug."

"Vera!"

She leaned down—he was sitting on the edge of the bathtub—and kissed the top of his head, and as she moved away she looked him long and hard in the eye. Nikolsky felt a chill run down his spine and thought, It can't last much longer.

In the main room things seemed back to normal, though people were still under the cloud of the incident and voices boomed louder, more raucous than usual. The most zealous among the guests— Slavik and Prebylov, who were old pals by now, the scholars, and the baby doll—were drinking heavily. When Prebylov caught Nikolsky staring at them, he returned his glance with an arrogant smile. It was clear from the look on their faces that they were talking about Vera and that Slavik was giving the poet a man-to-man, blow-by-blow account of what she was like. In the meantime, the ever-vivacious Lilia was providing a mezzo-soprano continuo for a discussion, taking place on either side of her, between José and Uncle Kostya, while Zhenya, standing behind them, tried vainly to attract their attention. Leopold Mikhailovich, Borya Khavkin, and Tolik were inspecting a series of drawings propped against the wall on the couch. Leopold Mikhailovich motioned to Vera and Nikolsky, his face full of concern. Vera hastened to make it clear that everything was all right. With a smile of relief and a broad gesture of welcome he invited them to join the group.

"We've been having a look at these sketches," he said. "Tolik here did them all today, and these three just now. He's got a good eye, don't you think?"

"What have I been telling you?" Vera cried triumphantly. "The talent is there. All it needs is a little training."

Tolik, embarrassed, tried to hide behind his girlish blond lashes.

"Perhaps," Leopold Mikhailovich muttered, "perhaps." And because Vera gave him a quizzical look, he felt constrained to add, "You know the saying, 'Talent is like money: some have it, others haven't.' But money is something you need to manage. And that's a whole other talent."

Vera was still confused. "Are you implying that artistic talent *doesn't* need to be managed, that is, developed, trained?"

"Actually, my dear," he said with a sigh, clearly less than eager to go into the matter, "I consider training a mixed blessing."

"I understand. The time, the drudgery. But how else can you learn technique, master the tricks of the trade?"

"True enough, true enough. But tell me, where do you propose he should study?"

Vera was taken aback. "There are teachers . . . I don't know . . ."

"Well, neither do I and neither does he."

At this point Nikolsky slipped off in search of Aaron, whom he discovered sitting on the kitchen floor, his head tucked between his knees.

"What in the world are you doing, Aaron?"

Aaron looked up at him like a little boy awakened in the night.

"Why are you sitting on the floor?"

The message was still not getting through.

"Why don't you sit in a chair like everybody else, you idiot?"

"You're the idiot, Lyonya," said Finkelmeyer at last, and with the utmost calm. "All the chairs are in the other room."

Only then did Nikolsky notice that Finkelmeyer had a pen and paper in his hands.

"You haven't been writing poetry, have you?" Nikolsky asked, when Finkelmeyer started stuffing sheets of paper into his jacket pocket. "Well, keep it up. I won't disturb you."

"No, no," said Finkelmeyer. "I was just putting something down on paper. I composed it in my head, at work." He made an attempt at standing, but twisted his foot and ended up back on the floor.

"You're a phenomenon unto yourself, you know that?" said Nikolsky, helping Finkelmeyer to his feet. "Was it something you didn't want to forget?"

"I *can't* forget, Lyonya. My head is a wastepaper basket. There's a lot I'd be glad to dispose of. Know what I mean?"

Nikolsky brushed off the baggy seat of Finkelmeyer's trousers.

"Merci."

They lit up.

"He's a good man, your Leopold Mikhailovich," said Nikolsky.

"A great man."

"I don't know about that, but I do know he's alive. I take an interest in life; he lives it. I enjoy art; he loves it."

"Leopold doesn't love art."

"What?"

"He doesn't. He can't."

"What are you saying?" Nikolsky asked, staring at him.

"It's hard to explain, but it's true. He knows everything there is to know about a painting—he does his homework—but he doesn't really *talk* about it; it's really only a glimmer of the moon, a glitter of the waters, the trill of a nightingale, in other words, a stimulus for his own thoughts. Take today's statue, for instance."

"What do you mean?"

"The fact that it's two thousand years old yet the image of a living person."

Nikolsky tried hard to understand. "Let's say you're right," he said. "Where does it get us? What if a man likes the moon because it puts a woman in the mood?"

Finkelmeyer gave Nikolsky an ironic look. "Admit you like it. Admit it helps you."

"Me? I don't need romanticism."

"You're a real man. Why love the moon when you can love a woman? Or to put it differently, 'When asked what he preferred, a nymph in a painting or his mistress, he replied, 'A bird in the bed is worthy any number on the wall.' "

"How coarse you can be!" Even though he suspected that Aaron either couldn't or wouldn't go more deeply into his feelings about Leopold Mikhailovich, Nikolsky was determined to keep the conversation on a serious plane. The complexity of what lay behind Aaron's clowning was on a par with Leopold Mikhailovich's statement about the two kinds of talent.

"I still don't see why you think that Leopold Mikhailovich, who lives in daily contact with art, doesn't love it."

Smiling wryly, Finkelmeyer fumbled with the buttons behind his tie and finally managed to pull out a piece of light blue material.

"See this undershirt? I don't love it, but I live in daily contact with it. Even if it were beautiful, it would still be just an undershirt."

"What about your poetry?"

"The undershirt at least keeps me warm."

At this point Nikolsky gave up entirely. "You can lay it on pretty thick, you know that, Aaron?" To which Finkelmeyer replied, "Oh, by the way, I've got the proofs for the Neprigen book in my briefcase. They must have set it before Manakin gave the go-ahead. There's a conference on national literatures coming up, and they wanted to have it ready in time."

"And you've waited this long to tell me, you bastard? Give it here! At least let me hold it!"

"All right, all right. You can read them. You can even do the cause of art a little service and *proof*read them. There are a dozen or so typos on every page."

VI

BEFORE they could cross the room to where Finkelmeyer's brief-case was lying, Zhenya grabbed Nikolsky by the sleeve with her usual overwrought enthusiasm and said, "Leonid! Leonid! Tell your friend it's his turn!"

Finkelmeyer flinched, and when others started chiming in—"Yes, yes! Do recite something!"—he muttered an excruciating "No, I couldn't . . . really . . . no!" They were like a band of torturers whooping in anticipation of their victim's agony, pricking his stom-ach, flanks, Adam's apple, spurred on by his pleas for mercy.

Nikolsky had an idea. He went over to Lilia and, putting his arm around the area he judged to be her waist, said languidly, "Why don't you sing something, Lilia dear?"

"Leonid darling, how nice of you to ask!" said Lilia, her mellif-luous mezzo rising and falling with each syllable. "But I've had so frightfully much to eat and drink, and then your friend over there—isn't he going to recite his poems?"

"Forget about him, Lilia! It's so long since I've heard you, and there are people here who haven't heard you at all. Leopold Mik-hailovich, for one. A man much respected in the world of art."

"But I'm totally unprepared, and my diaphragm . . ."

"Just a little chamber music. *Sotto voce*. Everyone will be so pleased!"

"Well, if Verochka agrees to accompany . . ."

"Fine!"

"Just two or three romances . . ."

"I kiss your hand!"

And having done so, he sprinted back to the siege of Aaron Fin-kelmeyer, shouting, "Just a minute! Just a minute! Can't you see he's had too much to drink? Besides, we have a worthy replace-ment! Our very own Lilia has agreed to sing for us!"

He started clapping, and others joined in, less rather than more enthusiastically. Zhenya looked surprised, Borya Khavkin groaned, and Vera walked submissively over to the piano.

Finkelmeyer, liberated, listened to Lilia with raised brows, a slightly open mouth, an extended neck, and an expression of rapture that rivaled José's. *Sotto voce* was not Lilia's forte, and when her conservatory voice came to "Tell me who is to blame" it sounded like a discussion of moral turpitude at a public forum. José shook his head and looked from one guest to the next as if calling upon them to share his emotion.

To everyone's relief the musical interlude came to an end after only three pieces and a polite encore. It was almost midnight. Uncle Kostya's head was nodding; a very pale scholar had just emerged from the bathroom wiping his mouth with a handkerchief; Slavik was trying to kiss his baby doll back to life; Prebylov was pouring the remains of a Stolichnaya bottle into his glass. Things were on the point of breaking up when Zhenya asked what had happened to the poetry reading. She'd been waiting all evening for it. Why didn't they ever do what *she* wanted to do?

All at once Prebylov pulled himself to his feet and, scouring the room from under his now sweaty forelock, declared, "Silence! I am going to give my recitation."

He delivered his verse slowly, rhythmically, leaning heavily on the accented syllables and drawing out the rhymes. He began with an autobiographical poem, informing all and sundry that he was not born in a maternity ward but in a haystack and therefore saw himself as a latter-day Antaeus: having made contact with Mother Earth at the moment of his birth, he had been constantly nourished by Her juices. Aggressive voice and aggressive message combined to form an *organic,* as the critics would put it, whole. It was impossible to tell where the text left off and his personality began; nor was there a hint of ambiguity, allusion, obscure imagery, or metrical, acoustic, or linguistic sorcery. The poems were about country sandals treading asphalt streets or boots on the dusty road or bare feet in rustling grain, about out-of-the-way villages so verdant in spring, villages that have upheld Russia's honor from time immemorial, and—lest his lyre be accused of ignoring the proletariat—about the miner's noble calling. The intelligentsia, the social stratum he was currently performing for, appeared in the asphalt-streets poem as "the rot of Arbat mold." It was also hinted at broadly in what turned out to be the final poem of the evening, a poem about "certain elements" that prefer things foreign to things Russian. In this poem Prebylov used the crane to represent simple, domestic values and the flamingo to represent the flashy, decadent West.

"Fla-*ming*-o," Finkelmeyer suddenly screamed.

Prebylov stopped short and looked up at Finkelmeyer, sincerely wondering what had gone wrong.

"The word is fla*ming*o, not fla*meng*o. You're conflating two words: *flamingo*, the bird, and *flamenco,* the dance!"

"What are you talking about?"

"If you don't know what I'm talking about, you have no business writing poetry. Either you know Russian or you don't!"

Finkelmeyer had pulled out all the stops; Nikolsky was ecstatic. Leopold Mikhailovich went over to Finkelmeyer, apparently hoping to calm him down, but it was too late.

"Who are you to tell me whether I know Russian or not?"

"What do you mean?"

There was a long pause.

"Oh, I get it! I see!" Finkelmeyer finally said. He looked as though he were about to aim straight for the jugular. "You mean *I'm* not Russian, is that it? Well . . ."

"Well, you're *not!* So don't try and teach me *my* language!" And he staggered out of the room.

"Why, you son of a . . ." Nikolsky shouted, rushing off after him, but Vera stood in his way, and although his first impulse was to push her aside he changed his mind when he saw her eyes and thought of what she had been through that evening. He realized he'd had too much to drink, but what he would have given to knock that bastard's block off!

"Hey, Aaron!" he called out. "Will you bring over my cigarettes?"

"We're going to be asphyxiated if we add any more smoke to this room," said Finkelmeyer, walking up to Nikolsky.

A double door led to the balcony. The inner one gave with no trouble; the outer one was frozen shut. But when Nikolsky rammed his shoulder against it, he flew out into the cold surrounded by puffs of steam and nearly toppled into the snow. While he was gulping down the icy fresh air, Finkelmeyer's shadow appeared behind him as if emerging from Hades.

They were about to light up when the front door beneath them creaked open, a beam of light ran up the trees and down again, and the door creaked shut. Then there was a short shuffle on the veranda followed by a short sniffle followed by a long stream.

Nikolsky knew who it was before looking down, but as soon as he had confirmed it he pulled Finkelmeyer up close and whispered in his ear, "It's him, Arosha! How about giving him a little shower?" Even as he spoke, he was feverishly unbuttoning his fly.

They were so excited it took a little time to get going, but soon one, then another golden stream was arching out into space. Without interrupting the procedure, Nikolsky inched up to the edge of the balcony—he wanted to see whether they were on target—and just at that moment Prebylov looked up.

"Son of a bitch!" he howled, and began spinning in place like a top. Nikolsky had evidently scored a bull's-eye.

"Give it to him, Arosha!"

"I can't! I can't! I'm laughing too hard!"

But by then it was too late. The last they saw of Prebylov he was running off into the night.

VII

FINKELMEYER and Leopold Mikhailovich were the last to leave. After Nikolsky had helped Leopold Mikhailovich on with his coat, the latter took Vera's hand and pressed it to his own.

"I have a confession to make. I was part of the escort that brought your statue back from Crimea. The Revolution kept it out of the Tsvetaev Museum, which it was meant for, and it ended up in the house of a University of Moscow history professor. I spent a good deal of time there. One day I was passing a political rally and noticed that the girl haranguing the crowd was the image of the statue. I don't recall what she was saying. What everyone said at the time, I suppose. But I waited till she'd finished, and walked her home. Eventually I persuaded her to come and see the statue. I'm sure I don't need to add that I fell madly in love with her. Yes, well, in any case, I was very close friends with your father, in the way people used to be friends. And it was at the professor's, seated around your statue, that your mother met your father.

"I saw this house in its earliest stages. Your father would ask me for advice. But once their relationship grew serious, I never returned. I never saw them again. I had no idea the sculpture had ended up here. It was a great pleasure. But meeting you was a much greater one. As you can see, I'm deeply moved.

"By the way, the tale about the woman and the stonecutter came to me when I first saw the statue, in the Crimea, and I once told it to your mother. I never dreamed I'd have the opportunity to tell it to her daughter." And with a weary smile he added, "Please forgive me for upsetting you so. You won't hold it against an old man, will you?"

"Oh, how could I? How could I? I *will* see you again, won't I?"

"There's nothing I should like better, my dear. Thank you, and good night."

The door closed, and Nikolsky turned the lock and went upstairs with the proofs Aaron had left him. As he deposited them in his briefcase, his hand brushed against something soft. It was Manakin's sables.

"Vera!" he called. "Come and see what I have for you!"

He gave them to her, but she was too tired to appreciate them, and the last thought that flashed through Nikolsky's mind as they got into bed was that they had made love during the afternoon and could now go right to sleep.

VIII

THE EVENING was not without its consequences.

The very next day the wife of the scholar couple knocked on Vera's door demanding an explanation for the scandalous treatment their bosom friend and talented poet—a real poet, a member of the Writers Union—had received at her hands. Vera, unlike her usual conciliatory self, told her in no uncertain terms she wanted nothing more to do with the poet or with them for that matter.

Then Slavik phoned and asked where she'd dug up that beanpole, the one her "current regular" was so taken with. To which Vera, again uncharacteristically, replied that if he ever dared to grace her with even a phone call she would immediately hang up, dial his wife, and give her an earful.

And so on and so forth, until she had made it clear to anyone with so much as a good word for either Slavik or the scholars that he was not to darken her door again. Nikolsky supported her wholeheartedly with shouts of "Give it to them! Give it to them! Don't let them get away with anything!"—diplomatically glossing over the fact that she should have chucked the lot of them long ago.

Leopold Mikhailovich's regular presence at the Refuge meant a radical change in its atmosphere. The way he looked at them, smiled at them, the things he said and did not say, made the snobs, the gossips, the brilliant conversationalists on the prowl for one-night stands so uncomfortable that they left after the first hour, never to return. The people who stayed were those still able to look within themselves and find a fragile shoot of something not yet smothered by the lying and cheating and primitive crudity of everyday life and to cultivate it in the company of like-minded people. Leopold Mikhailovich had a talent for attracting such people the way a distant magnetic field will slowly, gently attract the most faintly magnetic needle a child has stuck in a cork and floated in a saucer of water. As a result, the get-togethers grew more and more serious in tone, and although people no more than sensed the difference, breathed it in with the new fresh atmosphere, they now came not so much to entertain or be entertained as to rise out of the mire that otherwise engulfed them and to which they themselves unwittingly contributed.

Moreover, it soon became clear that even Vera, Nikolsky, Borya Khovkin, and the young Tolik—the core group—were merely guests in the Refuge, tourists who had wandered into a medieval castle and found it so pleasant they decided to stay on, while Leopold Mikhailovich simply *belonged* there; it was as much a part of him as his beret, his gray cardigan, his crumpled bow tie.

Vera soon pulled out her notes of Leopold Mikhailovich's lectures and offered to edit them for him. Leopold Mikhailovich accepted the offer more out of courtesy than interest: he had no use for anything he had said once before. In fact, when she showed him her version of the first lecture, he immediately began to expand on it, and Vera was quick to note it all down. They continued the process with the rest of the lectures, and the result was a series of variations on a theme, variations that were more often than not at loggerheads with the theme but always ironclad arguments in themselves. Leopold Mikhailovich delighted in attacking the seemingly indestructible bastions of his own arguments, smiled contentedly as they fell and he raised new ones on their ruins. The outsider might have dismissed it all as sophistry or a dazzling display of erudition, but it was actually something quite different: a refusal or, rather, an innate inability on Leopold Mikhailovich's part to hold to a single, predetermined line, a dogma that claimed to be the final word in art, that is, all realms of creative endeavor, and life, the life of the species and the life of the individual. At least that was how Nikolsky interpreted it as he listened to Leopold Mikhailovich going over the lectures with Vera. When he first asked permission to sit in, Leopold Mikhailovich not only granted it but admitted he enjoyed having an audience, and they took this admission of vanity as tacit permission to invite an audience.

From time to time they gathered at Leopold Mikhailovich's two-by-five-meter "pencil box," his section of the crowded five-room communal apartment where Finkelmeyer had spent so many happy hours. It all started very naturally. One day a young unknown artist came to show Leopold Mikhailovich his engravings. Leopold Mikhailovich phoned Vera and asked her to get in touch with Tolik because the two artists might like to meet—"and you come too, Vera, and Leonid."

When they got there, they found not only the artist but Finkelmeyer in his usual pose, that is, folded in thirds in a chair in the corner. Finkelmeyer duly nodded and had even begun to stand when Nikolsky pushed him back into his seat. He looked relieved.

Leopold was embarrassed, because all he had in the house was a packet of Ceylon tea and a stale roll. Vera immediately ran out and returned with a bagful of comestibles. She had no trouble finding her bearings among Leopold Mikhailovich's kitchenware: it consisted of a few miscellaneous cups, plates, knives, and forks, all of which fit easily on a single shelf in his wardrobe; a hot plate, a pot, and a pan on the windowsill; and a teapot on the floor. The only reason she needed to duck into the common kitchen was to fill the teapot with water, but she took the opportunity, under the inquisitive eyes of the neighbors, to give the dishes a proper washing as well.

With time Vera's ministrations became a regular feature of Leopold Mikhailovich's existence. She would appear in the middle of the day with bundles of food, then do the dusting or mop the floor. For the First of May she washed the windows and made him a gift of a frosted-glass lampshade to replace the paper fire hazard he had been using. At first he put up a front of protests, but they soon gave way to hand-kissing and words of gratitude. Moreover, when he stayed up late talking at the Refuge, they often persuaded him to spend the night. In the end, the Refuge and the pencil box off Kropotkinskaya shared both a way of life and a group of friends.

IX

ONE SUNDAY morning Nikolsky was lolling in bed with the newspaper. A word caught his eye as he rushed through the first pages to sports and international news, and although neither its sound nor its sense registered at first, it kept nagging at his groggy consciousness, reminding him of something—what? who?—in the not too distant past. On a hunch he turned back to the "Art and Literature" supplement, ran his eye down the first column, and there it was: Manakin.

Suddenly he was wide awake.

". . . the creative atmosphere so characteristic of our times . . . a great day in the history of our multi-national literature . . . Here is what Danil Manakin had to say to our correspondent."

No, this was too serious, he thought. He'd better read it straight through.

THINKING OF ONE'S OWN

Moscow, the capital of our multinational motherland, will play host this autumn to a conference devoted exclusively to the literatures of smaller nationalities. Poets, novelists, and playwrights will discuss problems common to writers from various regions of the country, summing up their achievements for the last few years and determining plans for the future in the light of the recent Party resolutions on cultural issues.

The Tongors live entirely in the inhospitable polar tundra. Nearly all the members of this small northern people are hunters, and they enjoy a well-earned reputation for bagging large quantities of "soft gold."

Danil Fedotych Manakin, the first Tongor poet, celebrates the hunters' hard but noble and romantic work; he describes the northern landscape and gives a picture of the simple people who inhabit it. Manakin, himself until recently the head of a team of hunters, draws directly on life in his verse, a volume of which will soon be published in Moscow under the title *Good Fortune*. Here is what Danil Manakin had to say to our correspondent:

"I am honored to have the chance to represent my small people at so prestigious a literary forum as the upcoming conference. I am looking forward to the day when my fleet-winged aircraft leaves the dawn behind and alights on Moscow soil. Whenever I am in Moscow, I think of how close it is to the heart of every Soviet citizen, no matter where he lives, because Moscow symbolizes what is best in our new way of life. But when I think about today, I cannot help thinking about yesterday as well. My people never dared dream of what they have now achieved. We Tongors long led an illiterate, semibarbaric existence. How things have changed! And we owe it all to the Party, the government, and the friendship of the Russian people.

"Today we Tongors can boast of a rich and fruitful cultural life. Each of us cherishes the creative atmosphere so characteristic of our times. It is the writer's duty to reflect reality and thereby become an integral part of it, participate in the activities and achievements of our heroic working class. Only then will the simple working men and women of our country find a worthy image of themselves in our works. We writers must never forget that ours is one of the most important sectors in the construction of Communism: the cultural and ideological front. I am not exaggerating when I say that the upcoming conference will be a great day in the history of our multinational literature."

Nikolsky could scarcely force himself through the article. There was no point in looking for any sense in a piece like that, of course, but the very fact of its publication was of the utmost importance: Manakin had made the national press; he was countrywide news.

Now all writers organizations would have to take him seriously. Yes, Manakin had made the big time.

Only then did it strike him. Manakin? Why Manakin? Why not Neprigen? What had happened to Aion Neprigen?

He skimmed the article to make sure. No, it was all Manakin: Manakin's verse, Manakin's volume. Something was very wrong.

It was early, and Finkelmeyer was most likely still in the bosom of his family. Nikolsky dialed his home number with a certain curiosity. He had stuck to the office number before, and we are different people at work and at home.

"Hello," a child's voice answered.

"May I speak to your father?"

There was no response.

"Is your father at home?"

Again no response, but this time the child's voice called out, "Pa-a-a! For you!" and another, more distant child's voice responded, "He's in the toilet!" Then a woman's voice started scolding the children, and as it came closer to the phone he caught the words, ". . . when there are grown-ups at home! . . . Hello? Did you want to talk to Aaron?"

"Hello. Yes, is he at home?"

"Well, actually . . . it might be better . . . are you calling from a public telephone?"

"No, I'm at home. I'll call back later."

"Can I take a message?"

"My name is Leonid. I'm a friend of his. I need to see him today. It's important."

"I see. Thank you. I'll be sure he gets the message. Or maybe . . ."

"Yes?"

"Well, I don't know if I should. Aaron will yell at me, I'm sure. But well, it's Sunday, and we'll be at home all day. You might want to come and talk to him here. We never have visitors. I work a lot at night, and Aaron's always busy or off on one of his trips, so we're not together very often, and it would be so nice. We could have lunch together, and then I'd take the girls out for a walk. You could sit and talk as long as you liked. Really, I'd be very happy to have you."

"Thank you very much. It's just so . . . unexpected."

"Oh, it won't be anything fancy. I'm not good at that sort of thing. Oh, and of course—how could I be so silly?—if you want to bring somebody, I mean, if you have somebody you . . ."

"No, no. Thank you. I live alone. . . . Why don't I talk it over with Aaron when he calls back?"

"No, no. We'll be expecting you. See you soon."

She seemed perfectly nice, this—what was her name again?—Frida. It's not easy to work and run a household and bring up two children on your own without an army of grandmothers and aunts.

Aaron returned his call about ten minutes later.

"She's already out shopping. Be prepared for a feast."

"I'm terribly embarrassed. She kept insisting. I hope she doesn't mind if we go off somewhere. We've got something important to talk over. Have you read today's paper?"

"I never read the papers. What's up?"

"I'll tell you later. When shall we meet? And where?"

"Maybe you *should* come. Frida has a real thing about hearth and home and the family table."

"She scrubs his underwear, and he condescends. Shame on you, Aaron Mendelevich!"

"Look who's defending womankind! See you soon."

He had to go all the way to the Taganka metro station and then take the bus to Kuzminki. Along both sides of the badly pitted road he studied Khrushchev's answer to the housing shortage, the same here as in Zaalaisk: endless, equidistant five-story boxes with graph-paper walls, windows, and entrances. Units. The family is the basic unit of society. Strange that people insisted on ruining the symmetry of prefabricated panels with trees and bushes. It went against the general scheme of things and led one to doubt the master plan.

Leave it to Finkelmeyer to land the worst unit of them all: a cheap ground-floor flat with low ceilings, a kitchen no bigger than a tabletop, a bathroom with the toilet squeezed under the washbasin, no hall space or closet space or pantry space, and no balcony. Yet it was not a communal arrangement: they did not need to share the toilet and kitchen facilities with six or seven other families.

While Nikolsky was taking his coat off, the tiny entrance nook filled with Finkelmeyers. He felt he was back on the crowded bus. Making his way past the pair of goggling girls, he entered what was really no more than an elongation of the nook—a kind of appendix or strangulated hernia—but bore the name of living room and provided access to the kitchen and the bedroom.

"So this is what Khrushchev's castles look like on the inside," said Nikolsky. "The bastards!" Noticing that the little girls were still staring up at him, he added, *"Mille pardons, mesdemoiselles!"* and tweeked their noses. They remained unperturbed. He then proceeded to unwrap a bundle he had carried in under his arm, and out came a doll with a chocolate bar tied round its waist. He had found it at a food shop—the toy shops were closed on Sundays. The girls immediately lowered their eyes from him to the doll, but when he held it out to them they made no move to take it.

"It's for you," Nikolsky said by way of encouragement, but the girls did not seem to hear him. At last the taller one, never taking her eyes off the doll, said in a soft, singsong voice, "*Which* of us?"

"I see," Nikolsky sighed. "You mean Uncle Lyonya should have brought two dolls, and right you are. But let me propose the following. Break the chocolate in two and eat it up. All right?"

"All right," said the girl in a barely audible voice.

"But don't break the doll in two and don't eat her up. All right?"

"All right."

"Good, because I want you to take good care of her, wash her, kiss her, take her to nursery school. And today you'll be the father—what's your name?—Anna, and you—what's your name?—Nonna will be the mother. And tomorrow Nonna will be the father and Anna the mother. And your humble servant Uncle Lyonya promises to bring the *demoiselles* another daughter the next time he comes."

The girls held out their hands, took the doll, and after a moment of thought, sang a pianissimo "thank you" in perfect unison and ran off to the corner near the window, the site of their modest fiefdom.

Meanwhile Frida had been flying back and forth between the living room and kitchen, assuring them that everything was just about ready. She'd be with them in a jiffy. Nikolsky thought of tempering her zeal by saying he wasn't hungry (though he was, and the smells wafting in from the kitchen didn't help), but he decided against it: she was excited by the whole idea of the meal. The sooner they took their places the better—for her, for Aaron, who had no idea what to do with Nikolsky, and for Nikolsky himself, who could feel his mouth forming an ironic smile.

"Our bedroom is in there, and this is where my father sleeps. And the girls, when they're home."

"When they're home?"

"They're at a five-day nursery, the nursery where Frida works. They stay there with her when she's on night duty."

There was a long pause.

"How'd you ever get a telephone in a new complex like this?" Nikolsky asked at last.

"Nobody wanted this place," said Aaron, happy to have something to talk about. "It's tucked away in a corner, it's on the ground floor, and the construction crew used it as an office and left a terrible mess behind. But when I saw they'd left a telephone behind too, I grabbed it."

They stood at their places like guests in a stranger's house.

"Tell me, what was that item in the paper you wanted to talk to me about?"

But before Nikolsky could respond, Frida burst in saying, "Everything's ready, Leonid Pavlovich! Everything's ready. Wash your hands, girls! Aaron, you sit here so I can be closer to the kitchen."

The formal meal began. Frida ran back and forth with a pâté, a salad, sprats, and an aspic mold; then she joined them for a small glass of sweet Kagor wine to celebrate the occasion; then she put out new plates and brought in *pirozhki* for the soup, pointing out which were filled with meat and which with cabbage and onions. Nikolsky praised them, and she said she was so happy to be able to have him as their guest; he asked whether she bought the dough or made it herself, and she blushed and said it was the simplest thing in the world. The girls stopped eating after the *pirozhki,* and Frida sent them off with some fruit syrup and water. Then she brought in a copper-colored goose still sputtering and sizzling in its own juice.

"Magnificent!" Nikolsky, exclaimed, filling Frida's glass with Kagor and Aaron's and his own with vodka. "To our hostess!"

Nikolsky was in a state of bliss: the food and drink were first-rate and plentiful. Frida was happy too: she had given her guest a worthy reception. Only Aaron seemed out of sorts—he kept raising his eyebrows and looking from Frida to the girls to Nikolsky—and Nikolsky knew why: Aaron was a *guest* at the table and extremely uncomfortable with the unnatural situation. Deep down Frida was doing this all for Aaron; she wanted to please Aaron by pleasing his friend. But even if I am a pawn in family politics, he thought, I'm not going to let it spoil my appetite. The reason Aaron's so thin is that he's hypersensitive to everything but food. What good is his big Jewish nose if it can't smell that goose? More important, why has he got a wife who can make so fine a goose when she's got a husband so indifferent to it?

A door slammed. Nikolsky had run out of cigarettes and asked Aaron for one. Aaron had looked first in the bedroom, then in the entrance hall.

"He's gone down to the corner shop," Frida said. "That's the way he is. Always disappearing. Oh, I'm not complaining. I just worry about him. I can't help wondering when I'm on duty whether he's off somewhere again. Luckily the nursery's not far and I can pop in and make sure he's had something to eat."

Now that Frida had stopped running in and out of the kitchen, Nikolsky sat back and took a good look at her. The fact that he had to remind himself to do so was significant. First of all, it meant she wasn't his type, but even so, if she'd had the slightest bit of what is commonly called "pep" or "go" in her, he would have noticed more than the sizzling goose in front of him. Yet she was a good, kind woman—it was written all over her. She must have put on weight after having the girls, and what with her being so short and Aaron being so thin she might have tried to lose it, but she was the type who looked after her family more than herself. He knew men who would find her attractive—her chubby little face, her dark eyes and full lips, her naturally curly hair. There was something Negroid about her and something countrylike, her rosy complexion, perhaps, the healthy glow she radiated. She couldn't have been more than twenty-five and would grow old slowly. Objectively speaking, then, she was a fine woman. Only who judges women objectively? Aaron, who could not be called a ladies' man, had no use for objectivity. He had Danuta.

"... I just wish we'd have some visitors from time to time. Oh, I know. Everybody's busy, everybody's tired, but why do people go off by themselves after work? There's always Sunday. Of course, Moscow's so enormous and we live so far out—it must have taken you forever to get here. What makes it worse is we have no relatives—mine were all killed by the Germans, and Aaron has nobody either. Maybe that's why I'm telling *you* all this."

"Of course, a family can be a burden," said Nikolsky, trying to comfort her, "more trial than pleasure. But I know what you mean. When you have no one, you miss the warmth of . . ."

"Warmth! Yes, yes! That's what I miss!"

"But so do people with families and friends. Because loneliness comes from within, basically. You can spend an evening in a group and never stop feeling alone. I'm out with friends all the time, and do you think I'm happy? I only *look* happy."

"Aaron's just the same," said Frida, "always needing to go somewhere, see someone. Oh, he doesn't hide anything from me, and he'll tell me where he's been or where he's going if I ask him. But you know what he told me once? He can't do without solitude. Have you any idea what he meant?"

Nikolsky said nothing.

"Tell me, are you married?"

"No."

"You'd be better off with a wife."

Nikolsky laughed and asked why.

"I don't know. Men have their own . . . concerns, but it's better to keep things in the family."

Danuta, thought Nikolsky, but put on a smile and said, "Don't worry about me. I've been seeing the same woman for several years now. We're as good as married."

"Oh, I didn't mean to pry. It's just that, well . . ." She looked over at the girls, who were safely involved with their dolls. "I sometimes wonder whether Aaron hasn't found somebody else. . . ." She forced a little laugh, then looked down, on the brink of tears.

Either she knows or she has reason to suspect, he thought.

"What ever makes you think that?" he said, disgusted at his duplicity.

"He's . . . he's so kind."

That sheepish look plays havoc with my feelings of male solidarity, he thought, yet Frida's constant solicitude clearly drives Aaron up the wall. She's the kind of woman you love as you love a child, and that is not Aaron's way.

"Yes, he is kind," said Nikolsky, and then suddenly asked, "Do you ever read his poems?"

"Well, I asked him if I could once, and he said, 'There they are in those folders.' " She pointed to a pile of folders lying on top of the wardrobe. "So I looked through them a few times, but what do I know about poetry? Are they any good? They certainly cause him enough grief. Getting up in the middle of the night to scribble them down. He dreams them, he says."

"I want you to listen carefully now, Frida," Nikolsky said, laying his hand on hers. "Aaron is extremely gifted, his poems are brilliant, and it's a great pity no one knows about them. But Aaron doesn't care about being known; all he cares about is what's going on in his head. You're right—living with any man is hard, and when the man's a genius . . . yes, there are times when I think that's what he is."

He paused when he saw how puzzled, even fearful Frida looked, and was relieved to hear a key turning in the door.

"You think it's easy to find decent cigarettes around here?" said Finkelmeyer, triumphantly waving his booty as he burst into the room. The walk had obviously done him good. "I hope you haven't had tea yet. I'm thirsty!" He called the girls over and started bouncing first one, then the other on his knee, and they alternately squealed with delight and whimpered with impatience. Little Nonna got the hiccups, and they ran off to the kitchen. They returned dragging their mother and whining, "But you promised!"

"What do they want?" asked Nikolsky.

"Oh, nothing. They're so headstrong. I told them once we could go for a ride on the Gorky Park ferris wheel, and bouncing on Aaron's knees reminded them of it. . . . Not today, girls. Today we're just going for a walk."

"Teacher! Teacher!" Nikolsky suddenly chirped, raising his hand like a child in school. "*I* want to go for a ride on the ferris wheel too." Then he laughed and added, in his normal voice, "Why not, after all? Can we get a taxi from here?"

An hour later they were piling into their seats—Frida and the girls in the front, Nikolsky and Finkelmeyer in the back—and the motor began to drone and up they went past trees still bare until the river climbed into view and the houses on the far side fell out of the gloomy sky and trees, river, and the houses again, swaying, rising, falling, growing, playing, teasing. Just as they reached at the top, the creaking mechanism came to a halt.

"Mam-ma-a!" cried a terrified little voice.

"Don't worry," said Nikolsky. "See? The people down there are getting out."

Aaron calmly twisted his head from one side to the other like a crow perched high in a fir tree. The sun had suddenly broken through the patchy gray of the sky.

"*Take heed to yourselves, that ye go not up into the mount, or touch the border of it,*" Finkelmeyer intoned. "*Whosoever toucheth the mount shall be surely put to death, whether it be beast or man. When the trumpet soundeth long, they shall come up to the mount.* You heard the trumpet, Lyonya, didn't you? *Be ready against the third day; come not at your wives.*"

With a jerk and a screech the wheel brought them down a bit farther, and as they swayed back and forth in their cradle, Finkelmeyer inquired of himself, "Why did I come at my wives? And why did I go up into the mount?"

The devilish contraption gave another lurch in the direction of the earth.

"*Sovev, sovev, holech haruah ve'al svivotav shav haruah.* Which means, *The wind whirleth about continually and returneth again according to his circuits,* and it must be true, because here we are, back where we started out from. *All go unto one place; all are of the dust, and all turn to dust again.*"

And they set foot on the earth.

X

AFTER making Nikolsky promise he would come and see them again, Frida took the girls and left the men to their own devices. They found a bench away from the main paths, and Nikolsky gave Finkelmeyer the newspaper.

"Well, well, well! A real celebrity!" he said, after reading the article. "And that nitwit didn't want a book."

"Nitwit, you say! Who does the article say wrote the book?"

Finkelmeyer glanced back at the article and whistled.

"Well, well, well!"

"Well, well, well is right! Not a word about Aion Neprigen. Tell me, what did he call himself at that first meeting in Siberia?"

"Neprigen. The editor and the Writers Union know it's a pseudonym, of course; otherwise Neprigen has always been the poet and Manakin the public figure. Now that I think of it, though, there was no title page with the proofs."

"Well, you can be sure it wasn't an oversight. Manakin wants to get rid of Neprigen because Neprigen is the ghostly go-between that links the two of you."

"Maybe Neprigen's usefulness is over," said Finkelmeyer after a pause. "He did get me into print, after all. What difference does it make if the rest of the poems come out in a book with Manakin instead of Neprigen on the cover?"

"How shortsighted can you be! The time will come, believe me, when you or somebody else, a critic, a scholar, will want to establish the truth. Aion Neprigen is you, Aaron Finkelmeyer. Manakin is Manakin." By now he was almost shouting. "What's the point of this fucking humility, eh, Aaron? You're the poet! *You!* Don't you see? People are going to read your poems. They don't belong to you anymore. They're mine and . . . and Leopold Mikhailovich's, and when the book comes out they'll belong to that couple over there, to anybody!"

"Keep it up and before you know it you'll be quoting Prebylov: 'Who do we write for if not the people?' "

"If you really think your poems have nothing to say to anyone, why have them published?"

"Oho! The cardinal question. Let me try and explain. It won't be the whole truth, of course, but here goes. First, because it's the done thing; second, because the Master talked me into it; third, because a little extra income always comes in handy; and fourth, because I'm afraid of death. You don't see the connection? The animal or mystical fear that when you die there will be nothing—a cold, dark void. And the concurrent hope that whatever it is you have written and sent out into the world will create the illusion that you still exist, the hope that just as your thoughts, made flesh by the magic of paper and ink and thereby fixed many times over have traveled far beyond the places you have been or will ever be, they will travel far beyond the space and time that circumscribe your life. Normal people long for the immortality of the body, the *body,* while people endowed with imagination—the dreamers, visionaries, fantasts, idiots, do-nothings of this world, its creative spirits, in other words—long for the immortality of the spirit. That's what makes art religious and close to God. But they are soon cured of their antiscientific illusions. They publish a book, and lo and behold! Life is as absurd as ever."

"Then why do they publish a second book and a third?" asked Nikolsky with a skeptical smile.

"For all kinds of reasons—except immortality. Actually, there are two issues involved: first, why they write, and only then, why they publish. They write because they get pulled into it, because they enjoy it, because it's the only thing they do well; they publish to earn royalties and be able to go on writing. What makes anyone decide on a profession? Vanity, inertia, peer pressure . . ."

"And are you cured of the desire for immortality?"

"I must have had an unusually light case," said Aaron, laughing, "because the moment I set eyes on the proofs I felt perfectly healthy. Manakin's a different matter: he will always be the first Tongor poet, and I'm green with envy. But the article was nothing to get upset about. I've got other *tsores.*"

"Other what?"

"Troubles."

Finkelmeyer fumbled though his pockets, and when at last he came up with a cigarette, Nikolsky struck a match. The flickering light of the flame revealed deep lines between Aaron's nose and the corner of his mouth and black semicircles under his eyes. He reminded Nikolsky of an Indian chief puffing on a pipe by the campfire. He kept his eyes glued to the ground, clearly unwilling to carry on the conversation.

Nikolsky went over it in his mind. His friend's viewpoint surprised—no, shocked him. Aaron had turned into a hard-boiled cynic.

True, Nikolsky was himself a cynic, but there was one area he refused to contaminate: art. Art was the only thing still worthy of respect in this world. When you picked up a classical novel or opened a volume of real poetry, you were never deceived. Now love—love deceived you left and right, the more so the higher you aimed. Art was different: art was immutable. What was written on paper or painted on canvas wouldn't abandon you. Besides, turning from one work of art to another didn't make you a traitor. No, the love for art was a polygamous love. Why couldn't he make Aaron see that as soon as a poem or painting or sonata was completed it belonged to its creator only formally? It was just as much the property of anyone capable of appreciating it. If reading Aaron's verse brought you closer to the mysteries of life, if the purity of his words soothed you as a prayer soothes—or at least as Nikolsky, who had never attended a church service in his life, imagined a prayer to soothe—then wasn't keeping it to himself tantamount to hoarding grain in a famine? Why did Aaron laugh whenever the subject came up? How could he be so indifferent? It was like fathering a litter of children and then leaving them to their fate.

"Granted," said Nikolsky, unable to keep his thoughts to himself, "you don't care about recognition, you don't care about publication as such. But what about the book as a means to an end? Wouldn't royalties free you to write, write more? Don't tell me you don't care about that!"

"Of course I care!" said Finkelmeyer, for once not trying to hide behind a wisecrack. "I couldn't begin to live on royalties unless I were willing to sell myself. There are ways and there are ways, of course, the most honorable being translation. But if you spend all your time and energy translating, you can dry up, draw a blank when it comes to your own work. Most people find it easier to sell themselves openly and write about whatever the Party line requires: construction sites, combines, the motherland, birch trees, calloused hands, memories of the glorious past, praise of the glorious present, intimations of the glorious future . . ."

"All right, all right! I understand!"

"You bet you do! Those poems are everywhere! Books, newspapers, radio, TV . . . Prebylov understands too."

"But *The Regiment Flag* . . ."

"*The Regiment Flag* was my introduction to the Devil. If you haven't met Him, you can't recognize Him. Well, I have and I can."

The streetlamps had come on, but the spot where they were sitting remained dark. Through the trees they saw the ferris wheel as a series of gaudy electric dots.

"You know what the money for a book would mean to me? Enough to give up my job for a year and a half, write day and night, clear my brain. If only I could forget! I've got too many words crowded up there. The pressure is like a tumor. I *have* to write whether I want to or not."

"And you do want to," Nikolsky intervened immediately, for fear of another break in the conversation. "You want to write, but you can't see your way to quitting your job. Could the reason for it have something to do with your . . . what did you call it?"

"My *tsores, meyne groyse tsores*. And you can guess what kind of troubles."

"The family kind," Nikolsky groaned, and with such vehemence he was afraid Aaron would take offense. But Aaron only sighed, and Nikolsky found a certain satisfaction in the thought that his friend's private life was as muddled his own. Confiding domestic troubles to one another brings men closer. But Aaron had Danuta.

"What do you expect from Frida, anyway? You don't need her to appreciate your poetry, do you?"

"I don't need anyone for that."

What about our encounter in the plane? Nikolsky was about to ask, but he was glad he bit his tongue.

"I live with a constant . . . with an unremitting sense of . . . guilt. I watch her suffer, watch her rushing around, trying to change this or that, make everything better, and I'm the guilty one. I am guilty because I . . . I'm not myself when I'm at home. I walk through that door and turn to wood, withdraw, and then try and make up for it by acting jolly. We have no peace, the two of us."

"Remember Pushkin in 'It's Time, My Friend'?

'There is no joy on earth but only peace and freedom . . .' "

"There is no peace."
"Then chuck freedom too."

"But there is freedom. Privacy is freedom. Real privacy. Physical and spiritual. By the way, is it true, as we are taught in school, that in 'It's Time' Pushkin is summoning his *wife* to share his 'remote enclave'? Could he have been so deluded as to believe he would find peace and freedom with the woman whose infidelity eventually caused his death?"

> "Long years, a weary slave, I've contemplated fleeing
> To a remote enclave of work and pleasure seemly,"

Nikolsky recited. "No, of course not! It's as clear as day he wasn't summoning her; he was *fleeing* her. Remember what you were taught about his simplicity and precision? Well, once he says 'weary slave,' he need say no more. I'd have those words engraved on a tablet and hung around the neck of every husband."

> " 'Long years a fine, an envious fate I've harbored dreams of,' "

said Aaron, reminding Nikolsky of another line in the poem. How glad he was to have someone he could talk to like this! "If all *he* could do was harbor dreams, how can *we* hope to succeed?"

"Aren't you asking a bit much? Why not settle for something more modest? A year, a year and a half, say. In a shack somewhere."

"To begin with, I haven't got a shack."

"You could have my place."

"Your place? Where would *you* live?"

"Let me worry about that." Although he obviously had the Refuge in mind, he was prudent enough—or superstitious enough—to add, "I have an aunt who will take me in." Which was only a white lie, becuase in fact he had a fine aunt who was always happy to see him and even put him up for the night.

"Aren't you carrying your philanthropy too far?"

"I've had enough of your idiotic questions."

"So you really mean it."

"Why you . . ." Nikolsky began, but he checked himself when he realized that Aaron had all but accepted. "Of course I mean it. I may be making some changes in my way of life, but that's neither here nor there. All you need to know is that the place is yours whenever and for however long you want it."

"A place of my own for a year, a year and a half! What bliss! But I don't know. I'll have to think it over. Thank you. If you haven't changed your mind by the end of summer . . . No! Don't be angry! I know you won't change your mind." Then he looked at his watch and said, "It really is time, my friend."

XI

ALL WINTER Nikolsky had looked forward to a month off for a canoe trip down the Inzer. The river had a good reputation among white-water enthusiasts. It had rapids, a swift current that made paddling a real art, and whirlpools that had been known to crack frames. June was the best month, because then the river swelled with snows from the Southern Urals.

They decided to take three canoes, two men to a canoe. Men, not women. The food would be worse, but whenever you took women along you said goodbye to your plans, your itinerary—everything. Besides, they were men in their early thirties, not randy youngsters on the make; in fact, they might even consider a month away from their wives and mistresses more respite than trial. What they needed most of all, those deskbound scientists and engineers, was some good strenuous exercise.

But just as Nikolsky was about to set off, the green box in Zaalaisk, where Nikolsky had left behind instructions on how to clean up the patent morass, started stirring. The semi-annual report was due, they were rushing to fulfill the plan, and telephone calls from the managers suddenly came fast and furious, begging, insisting, demanding they be allowed to minimize some changes, reject others, and cover up where nothing else would help.

In the end, they asked Nikolsky to put in an appearance. He refused. He had personal reasons to stay away from Zaalaisk, but he also knew that arriving on the scene in the midst of the final push meant exposing scandals and making enemies.

"Look," he said to the head of the green box, "I fulfilled my end of the bargain. You wouldn't need any last-minute patch-up job if you did your work on time. Talk to my boss. I'm not budging unless he orders me to."

His boss very politely agreed that without a new contract he was not bound to go, and very politely asked him to postpone his holiday to be available for telephone consultations. "It's a defense contract, Leonid Pavlovich. You understand. If they don't fulfill their plan, they could point the finger at us."

Goodbye, white water! Nikolsky's friends were indignant. In the first place, he was in charge of the itinerary; they had even nicknamed him "the admiral." But even more important, without him they had five men for three canoes. They called a meeting to discuss the situation. A gloomy Nikolsky showed up to hand over the map and pass his knowledge on to his successor.

"Wait a second," one of them suddenly cried. "Why not put it off for a month? I can change my dates without any trouble."

The funereal atmosphere dissipated instantly. Nikolsky was touched. He argued without much conviction that it made no sense for the five of them to change their plans for him and that the Inzer had been known to silt up in July; they said what good was a fleet without an admiral. It was decided to postpone their departure until Friday, the first of July.

Now there was only June to get through. Finkelmeyer had disappeared—the nursery school where Frida worked moved to the country for the summer and she had been allowed to bring Aaron and his father along—and the time had come to settle the issue he had hinted at to Aaron that day in Gorky Park, that is, whether or not he should move in with Vera and make a serious attempt at living with her. But things had changed between them. Theirs had been a carefree, on-again off-again kind of relationship, the kind where days or even weeks go by before you feel the need to be together. After all, they each had their own place, their own salary, their own friends, their own past. It was a vicious circle, really: each remained aloof because neither made a move towards a union, and no union developed because each remained aloof. Now, after three years, they seemed to have reached a watershed. Apparently Nikolsky was not the only one who felt their love suffered a setback that evening when Vera burst into tears on Leopold Mikhailovich's chest. Although they continued to see each other, they avoided ending up alone together as if by tacit agreement. At another time Nikolsky would have been highly indignant at a woman daring to pay him back in kind: *he* was the one who took the initiative in matters of sexual hide-and-seek. But this time it was no game.

Besides, Vera had changed, and Nikolsky instinctively kept his distance much as the parents of an adolescent undergoing rapid change stand aside, watching in amazement as a new personality unfolds. But Vera was no longer an adolescent or even young, and suddenly she felt a new desire, a desire to belong. She had always prided herself on *not* belonging—it was the trait that most impressed outsiders, the core of her happy-go-lucky character—and all at once she seemed gentler, more accommodating: she was less abrupt in her gestures, she spoke more softly, more slowly, she thought carefully about things she would formerly have dismissed with a brusque nod or an impromptu tirade. And the axis on which her new interest in people, her new views and attitudes, revolved was of course Leopold Mikhailovich.

Oddly enough, Nikolsky was not upset; in fact, seeing the attention she lavished on Leopold Mikhailovich he felt something akin to respect for her—insofar as he was able to associate such a concept with a woman, especially one with whom he was romantically involved. It was this new Vera who had made him rethink what a few months before seemed a relationship doomed to expire. There were times he felt that even as he entered his fourth year with her he had not had his fill of her body, her "classical" body, as he now saw it, smiling to himself, but then he would wonder whether he hadn't simply transferred to her the abstract desire that came of going through a womanless stretch.

In the course of his deliberations he was constantly visited by a phantasmic Finkelmeyer, who in a series of grotesque grimaces and gestures would intimate there was no way out, whereupon Nikolsky would argue that he was certain, well, he assumed that everything would turn out all right if only Aaron would take the first step and change *his* life—which was what he'd been dreaming of anyway, wasn't it?—and move into his place, which would mean that he, Nikolsky, would have to move in with Vera, and once Frida was out of Aaron's hair he might have *her* come and stay with him, which might mean . . . No, he must put all designs on her out of his mind and forget that silly word *hope*. . . .

By the end of the month the green-box people had stopped pestering him: they had either met the plan on their own or realized it was too late to do anything about it. He kept going to the office pro forma, however, and when Vera phoned him there one morning and asked whether he could drop everything and come to Leopold Mikhailovich's, he asked only whether he should grab something to eat on the way.

Leopold Mikhailovich started by asking if Nikolsky could take the rest of the day off. "I'm a lucky man, then," he said, when Nikolsky answered in the affirmative. "You're my last hope. First of all, it's summer, and half the town's in the country. And then this isn't something I can ask of just anybody. I'd have tried Aaron, but he's away, and Tolya's taking exams. I could explain it all in a few words, but I want you to understand the background, so please bear with me. You are, I assume, up to date on the latest—how shall I put it?—pronouncements concerning the state of culture in our country?"

"Oh yes. By the grace of Nikita we are now as astute critics of art as we are cultivators of maize, as up on twelve-tone rows as on . . . twelve-spotted asparagus beetles." He then took a deep breath and intoned: " 'Both the creative intelligentsia and the workers and collective farmers stand firm in the struggle against bourgeois influence, the influence of the decadent West, on our art, music, and literature.' Is that what you had in mind?"

"Exactly, though as you'll remember, when Khrushchev condemned the exhibition of the Nineteen at the Manège last winter, his language was a bit more crude. But that's neither here nor there. The point is, I am the keeper of several of the works that so provoked the ire of our esteemed leader. By the way, I also have some work by Falk and Sterenberg, whose allegiance to the avant-garde vexes the regime in no less measure than that of their younger compatriots. In fact, I have a considerable number of canvases—more than a hundred, if the truth be known—representing what I shall again call, for want of a term embracing the myriad varieties of art unacceptable to the official ideology, the avant-garde. You will understand, of course, why I've told so few people about them. I have seen all kinds of things in my day and have every reason to fear for my collection. The situation is complicated by the fact that the artists have on occasion—with my permission, of course—invited foreigners to view their works with an eye towards selling them. I should add that I am not so much the owner as the guardian of most of the collection. Because my circumstances enabled me to pay no more than a pittance for them, many of the young artists' paintings must be considered gifts. I have therefore always made it a policy to release a painting as soon as a suitable buyer presents himself.

"The collection is housed in a cottage outside Moscow. The cottage belongs to a fine young artist and one of those whom the authorities have decided to 'keep tabs on.' Kolya Begichev is his name. Kolya's charming wife, Varya, was here an hour ago. Kolya is off painting and fishing in her sister's village outside Yaroslavl, and just after he left, Varya had a visit from a neighbor, who said that some people had come and asked her where Kolya had gone and if Kolya's wife worked and if the two of them had drunken parties and who came to see them. The neighbor was a simple soul, but she understood at once what they meant when they asked what cars the people drove and if they dressed the way we do—everybody knew they kept an eye on foreigners.

"At first Varya paid no attention to the matter, especially as they'd had no visitors for the last two or three months. But this morning she'd been visited by two men who said they were architects from the local planning commission and needed to inspect the house. When after the most perfunctory look at the walls they asked to see the attic, she realized something was amiss and asked what the inspection was for. They told her there was a plan to build a road through the village and their job was to determine the amount she would be offered in case the house had to be demolished. Well, the only reason she'd let them in was that there'd been talk of bringing *gas* to the village. In other words, the operatives hadn't bothered to do their homework.

"Varya told them the attic was locked. They insisted she open it for them. She refused. Standing in the stairwell with her arms out to keep them at bay, she finally thought to ask for their warrant.

After showering her with insults, they said they could have one within the hour. By then she had come up with a plan.

"She told them her husband had left the key to the attic with some friends in Moscow and she had to go into town to get it. They said they'd be back that evening or at the latest the next morning and she'd better not try any tricks, because they could just as well break the lock.

"She was in a terrible state when she got here. We did what we could to reassure her and sent her home. Surely you've guessed by now what we want of you."

Nikolsky quickly fished the last piece of fruit out of his compote. He was sorry now he'd invited himself to lunch. His head was buzzing with plans.

"Is it far?"

"Nakhabino."

"And where do I take them?"

Before he had finished asking, he knew the answer.

"Of course," Vera nodded when he looked over at her. "Where else?"

"Nakhabino, you say? Let's see. That's on the Volokolamsk Road, isn't it? Couldn't be better. Now how big are they? Can they fit in the back of a Volga? Or in the trunk?"

"For the most part. But there are some bigger ones."

"I see. On the roof then. You know, one of those racks you attach to the roof. Say, one and a half by two meters."

"That should do it. Two or three are enormous. The main thing is to rescue as many as possible."

'What's the road like? To the house, I mean. Can you drive straight to the door?"

"Yes. There's a gate."

"Here," he said, handing Leopold Mikhailovich a pen and memo pad. "Would you write out the directions? Or even better, draw a map."

Vera beamed at Nikolsky with what could have been interpreted as either love or pride.

"How many trips will it take? Four? Five?"

"At least that, I'm afraid," said Leopold Mikhailovich, smiling apologetically as he scribbled.

"Well, I don't imagine the architects will make it back today, but if they do . . ."

"Lyonya!"

"Lyonya's dreamed all his life of a tête-à-tête with an architect," he said as he dialed a number, pressing the receiver to his ear with his shoulder. "Hello, fleet services? . . . Tell me, is Victor Kanakhin on duty? He's a driver. . . . Punched out this morning at nine? Thank you."

He immediately dialed another number.

"Sleeping," he said. "But I'll get hold of him if I have to go and pound on his door."

He hung up and dialed again. Obnoxious beeps filled the quiet room. All at once the receiver resounded with a thunderous "Goddam son of a bitch!"

"Vitek! Vitek!" Nikolsky whooped with joy. "It's me! Nikolsky! No, wait, Vitek! Don't hang up! Take it easy! Look, I'm sorry. I know you had night duty, but you don't think I'd wake you up like this if I— What was that? . . . Give me a chance! I *am* getting to the point. . . ."

Twenty minutes later Victor Kanakhin pulled up to Leopold Mikhailovich's door. Vera and Leopold Mikhailovich climbed into the back, Nikolsky into the front. Victor greeted Nikolsky with a chapped-lipped, freckle-faced, redheaded smile, and Nikolsky gave him a wink and shook his outstretched hand.

Friendships—male friendships, at least—depend largely on how much life the future friends bring to the incipient relationship. When they carry too much on their backs, they may have trouble straightening up and looking each other in the eye. And although a late-blooming friendship is possible (Nikolsky thought of his new bond with Finkelmeyer), things are so much smoother when they go back to the school bench or, as with Victor Kanakhin, to the lab, may it rest in peace, where the only goal was a thinking turtle and there were no complications or complexes, where the very word "complex" did not yet exist.

They stopped at the Refuge. Nikolsky refused to take Leopold Mikhailovich any farther: the architects were under no circumstances to catch a glimpse of the man who'd masterminded the collection.

Leopold Mikhailovich took it very badly. He had at least the remnants of what used to be called honor, he said, and he could not countenance putting others in danger while watching safely from the sidelines.

"Then I'm not going anywhere," Nikolsky snapped, looking Leopold Mikhailovich coldly in the eye.

"Varya won't open the door for you."

"Write her a message then. And make it snappy! Every minute counts!"

"You're a tough customer," he said after a pause, and took out his pen.

"You can say that again!" Victor quipped with what could have been either irony or pride.

XII

"WELL, RED, what've you been doing with yourself?"

"Nothing special. Can't even get fucking plastered when I feel like it. I'm on twenty-four hours, off twenty-four hours, and I finally get a drink in me when this bastard I know gives me a call and tells me he's got urgent business for me to attend to."

Nikolsky squinted over at him. Victor's chapped lips gave him away. Nikolsky laughed and said, "I bet you weren't alone, either."

"Damn right I wasn't, but it's not like you think. I live with my brother."

"Vanya? That little brat?"

"That little brat's just come back from two years behind bars."

"No! What'd they nab him for?"

"Got on the bad side of a cop. There was this Chink bigwig in town to see Nikita and, you know how it is, they rounded up a crowd to stand and wave? Well, anyway, they were roping off the street, and he decided to make a getaway, and he did, only he ran straight into this cop, see, and the cop grabs him and Vanya says, 'You take your mitts off of me! I ain't done nothing,' and the copper says, 'Obstructing justice, eh!' and shoves him up against a shop window. Well, Vanya tries to break loose and accidentally sticks his elbow through the glass, and, well, the cop gets a scratch or two in the face, lots of blood, but nothing serious. The thing is, the whole window comes down with a crash—and just when Nikita and his Chinaman are passing by. So the cops pounce on him and drag him off. Two years! Lucky he didn't get five."

"The bastards!"

"What about you?" Victor asked.

"Did you see the girl in the back? Well, I've been with her for three years. More. And now it's on the blink."

"Hey, maybe it's like you've blown a fuse and all you have to do is stick in a new one. Or do you think it's burned out for good? Three years! I can see why you stuck it out, though. When they're stacked like that and clean and don't run around, you're better off with one, know what I mean?"

He did, because there *was* only one he cared for, and when he thought of her—lovely, kind, and pure—he lost all interest in the conversation and began filling Victor in on the operation at hand.

"No problem," Victor said. "It's in the bag."

When they knocked on the door of the Begichev house, a fearful voice called out, "Who's there?"

"Open up, Varya!" said Nikolsky. "We're from Leopold Mikhailovich."

"Thank God!" said the voice, and after the clank of a sliding bolt and the rattle of a turning key the door flew open.

Varya *was* charming. The gray peasant scarf she wore was modest, yet the way it draped over her head, shoulders, and breasts was mildly flirtatious; in fact, everything about her was serene yet alluring. Victor immediately broke in to a silly grin, but Varya was still suspicious and asked why Leopold Mikhailovich wasn't with them.

"Vera and I—you met Vera at Leopold Mikhailovich's this morning, she's my wife—we wouldn't let him come. We didn't want him to be seen by anybody. My name is Leonid Pavlovich, and this is my friend Victor." Victor shook her hand with such a show of gallantry that Nikolsky nearly whistled in amazement and quickly followed suit. "Leopold Mikhailovich asked me to give you this."

She read the note, but remained on the defensive.

"How will I know where you're taking the pictures?"

"Has anyone ever told you you're a hard nut to crack?" Nikolsky laughed. "I know what. We'll load up in a hurry, and you can come with us on the first round. Agreed?"

"Agreed," she said, smiling at last.

Victor drove into the courtyard, and Varya motioned to him to take the car round to the back, where they could load the paintings without being seen from the street. She had also prepared rope, burlap, and a large tarpaulin to keep the frames from getting scratched en route.

They climbed up to a spacious attic with beams and rafters and three wide mansard windows that let in a wonderful soft light from three directions. Two easels and a cheap, paint-spattered kitchen table covered with brushes, a palette, a decrepit sketch folder, and a number of squeezed-out tubes stood near the middle of the room, and all along the walls—on the pillars supporting the beams, on the floor, face up and face down—were paintings.

"Oh my God!" Nikolsky muttered disconsolately, dazzled by the rows of rectangles. A good deal more than a hundred, he imagined. "How many trips, Vitek? What do you think?"

"As many as it takes," he said, unperturbed and still beaming at Varya.

"Where shall we start?"

"Here, I'll show you," said Varya. "First Falk, Drevin, and Sterenberg. Too many people know they're here. And then some of Kolya's work—Kolya's my husband—and these things by Gruberman and Daryushka. Don't think it's because he's my husband. He and Gruberman have done some rather wild canvases. They've been accused of pornography. And you've heard of Daryushka, haven't you?"

"Can't say as we have."

"You're not artists, then."

"Does it show?"

"Of course," she said matter-of-factly. "Daryushka has problems up here, if you know what I mean"—she tapped her head—"and she paints her dreams, her visions, her ravings. Just the kind of thing they're looking for. We may not manage to save all the canvases, so we've got to start with the ones they'd make the greatest fuss over. Like this one . . . and this . . . and that one over there . . ."

Victor went around picking them up while Nikolsky ran downstairs for the burlap, and within half an hour the trunk, backseat, and rack were filled to the brim. The car was an oven and they were all sweating from the strenuous packing job, but once under way they felt a refreshing breeze. Varya huddled next to Victor; Nikolsky had squeezed into the back. From time to time Nikolsky glanced into the rearview mirror at Victor's beatific smile, and when their eyes met they would wink like conspirators carrying off a secret treasure.

Vera and Leopold Mikhailovich were waiting for them outside the Refuge, and the unloading process started at once.

"Was I right to take the still life in gray?" Varya asked Leopold Mikhailovich with a worried look. "And the one with the eyes on the branches? . . . Watch out there, Victor! . . . And *Composition No. 7*—what do you think?"

Leopold Mikhailovich laid his hand on her shoulder to calm her. They all needed calming. He felt everything that they felt, but in him it was tempered with sadness, with the memory of something recalled from time past or yet to come, and he smiled the mysterious smile he'd smiled when talking about the two-thousand-year-old sculpture and its flesh-and-blood contemporary.

It was just after the summer solstice, and they managed to fit in two more trips before dark. Varya stayed at Nakhabino carrying the paintings downstairs and wrapping them, while the others— plus Tolik, who had happened along opportunely—made quick work of the previous cargo at the Refuge. After Nikolsky and Victor had loaded the car for the fourth time Varya called them into the kitchen for a snack. Nikolsky took his sausage and black bread and went back to work, but Victor just sat there, chewing and mooning over Varya.

"Hey, Vitek, get a move on," Nikolsky called out at last. "We've got at least two more trips. I'll take you to a restaurant when we're through, okay? My treat."

They scooped up some water from the water barrel and started off to the car. There were two men standing near it. One of them was trying to lift the end of the tarpaulin covering the paintings on the roof.

"Hey, get your paws off that!" shouted Victor, ready to tear across the grass.

"Take it easy, will you?" said Nikolsky, grabbing him by the sleeve. "Speak politely to the gentlemen."

Nikolsky stepped back over the threshold and said to Varya, "The 'architects' have come! Lock up and don't let them in for anything! You're not here, understand? Don't say a word. And don't worry. We'll be back."

When he reached the car, one of them, a heavyset man with a nasty, snakelike face, was still tugging at the tarpaulin; Victor had grabbed his arm and was being cautiously pushed and pulled by the snake's timid-looking companion.

"Take your hands off the tarp."

"Take your hands off *me*."

"I told you not to touch the tarp."

"Let go of my arm."

Nikolsky walked up and said, "Let him go, Vitek!" And squeezing his way between Victor and the snake, he managed to whisper into Victor's red stubble, "Hop behind the wheel and drive over to the gate."

Victor loosed his grip and yelled theatrically, "Well, why the hell was he fooling with the tarp?" while edging towards the front seat.

"Now what's the problem, citizens?" asked Nikolsky, moving between them with outstretched arms as if he were trying to keep them from going at each other. "Just what is the problem?"

"We've got a warrant!" the nervous one shouted, straining against Nikolsky's arm.

"There are warrants and warrants!" said Nikolsky, playing for time.

"Well, ours is from the local planning commission," said the snake. "Tell me, what do you think you're doing moving all this out of the attic?"

He was so involved in playing the architect that he failed to notice Victor ducking into the car.

"And what business is that of yours, may I ask?"

"Fire laws," said the snake. "What's this you've got here?" He was about to grab the tarpaulin with his other hand when the starter clicked, the exhaust pipe spat, and the car jerked forward.

Nikolsky came down hard with the edge of his hand on a hairy wrist. The snake let go of the tarpaulin and flew back into a corner between the wall and the porch of the house.

"Don't let him get away!" he cried, and his accomplice set off after the car. Then he narrowed his eyes and said to Nikolsky, "Who do you think you are, playing games with the law?"

"How do I know you're the 'law'?" said Nikolsky, unimpressed. "As far as I can see, you're just trespassers."

"He's got the warrant," he said, motioning to his colleague, whom Victor was pushing away with one hand as he opened the gate with the other.

Nikolsky shrugged, turned, and walked over to the man, who after a good deal of fumbling managed to produce the document.

"What good is this?" said Nikolsky, skimming the warrant. "You said you were here for fire laws, and this is about some new road that's going through."

He handed the man back the paper, hopped into the car, and told Victor to step on it, but almost before Victor could put his foot on the gas he slammed on the brakes with a "Son of a bitch!" The snake had run in front of the car waving his true credentials in the form of a little red book.

"Halt!" he shouted, confident in the hypnotic power of the dread booklet.

"Go fuck yourself!" Victor yelled, and barreled ahead, giving the ruddy face just enough time to jerk out of the way.

"Halt!" it went on shouting from behind as they bumped their way towards the main road.

Back at the Refuge they told the story of the confrontation as they unloaded, and the moment the car was empty they set off again. Leopold Mikhailovich advised them not to bait the architects: all that was left was Kolya's own work and a few inoffensive canvases by friends.

It was dark when they turned off the main road.

"Funny," said Victor as they passed a motorcycle policeman, "he wasn't there when we left." In the rearview mirror they could see him jotting something down in his pad.

There were no lights on at Varya's. The gate was still open, but the courtyard was empty. Varya had been on the lookout for them, and by the time they reached the porch she was sliding the bolt open. Apparently the uninvited guests had banged on the door, yelled out threats for a few minutes, and then gone off.

The loading process had just begun when Nikolsky called out, "Stop! Take them back! Varya, have you got any spare wood? Boards, laths, pickets—that sort of thing?"

"Why yes. In the shed."

"Show me."

His face lit up at what he found.

"Into the car with them!" he ordered.

"I don't think I understand," said Victor.

"You should have gone back to school when we told you to!"

Victor cursed and started loading the boards.

Varya locked the house up tightly. They had decided that for the time being she would stay with Vera or a friend.

As they turned from the dirt road running through the village onto the asphalt of the main road, their headlights slipped past the motorcycle policeman and instead of disappearing into a void lit up a Volga and two policemen in white tunics and caps.

"Listen carefully, Varya," said Nikolsky quickly. "We are your customers. You've just sold us this wood for twenty-five rubles."

"Not bad!" Victor barely had time to say as he pulled up to the black-and-white baton that had signaled him to stop. "Let me handle this."

He took his time getting out of the car and ambled over to the motorcycle policeman. The policeman saluted him, and the ritual was on: presentation of license, page-by-page perusal of same, explanations, gesticulations (at one point Victor pointed to the headlights and described a semicircle with one arm—in other words, the excuse they had used to stop him had something to do with blinding an oncoming vehicle). Then up came the two officers in white, as if they had just happened by, and the license was passed on to them. All three then set off in the direction of the car, and Nikolsky moved into action.

Jumping out, he lit up a cigarette. One of the officers, a middle-aged man, went over to him and saluted.

"Good evening," Nikolsky replied jauntily. "Cigarette?"

"Not while I'm on duty, thank you." He didn't quite know how to proceed. "Uh . . . out for a spin with the wife, I see," he said at last.

"With a *friend,* actually," said Nikolsky, smiling a confidential smile. "Nothing wrong with that, is there?"

"Not in the least, comrade," said the officer, smiling a reserved smile. "That's none of our business." He paused. "I see you've got something under that tarpaulin."

"That's right."

"Tell me, how are you paying the driver? Cash or vodka?"

Don't tell me they're only out for private drivers! Nikolsky thought. Could they have been stopped by chance?

"The driver?" he asked with great surprise. "You mean Victor?"

"I mean the driver," said the officer coldly. "The owner of the car."

"Oh, but Comrade Officer, there's been a terrible mistake!" said Nikolsky with a broad smile and open arms. "You wouldn't believe how long we've been friends!"

"I told them I only do it for friends," Victor said shrugging.

"Don't worry, Comrade Officer, there's no monkey business here. Vitek's a cabby with a good heart, that's all."

"All right, all right," he said. "Just let me have a look under the tarp and you can be on your way."

Oho! Nikolsky nearly said aloud, but managed to turn it into a howl and add, "It's not stolen, not state property. Believe me, Comrade Officer. I paid for every bit of it."

"Just a minute, just a minute," the officer said tensely. "Let me look first."

It was hard in the dark to make out what was under the tarpaulin, so the policemen unloaded board after board. At first the officer looked puzzled, then embarrassed.

Meanwhile Nikolsky was carrying on a heart-rending patter: ". . . and so I asked her, since her husband was away, whether she wouldn't sell me the lot—I have this new cooperative flat, and you know the fixing up that takes—and we agreed on a price of twenty-five rubles, and we were all set to drive the first load out when these two 'firemen' came up and started poking under the tarp . . ."

"Just a minute! What was that you said? They looked under the tarp?"

"Well, you know how it is. Two strangers come up to you and try to stick their noses into your business. Well, Vitek here and me, we shook them up a little."

"You may go now, comrades!" the officer hammered out, so furious that he couldn't hold back until he reached his colleagues, and shouted within earshot of the car, "Some agents they send out! 'Valuable goods!' 'Foreign currency!' They're *obsessed* with foreign currency!"

Nikolsky, Victor, and Varya laughed so hard that they were in Moscow before they knew it. They burst into the Refuge, interrupting one another's account of the incident. As soon as Nikolsky saw the meal Vera had prepared, he gave up the restaurant idea. For a while Victor was depressed: he had to drive home and wouldn't be able to drink at all—or, what was worse, would be able to drink only a little—but then Vera invited him to stay overnight. "No, *everybody* stay overnight!" she added. "It'll be a bit crowded, but we'll manage."

They sat down to supper full of spirit and remained at the table until well after midnight. The windows were open, and they could hear the leaves rustling, the wind rising and falling. They were in for a storm. When at last they lay down to sleep—Vera and Varya in the alcove, Nikolsky and Victor at the other end of the room on some chairs, Leopold Mikhailovich on the entresol couch with Tolik on a camp bed beside him—there was a good deal of murmuring and sighing.

"How about making a switch, eh, Lyonya?" Victor whispered in Nikolsky's ear. "You go over and sleep with Vera and send Varya back here." But by the time Nikolsky finished his joke about the bed over there being softer, he saw that Victor was asleep.

All at once the sky was alive with white-and-blue flashes. The wind picked up noticeably. Nikolsky got up to close the windows. He was joined on the entresol by Leopold Mikhailovich, and together they made the rounds of the house. When they found Tolik in the kitchen guzzling water, they realized they were thirsty too. Then all three of them had a smoke and started discussing the paintings. In the end, they tiptoed up to the entresol and covered two lamps in such a way that the light would not disturb the sleepers, and Leopold Mikhailovich, his eyes burning like a naughty boy's, brought out one after another of his favorites.

The rain came down in buckets, thunder roared, lightning flashed. "Not sleepy yet?" he kept asking them.

"No, no! Show us another!"

Vera got up at dawn and made them some strong black coffee. "You men," she kept muttering.

XIII

Dear Admiral (if you haven't been demoted for some character defect),

I don't know if you'll ever get this letter. I have no idea where the Inzer is. It's hard to write someone a letter when you can't picture where he is or what he's doing. So let me imagine you in a far-off land a-roving across the seas, heigh-ho, with a galleon grand and a merry band and a maiden all comely and fair, heigh-ho!

But enough of that. It's two weeks since you left. Life has continued apace, and for the first time in ages I feel a real part of it, part of the flow of things, so to speak. (Funny I should think of that analogy when you're off on the rapids.) But it's more than that. It's even a bit frightening. Remember the excerpt from Gogol they had us memorize in school? "It was as if an unknown force had taken you on its wing and you were flying, everything was flying!" I've always found Gogol a bit frightening, that passage in particular.

What is there to tell you? First of all, Leopold Mikhailovich has been having trouble with one of his legs—terrible pains that keep him off his feet for several days. The awful thing is, he won't go to see a doctor. He laughs at the idea, and it's no laughing matter. We finally dragged out of him that he was wounded in the war, in 1916, and was operated on at a field hospital. Then in the last war he was in the home guard. Living outside in the cold and wet must have got to the wound, because since then it has acted up more or less regularly.

The reason it's so bad now is that he strained it while unloading the collection. For a while he stayed here with me, because there was so much to be done in connection with the paintings. But then he did a silly thing. To "keep me from worrying," as I found out later, he sneaked out one morning and took a taxi home—just when his leg was at its worst too. I kept phoning him, but all he would say was that he felt fine and didn't need to see me, and I, fool that I am, thought he was annoyed with me for some reason and decided not to force myself on him.

Then one day Aaron came and told me he'd found L.M. in a terrible state. Practically starving! He couldn't even get out to the bakery for bread. Well, of course we brought him back here at once and I made him promise not to run away again. I don't see how he can live in that place anyway—those neighbors! When Aaron and I went there last Sunday for some of his things, one of the sharp-nosed biddies gave me the third degree. I told her I was his niece and he was living with me now, and she finally let us be. Well, I went out to the bank to pay his rent for him, and when I got back, there was Aaron dragging L.M.'s table out of the kitchen! *She'd* told him to; she said he wouldn't be using it while he was gone. Your friend Aaron's unbelievable! Well, I lit into him, let me tell you, but he looked so crushed I pulled back. It isn't his fault, after all; it's those damn communal apartments. How people can have lived in them all these years I can't imagine!

A few days ago your other friend, Victor, came to see you. I had the feeling something was wrong, so I asked whether he'd had any trouble on account of the paintings, and though he didn't give me a straight answer I could tell that was bothering him. He wanted to know how Varya was, and I told him she was staying with a friend in Moscow. He perked up immediately and said there was nothing to worry about, but then he asked me to have you call him when you got back.

To tell the truth, I don't want L. M. to hear about any repercussions. I've told Aaron the whole story and he agrees. He's come and recited his poetry once or twice. You have to get used to his manner—he tends to forget there are other people around and starts mumbling to himself—but it can be a real experience.

What else? Tolik. Tolik can sketch for days on end. He sits at the foot of the statue; she is his muse and his model. And all his sketches—he's done hundreds of them by now—are of ballet dancers! A man and a woman, naked or in togalike affairs, dancing their dance of love. You know, I don't believe Tolik has ever held a woman in his arms. (Don't tell him I said so.) Why else would he be so attached to the statue? I can't quite tell if it's sad or charming.

Well, that's it for today. If I go on, I'll have to add another stamp. Since you'll probably be back before any letter you could send, I won't ask you how you are, but I do hope you'll bring home a snapshot or two.

Shall I be honest? You haven't been on my mind all that much, but I enjoy it when you do pop in. Really. I like hearing your friends talk about you, about missing you. I owe you a lot, you know. I've never told you that before, but I'm telling you now.

Love and kisses,
Vera

XIV

IT WAS Sunday in Moscow; it was Sunday over half the globe. People were at rest. True, there are people for whom Sunday and, say, Wednesday are very much the same, and not so much because they do not keep the seventh day holy as because they do not take part in the inexorable work week; in our society, however, where everyone eats and therefore labors, summer holidays are the only time when one can allow oneself the luxury of disconnecting the cruel mechanism that clicks off Thursday, Friday! SATURDAY!! SUNDAY!! Monday, Tuesday, Wednesday . . .

Nikolsky had arrived back from his trip in accordance with the unwritten law that places Sundays on either end of a vacation, thereby stretching the delights of leisure to the limit. But the moment he and his crew stepped from the train onto the filthy platform, Nikolsky rewound the rusty mechanism and started thinking about going to work the next morning, which meant shopping, though what could he hope to find on a Sunday evening—no sausage, no butter, no eggs, no milk, and certainly no tomatos or cucumbers—and shouldn't he stop in at the Refuge? No, there wasn't time, he had to put the canoe out to dry and get cleaned up and throw his grimy clothes into the bathtub to soak—if you want to be a bachelor, you've got to do everything yourself.

Yet somehow at nine-thirty sharp Nikolsky entered the office with his head held high. A good thing too, because amidst the hellos and welcome backs, he was informed by the secretary that the boss had asked for him.

The secretary followed Nikolsky into his office and showed him how pleased she was to see him by smiling with her deep cherry lips and perching on the edge of his desk in such a way as to bring out the quasi-ellipsoidal line of her thighs. She and Nikolsky had had a quick fling several years before, one they both looked back on with pleasure. The only reason it was so quick was that she had previously agreed to marry a suitable prospect. Nikolsky, though without a suitable prospect for some time thereafter, put no pressure on the blushing bride, and her appreciation of his prudent policy boded well for the future. It hadn't been so long ago, either: first the secretary, then the fallow period, then Vera. You might even say it was only the day before yesterday—if Vera was yesterday, that is.

"Hey you've got a date with the boss first, remember?"

The boss? Fine, I can handle that.

Glad to see you. Same here. Let's cut the play-acting, shall we? Who's glad to see the boss on the first day back to work? By the way, your return has been anxiously awaited. They need you in Zaalaisk again. The commission has given them a verbal go-ahead, but they're afraid of last-minute hitches. They want a clean bill of health, and they want it from you. Here's the contract, paid in advance. Sorry, but . . .

While the boss went on apologizing, Nikolsky felt his throat go dry. He wondered what emotion his face showed, and turned his head slightly just in case.

"Well, if I really must . . .
        I'll see her I've been dreaming of telling her about
. . . I want a decent room . . .
her the other side of the wall with him private room no you bastard
. . . a private room."

"I'll send a telex immediately."

He pressed a button and the secretary came in.

"Telex the head of the institute and tell him to reserve Leonid Pavlovich a private room starting . . . starting when, Leonid Pavlovich?"

"Wednesday? Or even Tuesday, if I can get a ticket . . .
        now crazy there night tomorrow evening her
. . . for tomorrow."

He went to bookkeeping and waited for his ticket money, then to the ticket office and waited for his ticket, then to the cafeteria and waited for his lunch. He started dialing Vera's number, but decided to dial Victor's instead, and when Victor didn't answer he went to the bank, made a sizable withdrawal, then bought a set of amber beads and earrings, a new electric razor, ten condoms, a notebook, some Koh-i-noor lead, and a mechanical pencil. Then he remembered he needed a shave and a haircut and flew off to his favorite barber in a tiny old-fashioned "shaving parlor" near the Shockworker Cinema.

"Well, look who's here! Long time no see. Late today, aren't you? I was about to close."

"I'm terribly sorry, Israel Markovich. I'm just back from holiday and off again tomorrow."

"That's some stubble you brought back with you. Head down. You like it straight, if I remember correctly. That reminds me of something that happened back when I was an apprentice in Odessa in 1926 I think it was, yes, during NEP—you *have* heard of the New Economic Policy, haven't you?—well, anyway, the master barber, who was still a young man, mind you . . ."

Israel Markovich strutted back and forth in the mirror behind a white cone sliced off at the apex and revealing the long neck and head of an actor running through his roles—Karl Moor, Romeo, Horatio, Iago—you're a cad of the first order if you don't get in touch with Aaron, though what will you say to him? What will he say? What will you say to *her?* "Yes, Israel Markovich, even for a place like Odessa that was a strange thing to happen." Smile. Go on, smile.

The actor in the mirror smiled unconvincingly.

Nikolsky did not get in touch with Aaron. It never quite worked out. He had so much to take care of that evening he couldn't get to the phone, and all he had time for the next morning on the way to the airport was a hasty telegram to Vera: "RETURNED LATE YESTERDAY FLEW OUT URGENT BUSINESS TODAY GREETINGS LEONID."

How long was it—six months? no, five—since Nikolsky had found himself next to a spindly-legged scarecrow with a journal in his lap, its broad-margined pages like the fluttering pinions of a tundra bird shot out of the sky. "Go fleetly, do not stumble, hunted stag . . ."

After running through the poem—all the poems—in his mind, he wondered how his life would have been different had he . . . had he ended up sharing a room with Aaron without knowing he was a poet (he would have been disgusted by him); had he not invited

Aaron to the Refuge (he wouldn't have thought of marrying Vera); had he not been introduced to Danuta, had he not noticed her breasts when her blouse stretched taut over them, had he not dreamed of her in those humiliating dreams that come to a man who has abstained for too long (he would have gone on living as he'd lived before and the whole mushy *hope* thing would never have come up); and finally, had he not been involved with such incompetents at the green box (he'd be at the Refuge and his ears wouldn't be about to burst). They must be descending.

It was daylight saving time and still light when they set down. Nikolsky was lucky: he was able to hitch a ride from a green-box driver who had just let off an engineer at the airport and took him straight to the hotel.

Everything was just as he remembered it: the glass door to the restaurant on the left, the manager's counter on the right, a sullen cloakroom attendant under a row of nickel hooks at the entrance. The suffocating atmosphere that had engulfed him the moment he set foot on the gangway now entered his throat; he felt he was moving through a tightly packed bale of cotton whose fibers a swarm of the most repulsive flies had penetrated solely for the purpose of attacking his pupils and nostrils.

The cloakroom attendant hobbled over to the restaurant door and called out into the empty room, and a middle-aged woman appeared, glanced quickly at Nikolsky, and shuffled over to the counter.

"I'm from Moscow. I have a reservation for a private room."

"Yes, yes. It's all ready."

When he reached the alcove with the two armchairs, he realized it was the same two-room suite he and Aaron had shared. Of course. It was the only VIP room in the place. Same bed—he gave it a kick. Same couch—another kick. Same plates and glasses he and Aaron had put to such intensive use. After a glass of water Nikolsky set off down the corridor to find the fateful cubicle. He knocked. No one answered; the door was locked. He decided not to make inquiries for the time being and went back to his room, peeled off his clothes, and had a cold shower, singing gleefully all the while. It was Nikolsky's firm conviction that modern man belonged to himself only when in the shower or on the toilet. He made it a practice of referring to the latter as "the life preserver" and never tired of confounding his hosts with the question "Would you tell me where I might find your life preserver?"

Afterwards he lay down on the couch and would have slept through till morning if he hadn't been woken by the shower. Though annoyed with himself for forgetting to turn it off, he decided, now that he was up, to have something to eat. When he went to take care of the shower, however, he found the bathroom door locked from the inside. Only then did he notice a serene melody accompanying the sound of water. So there was another free spirit in the vicinity.

Suddenly he was wide awake. He noticed a key in the outer door. He tiptoed up, removed it—it was the same as his, only it had no number plate—and slid it into his pocket along with his own. Then, full of playful fantasies, he turned off the light in the main room and sat down to wait.

At last the water stopped, and after a few noises—a comb hitting against the enamel sink? a perfume bottle clicking against the glass shelf?—the door flew open in a streak of light, a body flashed before his eyes for a split second, and the light went out. He heard two confident steps in the direction of the door, a hand feeling for the key, a moment of indecision—maybe you put it in your bag—the click of a light switch, then endless rummaging through house keys, lipsticks, earrings, compact, handkerchief—why not just empty it onto the shelf?—a loud jangle as the contents came out, a few nervous scrapings as they moved on the shelf, another loud jangle as they went back in—now down on your knees to check the floor under the lock, that's it, and over to the bathroom floor, good girl—now up you go, right, and try the door once more, just to make sure, give it a yank, no, not too hard, you don't want a black-and-blue mark on your shin—now the only thing left is to broaden the search, which means the main room—even though you don't remember going in there—and at last you turn on the light.

Where had he seen her before? Why of course! The restaurant! What was her name? Galya! Galochka!

Meanwhile a pouting Galochka was scrutinizing the floor beneath her, one hand still on the light switch. Nikolsky, unable to hold back his laughter, let out a sputter. Galochka gave a start, looked up like a stalked beast, made a beeline for the hallway, and for want of anything better to do desperately jiggled the door handle.

"And where might you be off to, Galochka?" Nikolsky asked in a booming baritone, still trying not to laugh.

She turned to face him with a brief "Oh!" and although her legs were buckling she made a last-ditch—and rather lewd-looking—attempt to escape by bumping her hindquarters against the door.

"Good evening, Galochka. Don't tell me you're afraid! Afraid of an old acquaintance?"

She straightened up a little, and he noticed she was trembling.

"You mean you don't recognize me?"

"No. I mean, yes," she whispered and tried to smile.

"Fine," said Nikolsky cheerfully. "It's good to see you. Really."

"The key? Please?"

She was about to burst into tears, which was the last thing Nikolsky wanted.

"The key? Why, of course. Now where did I put it? Oh yes, the other room."

He turned as if to go and look for it, then turned back and said, "Come in! Come in! Take a load off your feet!"

By the time he had returned with the key in his hand, Galochka was perched on the edge of a chair, clutching her bag.

"Well, Galochka?" said Nikolsky, pulling up a chair for himself. "You see, I remember your name. Do you remember mine? Leonid. Leonid Nikolsky. Place of residence: Moscow. Wife: none. Children: none that I know of."

Galochka tilted her head back and, showing her gold tooth for the first time, laughed. She had forgotten about the key, which now lay on the table between them.

"When I think of you watching me poke around on the floor! I could die! And then, if they caught me here, they'd fire me on the spot!"

"*I* caught you here."

"Yes, but you're different. I remember you from the restaurant. Want me to tell you a secret? I always come up here for a shower after work. I live in one of those old wooden houses, and by the time you haul in the water and heat it up . . . You know, this is the only room in the place with hot water."

"But how did you get a key?"

"Promise you won't tell? I took the master to a friend of mine, a locksmith; he made me a duplicate!"

"Pretty clever. And nobody knows you come up here?"

"I had to let the Lithuanian girl in on it, but she won't tell."

"Who?" he asked, suspecting the answer.

"The Lithuanian girl. The one that Jew you were with comes to see. You know. Aaron? The tall funny-looking guy?"

"Oh, you mean Danuta," Nikolsky said at last. So the accent was Lithuanian, not Polish.

"That's right. The 'lost Lithuanian,' they call her."

"Why lost?"

"Gee, I thought everybody knew." She inhaled deeply, ready to launch into what Nikolsky feared would be a breathless, garbled version of the story.

"Wait a minute, Galochka. Tell me, are you free now? . . . You are? Well, I haven't had a thing to eat since Moscow. Think we can get some room service up here?"

"Sure. Just dial sixteen. They'll charge you an arm and a leg for it, though."

"Money is no object."

"What if they see us together?" she added, blushing more with pleasure than with shame.

"Don't worry. You can run and hide in the bathroom when they knock. I'll say I don't want to be disturbed."

"Ooh!" Galochka squealed with delight. "Let me tell you what to order, okay?"

"The sky's the limit!"

His plan was to use the dinner—the friendly ambiance of food, drink, and chitchat—to probe beneath the surface, learn as much as possible about Danuta, and Aaron and himself or, rather, *experience* what there was to learn from Galochka. But Galochka had other plans. Excited and exhausted after a day's work, she was soon giggly drunk, feeding "her little Lyonechka" with a spoon and going off into gales of laughter when she missed his mouth and hit his cheek or nose. Then all at once she jumped up, switched off the lights, and started smothering him with kisses.

At first she aroused no more than pity in him, paternal pity actually, because how old could she be? But she kept pushing herself on him, rubbing herself against him, and in the end she managed to drag him, stumbling over table and chairs, to the bed, where under the covers she let her hands roam nervously—touching, stroking, clasping, squeezing. As he returned her caresses, he became obsessed by the image of a man and a woman in that same bed and himself lying on the couch on the other side of the wall, and he said to himself, No, I'm not going to let this happen, and to Galochka, "You're a resourceful one, you are," and suddenly it was upon him, and he took her so wildly that she let out a long whoop of exultation when it was over. But it wasn't over, because he was making up for all the previous months and for a desire that had nothing to do with her, and long after her own desire was sated he made her pay and pay, pay against those other accounts. Afterwards she cried. She couldn't quite say why, but it had something to do with happiness.

All Nikolsky wanted was to sleep, sleep by himself, woman-free, but Galochka lit a cigarette and was soon whispering, sighing, breathing her life story to him. She was twenty-two. She had no father and a mother who slept around. She had a three-year-old daughter in a five-day nursery. She didn't love the girl's father—he had got her pregnant on the eve of his military service, and the doctors had scared her out of an abortion—but she didn't mind having the girl. There were plenty of men around, and she intended to get married eventually, but she wouldn't settle for a drunk, and the men who came to Siberia to work in construction were all drunks. They drank so hard they started beating their women *before* they married them. Lyonechka was different. Dear, sweet Lyonechka.

The next morning, or rather noon, there she was, fresh and resplendent in her white apron and white-lace crown, beaming at him with such goodwill that he could only respond in kind.

"Coming up for another shower tonight, Galochka?" he asked under his breath after she had taken his order.

"You mean I can?" she said with a gasp.

O Lord who hast created us. We crave so much and need so little. Galochka is radiant, Nikolsky calm. The prospect of a night of physical bliss is enough to make us scorn the rational. Is that what Thou expected of us? Well, that is our nature, O Father, and we thank Thee for it.

XV

ALTHOUGH Galochka talked a lot that evening, she kept pausing and staring at Nikolsky with lovesick eyes, and he was unable to steer her in the right direction. Then he had the idea of taking her for a walk. He asked her where people went. She pointed at the window and said, "To the steppe."

They left the hotel separately. After passing some sheds, straggly garden plots, and a fence, they suddenly felt the cool absinthe wind of the steppe on their faces. It seemed to bring Galochka back to normal, and soon she was going on about how her boss, a respectable married man, disappeared for an hour every day into the office of the hotel directress, a Party member and Workers Deputy married to the chief of police, and about all the stealing that went on in the kitchen—the cook had been caught red-handed and they'd taken up a collection to get him off the hook, but she'd been broke at the time because her daughter was ill and she'd had to take off a few days, and when she said she couldn't contribute they threatened to have her fired, and if it hadn't been for the lost Lithuanian, who lent her the money . . .

"Speaking of Danuta, when is she on duty? I have a message for her from Aaron. We're friends, you know."

Now that he had an entrée, he was determined to make the most of it. Guiding her with carefully calculated questions, objections, and exclamations, he was able to learn enough to keep him awake with a splitting headache and a feeling of self-disgust long after she had fallen into a sweet, peaceful sleep, exhausted from the pleasures of the flesh. Somewhere on the outskirts of town a dog was howling.

"Danuta's at home," she had begun in answer to his question. "Her sister died last week."

"She had a sister?"

"Yes, and God forgive me for saying so, but her death was a blessing."

"Why?"

"Because she was completely paralyzed, that's why!"

"I see. Has she any family? Mother, father?"

"No, no! Only your friend Aaron, who brought her here after she was lost."

"Oh, that's right. The 'lost Lithuanian.' Tell me, how did she get her nickname?"

"You mean your friend never told you her story?"

Little by little Nikolsky pieced together a picture so chilling he could scarcely absorb it. Galochka clearly took it as a matter of course.

Danuta had been "deported." When Nikolsky asked her what that meant exactly, Galochka clasped her hands and raised her eyes in wonder at the things these Muscovites were ignorant of. "You didn't know they sent droves of Lithuanians into exile?"

"Oh, that," said Nikolsky. He had in fact heard some vague reports about nationalities being shuffled about, but he hadn't remembered which ones they were, and he certainly didn't remember anything about the Lithuanians. He'd been to Lithuania. To Palanga, on the sea coast.

A few hundred kilometers from Zaalaisk there was an island of Lithuanian exiles. Danuta had lived there with her sister. One day when she was coming home from work, the neighbor's boy ran up to her and said that his grandmother had told him to tell her not to go home: a convict had lost her at cards. (Apparently convicts used people as stakes when they ran out of money, and if they lost, they were duty-bound to kill them. She said not to worry about her sister, they would take care of her, but Danuta had to leave town.

The convicts were exiles too, but Russians, and they'd been deported for criminal acts, not political ones—in other words, they were dangerous. So Danuta ran to the station and jumped a freight train and rode it for a day until it came to a fairly big station and they broke it up. By that time she was half frozen and had no money or papers of any kind.

"Couldn't she have gone to the police?"

"Are you crazy? An exile? They'd have sent her back lickety-split, and those crooks would have torn her limb from limb! She doesn't know how long she spent in that station. Two or three days.

To keep from looking suspicious, she would walk into town, sit a few hours in the post office or cafeteria, then rush back each time a passenger train was due in to plead with the conductor to let her on. But all she got was the cold shoulder or a filthy mouth. Where would she have gone to, anyway?"

"How did she survive, then?"

"I told you. Aaron saved her."

"But what was he doing there?"

"How should I know? She never says a thing about him. She doesn't really know what happened herself. She kind of . . . fell. That's it. She was in town and she fell and he saw her. Yes, and there was something about a plane, the plane he brought her here on."

In the end Nikolsky managed to determine that weather conditions had forced Aaron's plane from Vladivostok to make an emergency landing near the town, and while he was stuck there he happened to see Danuta faint in the street. He took her to his hotel room, and given his complete and utter helplessness in practical matters it was a miracle he succeeded in reviving her. But having taken on the role of savior, he played it to the hilt, and when the plane was ready to take off he bought her a ticket and brought her with him to Zaalaisk.

"Why Zaalaisk of all places?"

" 'Cause this is the district she's registered in. She can't live outside the district. Or her sister, for that matter. She had to think of her sister, after all."

"You mean her sister came too?"

"Her sister couldn't come, stupid! Don't you remember? Her sister was paralyzed. No, Aaron went and brought her here. Had to fly again. You can't get there by train. The stories he told! The convicts slit the guy's throat, the guy who lost Danya at cards. Then they shoved him feet first through Danya's window. Why? Because he didn't kill her, of course. Only he didn't go in all the way, and the next morning there he was, his head hanging out, upside down, all blue-like, with a pool of blood on the ground below. Pretty creepy, eh?"

How's that for local color! Oh, the terrors Danuta would have gone through before the hoodlum's knife finished her off. Nikolsky shivered as he pictured a gorilla-like band swarming over Danuta, screaming and howling, mauling, molesting, smothering . . .

He awoke in a sweat, leaped out of bed, raced back and forth between the two rooms until he found some disgusting vodka to put out the fire. Climbing back in, he inadvertently brushed against Galochka's thigh, and immediately she was up and whispering, "Want to do it again, Lyonya? Want to do it again?" But he told her to go back to sleep, and she returned to her dreams as if she'd never left them. He slept fitfully until sunrise, afraid that Galochka would slip away, as she had the last time. He needed her; he needed her to tell him where Danuta lived.

As soon as he got the information out of her, he left for the green box, where he spent the morning. At lunchtime he drank a glass of soda water in the street, then found a place for himself on one of the few benches in the sorry little park opposite the front gate. For a while he watched the workers chew on their newspaper-wrapped sandwiches, play dominos on the dusty grass, and peel off their shirts to the merciless sun, but his nervous, almost nauseous excitement soon got the better of him, and he set off with the presentiment he was about to be swept away by events that had long been moving in a predetermined direction and were now ready to merge into something vitally important. Then he laughed. How ridiculous! Why *that* presentiment and not one of things happening with no discernible reason, no cause and effect, rolling together into one gigantic unravelable, uncleavable ball with him in the center forever and ever, world without end. Amen.

The old lopsided peasant hut in which Danuta had rented a room had a padlock hanging on the door. In the neighboring courtyard an old woman was scattering feed to a flock of chickens, calling, "Here chicky chicky chicky chick!" as she stared at Nikolsky.

"Anybody at home next door?" Nikolsky shouted, walking up to the rusty fence that surrounded the courtyard.

"Here chicky chicky!" the woman called, turning over the feed bowl and shaking it. "Polina's gone to see her son. In Irkutsk."

"I was wondering about her tenant, actually. Danuta."

"Oh. Her sister died last week, may she rest in peace, though she wasn't one of us."

The woman crossed herself slowly.

"What do you want with her?"

"I'm a friend. From Moscow."

"What about the other one? The Jew."

"Aaron. We're friends too."

"Is he with you?"

"No, his boss wouldn't let him come."

"Hm." She paused. "She can't stay here. They'll get her. They're all after her. It'll be worse now, with her sister gone. Danya, I told her when she came here, Danya, I said, you sleep in the bed with your sister. They'll be scared to do their dirty work in bed with a paralytic. You should have seen how they fixed that Jew, the bastards! She can't stay here."

She started off, then turned and said, "She's at the District Council. Probably be back for lunch. You can wait in my kitchen if you want."

"Thanks. I'll wait here."

He sat in the shade of the hut, feeling more and more nauseated, the effect of a bad night, warm soda water on an empty stomach, and a growing store of pent-up anger. He pressed his temples with a groan and let out a stream of noxious curses, then shook his head violently and ran his fingers through the dirt. Feeling slightly less queasy, he stood up, leaned back against the wall, and closed his eyes. When he opened them, there was Danuta, standing at the other end of the hut with a puzzled look on her face.

"That's him," he heard the old woman say. "Didn't want to come in. Well, I'll be off."

"Do you recognize me?" Nikolsky asked.

"*Jèzus Marija!*" she said with a quivering voice. "How glad I am to . . . How did you know I . . ."

Her hands were clasped. He took them with a purity he did not know he had in him and pressed them to his lips. It was a moment free of the flesh, a moment of unadulterated feeling.

"I'm sorry. Please come in."

They went into the house. It had low ceilings, a whitewashed Russian stove, a round oilcloth-covered table, and a window graced by a plant with pale pink blossoms and covered by a curtain with a flounce running along the bottom. They sat down at the table, and

Danuta said, "You've heard, I imagine . . . about Ruta, my sister. . . ."

She paused, on the verge of tears, and asked his forgiveness with the trace of a smile.

"Yes, Danuta," he said. It was the first time he had called her by her name, and he felt it brought him immeasurably closer to her. "But now it's time to think of yourself. Have you anyone . . . is there anyone besides your sister? Besides Ruta." It was important for him to say her name too.

"No one."

"Not even in Lithuania?"

She shook her head.

"Could you really have lost everyone? When did you leave?"

"Lithuania? It was . . . they took us away in 'forty-one. A whole life ago. I as still a baby."

All at once she laughed.

"The only person I remember from there is the *kunigas*."

"The who?"

"The priest. We were in one of those freight trains they deport people in, you know? We'd just gone through the station after Vilnius—have you ever been to Vilnius?"

"No, I haven't."

"Well, all I remember is a wall and our hair blowing in the wind—I liked that. But then all the women began to cry and stretch their arms out of the window. 'Look, Danuta! Never forget this!' And I looked and I saw a *kalnas*—oh, sorry! a hill, a little hill—it's very hilly there. And there on the hill stood a man dressed in black. The *kunigas*. And he held a large cross in one hand, held it high over his head. And with the other, this one, his right hand, he—oh, suddenly I'm forgetting all my Russian!" She made a sign with her hand going first up and down, then from side to side.

"He blessed you!"

"He blessed us. I was terrified of him. He had long hair, down to his shoulders. It was blowing in the wind like ours."

Nikolsky stood abruptly, and the stool he had been sitting on made a loud scraping noise.

"The bastards!" he shouted, starting to pace. "Sorry for the language, Danuta, but I mean, rounding you up like sheep, women and children, and packing you off! And you had no idea where they were taking you, right? No, of course you hadn't. What a thing to ask! And then the priest, who saw you as *his* sheep, his flock! Blessing you, though he knew what they'd do to him! It was all symbolic, if I understand it correctly. He is given . . . His flock comes . . . from God. And he must tend his flock, go where it goes. No, you won't find him when you go back! I bet they took care of him then and there, on the spot."

"What was that you said? When I go back?"

Nikolsky stopped in front of her.

"You're not staying here, are you?"

She hung her head and retreated into herself. He sat down again in silence. If the table had been smaller, if he had sat closer to her, if he had dared, he would have taken her hand. He took her hand mentally and began talking with an animation he had rarely experienced, and he realized that the cold, calculating reason he had always trusted was giving way to something sounder, keener, and he let it take over his words and his deeds, both reveling in its power and fearing it.

He told Danuta she had to leave this place, leave it no matter what. She said she had lived only for her sister, her sister was her life, her sister had brought her up, she was a saint; she was as happy with her when she was ailing as she had been when she was well, and looked upon her sister's illness as simple, natural, inevitable, never felt it a burden; they had lived for each other, shared a common fate.

"Yes, but banal as it sounds, life goes on."

"Well, not for me."

"But life is holy! Holy, don't you see?"

"Maybe, but when we were in the boat on the Arctic Sea and we thought it was taking us to freedom, to America, the people who died of dysentery were tossed overboard. And later, when we settled at the mouth of the Yana, the bodies of the dead were propped up outside the yurts, and even though the dogs weren't supposed to eat them, they did. . . . But why am I telling you this?"

"Because I said life is holy."

"Oh yes. I don't agree. Life just is. It as holy when I had Mother, it was holy when I had Ruta, but now . . ."

"May I ask you a question, Danuta? Do you believe in God?"

"I believed while I prayed to Him to save my Ruta, but I'm not so sure anymore. When He turns His back on you, He ceases to exist."

"But He can turn to you again and give you strength."

"I can't live alone with God."

"But what about . . . you know who I mean."

"Yes, Aaron. He's a fine man; he's been a brother to me. But it's been hard for him having me here and a wife and children in Moscow. You've seen his daughters, haven't you? They're good girls, aren't they? And I don't want to cause him more grief. I live without him now and I'll go on living without him. Will you have some tea?"

She put the teapot on the hot plate, and the water was soon boiling. While the tea brewed, she put some biscuits in a saucer, and when the tea was ready, she poured it into large bowls. They drank in silence, Danuta sipping hers, Nikolsky gulping his down avidly, asking for a second, then a third bowl. His head was awhirl with all the fortuitous—or not so fortuitous—events drawing him in, walling him in, with all the names and places rising and falling in his consciousness: Danuta—Moscow—Zaalaisk—Aaron—Vera— the Refuge—Leopold Mikhailovich—Aaron—Frida—Moscow— Lithuania—Zaalaisk—Aaron—Vera—Danuta—Zaalaisk—and— Galochka—oh!—Danuta, Danuta, Moscow!

He put down his bowl and looked Danuta straight in the eye. She had a large tea leaf on her lower lip, and he wanted nothing more than to brush it off with his finger, no, with his tongue, and coddle it against his cheek. Only after a deep breath could he steady his voice enough to say, "Come with me then. I'll take you away from here."

At first she seemed not to have heard him.

"No," she said at last. "Thank you, Leonid." Her diffident smile returned, accompanied by tears. "But there's no point in even talking about it. I'm a deportee. I can't—"

"Sorry to interrupt, but let's begin at the beginning, shall we? Your residence permit, is it temporary or permanent? See what I have in mind? Facts. Cold, hard facts."

Behind every answer he could feel her "what's the use," "what's the point," her certainty that all his talk about things she had thought through many times over would get them nowhere, but he pushed on, phrasing his questions in such a way that she could answer only yes or no. Gradually he learned where deportees were permitted to live, how they managed to move from one place to another, why not all Lithuanian deportees had returned to Lithuania, what sort of a reception they could expect when they returned, and gradually it became clear that the life of a deportee, much like the life of an ordinary citizen, centered on two elements: residence permit and work permit.

The two were inextricably connected. You were eligible for a new residence permit only if you were officially employed in the new place of residence; you were eligible for official employment in a new place of residence only if you had the requisite residence permit. For deportees this vicious circle was complicated by the sometimes hidden, sometimes open opposition by authorities to the idea of ending a Siberian exile. Granted, the opposition had eased somewhat in the post-Stalin years, but what if, like many Lithuanians, they had long since lost their homes and perhaps families and friends as well? Hard as life was in exile, they had somehow made a go of it, begun to belong. Where would Danuta go? Who would take her in, find her work, register her?

"There's only one way out," said Nikolsky, and when he saw her about to retreat into herself again his voice grew firmer. "You must marry me, Danuta."

He knew what would happen when he said the words "marry me," though a moment earlier he had not known he was going to say them; he knew her eyes would fill with fear and her throat with a tortured "What?" It was all starting to seem inevitable, predestined.

The ensuing dialogue—"How could you think I would do such a thing?" "You have no choice"—would have gone on and on had he not cut it short with a diatribe aimed at either himself or her or Aaron. He couldn't be sure which.

"It's all a terrible embarrassment, I know! You're a fine woman, a pure woman, and you can be certain I will treat you as such. I promise not to touch you. I won't even hold your arm as we climb

into the plane. I swear I won't! It will be a purely fictitious marriage,
a piece of paper, a rubber stamp to spring you from this grave!"

The word "grave" sent her into fresh tears of mourning.

"How stupid of me! I'm sorry, Danuta! Forgive me! Forgive me,
please!" He paused to catch his breath. "Once you're in Moscow,
once you're out of this place"—and he looked out of the window
at the chaos of blind, burning shadows along the dusty steppe—
"you can live as you please. You can take a trip to Lithuania, see
what it's like, come back to Moscow if it doesn't work out. But if
you stay here . . ." Suddenly he all but screamed at her, "Look, you
barely got away with your life the last time! Do you want to hand
it to them on a silver platter?"

By now she was racked with sobs, and while stroking and kissing
her wildly in his fantasy he tore at his stomach, liver, intestines to
keep from touching her, hugging her, *crossing the boundary!*

'I'm sorry. Will you . . . will you come back tomorrow? Tomorrow, *gerai?* All right?"

"Yes, yes," he said, grasping desperately at her "all right." "Forgive me, Danuta, but everything will work out in the end. I'll leave
you now, but tomorrow morning, all right?"

He had no idea how he made his way back to the hotel. The next
time he was aware of himself he was stretched out in his bed, staring
dully at the ceiling, a swarm of lazy, end-of-the-day flies hovering
just above his face. Had he been told that remaining in that position
meant certain death, he could not have budged. Not until much
later, when it was completely dark, did he attempt to lower his
enormously heavy eyelids over their empty globes. Nor did he raise
them again until he felt himself emerging from the abyss in which
he had been submerged, felt Galochka taking off his shoes and socks,
unbuttoning his shirt, and then, to remove the shirt from his trousers, unbuckling his belt, her fingers trembling as she touched his
bare stomach and then caressing him there and beneath the clothes
he still had on. And he thought, Thank God he was still a man,
thank God she meant nothing to him, this woman, thank God their
fleshly, beastly, bawdy games required no burning, chaste, or other
brand of love, and all he had to do was take her on him, under him,
in front and behind, to breathe, scream, press, squeeze all this out
of him. Which he did.

Gazing the next morning at her pointy breasts as she sat cross-legged and naked before him, he said, "I have something to tell you."

"Shoot."

"But first promise you won't tell a soul."

"No go!"

"What do you mean?"

"When I say no go, I mean no go! I'll tell whoever I feel like. So there!" And she made a face at him.

"How about this, then? Promise you won't say anything till I leave."

She detected the hint of a threat in his voice and answered, half curious, half alarmed, "All right, I swear." And with the instinctive rapidity that comes of learning something as a child, she made the sign of the cross over her naked body.

He *had* to let her in on his plans for Danuta. If Galochka heard through the grapevine that her brand-new Moscow lover was tying the knot, she might cause a scandal. So he told her he'd phoned Aaron about Danuta's sister and Aaron had asked him to do him a big favor and go through the motions of a marriage so Danuta could move to Moscow. It wouldn't last long. Divorces were simple. He knew. He'd been through one.

He looked up at her with a nervous laugh. Her hands were pressed to her cheeks, and she was staring at him with shining eyes.

"Well, well!" she said. "Ooo-hoo! The things you men come up with." Then she looked away. "That Danuta's a lucky duck! Why her and not me? I know why! I've got a kid and an alcoholic mother, that's why. And, well"—she glanced down at her body—"I'm not as pretty as her. But you should see me in the kitchen!" She tried to laugh.

Nikolsky felt sorry for her, but he was relieved things were moving in the right direction. He reached out to put his arm around her, but she shied and jumped off the bed.

"What's done is done," she said, her lips trembling. "What happens now?"

"Don't be silly, Galochka! I told you. It's all on paper! It's got nothing to do with reality."

"We'll see when you come back," she said, turning away, as if suddenly bothered by her nakedness, and started throwing on her clothes. "*If* you come back."

He stood up, washed, and dressed quickly, then dialed the operator and asked for Moscow. It was five in the morning, in other words, midnight in Moscow, and he was quite certain to reach his neighbor, a dentist who did a lot of moonlighting and always had plenty of cash on hand. The call went through, and annoyed as the dentist was at being woken he agreed to wire Nikolsky two hundred rubles. Galochka said goodbye by kissing him on the cheek as he shaved.

After a quick trip to the institute to say he would be away all day, he ran off to Danuta's. The dark circles around her eyes and the reproach (or submission or prayer) in them told him before she said a word that she would put up no more resistance. He decided he would best spare her feelings by resorting to his businesslike stance again, and started with the pettiest matter: her possessions. Danuta smiled sadly. The furniture belonged to her landlady. Dishes? She would give them to the woman next door. All she had was her clothes and a few keepsakes from her mother and sister. In other words, enough for two or three suitcases. Fine, he would buy her the suitcases. What about her job? She would write a letter of resignation. "I hereby request to be released from my obligations . . ." He would talk to the directress himself. What else? The registry office, the police. We'll do those together. Oh, I know. You probably owe your landlady some rent. How much? . . . Here, go and ask the woman next door to give it to her when she comes back. . . . Don't be silly. Don't even think about it. Really. . . . Now you start getting things ready to be packed, and I'll deliver the letter of resignation and find out about the rest of the formalities. You can expect me back by noon. No, later. I want to go out to the airport and see about our tickets.

Things started off smoothly enough with the "Russian Venus" of a hotel directress. He immediately fell into the cock-of-the-walk pose he could see she expected of him. But not even the suggestive squeeze he gave her hand sufficed to avert a frown when he made it clear that the man who was whisking her Danuta off was none other than himself. So he had to go into a song and a dance about how he couldn't get a flat of his own unless there were two people officially registered for it.

"And a friend of mine—oh, of course, you know him, the one who brought her here—"

"You mean the Jew?"

"That's right. Well, he was the one who put me up to it. . . . You know, that's an exquisite wool your sweater's made of."

"Really, you should watch your hands."

"And I have just the thing that would set it off. It's just up in my room. Don't go away now!"

What a waste! he thought. But I can buy Danuta another one back in Moscow.

"There! See how beautiful it looks on you! Real amber!"

"I don't see how I can accept it, though I don't see how I can bring myself not to. You're a lucky find for our lost Lithuanian. Now let's see, what date shall I put?"

"Well, I am in a bit of a rush. It depends on what the police require."

"Oh, that's no problem. Know who my hubby is?"

"No, who?"

"The chief of police!"

"No! You're an angel!"

"Hello, Grisha? It's me. Look, there's a man by the name of Nikolsky, Leonid Pavlovich Nikolsky, coming to see you. Got it down? . . . Tell Lyuska to show him right in, and do whatever he asks, all right? . . . He'll tell you himself. By the way, are you coming home for lunch? . . . Fine. Bye."

"I don't know how to thank you!"

"It was nothing. Will you be back this way again soon?"

"Oh, yes."

"Well, just send me a little wire, and you'll get personal treatment, I assure you."

The hotel directress's husband turned out to be a malicious little bastard, but to give him his due he managed to have everything signed, sealed, and delivered by the end of the day. Then Nikolsky got the two engineers he had worked with to give him a few hours, and they finished what needed finishing in plenty of time for him to meet Danuta in front of the registry office at the appointed hour. Just as they were coming down the creaky wooden steps, who should run up to them but Galochka. Nikolsky could smell the vodka on her breath. With a strange smile she thrust a few hollyhocks at Danuta, and when Danuta began to thank her she darted off to the side and cut her off by yelling, "I slept with him, you hear? I slept with him three nights in a row!" And she ran off.

"The little fool! She came up to the room to use the shower!" At that moment he really thought there had been nothing between them. Danuta made no reply.

That evening they flew to Moscow.

PART THREE

His life could have been perfectly pleasant, but he had the misfortune to write and publish poetry.

—*ALEXANDER PUSHKIN,*
Egyptian Nights

I

TWO OLD MEN were playing chess on a Nativity Boulevard bench. A third man stood behind them looking on. He had an unobstructed view of the board, the straw hat of one of the players, and a newspaper with a banner headline reading SPEECH BY NIKITA KHRUSHCHEV, which the second player was using for the same purpose as the first player his hat.

"Let's ask the young man," came a voice from under Khrushchev's speech, and the newsprint tilted to reveal a gray, stubble-covered chin, two hairy nostrils, and a pair of tortoise-skin eyelids rolling up over sclerotic corneas. "Does the rook castle under fire?

Aaron-Chaim Mendelevich Finkelmeyer shrugged his shoulders and said, "What a question!"

With that, the bright-yellow circle of straw began twisting and turning, and although the player beneath it kept his eyes on the board—it was his turn—a thoughtful, melodious voice purred, "So you're an expert, eh?"

"What a question!" Finkelmeyer repeated with great authority.

One Jew, or so the old joke goes, is a pushcart, two Jews a chess game, three Jews a symphony orchestra. As Finkelmeyer felt no music welling up out of the encounter, he decided to move on and give the joke another crack at reality.

He moved on in the direction of Trubnaya Square, conscious of every step. He also needed to be conscious of carrying a briefcase in one hand, because otherwise it listed dangerously groundward and he had to increase the pressure under his arm and inch it forward. At the square he turned left past the tram tracks and crossed Neglinka. By the time he realized he had made a mistake, the light had changed and a stream of cars was rushing by, and he stopped to examine the pattern on a glazed sign outside an Uzbek restaurant. Just then a fat Uzbek wearing a prewar service jacket, jodhpurs, boots, and a skullcap came through the door.

"Ha?" said the Uzbek to Finkelmeyer, pointing to the sign. "Good!"

"Yes, very good," said Aaron in broken English, and translated it into broken Russian.

"Oh! Oh!" said the Uzbek, rolling his eyes. "American, yes? Peace! Peace and friendship!" Then he beat a fast retreat. ("Peaceful coexistence" had been shot down together with the U-2 spy plane that spring, and Americans were once more to be feared.)

He proceeded to Rakhmanovsky, waited while a row of ailing trolley buses passed like a herd of cows, and finally retraced his steps across Neglinka to his immediate destination: the savings bank.

A. M. Finkelmeyer was not an important customer. He pulled a spanking new bank book out of the briefcase, opened it, and slipped it under the window. The girl behind the window divided her scorn in two equal portions: the first for the bank book, the second for its owner.

"Hey, there's only one ruble in this account. You want to make a withdrawal?"

"No, no! I was told I had a transfer waiting."

"Well, why didn't you say so!"

The girl starting twirling her roll file, and when she came to the account of A. M. Finkelmeyer she turned to the customer as though the card contained a complete course in etiquette.

"I see! Yes, you do have a transfer! Quite a sum too. That's a big publishing house, isn't it? I'll enter it into your book, and if you wish make a withdrawal, all you have to do is—"

"Oh, I won't be making a withdrawal. I only need to know how much it is." He was in a good mood, and decided to tease the girl a little to get back at her. "You enter the amount. I just want to look at you."

Uncertain of how to respond, the girl grabbed her pen and started writing assiduously.

Aaron took a trolley bus to Pushkin Square, where he circled the statue of the poet, thinking of his favorite line: "There is no joy on earth but only peace and freedom." The statue always looked aloof to him and far from free.

He sat down on a bench and watched a little girl in yellow underpants and a big white bow prancing up and down near the fountain. He listened to her shriek whenever a drop of the spray landed on her; he listened to her grandmother puff after her, threatening her with a cold; he listened to the tires whiz and whistle past. And everything came together and resounded and broke up into short voiceless sounds and long-drawn-out-voiced ones and teamed up with deep, round vowels and formed prefixes and suffixes, participles and gerunds. One poem more, one poem less, Aaron thought sardonically, but in the end he gave in to the sounds, the sounds in his head, because he loved how they engulfed him and turned into rhythms and rhymes, odd even, odd even, Ira, Irina come back here this instant, the pigeons, the cooing, the sun beating down on the fountain, down on my head, head of the section or head of the ministry . . .

At this point Finkelmeyer's fate took another turn for the absurd. He removed a blank sheet of paper from his briefcase and wrote:

To: Head of the Economic Section

From: Senior Inspector A. M. Finkelmeyer

This is to inform you that I shall be leaving my post for personal reasons.

He decided to not to date the letter. He would wait until they told him when was best for them. Though, of course, the sooner the better.

Then he took out another blank sheet and wrote the word "Income" and the sum the girl in the bank had entered in his bank book. It looked different on the virginal sheet, indecently large, perhaps because its first digit was round and paunchy, not the dry stick he was used to when signed for his monthly pay packet. But he couldn't tell what it actually meant to him—much and little are relative concepts—until he had worked his way through a series of complex calculations.

The paper was soon full. Columns of figures alternated with columns of letters indicating the months from August to August (ASONDJFMAMJJA). Also dotting the paper liberally were the abbreviations *Fr, Fa,* and *Aa:* Frida, Father, and Aaron. He was trying to stretch the amount as long as possible—to the second M or maybe even the third A—while allotting Fr and Fa their due.

The longer he worked on the accounts, the more confused he

became. He'd never last a year, and even eight months seemed doubtful; he'd either have to settle for six or augment what he had by earning a little something on the side. But if what he really wanted was to be off on his own, he couldn't bother about outside income. No, it was all or nothing.

Aaron sighted Nikolsky, who had approached the statue from behind, before Nikolsky sighted him.

"Look at him!" Aaron exclaimed as they shook hands. "Slim, tan, muscles aripple! Doesn't help my complexes, let me tell you. I've been in nature too, and look at me: the picture of urban pale!"

"Look," Nikolsky interrupted, frowning as if he had a tooth-ache, "could we find a nice cool place to have a beer?"

"Beer, beer! Three cheers for beer!" Finkelmeyer squealed like a child. "But the only bar near here has gone from beer to milk."

Nikolsky took him by the elbow and turned him in the opposite direction. As they walked, Finkelmeyer thought that even the bags under his eyes added to his charm: wine, women, brawls, duels.

"No," he said with a sigh, "you're out of your element."

"What was that?"

"You weren't made for Moscow beer or even Moscow vodka; you were made for burgundy, claret, and . . ."

"Hemlock."

Lyonya was definitely not himself today.

By then they had reached the cinema behind the statue. Nikolsky went up to the cashier, who turned and shouted, "Hey, Shura! Got any beer today?"

As soon as the answer came back, Nikolsky bought two tickets, and in no time they were sitting in the empty snack bar, taking long slow drafts of the bitter liquid from ice-cold glasses.

Aaron was in bliss. Having quenched his initial thirst, he threw open his briefcase and with the theatricality of a fakir produced his bank book.

"Take a gander and turn green!"

Then he handed Nikolsky the letter of resignation.

As Nikolsky glanced at one, then the other, Aaron observed something he had never seen before on his face: a preoccupied, even frightened look. His spirits immediately plummeted, and everything lurking just beneath the surface—the misery, the fatigue, the uncer-

tainty in himself and in life, and the certainty that events occur of
their own volition and cannot be altered—came out in his voice: "I
haven't told anybody yet . . . about your place, I mean. So if you've
changed your . . . It was a silly idea to begin with, a whim, really . . .
I just thought . . ."

Aaron stopped short when Nikolsky lifted his head. they looked
each other in the eye.

"I . . . Forget it, Aaron. It . . . it doesn't matter. I . . . I've . . .
Danuta's here."

He didn't understand at first. Then he did. Then he didn't. And
did and didn't.

"And . . . you brought her here."

Suddenly that other man's face was full of self-assurance again.
His fingers dug into the man's wrist.

"You? You?"

"Yes. Let go of my hand."

"You?"

"Look, I've asked you to forgive me, haven't I?" Nikolsky snapped
and jerked his hand free. A glass toppled over.

"Take it easy there!" the waitress shouted from behind the counter.

Aaron was shaking. "Let's get out of here," he said.

"Nothing doing, Aaron my boy," said Nikolsky with forced lev-
ity. "I paid for this beer and I'm going to drink it. I advise you to
do the same. I also advise you to hear me out. We can bash each
other's heads in later."

Nikolsky went over to the counter and returned with a rag. He
wiped away the puddle of beer, took the rag back to the counter,
returned to the table, wiped his hands with his handkerchief, sat
down, picked up the glass that had fallen, and poured out the rest
of the beer.

Finkelmeyer watched him, trying to decide whether what he felt
for the man was hatred or the hostility a younger brother feels for
an elder one, a hostility born of affection.

He cared for him deeply.

He saw his difficult side.

He understood his complexity.

Nikolsky spoke in a businesslike monotone, looking off to the side, as if he had written his speech out beforehand and were simply reeling it off: Galochka told me that her sister . . . I went to see her and she said . . . And I thought the only way out was . . . Of course she put up a fuss, but . . . And when I went back the next morning, she . . .

"You could have let me know," said Finkelmeyer softly.

"What good would that have done? Think of the agony it would have caused you. You might even have dropped everything and flown out there. Look, tell me, was I right to pull her out of that place? Yes or no!"

"Yes." Finkelmeyer nodded wearily.

"Could you have done it? Could you have arranged for a divorce? On the spot? From one day to the next? Well?"

"Don't push me to the wall," Finkelmeyer pleaded. He was weak, Nikolsky strong; he was ashamed.

"It's the farthest thing from my mind," Nikolsky said, trying to sound affectionate. "Look, I . . . it's ridiculous for me even to . . . to put this into words, but . . . well, I . . . haven't touched her." He squeezed his fingers together as if to cross himself. "There, I've said it. And I won't touch her, either. She's . . . too good for me. So you can rest easy on that account. The first thing to do is get her a residence permit. That's my job. I have the papers. Then you take over. Whatever the two of you decide is fine with me. I'm willing to start divorce proceedings at any time."

"She'll go to Lithuania."

"That's your business. I can give the place to you, I can give it to her, you can live there together."

"Where will you live?"

"At Vera's."

Finkelmeyer, who still felt weak, looked over at a man only slightly less weak than he.

"The problem is . . ." he began, taking a deep breath.

"Leopold Mikhailovich?"

"Right," he said, exhaling all at once.

"Maybe it's all for the best," said Nikolsky, "though I seem to have developed a talent for being late." He gave a sardonic laugh. He had buried his hopes. He saw a deep pit, no, two, and a pair of jolly gravediggers shouting Allez-oop! and again Allez-oop! and shoveling the dirt in, their blood-curdling curses mingling with the heart-rending female screams rising out of the coffins. "Why has everyone without regard to sex, age, and national origins a right to love and the quiet joys—everyone but me?"

"And me," said Aaron, ready to embrace, embolden, enhearten this poor specimen, now every bit as weak as he.

"Stop sniveling, you bastard. You've got Danuta, haven't you? I've delivered her to you, haven't I?"

"Not to me."

"What?"

"She'll be gone soon. Her wings will heal and—"

"—she'll fly off into the sunset, is that it? What you need is a divorce."

"No. Out of the question."

"You're an idiot." Nikolsky sighed. A sigh of relief, perhaps. Perhaps a phantom of hope still haunted the graveyard. "Here's the key," he said, tossing it over to Aaron. "She's got her own."

"What about you?"

"I've told you. I'll move in with my fairy-tale aunt. I'm all she has left. Her son's climbed so high he can't see his mother for the clouds."

"Look, take the key back."

"You don't want to live with her, you moron?"

"Of course I do, of course I do. But . . ."

"But you want *her* to open the door, is that it? Fine. But take the key just in case. Just so I don't have it."

"You know what I thought when I heard your voice on the phone?" said Aaron picking up the key and turning it this way and that. "I thought, Even if his aunt is just a fiction, I can still go and live there. I remembered what you'd said in the park about Vera, but I knew that was out because of Leopold Mikhailovich. So I thought, We'll be roommates. You'll go off in the morning, and I'll have the place to myself all day."

"Well, now you can live with her, dammit! And you'll still have the freedom you need. Come on, let's go! I'll take you there!" So saying, he burst into a song he had picked up on his canoe trip: "If you haven't got an auntie . . ."

"Take it easy there!" the waitress called out again.

But Nikolsky was past caring, and as they made their way to the exit he sang it at the top of his lungs:

> "If you haven't got an auntie,
> You won't have an auntie to lose!
> If you haven't got a doggy,
> Your neighbor won't poison its food!
> If you haven't got a wifey,
> Your wifey won't cheat you and lie!
> If you haven't got a lifey,
> You won't have to lie down and die!"

"Listen to them, will you!" they heard the waitress call to the usher. "After one beer!"

II

NOW THAT Danuta was in Moscow, Finkelmeyer's life was more complicated than ever, and he postponed handing in the letter of resignation until he could mull over the situation.

One factor he no longer had to take into account, of course, was how to get to Zaalaisk. He had planned to go once or twice on his own money and then find a publishing house to send him for consultations with the first Tongor poet. But how would his relationship with Danuta develop now that Nikolsky had brought her to Moscow, now that he could see her every day? There was another issue as well: had he any claim on her love?

By bringing Danuta and her sister to Zaalaisk, by saving them from certain death, he became her friend, brother, and in the end, her man, that is, the man every woman in those parts required to keep other men from grabbing at her blouse or stomping across her threshold. Not that they didn't go on grabbing and stomping. One day Aaron clashed with a pair of them, and as they were about to toss him, half dead, into a ditch, he managed to grab a piece of lead piping and strike out at them with a last bit of fury. He was rewarded for his pains. After three days in agony on Danuta's couch, he nestled up to her and stayed the night. And should not the lonely, the unfortunate, and their saviors come together in that higher expression of gratitude known as love?

Yet what did it all mean in Moscow? First, there was his family, and Aaron knew that Danuta would be burdened by the thought of its proximity. And then, what would she be here? His mistress, pure and simple, receiving him in Nikolsky's apartment, no, *her* apartment, because, no matter how fictitious their marriage was, she was Nikolsky's wife. What is more, he was clearly in love with her. True, he behaved with perfect nobility, but how long would he keep it up? How long would it be before, calculatedly or not, he took advantage of his own flat, the stamp in his papers, a poor girl's helplessness, and —let's face it—his brute masculine appeal to have his way with her?

The whole thing was so ambiguous. Ambiguous and trite. How could he turn his back on Frida and girls? All he wanted was a little peace and quiet, a bit of relief from his everyday worries which, though different at home and at work, had the same depressing effect of stymieing him, making him unsure of himself, forcing him to wonder whether he wasn't defective in some way, even a mental case. If he could somehow find release from this hopeless situation, then he would love his children, care for them without the nagging feeling of dependence and guilt he now felt, then Frida would stop torturing him as she did every evening when faced with his misery. So far so good. But there was something every bit as important and even more complicated at stake: his verse.

Aaron had long felt something important ripening within him, something ready to emerge, like a creature from a womb, and in some instinctive way he was seeking a corner to crawl into so as to give birth to it, lick it, feed it, and rest. For a while everything seemed to be coming together: he had the money from the book, he had Nikolsky's place—and then this had to happen.

Nikolsky took him home, and she shook hands with him and kissed him on the forehead as she always did. The three of them had a meal together, and then Nikolsky said he was going into the hall to work on his canoe. A few seconds later they heard the lock click, and Aaron ran out to find a note that said: "Gone to Auntie's. Will phone tomorrow evening." Aaron went up to Danuta and put his arms around her, and everything was as it had been except that he had to make sure to catch the last train to the country, where

Frida was waiting for him, and he had to keep asking himself why they were where they were and where they were going.

In other words, nothing was as it had been. All Aaron knew or, rather, felt was that he should not stay on with Danuta. What he needed at that point was not her warmth but cold solitude; even if it gave him pneumonia, he needed the tart taste of freedom.

Aaron finally poured out his misery to Leopold Mikhailovich. Leopold Mikhailovich agreed it would be "precipitate to tie Danuta down" (those were his words) and asked Vera whether she thought Aaron could live in his pencil box. Vera thought it was a wonderful idea, but advised him to stay out of the kitchen.

Finkelmeyer's spirits soared. His resignation was accepted with a look of surprise but no attempt to talk him out of it. He informed Frida of his decision in a halting monologue on the day he brought the family back from the country. He had told her in the spring that he dreamed of quitting his job once the payment for the book came in. She failed to grasp then as she failed to grasp now how much was at stake for him, and she was crushed when Aaron announced he would be moving into Leopold Mikhailovich's flat. Yet the mere mention of Leopold Mikhailovich served as a balm, and soon she was resignedly emptying the suitcase of things they had brought back from the country and filling it with Aaron's things, carefully enumerating the items she included and the items she did not. By the time she had finished, Aaron was ready to hang himself.

But one day passed and another and another, and Aaron was in heaven. Things going on around him reached him in subdued tones, with fuzzy edges, smaller than life; everything lost its former significance. There were times when he felt like a giant green leaf whose only responsibility was to catch air, light, and moisture; or a silkworm in its cocoon with nothing to do all autumn (which was upon them) or winter (which was coming) or spring (which was still far behind); or an apple core tossed in the river and carried swiftly downstream, unconcerned at being chewed a bit, gnawed a bit, as long as its heart was intact and it could float on unhampered, unseen.

There were stretches when he did not leave the house, when, sitting at the desk writing away, he would experience an unconscious hunger, reach for the bread that had been sitting on the newspaper, but, not finding it, forget what he had reached for and go back to writing. Late at night he might notice a dull pain in his head, an empty nauseated feeling, but by then the shops were closed and he would drift off to sleep.

Then there were days when he roamed through the city, never stopping, peering at rounded moldings, spirit-level facades, trapezoid roofs, the Arbat's maze, the boulevards' rings and radii. He would knock on her door at nightfall or well into the night—"Who is it?" "Aaron"—and she would open and he would enter, eat, drink, make love, fall asleep, sleep late, wash, and leave, and mutter and stumble and sit down to write and forget about eating and drinking, a hand floating off the desk, a paper fluttering to the floor, a car roaring past, the crashing of glass in a corner, and rain, rain, the reign of God, give us this day, our Father . . .

One day, some time between evening and night, there was a knock on the door, but before he could answer, before he could turn in his chair, the door flew open.

"Inspection!" he heard in a fog.

"What was that?" he said, rubbing his eyes and trying to stand at the same time.

"Inspection! Your papers."

His eyes focused first on a police lieutenant, then on the neighbor for whom he had moved Leopold Mikhailovich's table. She was chewing on her lips like a rabbit while the lieutenant took stock of the desk, the floor, the corners.

"Hot plates are forbidden. You will be fined accordingly."

"What did I tell you?" said the old woman in a singsong voice. "What did I tell you?"

"I'm still waiting for your papers."

"My papers? I'm sorry, but . . ."

"You're sorry? You are obliged to have them on you at all times."

"I'm sorry, but I don't happen to have them here. I can have them for you tomorrow or the day after if you really need them."

"*You* need them, not *me* understand? And tomorrow, first thing, is that clear? Now tell me, what kind of residence permit have you got?"

"What kind?"

"Moscow proper, Moscow district, or other?"

"Moscow proper."

"Permanent? Temporary?"

"I was *born* in Moscow!"

"How was I supposed to know?"

"Permanent."

"Now let me have your name, patronymic, and surname; year and place of birth; and place of employment."

The lieutenant sat down at the desk, and Aaron dictated the data in a monotone until he came to "place of employment." He looked up. Both the police officer and the old woman were staring intently at him.

"Place of employment . . . none."

" 'None,' eh? How long have you been unemployed?"

"A month or two I don't know."

"You don't know!"

He picked up a sheet of paper with distaste and cast an eye over the squiggly lines.

"And what is this supposed to be?" he asked.

"Put it down," Finkelmeyer said with a threat in his voice. "I did not give you permission to look at it."

The lieutenant eyed the paper for a moment or two more, then placed it back on the desk.

"Marital status?"

"I have seventeen wives and two hundred children. What do you need to know for, anyway? I told you I'd get you my papers."

"Just make sure you do. Now one more question. The officially registered tenant does not appear to be in residence. Are you a sub-lessor?"

"No, I am not, and he is ill and being looked after elsewhere."

"I see," said the lieutenant, noting it all down and then standing. "Tell him to pay us a visit when he's feeling better, will you?"

He saluted, turned on his heel, and left the room. The old woman tagged behind, still chewing on her lips.

III

AFTER moving into Leopold Mikhailovich's flat, Aaron found it painfully difficult to speak to anyone but Danuta. He had always had a tendency to withdraw into himself, into contemplation, the signs of which were a fixed stare, raised brows, and a vague half-smile. Now, left to his own devices, he rarely came out of it.

Still, Nikolsky kept in touch by phone, as did the Refuge. From early September the Refuge regulars had gathered every other week, but whenever Leopold Mikhailovich or Vera invited him to join them he would give a vague response, then fail to show up. They didn't hold it against him; they understood his need for privacy.

Frida phoned often. She asked how things were; she wondered whether he was eating well, whether he wanted her to buy him warm shoes for the winter; she told him about the girls. She always sounded nervous, and as the conversation wore on her voice would fill with tears.

One morning the phone rang, and Aaron, who was still half asleep, heard a muddle of unintelligible syllables that he took for "Leopold Mikhailovich." He was about to launch into an explanation of Leopold Mikhailovich's whereabouts when the voice repeated its request and Aaron caught the inimitable "Aronmendelch." Frida had evidently made free with his number.

"Ah, Manakin! A pleasure to hear your voice! Where are you?"

"Moscow. The Metropole. We must talk."

"I'm afraid I can't just now, Comrade Manakin."

"Can't is no good. We must talk."

"What would I have to say to so important a personage?"

"You are making fun of me, I know. But we have business to talk."

"When we talked business before, I talked to Aion Neprigen. What have you done with him, Comrade Manakin? Is it true that the name on the cover . . . By the way, is the book out yet?"

"Author copies only. Soon there will be more."

"I suspected as much. Why else would you have come? Well, what is the name on the cover?"

"Manakin is better to sell books."

"Thus spake the 'first Tongor poet.' Well, you know where you can go!" And he slammed down the receiver.

The phone rang again immediately, but Aaron had no intention of answering. He was through with Manakin. The past was dead. Long live the *vita nuova!* Aaron Finkelmeyer belonged to himself and himself alone.

But a few hours later Nikolsky phoned from work. "I know you don't read the papers, so I thought I'd tell you: that conference has opened. Remember? Literatures of small nationalities. The article says it's a five-day affair and mentions Danil Manakin's *Good Fortune*. He must be in town."

"He is. And on my back."

"Where's he staying?"

"The Metropole."

"I see. Well, goodbye."

A few minutes later the phone rang again, and Aaron immediately recognized the world-weary modulations of the Master.

"Congratulations, my boy! I hear you've left your job. Your poor wife's in a tizzy, of course, but I calmed her down. 'Ah yes, the poet's lot, the Muses' fateful call'—that sort of thing.

"Now listen, my boy. I've just met your abominable snowman. What's his name? . . . That's right. He's terribly upset with you, you know. They're clamoring for new poems. I gave him my word I'd get you over there. By the way, when are you going to throw your party? I mean, it's your first book, and into every life a little champagne must flow. Now what were we talking about? Oh yes, Manakin. Dash him off a few poems, will you? They're for the conference volume. Come down to the conference with me, my boy. Come down to the conference with me. I'll find a pass to get you in, my boy, and introduce you with a grin, my boy, to the powers that be and their kin, my boy, to the powers that be and their kin. . . . How can you be so pig-headed! There are ways of earning a perfectly decent living without doing translations. . . . Now you listen to me, you son of a bitch, you be at my place at ten on the dot tomorrow. You find the taxi, I'll pay for it. Oh, and I'll chip in for the champagne as well."

The Master was growing old. He'd always been insufferable, but now he ran on like a millrace. Was there any point in going to the conference? Damn the conference! Damn Manakin! But the Master was right about the champagne. How could he have been such an ingrate! He hadn't talked to the Master in six months. And how long was it since he'd seen Leopold Mikhailovich? And Nikolsky? The only way to make up for his inexcusable behavior was to gather everyone around a table and get them to drink, smoke, and talk themselves into forgetting it.

Aaron asked Vera to see how Leopold Mikhailovich reacted to the idea, and in no time Leopold Mikhailovich informed him he had taken the liberty of contacting his old colleagues at the National and if Aaron was willing . . . Of course he was willing! Well then, all he had to do was fix a date and tell him the approximate number of guests.

"You and Vera, and Nikolsky too, I hope."

"Definitely."

"And the Master. At last you'll have a chance to meet him."

"I'm looking forward to it."

"I'd really like to have Danuta, but . . ."

"Do try to persuade her, Aaron."

"I will. And who else would you or Vera like to have?"

"Would you mind asking Tolik?"

"Excellent idea!"

"Which means we'll be approximately ten in all."

"Thank you, Leopold Mikhailovich! Thank you."

Nikolsky did not respond immediately when Aaron phoned to invite him. He had kept his distance from the Refuge and wasn't sure he would feel at home with the group.

"Are you bringing Danuta?" he asked suddenly.

"Yes, I want to introduce her to everybody."

"Of course, of course," he said impassively. "Would you mind if I invited another couple? A friend of mine and his new flame. Vera and Co. know them, and I'd feel more a part of things if they were there. His name is Victor and hers is Varya."

"The Varya who used to come to Leopold Mikhailovich's? The artist's wife? What happened to the artist?"

"Oh, he's still off in the country, drunk most of the time probably, and Victor's gone gaga over her. By the way, I've got some scuttlebutt for you. I've been to see Manakin."

Manakin again! It was an obsession! The Master too had gone on about him when Aaron phoned about the party. He gave Aaron hell for failing to show up at the conference and meet the influential editors and publishers. "You think you're the cat's bloody whiskers, prancing around on those pristine paws of yours. Well, you'll starve if you don't get some work soon, you . . ."

At that point the Master was seized by a coughing fit, and Aaron was able to issue the invitation. The Master immediately came round, and before long he was threatening to drop his trousers in the midst of the festivities.

The National still shone with the art-nouveau opulence of the reign of Nicholas II. Of course, the paint was cracked and utterly inappropriate, the sconces and chandeliers had been fitted with puny shades, the marble floor was covered with threadbare government-issue rejects—in other words, it was suffering from a bad case of *tempora* and *mores*. The room Leopold Mikhailovich had reserved, however, was encumbered with neither tarnished Muscovite majesty nor tawdry modern glitter; it was moderate in size, comfortably appointed, subtly lighted—the perfect combination of decorum and intimacy.

He and Vera arrived first, with Zhenya. Leopold Mikhailovich thought of himself as the master of ceremonies. His goal was to impart a certain dignity to the proceedings, yet preserve a family atmosphere, and he and a middle-aged waiter immediately began consulting in hushed tones like chess players discussing a match.

Meanwhile, Aaron arrived, awkwardly ushering Danuta through the door. Danuta was nervous about meeting so many new people in a famous restaurant in the middle of the big city, but Leopold Mikhailovich put her at ease in no time, and Vera, who immediately took Aaron aside and told him how "lovely, really lovely" Danuta was, took her under her wing.

Next came Tolik, all indignant because they had refused to take his battered briefcase in the cloakroom and then wouldn't let him up the main staircase with it. Having dropped the scandalous object in a corner, however, he forgot everything and everybody and began examining the moldings around the ceiling, the dazzling pendants in the chandelier, the gilt on the furniture. It was all new to him too.

Victor and Varya, who came with Nikolsky, were a bit overwhelmed at first, but Victor was not one to let anything get the better of him, especially when Varya was around, and Varya—the picture of a Russian fairy-tale princess in her *sarafan,* white embroidered blouse, and long blond braid—calmed down once she saw that even amidst all the pomp her cavalier never took his eyes off her.

Nikolsky decided in favor of an all-inclusive wave, but Leopold

Mikhailovich came up to him, held out his hand, and, looking him straight in the eye, said, "Glad to see you."

"Glad to see you too, Leopold Mikhailovich."

As they went their separate ways, Leopold Mikhailovich gave Nikolsky's elbow a friendly squeeze.

Then Nikolsky noticed Vera looking over at him, biting her lip, and while he was making up his mind whether to go up to her, she came up to him.

"Hello, Lyonya. It was good of you to come."

"You don't think I'd miss a spread at the National, do you?"

Vera frowned. She had hoped for a different tone. "I'm sorry we . . . I'm sorry nothing's been said."

"What's there to say?" he asked, in just the tone he had hoped to avoid.

"I only wanted you to know that what I have now means too much to me to . . ."

He knew exactly what she meant: I'm afraid of you. Go easy on me. Don't ruin things.

He moved closer, took her by the arm, and said, "Don't worry. You're a fine person, Vera."

"You know, we miss you at the Refuge. Come back. Not only on Thursdays for the gatherings. Any time. Just give us a ring."

"I will."

Nikolsky then moved on to Danuta and Finkelmeyer. He bowed and said with a sardonic smile, "And how is my charming wife doing without me?"

He immediately felt Aaron's bony fist in his side.

"Always looking for a fight," said Nikolsky, clutching his rib. Danuta looked at him helplessly, the tears welling up in her eyes, and for a moment he took malicious pleasure in the scene. But then he thought in horror, Is this what I really want? and said contritely, "Don't mind me. I'm a little unhinged today. But there is something I've been meaning to talk to you about, Danuta." He took out his wallet. "This is for the rent." And he began explaining where and how to pay it. Aaron interrupted and said he would take care of it, and Danuta modestly proposed that since she was now working (she had found a job at a dry cleaner's) *she* could take care of it, but Nikolsky brushed their protests aside: the place was still his, he hadn't given it away; he was only asking Danuta to do him a favor, save him some time.

In fact, it was all just a ruse to show he intended to keep his distance as promised.

"Thank you," Danuta whispered, tucking the money away in her bag. "And thank you for being . . . such a good friend," she went on without raising her eyes. "Good friends are rare . . ."

Un-be-liev-able! Women taking pity on Nikolsky! What was the world coming to!

Only the Master had yet to arrive, and the old fox knew how to make an entrance. Just when people started wondering whether something had happened to him, in he hobbled on his cane, calling out, *"Bonsoir! Bonsoir!"* and dismissing with princely majesty the "page" who had shown him the way.

No matter where he appeared, the Master held the stage. If the spectators had eyes to see, they watched him; if they had ears to hear, they let him speak, or, if they spoke too, accepted the subsidiary role of conversation partner.

He was exceedingly angry with Aaron and attacked him with both word and cane. Though refraining from his more salty vocabulary, he berated him with avuncular (as he put it) gusto and peppered his monologue with scathing witticisms. Then suddenly he looked up and said, "I say, aren't they ever going to feed us? I'm starved!"

As people started taking their places, the Master poked Aaron in the stomach with his cane. "Don't think you're off the hook, my boy. As soon as I get a little sustenance in my gut, I'll have at you again."

"Mind if I join you?" asked Nikolsky.

"Welcome aboard!" said the Master. "Tell me, you know everyone here, don't you? Then please arrange to have a ravishing woman on my right hand and a captivating woman on my left."

He was placed between Vera and Varya.

"Now tradition requires that the book, the book we are here to celebrate, be displayed on the table. Have you got a copy, Aaron?"

"Just a second," said Nikolsky and ran out. He returned carrying a briefcase.

"You mean they let you put *yours* in the cloakroom?" Tolik lamented.

"Tolik, Tolik!" Nikolsky said, carefully removing a bundle from the briefcase. "When will you learn to make a scene!" He handed the bundle to Aaron and said, "Here are ten copies. You may distribute them as you see fit."

There was a joyous uproar.

"Where did you get them?" Finkelmeyer asked, gazing at a copy with an absentminded smile and flipping through the pages with a less than obedient finger.

"Manakin gave them to me."

"Manakin? Oh, that's right. You said you saw him."

"I'll tell you the whole story later."

The Master picked up a copy, waved it in the air, and said to Vera, "Display it artfully, will you, my dear?" Vera turned a long, slender vase into a pedestal on which the half-open book was esconced in red and white carnations.

Then two corks popped, and after Leopold Mikhailovich and Nikolsky had filled the guests' glasses with champagne the Master rose and launched into a flowery toast. But suddenly his voice began to shake; suddenly he sounded like just another nice old man. "My, how you've grown since we met ten years ago and you were in the army. Remember? Come and give me a hug, my boy!"

Aaron nearly knocked the table over as he ran up to him. It was a touching scene, and the Master had to wipe his eyes before he raised his glass again. Then everyone toasted the man of the hour and drank. Aaron was thrilled. Everything was going well; everyone was having a good time. He loved them all, even carrot-top Victor, whom he'd never seen before in his life. But of course the Master, who had just shown his true, sentimental colors and was now teasing Varya by calling her "the boyar maiden," and testing Vera's Italian, French, and even Latin; and Leonid, a dashing, dying breed (epaulettes, pistols, punch, and gypsies) or a portent of things to come (space suits, astral beams, artificial intelligence, and infinity); and Vera, who was looking radiant; and Danya, Danechka, Danuta, Danusha; and of course Leopold Mikhailovich.

The waiter kept coming up to Leopold Mikhailovich to find out how he wanted things done, but from time to time Leopold

Mikhailovich would stand and serve the guests himself. Although he did not take part in the conversation, he kept an eye on the Master and followed his eloquent tirades with a smile meant only for himself.

"You look familiar," the Master said to Leopold Mikhailovich at one point. "Where could we have met?"

"Here. At the National."

"No, I really mean it."

"So do I. Just after the war you were one of our regulars. You and writers like Olesha—"

"Amazing! But why 'one of *our* regulars'?"

"Because your humble servant was your humble servant, your waiter, to be exact."

"No, it was before that," the Master said, his yellowed parchment of a forehead crumbling into wrinkles. "I'm certain of it."

"Then as well," said Leopold Mikhailovich calmly, "when you read your early works at the Circle, though you were a rising star and I just an amateur actor with YSCET, one of the many organizations and abbreviations of the time that have been lost to history."

"What does YSCET stand for?" asked Vera. "Tell us about it."

By this time everyone's attention was focused on their conversation.

"Well," said Leopold Mikhailovich with a twinkle in his eye, "officially it stood for the Youth Studio for Communal and Experimental Theater, but we liked to think of it as Youth against Shoddy, Conventional, and Elitist Theater."

Everyone laughed.

"And among ourselves, if the truth be told, we sometimes replaced 'shoddy' with a similar but much less civil word."

Again they laughed, and no one louder that the Master, the tears rolling down his cheeks as he recalled the days when everything was or at least seemed to be permitted. But he was still dissatisfied with Leopold Mikhailovich's explanation of where their paths had crossed.

"Somehow, I don't know why, I connect your face with art."

"Leopold Mikhailovich is an art critic," said Vera. "He used to lecture at CEWA. Though he was trained as a historian."

"What's going on here?" cried the Master, grabbing his head. "Actor, critic, waiter, historian! No, what I have in mind is a canvas, an oil painting!"

"Then I believe I know what you're getting at," said Leopold Mikhailovich. "You're a friend of Zhilinsky's, aren't you?"

"Of no less than thirty years' standing."

"Well, his collection includes the portrait of an artist working with a brush and palette on the canvas of a nude."

"Eureka! Bravo! That's it! Of course! The artist in the painting! Tell me, who did it? It's a fine piece."

"It's a self-portrait, actually."

"A self-portrait! My judgment may not count for much, but our mutual friend does not collect mediocrities."

Leopold Mikhailovich's only response was to announce that there would be a short break before the final course. They opened the door to the neighboring room, where couples were dancing primly to an orchestra. Zhenya dragged Tolik out to the dance floor, and Victor plucked up his courage and invited Varya. The Master rose and retired to an armchair in the corner under a gigantic lamp-shade, asked for a copy of the book, and put on his glasses. The guests all gathered round him. He opened the book at random and read out lines or stanzas that particularly appealed to him, caressing each syllable with his richly modulated voice and surveying his audience with a proud glance. It was as though they had forgotten the poems were Aaron's. Aaron himself sat entranced, clasping his long arms under his knees, leaning forward now and then—Ulysses, lashed to the mast, craving to hear the Sirens.

"The lightness, the freedom!" the Master exclaimed. "Caesuras, *Luftpausen*, melody, rhythm! It's Mozart, late Mozart! All hail Aion Neprigen!"

"May he rest in peace," Nikolsky said sarcastically under his breath.

"What was that?" the Master snapped.

"Aion Neprigen is dead and buried," said Nikolsky with an insolence that bordered on disrespect.

"On the contrary," said the Master. "He's very much with us. He is life itself, in a manner of speaking. You wouldn't deny the existence of Neprigen's *book,* would you? Neprigen is a pen name, a mystery, a game that literature has played many times before and will go on playing. Literature is mysterious by its very nature, young man, but there will come a time when Finkelmeyer takes up his rightful place beside Neprigen."

"But Aion Neprigen doesn't exist!" Nikolsky objected again, even more boldly. "The name on the book is Manakin."

Puzzled, the Master stared at Nikolsky, then at the cover illustration—a stylized deer head with the sun rising out of its antlers—and finally, after readjusting his glasses with a trembling hand, read out loud, his lips barely moving:

Danil Manakin
Good Fortune

He opened the book to the title page and read:

Danil Manakin
Good Fortune
POEMS
Authorized Translation from the Tongor

"How . . . how could you?" the Master asked, his voice cracking. "How could you do it, my boy?"

"It's . . . I . . . I didn't realize . . ." Finkelmeyer responded, like schoolboy to schoolmaster. "I . . . had no idea. Really . . ."

"A poet must live his own life," the Master said, even as Aaron spoke. "He can't let others run it for him, ruin it for him. That's treason! A betrayal of poetry, of art! How could you do such a thing? You were on your way. I'd have helped you along. Word would have spread. . . . How could you, my boy?"

He stopped there, looking very sad. Leopold Mikhailovich glanced over at him inquisitively and with no sign of pity for Aaron. As someone who had taken his fate into his own hands, he could feel nothing more than a certain discomfort at having upset the Master so.

Nikolsky recalled the indifference with which Aaron had reacted to Manakin's ploy, and began to wonder whether it wasn't somehow related to Leopold Mikhailovich's actually quite attractive practice of reworking his lectures to refute and thus reject one another. Aaron had made a special trip to Zaalaisk to talk Manakin into submitting the book for publication, yet no sooner did he learn it had been accepted than he rejected it. He had renounced his offspring, destroyed, devoured his very self!

"Perhaps *I* can shed some light on the matter," Nikolsky said out loud. "You see, I had a little talk with Manakin when he gave me the book."

"You know him?" the Master asked.

"I met him at the same time I met Aaron, early last spring in Siberia. I gave him to understand I was a big shot in the Ministry of Culture and basically bullied him into allowing the book to come out."

"In other words, I talked Aaron into it, you talked Manakin into it," said the Master.

"You might put it that way. Anyway, when I read in the papers that the book had appeared, I phoned Aaron to let him know and learned he'd had words with Manakin. I decided to take matters into my own hands. I went to the Metropole, where Manakin was staying, and we did our Siberia number again, only in Siberia *he* spied on *me* and here *I* did the spying. I found him in the dining room and stood there staring at him, as if trying to remember where I'd seen him before. And sure enough, up he bounded, beaming, and pumped my hand. 'Comrade Nikossky! Comrade Nikossky! It's Comrade Manakin!' 'Of course! Of course! Comrade Manakin! Imagine meeting you here!' Stanislavsky would have been proud.

"I sat down at his table and told him that the Moldavian Minister of Culture was waiting for me upstairs so I could only stay a few minutes—and proceeded to grill him on the book. The first thing he did was to pull a copy out of his briefcase. I immediately requested ten more for the Moldavian minister, and he obediently ran up to his room and brought them back. I asked how it was he had used his own name on the book when he had published the poems under a pseudonym. Aion Neprigen, wasn't that it? Oh yes, he smiled, but in fact I was the one who had made him see the light. I had told him that a book would strengthen his position as the leading functionary of Tongor culture, and he had concluded on his own that there was no advantage to hiding his light under a pseudonym. Besides, the local officials might not grasp that Neprigen and Manakin were one and the same person. Things were a lot simpler this way.

"But there was a new development as well. Apparently the officials at the conference had told him he had to justify their confidence in him. 'We understand that all this emphasis on the taiga and the tundra, the sun and moon, all this pantheism'—he had tried to learn the word, but in his mouth it sounded like 'pantyism'—'has its roots in your folk heritage, but what we need is something with a more contemporary ring to it, something that will give our readers an idea of the lives of the men and women who work in the fur industry, their day-to-day concerns, their aspirations, the growth of their culture—you know what we have in mind. Give us ten or twelve poems in this new key and we'll splash them all over the national press. Just remember: easy on the pantheism. Or even better: get the pantheism out of your system in one or two and keep the rest of them pure.'

"Manakin was scared stiff: orders were orders, after all. But all was not lost. He had been told—*nota bene,* he had been told—that part of the problem was with his translator: the translator had been overstating the pantheistic elements in his work. 'How do you plan to take care of the problem?' I asked. 'The Writers Union takes care of the problem,' he said. 'They give me a *new* translator, a good translator.' And guess who it is, guess who's taking Aaron's place."

He ran his eyes over the assembled guests.

"Well, who?" asked Vera impatiently.

"Prebylov."

Finkelmeyer doubled over in a guffaw, Tolik whistled, Vera and Zhenya waxed indignant. Of those who had met Prebylov, only Leopold Mikhailovich seemed unperturbed. The Master was livid.

"Prebylov?" he shouted, shaking his fist. "That bastard! That jingo bastard! They're a pack of jackals, he and his kind. They'll take over if we let them! And you had to play the prima donna!"

"But why should Aaron keep giving Manakin his poems?" Nikolsky protested.

"Nobody says he should. He wouldn't have had to this time either if he hadn't let them bamboozle him. If he'd just let me know what they were up to, I'd have forced them to put his name on the book. Prebylov! That's the last straw!"

Although he continued to rant as they moved back to the table for dessert, down deep the Master must have realized that he had been duped as much as Aaron: his original idea of publishing Aaron's poems as Russian translations of a nonexistent Aion Neprigen had fallen flat and with it the chance of capping his half century of fame—raucous and scandalous at first, then suppressed and all but underground, and now glittering with legend and academic respectability—by presenting Russian poetry with an unrecognized genius and leading him up Olympus by the hand. But he directed his ire outward, and after running through Aaron and "that self-satisfied primitive," and his new translator, he began to wonder whether that self-contained gray-haired gentleman hadn't had a part to play in the affair.

"What's your opinion?" he asked of Leopold Mikhailovich. "I understand that you two"—he nodded in Aaron's direction—"are quite close. You're getting on in years; you've been through a lot—outside the kitchen as well as in, I imagine."

Leopold Mikhailovich intercepted the sally with a smile. "I do not share the conviction that one's life may be reduced to one's profession," he said, "but I should be less than sincere were I to deny that my own profession has been instrumental in my understanding of life and human nature." Not until this point did he allow himself a spark of irony: "One is never so much oneself as when one is at table."

The Master's parchment forehead wrinkled again, but he said nothing.

"As for the question of influence,

> 'We are not given to discern
> How our advice performs its task.

"I know my Tyutchev as well as the next man."

"I am certain you do, which is why I hope you'll understand my meaning. I have never been one to give advice; I prefer to discuss possibilities."

"In other words, evade responsibilities. Or do I fail to understand your meaning?"

"Perhaps, but how much can we know about others when we know so little about ourselves? At best our advice will be useless, but it can also do great harm, especially in the context of strong emotions like love or artistic creativity."

"Hogwash!" shouted the master, high on his horse and very much in his element. " 'Love can't be taught'! 'Love can't be learnt'! Philistine tommyrot! Malarkey! Love without a confidant isn't love at all."

"Well said!" Leopold Mikhailovich interjected while the Master struggled a bit with his breathing apparatus.

"As for artistic creativity, it's only half the story. An artist needs to create, true, but an artist needs to eat as well. I may have had some meals at the National, but I had plenty more in the lowest dives imaginable."

"Your point is of course well taken: both love and art have their practical sides. But I must admit I am less broad-minded than you. For me love is pure emotion, stripped of the carnal element; creativity is a process, independent of what comes of it and certainly of fame or fortune."

"Well, for me love is always a compromise, even when only two people are involved—"

"Clever."

"—and creativity a compromise between idea and realization."

"Granted."

"But life—life is one long string of compromises. Do you really think your pure ideals of love and art can protect you from them?"

"I do."

He said it loudly and clearly. It made a great impression.

"You admit that compromises exist, yet you wish to avoid them."

"I do."

"I see. Jesus said, 'He that is able to receive it, let him receive it.' Some people make major compromises, others minor ones. Surely you don't feel you can avoid any and all of them."

And for the third time Leopold Mikhailovich said, "I do."

"But how? How do you propose to go about it?"

"There is only one way: abstention."

Silence.

"Abstention? Abstention from love? Abstention from art? Just to avoid a few compromises? Where's your sense of reality? Who ever heard of anyone—" He stopped short. Then, breathing heavily, he looked Leopold Mikhailovich in the eye and said, "What you mean is, that's why the actor, the artist—the gifted artist—the historian, the critic, spent all those years . . . as a waiter."

The Master turned his head. A teaspoon tinkled in a cup.

"I . . . That's . . . Had I known, I'd have come to the National and bowed before you, sinner that I am. There isn't a compromise I haven't made. I don't remember how it began, and I know for certain it hasn't ended. In both art *and* love. I never married. And you?"

"I was married for a short while."

"Have you any children?"

"A daughter."

"I have none. Do you think it's better that way?"

"Perhaps. My daughter turned out badly."

The Master shook his head, or perhaps it shook of its own accord.

"Voluntary abstention, you say," he muttered to himself, no longer concerned with the presence of the others. "Self-abnegation. That's it. You've had fewer illusions than most, and it will be easier for you to face . . . to pass on. Oh, the burden of age!"

"Burden!" Leopold Mikhailovich cried. They all riveted their eyes on him. To Vera he seemed to light up from within. "This is the happiest time in my life! Each day is an unearned gift, each moment a flower brimming with nectar. I was young when I stopped making demands, I let life sweep me along. And now it is paying me back."

The Master nodded, Finkelmeyer swayed as if in prayer, and Nikolsky found the canoe-trip ditty running through his mind: "If you haven't got a lifey, you won't have to lie down and die."

"Did you and the boy often . . . talk about these things?" the Master asked with something closely akin to jealously in his voice.

It was Aaron who answered.

"I . . . You . . . It's not really something . . . I mean, you don't need to talk about it. It's something . . . you feel . . . feel on your own."

The Master understood. He nodded.

"Now you understand why I never try to influence anyone, why I refuse to give advice."

"I see," muttered the Master. "I see." Pleading exhaustion, the Master rose to leave. Victor immediately offered him a ride home— he was clearly eager to make a getaway with Varya—and since the Refuge was on the way to Varya's he agreed to take Vera and Leopold Mikhailovich as well. They all said their goodbyes outside the National, under the gaze of its bronze griffins, who had seen it all before, and in close proximity to the Kremlin's red-brick wall. But both the wall and the entire Manège Square that separated them from it were set off by a gauze backdrop of mist, whose individual particles glittered in the light of the streetlamps. And in the cold silver gleam of this rather tawdry set the main entrance to the restaurant served as the proscenium for some rather commonplace stage business: sleepy revelers jostling one another, cars sporting less than shiny finishes, stop signals flashing blood-red, people babbling in tongues, painted Columbines hanging picturesquely on the necks of Harlequins both Russian and foreign, yesterday's schoolgirls, today's call girls, all prank and caprice, the world at their feet and the skirt at their bottom, careful to show plenty of thigh as they enter their cabs and none too quick about closing the doors either, oh là là! And there's a Citroën with diplomatic plates! They stand like hounds, their noses pointing in its direction; one of them nearly rushes after it: a morsel of a charmed life has just passed them by. . . .

Vera, Leopold Mikhailovich, and the Master piled into the back of Victor's car; Varya snuggled up to Victor in the front. Tolik gallantly offered to see Zhenya home, and off they went. Finkelmeyer was talking to Leopold Mikhailovich and holding Danuta by the arm. Nikolsky went around to Victor's side of the car and stuck his hand inside.

"Good night, Red."

"So long, boss. Remember you promised to come and see me."

"I won't forget."

Just then Nikolsky noticed an unsavory-looking type with an unsavory-looking smile who was all but hanging out of the window of a nearby Volga. Nikolsky turned away, disgusted, and saw Finkelmeyer and Danuta coming up to him.

"There you are!" said Finkelmeyer. "I was afraid you'd run away."

"Run away from you? You mean because of that ridiculous beret you're wearing?"

At that point the doors slammed shut, everyone waved, and the car shot off across the square. The Volga pulled out after it. Nikolsky had the feeling that he'd seen the driver before and that the man had recognized him, but the hell with it, he had more pressing problems.

Danuta walked between Nikolsky and Aaron, but only Aaron held her arm. Nikolsky saw immediately that he was less than skilled in the art of strolling with a lady: Danuta kept having to readjust her stride and jump out of his way. Nikolsky longed to take her arm and glide down the street with her as she deserved.

They were crossing from the Okhotny to the Sverdlov Square metro station when Aaron gave Danuta such a jolt she nearly dropped her handbag. First he stopped dead in his tracks, then he ran in front of Danuta and Nikolsky to cut them off.

"My father! He mustn't see me. Try and cover us somehow, Lyonya. We'll wait for you farther on."

"What in the world are you talking about?"

"That man selling newspapers—he's my father."

Between the two arches at the end of the corridor there was a man standing behind a rickety table piled high with newspapers. Nikolsky could hear the clink of the coins as he counted his change.

"Your father?" he asked, trying to peer over Aaron's shoulder.

"Go on! Quick! Buy a paper from him!"

Nikolsky made his way around Aaron and went up to the table. While taking out his wallet, he got a good look at the man. He was far from tall—where did Aaron get his height?—and had a round face, prominent rosy cheeks, tiny slits for eyes, and a beard running down to his chest in long grayish curls. He wore a shiny black skull-cap and a nondescript dark gray overcoat buttoned all the way to the collar.

"Out late tonight, aren't you? Business slow? What paper are you selling?"

The old man did not answer, but his sparkling eyes and the rise and fall of his eyebrows—they had the same fine shape as Aaron's—showed that Nikolsky's banter had registered with him.

"I see. *Izvestia.*"

Nikolsky felt Aaron and Danuta slipping past behind him, but he didn't want to leave without hearing the man's voice. "Another speech by Nikita, eh? Three columns' worth. No wonder you have no customers. Or did they hold up delivery on account of the speech?"

As the old man held out the paper in one hand and brought the other one up to receive payment, Nikolsky heard a soft, high-pitched melody and some garbled syllables spiraling up and around him.

"All I have is a ruble," he said, "but, well, I'm doing some repairs at home and I'll be needing a lot of newspaper. Why not give me the whole pile."

Without a hint of surprise the old man scooped up the pile, took the ruble, and handed Nikolsky the papers and two coins in change.

"Thank you very much. Be well!"

The old man bowed his reply, and Nikolsky ran down the stairs with the image of the black skullcap in his mind.

"What took you so long?" asked Aaron, when Nikolsky all but bumped into them at the foot of the staircase. Then he saw the pile of newspapers under Nikolsky's arm and broke into a smile. "You're really something, you know?"

Danuta also graced him with a smile.

"But don't think you did him a favor. He enjoys selling those papers. It's a way of passing time and adding a few kopeks to his pension. He's probably upset."

"What kind of nonsense is that?" Nikolsky snapped, annoyed that Finkelmeyer's smile had turned into a laugh and that he would now look ridiculous in Danuta's eyes. "How can he be upset about selling them all at once?"

"It's like this," said Aaron, suddenly serious. "My father spent his whole life in trade; he was sent to prison for it. And now that he's back—at least this is how I see it—he needs to . . . how shall I put it . . ."

"I know what you mean," said Danuta softly.

"Rehabilitate himself?" Nikolsky suggested. "In his own eyes?"

"Exactly," said Aaron. Just then a train came roaring in, and when the racket had died down, Aaron asked, "Did you try to have a conversation with him?"

"Yes, I did. Why doesn't he answer?"

"Well, first of all, he's a little . . ." He tapped his forehead. "And then in prison he met up with a rabbi or fanatic or some sort and vowed to speak only in the language of the Torah. So he doesn't speak at all. Convenient, isn't it? He hears and understands everything; he just doesn't respond."

"I know exactly how he feels," said Danuta in the same soft voice as before.

"You mean he was singing in Hebrew?" Nikolsky asked.

"So he sang for you, did he? You must really have upset him.

You see, he knows a few Hebrew prayers by rote, but he only sings them as a kind of defense mechanism, when he's afraid he might say something."

"Well, well, well," said Nikolsky, "or, as Leopold Mikhailovich reminded us today, the things 'we are not given to discern'!"

Suddenly he was in a foul mood. "Look, what are you hanging around here for? You've got a much longer ride ahead of you than I have! Oh, and here's my train." He quickly shook Danuta's cold hand, joggled Aaron's dry bones, and stepped into the train with a "See you soon."

Just before midnight on that misty evening the last couples rushing along Gorky Street to reach the metro station by closing time were accosted by a respectably dressed though perhaps not quite stable gentleman in his thirties calling out, "Read all about it, citizens! Read all about it! An Italian signora gives birth to sextuplets, all healthy, and our own dear Nikita Sergeevich gives a speech! Special offer! Tonight only! *Izvestia* free for the asking! Step right up! Thank you. Step right up! Two? That's right, absolutely free! And the best of health, wealth, and happiness to you!"

After a while the gentleman either regained his senses or simply lost interest, and tried to stuff the remaining copies of the newspaper into the much-suffering waste receptacle at the entrance to the metro, but the sextuplets protested so violently that the papers fell out into the street. Nikolsky imagined the policeman watching him from a distance to be racked with doubts of a "to nab or not to nab" nature, and his first impulse was: Just try me. But then he thought better of it: What the hell. You've had your fun. Think of the poor honest street cleaners and newspaper vendors and journalists. He picked up all the newspapers, turned to give the policeman one last nasty look, and—the same feeling as at the National: that man in the Volga and now this cop—set off at a swift clip. Dammit! Dammit to bloody hell! How could I have forgotten his face. The "architect" that day at Varya's, the bastard who tried to stop us by running in front of the car! He must have been tailing Victor, followed him to Refuge! God, what do I do now?

He was about to dash off to the Refuge when he realized there was no point in raising a hullabaloo in the middle of the night. What could happen before morning? Besides, he'd had enough for one evening—wine, women, poets, a Hebrew prayer, and now cops and robbers.

Walking home, he tried his trick of purgation through fulmination and ran through all the curses in his repertory. It didn't work. Then he remembered the bottle of Stolichnaya he kept in his aunt's refrigerator. It was his only hope.

IV

NOT LONG after the operation by which Leopold Mikhailovich's collection was transferred from Nakhabino to the Refuge, Victor had been summoned by the Motor Vehicle Inspectorate and asked whether he had witnessed a certain accident on the Volokolamsk Road. No, he hadn't. Had he traveled along such-and-such a stretch of the road on such-and-such a day? No, he couldn't say he had. "Well, we have a record of your having been stopped." "Oh, *that* time! Of course!" "And what were you doing there?" "Transporting some boards." "Where to?" "A favor for a friend." "Name? Address?"

Victor realized from the start that the "accident" was a smoke screen. He also saw that he was just an accessory; their real target was Nikolsky, and he was not about to rat on a friend.

"Your friend's name?" "Volodya. Volodya Yevdokimov." "Where did you take him?" "Somewhere over in Maryina Roshcha. It was dark and he just gave me directions. You know: left here, straight ahead, that kind of thing." "How many trips did you make to Nakhabino?" Victor remembered they had been observed only twice. "Two." "Anything valuable in either of the loads?" "Valuable! I told you—it was just a pile of boards: plywood, laths . . ."

Then they told him that some valuable state property had disappeared—they weren't at liberty to be more specific—and that it was his civic duty to tell them everything he knew. He said he had nothing to hide.

They switched to threats. "You know, we gave you your license, and we can take it away." Whereupon Victor let loose a volley of the choicest abuse at the Motor Vehicle Inspectorate, Volodya

Yevdokimov, plywood, and "your bloody valuable state property."
They immediately backed off, gave him back his papers, and let him
go.

If Victor related the incident to Nikolsky with a certain pride, he
was positively bursting with it when he told him what had happened to Varya after the stormy night they had all spent together at
the Refuge. Apparently Varya had gone to stay with her friend, but
at the end of a week or two she got worried and asked Victor, who
had been visiting her every evening, to take her home. Victor then
started making regular trips out to Nakhabino, and one day Varya
told him that the architects had been back, that they'd insulted her,
said outright they knew what was in the attic, and threatened to
make things hot for her and her husband. So she wrote to her sister
and asked her to tell Kolya what was up, and her sister wrote back
that Kolya was drinking heavily and carrying on openly with the
local schoolmistress. Well, Varya had a good cry, and before he
knew it they were in bed together. That was the first time too, because
she was a good girl (even though he could see she was dying for it),
but the minute she heard Kolya was two-timing her she only had
eyes for Victor, and now . . .

"Wonderful, Vitek, fine," said Nikolsky, "but what about the
architects?"

"The architects? Oh, they came and poked their noses around
again, hassled the neighbors, but that was that. We really fucked
the bastards over, didn't we?"

But he who laughs last laughs best, thought Nikolsky on his way
to the Refuge the next morning. And the bastard he'd seen the previous evening wore a smile that said, "So you think you've fucked
us over, eh?"

Everything was clear as day, the beautiful day that followed the
bleak night after the party at the National. The sun shone bright,
there wasn't a cloud in the sky, the yellow leaves were brushed by
a fine layer of snow. The frost had performed one of those magnificent transformations of nature that are visible to the naked eye and
can even be fixed on paper with charcoal, sepia, pen and ink, and a
sheet of white paper under a moderate but even light.

It was eleven by the time he arrived—he had stopped at the office
first to tell them he was taking the day off—and Vera and Leopold

Mikhailovich were drinking coffee. He immediately filled them in on the details and concluded by warning them that since *they* had found their way to the Refuge, Vera should be expecting a visit from the fire department or state insurance or the local choral society.

"But how could they have known that Victor would come here after the party last night?"

"They didn't. All they knew was that Victor regularly drove out to see Varya and—it only takes a single vigilant neighbor—that he'd called for her last night. Then they simply tailed the car and noted all the stops."

"Didn't he stop for you on the way to the National?" asked Leopold Mikhailovich.

"Oh, my God, you're right! I never thought of that! Looks like poor Auntie's going to have her own little talk with the fire brigade."

"But what if you're just imagining things?" Vera interjected. "You said yourself you didn't recognize the man in the car right off."

Nikolsky was ready to jump down her throat.

"No, it's clear," said Leopold Mikhailovich. "Things are a good deal more serious than we thought."

"Why did Vitek have to fall in love with Varya!" Nikolsky sighed.

"Varya's charming," Leopold Mikhailovich replied with a smile, "They would have caught up with us some other way."

Nikolsky was surprised at the—what was it?—exhaustion, resignation, in Leopold Mikhailovich's voice. Vera too looked up in alarm.

"I've nothing specific in mind. I've just had my share of experience, that's all." He smiled to himself: always going on about experience.

They finished their coffee in silence. Then Leopold Mikhailovich said he had an appointment to keep and Nikolsky made them promise to let him know the moment anything new came up.

Later on that day Nikolsky reached Victor by phone. He was just back from Nakhabino and happy as could be.

"Listen, Vitek, you did pick Varya up last night at Nakhabino, didn't you?"

"Of course. My place is off-limits on account of Vanya, and she doesn't like to leave hers for long. She's afraid that husband of hers will show up. The house is in her name—her parents left it to her—and when he's been away for six months she can cross his name off the deed."

"I see," said Nikolsky thoughtfully, though all he really cared about was that they had in fact set off for the party from Nakhabino.

A few days passed uneventfully, but Nikolsky was still worried and in the end phoned the Refuge to find out if anything had happened.

"Nothing," Vera answered almost triumphantly. "Didn't I tell you?"

There was no sense in arguing the point. She believed what she needed to believe, and consciously or not she was also trying to make things easier on Leopold Mikhailovich. He knew her well enough to understand that since he had been the bearer of bad tidings she saw him and not the bad tidings as the cause of all the trouble. He did not phone the Refuge again.

When another week went by with no repercussions, he began to catch himself wondering whether he hadn't in fact jumped to conclusions, whether he hadn't simply imagined that smile—that insolent, yet mysterious, even mystical (had he been a mystic?) smile—in his post-National, sub-drunken stupor.

He decided to look in on Aaron. He tapped at the window as he had done when visiting Leopold Mikhailovich in the spring—it seemed a different life now—and Aaron let him in with one of his broad toothy grins. They talked about this and that, about how the Master was going downhill and Leopold Mikhailovich seemed to be holding on, though of course he was younger.

"How old is he, anyway?"

"Under seventy."

Nikolsky was itching to tell Aaron about how they'd been followed, but he realized it would only make Aaron worry about Leopold Mikhailovich. So he drank weak tea and munched rock-hard biscuits and listened to Aaron's marvelous new creations, a dense, untrammeled flow of words not always accessible to the consciousness but visually, audibly, tactilely stimulating, clashing, swirling, scaling, dispersing, purling, whispering, glowing in fire, dying in silence, and coming alive again in love. Nikolsky listened motion-less, and when his brain could no longer stand the tension of con-stant communication with the divine spark, he found himself looking for points of reference: Dante? the Apocalypse? the Prophets? Yes, yes, the Bible, definitely the Bible. He remembered the horror and the ecstasy of pale horses and riders, of waters divided, of inscrip-tions appearing magically on walls, and people made pillars of salt.

One day Vera phoned Nikolsky at work.

"Stop in and see us on your way home," she said in a voice that implied, And don't be too hard on me.

Apparently she had been visited by a team of wiring inspectors. Two men and a woman. The woman, clearly nervous, had asked her how many sockets there were in the house and how many lamps: the meter gave suspiciously low readings for so large a dwelling and would probably need to be replaced. Meanwhile, the men scruti-nized every inch of the place, and one of them, fingering a pile of paintings on the entresol, inquired, "Are you an artist?" and, when Vera shook her head no, sneered and said, "Oh, an a-a-amateur." In other words, they wanted her to know that the wiring inspection was only an excuse for an inspection of a different kind.

"So you were right," said Vera gently, and suddenly Nikolsky, who had come prepared to preen himself on his victory, felt the wind go out of his sails.

"I've heard rumors of an investigation," said Leopold Mikhai-lovich, "a large-scale effort, in which case my collection is only sec-ondary. But we can only guess whether it's a routine antiformalist campaign or whether they're seriously cracking down on contact with foreigners and—worst of all—hard-currency transactions."

Leopold Mikhailovich paused for a moment and laid his hand on Nikolsky's arm.

"I want you to know, Leonid Pavlovich, that my only interest in all this has been to preserve fine art, my only role a philanthropic one—and a necessarily modest one at that: I live on my pension and paid the artists no more than what I managed to earn as a lecturer. True, during my years at the National I amassed a considerable amount in tips, but that all went long ago on my Dutch and Flemish collection."

"I know your motives are pure, Leopold Mikhailovich!"

"I realize that, and I'm grateful to you for it. But you, that is, you and Vera"—he looked over at Vera with great suffering in his eyes—"must also know that I have never done anything illegal. I say this because you will undoubtedly be questioned about me, and we cannot know how it will end."

Vera tried to say something reassuring, and Nikolsky wondered aloud how *they* could know that the paintings belonged to Leopold Mikhailovich. Why couldn't they belong to him, Nikolsky? After all, he was the one caught transporting them.

"They're not so naive as that. Nor are you, for that matter. No, in the long run they'll trace them back to me."

In the short run, however, Nikolsky proved perspicacious, because shortly thereafter Nikolsky's aunt had a visit from her son. Nikolsky's elder cousin was also Nikolsky, having taken his mother's surname to avoid the stigma of his father's German one (although his father's family had come to Russia during the days of Peter the Great and provided Russia with military physicians for two centuries). The elder Nikolsky (who was successful in the sense that he was high enough in the *apparat* to be mentioned in all the newspapers on the same day) burst into the flat and, without even acknowledging his mother's presence, started haranguing the younger Nikolsky, that is, raking him over the coals for the standard infringements of socialist morality: improper work habits, frivolous use of leisure time, lack of respect for women and the collective, and so on and so forth. When he looked up to see his younger cousin laughing and holding out a bottle of vodka, he let out a stream of invective, which only increased the younger cousin's merriment. The younger cousin then began picking at his elder cousin's grammar and asking him whether he thought Comrade Stalin's grammatical mistakes should be incorporated into the language. The elder cousin took a different tack: How dare he exploit his poor defenseless old aunt?

But the poor defenseless old aunt sprang to her own defense, shouting, "What right have you to tell him whether he can live here or not?" She burst into tears. "Where's your conscience?"

The elder cousin, not in the habit of hearing the word "conscience" in connection with himself, listened pensively while his mother went on and on about a third person, "he," who kept supplementing her minuscule pension. The only effect her ranting and raving had on him was to make him realize how old she was and what an outdated concept "conscience" was. Then he thought to himself, What a relief to have a huge apartment of my own, and he walked over to the window to make sure his chauffeur was at the wheel. As he threw on his coat and scarf and positioned his fashionable deerskin hat on his head, he couldn't help sputtering, "You watch your step, Leonid! I can't be expected to. . . . After all, specu—" But he stopped short and stalked off, slamming the door.

So that was it! Dear cousin couldn't keep it to himself: speculation, speculation in foreign currency! That's what they were trying to pin on him! And the only reason they hadn't nabbed him was that they wanted to have a talk with his bigwig cousin first.

"Who is this relative of yours? We don't want any trouble we can avoid. We know you're not mixed up in it, of course, but it's our duty to look into these things."

"What's the charge?"

"It's rather vague as yet. Something to do with hard currency operations—but not a word to anybody."

"Of course not! Of course not!"

Worried that his good name was in danger, cousin bigwig had rushed off to find out what he could, issue a warning, and perhaps even hush up the affair. It didn't work.

Within a few days Nikolsky found himself seated in the armchair his ever so considerate boss reserved for serious conversations.

"Tell me, how are things going in Zaalaisk?"

"You know perfectly well we've kept our part of the bargain."

"Yes, yes, of course. Tell me, don't you think you deserve a promotion?"

"Anything you say, boss."

"The trouble is, there's no money for it."

"Then why bring it up in the first place?"

"I just thought you might be a bit . . . well, dissatisfied in general. I mean, you have the highest qualifications, and the work here isn't always as challenging as it might be; in fact, I foresee a period when . . ."

What is he driving at? Nikolsky wondered. But not for long. He leaned forward, looked the boss in the eye, and said, "Has anyone been talking to you about me?"

The boss looked away.

Nikolsky stood and said, "Yes or no?"

The boss made a helpless gesture. "Just don't tell anyone I said so."

"I understand. You're under oath. Well, the whole thing's a lot of hooey! And you won't gain anything by giving me the chuck. You need me here."

"We do a lot of top-secret contracts, Leonid Pavlovich. . . ."

The boss cut a pitiable figure.

"May I go?"

"Yes. Oh, and one more thing. Try not to stay away from work so often. It's in your own interest."

They started closing in on Vera too. One day Borya Khavkin showed up at the Refuge all excited. He had been called to the personnel office of the institute where Vera and he had studied and where he now taught part-time, and before he knew it he was being grilled about Vera. At first he assumed they were thinking of hiring her and was even hurt she hadn't told him anything about it, but before long the questions veered into areas having nothing to do with Vera's qualities as a teacher: whether Borya was a regular guest at her house, whether there was a regular group that gathered there. What did they talk about? Besides poetry and singing. Painting? Ah, painting. How did she come by all the paintings in the house? No, besides the ones she inherited from her parents. You don't know. I see. And do you know how she earns her living?

"Excuse me, but who are you?"

"An investigator. Now you will write us up a detailed report including everything you've told me and anything else you know about her and her circle."

"And if I don't?"

"You have the right to refuse, but we can summon you officially, and then you will have no choice."

"Summon me where?"

"Why, to the public prosecutor's office."

Borya paused.

"Well?" asked Vera.

"I refused. Let them summon me if they're so eager. You don't think I said too much, do you?"

"You've no reason to feel guilty," said Leopold Mikhailovich.

"I always feel guilty. I've got a Judas complex."

"I wonder how they knew to talk to you," said Vera.

"Simple. Shurik told them. I literally tripped over him as I was going in."

"Who is this Shurik?" asked Leopold Mikhailovich.

"Another of our classmates," said Borya, "and now an assistant dean. You can be sure Shurik gave the investigator an earful!"

"What could he have said?" Vera objected.

"Plenty. He's been here often enough."

"Oh, he's not so bad."

Borya and Shurik had once been rivals for Vera's attention.

"*Wasn't* so bad, until he took over our Komsomol group and wormed his way into the Party bureau."

Their squabble would have gone on had Nikolsky not appeared on the scene and confirmed Borya's suspicions about Shurik. "Look how often he's been to the Refuge and how many of the regulars he knows. In fact, he's the one who introduced Slavik to the group. Slavik! God's gift to television! Congratulations, Leopold Mikhailovich! You have just entered the ranks of the suspicious."

"But why?" Vera cried.

"Who else was here the evening Aaron and Leopold Mikhailovich came for the first time? Got a sheet of paper? Let's make a list."

It all came back to them: the people—Slavik and his baby doll, the scholars and their friend Prebylov, Carmencita and her José— and the scandalous way it ended.

"A pity," said Leopold Mikhailovich. "Now Aaron will get involved."

"Prebylov will see to that! Really, Vera! How could you have invited such a—"

"Leonid Pavlovich!" Leopold Mikhailovich broke in.

"I'm sorry. Forgive me, Vera. It's just that everything looks so bleak." Then he had a good idea. "Have you heard the one about the time Nikita went to inspect one of his new blocks of flats? Well, he went into a bathroom, and . . ."

V

WHAT WITH the recent events, the Refuge get-togethers had fallen by the wayside. A group of regulars decided to reinstate them and meet every other Friday, but there was some disagreement over where to hold them now that the Refuge was under surveillance. Then Tolik, blushing with emotion, pointed out that avoiding the Refuge in such circumstances was tantamount to betrayal. He promptly received a noisy kiss on the cheek from Vera. There was also the pencil box to consider, first, because Finkelmeyer lived there and if they didn't keep in touch with him he'd turn into a real hermit, and second, because Leopold Mikhailovich needed to put in an occasional appearance to show the neighbors—and thus, indirectly, the police—that he deserved to maintain his residence permit. They decided to alternate between the two.

The theme Leopold Mikhailovich chose for the first get-together was "The Russian Avant-Garde." He placed a large pile of reproductions and photographs in front of him and began with the Itinerants, moved on to Vrubel and the Lithuanian artist Čiurlionis, and by the end of an hour and a half reached the artists whose work was being stored in the Refuge—that is, the artists whom Khrushchev—and then all officialdom—had condemned so roundly.

For the next get-together, the first in his flat, Leopold Mikhailovich chose the theme "The Evolution of the Nude in Western Art." All along one side of the room, on the walls, floor, bed, and chairs, he placed reproductions—some in black and white, others in inviting pink—of Greeks and Romans, especially frescos; ascetic medieval Germans; Renaissance Italians starting with Botticelli's Aphrodite; neoclassicists and romantics; Renoir, of course; Picasso's drawings; the sculptures of Maillol, Rodin, and Moore; a "Nude" by Falk that had recently been run down in the press; and last but not leas*—and to general acclaim—Tolik's ballet series (pastels, charcoals, sepias, and watercolors on colored paper).

"If only I had a model, a live model," Tolik kept saying, and at one point Vera couldn't stand it any longer and shouted, "Down with convention! *I'll* pose for you, Tolik! As many sessions as you like! What do you say?"

They all cheered, Tolik beamed, and someone proposed they should all drink to it. Borya ran out to see if the corner shop was still open, and in the meantime Leopold Mikhailovich selected works from Tolik's series to place next to Venus, Psyche, Bathsheba, and Olympia. Soon Tolik's sketches were everywhere, and suddenly it was clear to all those assembled, even through the thick gray screen of cigarette smoke: Tolik was a fine artist. Just as somebody put it into words, there was a loud knock on the door.

The mystery of art does not reside in its beauty, for nowadays beauty can be measured and expressed in figures; no, the mystery of art resides in its banality. Should we then avoid banality like the plague? Should we venerate it as a revelation? Is there a golden mean between the banal and the unique? We might ask what life, art's great provider, has to say in this regard, but what can life teach art if it is capable of using the cheap, banal contrast between a moment of spiritual joy and the appearance of the local police lieutenant flanked by a janitor and an old woman chewing on her lips? No, art had better forget about life if life is no more original than that.

Leopold Mikhailovich was invited to explain what was going on. He said he was giving an art lecture to friends. The policeman replied that there were institutions specially set aside for such cultural activities. Leopold Mikhailovich thought it the better part of valor to hold his tongue. Then what should ring out in the silence but Borya Khavkin's footsteps. The policeman stepped aside, the door flew open, and in bounded Borya with a string bag bulging obscenely with bottles.

"That's the art the lecture's really about," said the policeman to the two witnesses. "The art of drinking vodka."

He was immediately attracted to Tolik's sketches: he had never seen such a wealth of naked bodies in such a variety of poses, and was clearly disconcerted.

"What do you call that?" he said, picking up one of them at random.

"It's called a nude, which is the term for the whole genre."

"Well, I can tell you another term for what the two of them are doing."

Actually they were rather too far apart to be doing what he had in mind.

"Well, I say they're just people with no clothes on," said the old woman, "and all *these* people ought to be ashamed of themselves!"

"Right!" said the policeman. He turned to Leopold Mikhailovich. "Do you live here?"

"I do," said Leopold Mikhailovich.

"Well, tell your 'friends' to get their papers out. And if some of them 'happen to have left them at home,' I hold you responsible for the accuracy of their statements."

"Would you mind telling me the basis for your request?" said Leopold Mikhailovich in an even tone.

"The law. Which you and the tenant living here in your place are breaking, by the way."

"Tell me, what is illegal about having in a few friends?" Leopold Mikhailovich continued in his mild voice.

"Let's see who your friends are first," he answered sullenly.

Finkelmeyer produced his papers, but the policeman knew him and waved him off; Leopold Mikhailovich produced his, and again the policeman gave them only a cursory glance; Danuta, who as a former deportee was never without her papers, did not get off so easily.

"So . . . You are the wife of . . . Nikol . . . Nikolsky."

He's in the know, all right, thought Nikolsky. If he knows my name, he knows Vera's too.

"I am Nikolsky," he said, "and this is my wife. She has a Moscow residence permit and works at a dry cleaner's. What more do you need to know?"

"Don't rush me," said the policeman, copying out something from Danuta's papers. "So you're a Lithuanian."

"That's right." She had been through it hundreds of times.

The policeman then moved on to each guest in turn, asking for last name, first name, patronymic, place of residence, place of employment . . .

The janitor looked longingly at the bottles; the old woman bit her lips and mumbled to herself. When at last the process was completed, they followed the policeman out of the room.

At first they drank without much enthusiasm, but things picked

up and soon they were cracking jokes at the expense of the uninvited guests. The old woman had had it in for Leopold Mikhailovich from the start. Apparently his room had at one time belonged
to her family, and although her children moved away and her husband died and the room disappeared from her residence permit long
before Leopold Mikhailovich arrived on the scene, who else was
there for her to vent her ire on?

The guests stayed late; Danuta stayed the night. At seven the next
morning, when she was trying to slip out quietly, the old woman all
but pounced on her and cried, "Really, I ask you! One husband in
her papers, another in her bed. Shameless hussy!"

Aaron was in his underwear and couldn't do anything to help.
As soon as the door clicked shut, he ran to the window. It was some
time before Danuta appeared. She didn't want to go out into the
street until she had regained her composure, and when she did scurry
past through the winter dawn, the streetlamp cast her shadow on
the windowpane, then drew it off to one side, and finally swept it
out of sight.

A week later, the next Friday, Leopold Mikhailovich, Nikolsky,
and Vera all received summonses. Finkelmeyer signed for Leopold
Mikhailovich's, Danuta for Nikolsky's; only Vera received hers in
person. All three were requested to appear at the public prosecutor's office on different days, Leopold Mikhailovich first, on the
following Monday, then Nikolsky, and finally Vera.

The worst part was the waiting. All three kept imagining what
was known about them, and wanted from them, but it was like
fighting an army of ghosts.

Anxiety lies within us; whatever comes from without, no matter
how threatening, brings relief. Gradually they realized that the only
way to breathe more easily was to picture something concrete, like
the investigator wearing a crumpled suit that didn't quite fit, worrying about whether his questions were logical, grammatical, and
to the point. . . .

Leopold Mikhailovich answered slowly; he gave himself ample
time to think. When asked to speed up his responses, he replied, "I
am no longer young, and I find our conversation rather trying." The
investigator could say nothing.

The questions dealt mainly with Leopold Mikhailovich's past.

He kept expecting them to veer around to his original collection—
the one his daughter had sold piece by piece—and the "unearned
income" he had used to assemble it. It never came to that, however;
in fact, the investigator appeared to have no knowledge of the collection. Then why did he keep harping on Leopold Mikhailovich's
days as a waiter? He asked whether Leopold Mikhailovich had any
acquaintances from the National. Leopold Mikhailovich named the
man who had helped him to set up the party for Aaron. Clearly the
investigator had another kind of acquaintance in mind. "Did you
have occasion to serve foreigners?" he asked. Yes, he did. "Well, I
don't wish to wear you out with my questions," he said immediately. "You will receive another summons within a few days."

Unlike Leopold Mikhailovich, Nikolsky answered each question
instantly, doing his best to make the investigator sweat. Nikolsky
never missed a chance to mock a dullard, and the investigator was
a sitting duck. Either he answered "yes" or "no" to "when" and
"where" questions, and the investigator, not quite grasping he was
being had, would simply repeat the question, at which point Nikolsky would say, "I don't understand"; or he went into great detail,
even philosophizing over some minor point, until the investigator
stopped him in desperation. Secure in the knowledge that Leopold
Mikhailovich hadn't been asked about the pictures, he had a whale
of a time. Then the investigator came to Victor.

"You mean Red? Of course I know him. We worked together.
What's he done now?"

"Now? What do you mean exactly?"

"So he likes his bottle. Look, I once saw him give a passenger a
sock in the jaw."

"Why," the investigator asked, "did he say you lived in Maryina
Roshcha?"

"Are you sure you're not mixing me up with somebody?"

But when the investigator brought up the nonexistent Volodya
Yevdokimov, Nikolsky simply said that Victor had made it all up.
Why? Because—don't you see?—he couldn't be absolutely sure
whether those boards had been stolen or not. He didn't want to rat
on a friend.

"Boards?" said the investigator. "Who said anything about
boards?"

No you don't, fellow. Not with me!

"You think I don't remember? These two guys tried to stop us. An architect and a fire inspector. We almost knocked their blocks off."

"Why did they try to stop you?"

"Ask *them*!"

But the investigator wouldn't let go, and after protesting for a while Nikolsky was forced to admit that he did have an idea why the two of them tried to stop them: "Because the boards *may* have been stolen." The sigh with which he prefaced these words made it absolutely clear to the investigator that he didn't like betraying a friend, but, well, he, the investigator had pushed him, Nikolsky, to the wall.

"I see, I see," said the investigator, as he thought how to get back on the right track. "Tell me, how, when, and where did you meet Varvara Begicheva?"

Nikolsky began searching his memory. No, his mind was blank. All he could remember was that they had worked out the deal with the boards at Leopold Mikhailovich's. When? Oh, two weeks or so before they drove out to pick them up.

"How many trips did you make?"

"Two."

Pause.

"When did your friend enter into cohabitation with Begicheva?"

"Vitek?" said Nikolsky, flustered. "I don't know. I mean, I don't know about any cohabitation." His whole being seemed to say, One betrayal a day was enough; Vitek hadn't given him away and he wouldn't give away Vitek. No, there was no friend more noble than Nikolsky!

And on that note the session came to an end—until further notice.

Vera was testy and aggressive with the investigator even though Leopold Mikhailovich, Nikolsky, and Borya Khavkin (who had taken to stopping in at the Refuge on a daily basis) all advised her to keep a low profile. Whenever he tried to pry, she would challenge him with a "What difference does that make?" or "What business is it of yours?" Moreover, she insisted on smoking even after the investigator informed her that cigarette smoke made him sick. Perhaps because she irritated him so or because she was the owner of the house to which all the evidence led, Vera was the first to be asked point blank about art. Yes, she had a number of paintings. No, over a long period of time. Gifts mostly. A *complete* list? Impossible. Oh, people like Benois, Korovin. If the investigator needed to know the exact number, he was welcome to come and count them, only he would need a warrant, wouldn't he? Visitors? Oh yes, all the time. She liked company. Foreigners? He must be joking! The only ones she came into contact with were the ones she met professionally as a guide at exhibitions or as an interpreter—he'd heard of simultaneous translation, hadn't he?—at scholarly conferences. Was that clear?

Vera was very proud of herself. If they thought Benois and Korovin were contemporary abstract artists, that was their problem.

Borya was terribly upset at not having had a go at the investigator, but before long he too was called in. Then Zhenya, who came back in tears; then old Uncle Kostya, Leopold Mikhailovich's coeval, new neighbor, and for the last three months fast friend; then Tolik, who proclaimed at an institute Komsomol meeting, "Go ahead! Kick me out! I won't say a word against Leopold Mikhailovich! He's worth more than all of you put together!" and was soon thereafter, in the course of a reprimand for being late to a lecture, told that his days at the institute were numbered; and eventually Citizen Nikolsky's wife. The investigator proved particularly well informed about her circumstances: he knew about Zaalaisk, he knew about the hasty marriage, he knew about her cohabitation with Citizen Finkelmeyer both before and after the marriage, and he knew that she and said Finkelmeyer used both her husband's flat and the flat of a certain retired waiter for their illicit meetings.

New Year's Eve was rather subdued at the Refuge. Behind all the standard wishes was the hope that the bleak period they were going through would soon be over. In the middle of the night they trooped outside and Vera lit a candle in the branches of an old fir tree.

Just before dawn Danuta went up to Nikolsky and said, "Aaron wanted to tell you himself, but I thought, No, that's not right. What I mean is, thank you for everything, but the time has come . . . I . . ."

"Of course, of course, I understand," Nikolsky inserted nervously. He understood everything, he had a fine sense for what a woman needed, and women had always noticed that about him and been appreciative of it. "I promised it was dissolvable at any time. But remember, you can keep your Moscow residence permit even after the divorce. That's the law."

"Thank you, Leonid. You are a true friend. But I want to go to Lithuania."

"I see. Yes, this is the time. What does Aaron think?"

"That I should go."

Then Nikolsky went over to Aaron, and they performed a canon (a contrapuntal device dating from the Middle Ages whereby a melody stated in one part is imitated strictly in one or more other parts) on the following text: *Oh holy Danu— O holy Danuta— ta—why hast thou—why hast thou forsaken me—forsaken me in this my hour of need—in this my hour of need?*

"I feel rotten," said Nikolsky.

"So do I," said Finkelmeyer.

"Idiot! Why don't you marry her?"

"Moron! I can't."

"What will become of her in Lithuania?"

"She can't stay here."

"They'd never let her alone."

"Right."

"Funny they've left you alone."

"Frida's been called in."

"Frida!"

"First Nikolsky's wife, then Finkelmeyer's."

"Terrific."

"They've left me for dessert. I've known Leopold Mikhailovich for more than ten years."

By then Leopold Mikhailovich was on the stand two or three times a week. The investigator was after the names of artists who had sold Leopold Mikhailovich their works or whose studios he had visited; Leopold Mikhailovich sidestepped the questions skillfully, and the investigator was occasionally forced to reveal facts he could have obtained only by interrogating definite individuals. By carrying out a discreet investigation of his own, Leopold Mikhailovich was able to determine that the case dated back to the days immediately following Khrushchev's antiformalist, anti-abstractionist tirade at the Manège exhibition of the Nineteen, when an exhibition including some of the Manège's abstract canvases was mounted in the West and widely commented on in the Western press. The publicity was such that the culprits had to be found.

The lawyer Leopold Mikhailovich consulted informed him that things could easily take an ominous turn. "Granted, you have not done anything illegal: you buy a painting from an artist—for practically nothing, as you say—and then sell it to back to him for the same nominal sum; he is the one who sells it to a foreigner for hard currency. But what does the outsider see? The outsider sees only that you buy paintings which later show up abroad. The outsider knows nothing about your dealings with the painter, and the painter can easily deny that you sold the work back to him."

"But how can they prove I sold something to a foreigner?"

"The presumption of innocence is not one of the cornerstones of our judicial system," he replied, speaking as a venerable practitioner of the law (whose many years on the bench had acquainted him as intimately with its minuses as with its pluses) and in the privacy of his own home. "Given the circumstances, you could go from witness to defendant overnight. My guess is that the prosecution has run into some snags. If each of the artists says, 'I sell my works to Russians for rubles; what happens to them afterwards is none of my business,' there is no end to the investigatory work involved. It is much simpler to posit an operation and pinpoint its guiding light, its *organizer*. And you, my dear fellow, are an ideal target. What did you do upon retiring as a waiter? Lecture on the history of art. Where did you work as a waiter? In the fashionable National, where you were in daily contact with foreigners and could easily set up meetings between artists and prospective clients. Where do you live? At an address which is not in your residence permit and with a woman half your age who collects art and works on a day-to-day basis with foreigners."

"But the facts will show—"

"All I'm saying," the lawyer said wearily, "is that you may find yourself a defendant soon. For that no facts are needed."

Leopold Mikhailovich thanked the lawyer and made ready to leave.

"So you have trouble with your legs," he said, nodding at the cane, without which Leopold Mikhailovich could no longer walk.

"Yes, they have been acting up lately."

"Take my advice and have a doctor certify you as incapacitated, in need of special treatment, something along those lines. The best thing for you to do now is vanish, disappear. Do you think you could arrange for a month or two at a sanatorium?"

"Wouldn't that make me look even more suspicious? And only prolong the agony in the end?"

"The case has been dragging on for some time now; they want to get it over with. According to what you have told me, they are on the lookout for a scapegoat, and if you drop out of the picture they will have to go elsewhere. You are in a dangerous position. Make yourself scarce. And ask your friends to keep me up to date."

"Thank you. I'll think it over."

"One more thing. If my worst fears come true, I am willing to defend you."

When Leopold Mikhailovich told Vera and Nikolsky about his talk with the lawyer, he passed over the lawyer's recommendations in silence. He recognized flight as a sensible option, but considered it none the less ignominious therefor. He still hoped that the investigator would come to see that neither he nor his friends had done anything wrong, and would leave them in peace.

Then late one Friday Victor brought a red-eyed Varya to a Refuge get-together. Her husband, Kolya, had turned up at Nakhabino, banging on the door with threats, curses, and drunken sobs. She refused to let him in, and eventually he spent the night at a friend's, but on the next and following mornings, as soon as his hangover let him, he renewed his siege on the house, leaving only when Victor drove up.

The wife of the friend Kolya was staying with, tired of their non-stop spree, visited Varya at Nakhabino one day to commiserate and pour out her soul. She said she couldn't go to the police because Kolya kept bragging about having them in his pocket now that he'd told them the whole story.

"The whole story? What did he tell them?"

"He was so drunk I could hardly make it out, but something about getting himself and all his friends off the hook and pointing the finger at 'the old fathead.' "

"That's *you*, Leopold Mikhailovich! After all you did for him!"

"What else, Varya?" Vera asked nervously. "What else?"

"That's about it. He just kept boasting about getting back at Leopold Mikhailovich for bringing me together with Victor here, getting even with all those bigshot professors and critics—they had it coming to them whether they'd done anything or not." She burst into tears.

Vera did her best to console her; Leopold Mikhailovich phoned the lawyer.

"What?" the lawyer shouted. "You still here?" And when he heard about the new developments: "You will do as I told you at once, do you hear? At once! I will not go into details over the phone, but there is not a moment to lose!"

Leopold Mikhailovich hung up. They all looked at him expectantly, but for a long while he could not bring himself to speak up, and when he did speak he did not come straight to the point. He reiterated his conviction that he had done no wrong and stated how sorry he was to put them through all this pain. But he was grateful to them and happy. . . . (He never said why he was happy, but he did say the word, and the *why* resounded tacitly in the pause that followed.)

At last he was able to broach the subject of his departure and set forth the lawyer's fears.

"You must go," said Nikolsky in a tone that brooked no resistance. "What's holding you back? You don't want to leave us in the lurch, is that it? Really now! You're the center; we're the periphery. They'll forget about us once they leave you in peace."

"If I didn't think that was the case, I'd never entertain the thought of leaving."

The next issue was where he should go. Leopold Mikhailovich didn't care in the least, and no one else could get past the standard Crimea/Caucasus combination.

"Danuta's up in the air too," said Nikolsky pensively. "She's going to Lithuania, but doesn't quite know where to start."

"Lithuania?" asked Uncle Kostya. "Palanga's in Lithuania, isn't it? On the sea? We've got some cottages there. My factory, I mean. I can sign up for one tomorrow. This is the off-season; they're all empty. I have a few weeks coming to me. What do you say, Leopold?"

"And if you took Danuta with you . . ." Nikolsky prompted.

"Oh, wouldn't that be wonderful!" said Vera. "With Danuta looking after you I wouldn't worry at all."

The next day Nikolsky went to see Danuta, praying all the way that Aaron would not be there. Just half an hour together, no, an hour (two—three—a day—eternity to say—tell—once—all). Watch out, Nikolsky; you're out of control. Hopeless. *Hope*less. Even though he was in a hurry, he stopped for a moment at the place where he had stood with his back to the church and turned to admire the golden crosses shining in the sun. They weren't shining. It was a winter evening, not a spring day. How many days had passed, how many pages had turned, how much water had fallen and seeped into the earth from the time he first connected the word *hope* with the name *Danuta*.

They sat at the table (*face à face,* Nikolsky kept thinking for some reason, *en tête-à-tête*), talking calmly. The first thing he asked was when she expected Aaron. Not for a while yet, she answered, embarrassed. (So he's staying overnight, thought Nikolsky.)

"I have many addresses, people who came back from Siberia long ago. Kaunas, Vilnius, Anykščiai, Telšiai . . . But I want to be on my own. I don't want people to feel sorry for me. Don't you agree?"

"Yes, Danuta, I agree."

"Life is the best teacher, they say. . . . Oh, yes. I wanted to know: was the trip to Palanga your idea? I am very grateful. You are so . . ."

". . . so? . . ." Nikolsky felt his heart race.

". . . so un . . . un . . . I can't remember the word."

". . . selfish? Unselfish?"

"Yes, that's it!"

Oh, Danuta. How can you . . . I mean . . . Can it be selfless when there's still hope . . . You see, I've always hoped that . . . Oh, Leonid, you are a fine person, but that is not what . . . A fine person is fine for everyone, but I have something else in . . . What does it mean for us? You see? I use the words *for us*. . . . I can put on water for tea if you . . . Not now, though do you remember when we had tea together in Zaalaisk? . . . I do, Leonid. . . . Well, the reason I'm telling you all this is that a whole year has gone by, and I never even noticed the only thing that's mattered since then is that I love you.

There was agony in her face. She went and put the water on for tea. Nikolsky lit a cigarette, greedily inhaling the bittersweet smoke to fill the void where only a few minutes earlier he had felt his heart pounding.

Danuta took her seat again. Nothing happened.

"Tell me honestly, Danuta," said Nikolsky after a pause. "Are you planning to come back to Aaron?"

She hesitated, wondering whether to answer, then—if only to console him and besides, didn't she owe it to him to be frank?—replied, "He does not . . . need me. He does not need any of us. He does not even need himself, do you see?"

"Yes, I see."

"A child left alone in the woods—he does not know what he needs. If someone finds him and warms him he will be warm; if not, he will sit under a tree and be cold. No one will know what becomes of him."

Nikolsky did not quite understand what she meant, but her story made him uneasy.

"I need someone who needs me," she said softly.

"I understand. You want to have children."

"Yes. A simple life. Where can you find a simple, beautiful life? I have never seen one. Not there. But at least I had my sister."

"What about here?"

"It has been good. I have rested. I am ready now. To live."

"And you think you'll find that life, that happiness, in Lithuania?"

"I will see. Here"—and she touched her right temple through a lock of auburn hair that shone in the suffused light—"a voice tells me things will not be good in Lithuania, but here"—and her hand slid down to the gentle swell in her sweater—"it tells me that I will not be at peace until I go."

"Well, no matter how things work out there, Danuta, or as they say in old-fashioned novels, 'no matter what fate has in store for you, remember that no distance shall extinguish the feelings you inspire in your faithful servant, that come what may he will always consider it the greatest of joys to fulfill your slightest wish.' I really mean that, Danuta."

She vouchsafed him one of her rare laughs—it was the first time he had seen her face light up—but immediately turned serious again. "Old-fashioned novels . . . I have read so little. I want to read and read and read. In Lithuanian and in Russian. You must think I do not read Russian well."

"No, I don't!"

"I read very well. And I understand everything people say. I only speak poorly."

"No, you don't!"

"I speak poorly, because I speak so little. I speak little to people I do not know well. The people I knew well were Lithuanian, and we spoke Lithuanian. But I had few Lithuanian books, so I read Russian ones. Now I will read more."

At that moment the phone rang. Aaron would be arriving soon. Nikolsky tried to go back to where they had left off, but the spell was broken and all he did was ask Danuta to write to him from Palanga and from wherever she happened to go after Palanga. He didn't want to keep asking Aaron about her; it might be painful for him. A few lines would do. Would she promise?

She promised.

Suddenly Aaron appeared in the doorway. "You may congratulate me," he said. "Today was my turn."

They guessed immediately where he had been.

"Well, tell us all about it!" Nikolsky cried out, through he had resolved to leave as soon as Aaron came and avoid the pain of seeing them together.

Aaron shrugged. "There's nothing much to tell, really. The standard questions. He was more interested in why I had no job and was living at Leopold Mikhailovich's. Then we had a long talk about literature, how it swallows you whole, distracts you from the kind of work society deems useful. My prime example was a doctor by the name of Chekhov, and although he indicated he had heard of him . . ."

When Aaron got excited, he couldn't stop talking.

"All right, Aaron, we get the picture," Nikolsky interrupted. "Now listen carefully. After you've seen Danuta and Leopold Mikhailovich off tomorrow, I want you to remove all your things from the pencil box and bring them here. Danuta will give you her key."

"Thank you, Lyonya, but do you really think it's necessary?"

"It's for your own safety, you idiot! If we don't lock up Leopold Mikhailovich's place after he leaves, they'll never stop snooping."

"Thanks, Lyonya. You're a real—"

"Shut up, will you, Aaron? Well, I'm on my way. Goodbye, Danuta. Forever, perhaps, or is that too—"

Before he could say "hopeless," Aaron jumped in with "You mean you're not coming to see them off?"

"Goodbye," said Danuta. "Be well."

She went up to him and placed her hands on his shoulders.

"My mother used to say that in the old days a man and a woman who were friends would say goodbye like this." She leaned over and touched his left shoulder near the neck with her lips, whereupon he placed his hands on her shoulders and carefully, his head whirling from the gentle aroma of her hair and neck, completed the ritual.

VI

SCARCELY two weeks later, Nikolsky boarded the Kaliningrad train that Danuta, Leopold Mikhailovich, and Uncle Kostya had taken to Lithuania. After politely declining the offer of the soldiers in his compartment to drink to the last hours of their leave, he climbed fully dressed to a top berth and lay there listening to scraps of their coarse conversation intertwined with the rumble of the wheels and an occasional screech of the buffers and breathing the pungent smell of vodka mixed with fumes from the fanless, latchless toilet next door.

If only he could sleep, suppress, repress what the infernal funnel of memory kept spewing to the surface—where is Leopold Mikhailovich?—the investigator's furious tight-lipped face—well, find him, find him—where is Leopold Mikhailovich?—Vera's sobs—why can't they leave him in peace?—where is Leopold Mikhailovich and why have you moved to Nikolsky's flat?—I'm the one they're after now, Lyonya—you're all he has left, Leonid Pavlovich; save him, save my poor Aaron!—then the telegram—PALANGA 16306 9 26 1745—the first number the message, the second the word count, the third the day of the month, the fourth the time (hours + minutes)—more

than twenty-four hours ago— COME IMMEDIATELY PALANGA VITAUTO
6—how did they know Auntie's address?—didn't I tell Danuta to
write to—oh, I gave it to Leopold Mikhailovich just in case—Uncle
Kostya knew that Vera was not the one to—so they sent the telegram to him, that is, me! Nikolsky!—luckily I still had the key—
who is it?—me!—what's wrong?—soften the blow—are you
dressed?—part the fossilized folds of the curtain—Vera in her night-
gown—here, come to the window, find someone to stay with, there's
no reason for you—tell her, you bastard!—no, you show it to her—
she knew anyway—I knew it! I knew it! when?—but it didn't say
when, it said COME IMMEDIATELY PALANGA VITAUTO 6 LEOPOLD
MIKHAILOVICH DECEASED KONSTANTIN—but why send it to you?
why you? I'm going—no, you must stay—he was ready for hysterics—suddenly she was all submission—the droopy-headed toy don-
key he had had as a child—nodding, crying—I promise, promise to
bring back his ... bring him back—O God—but not a word to
anyone! anyone, you hear? especially Aaron, Aaron might ... you're
stronger—yes, we'll bury him ourselves, just you and me, or, rather,
we won't quite bury him.

There was something odd about her reaction. What had she meant
by statements like "I'll be with him anyway" or the even more curious "He will live on"? Why did her smile, mournful at first, turn
tranquil so soon? Could she really have gone off her head? No, their
talk had been perfectly rational; in fact, he'd been slightly put off
by her matter-of-fact references to cremation and her mother's plot
at the New Virgin Cemetery, where they could bury the urn. But
then she came out with "I'm sure he'll be satisfied," and he couldn't
help wondering at the combination of mysticism (in Vera of all people!) and—yes, there was no other word for it—*triumph!*

Dozing off at last, calmed somewhat by the fact that the idea of
triumph, though it explained nothing, at least defined what needed
explaining, he returned to the thought that had flashed through his
mind the moment he read the telegram—namely, that Leopold Mikhailovich was no longer either witness or defendant and that his
death had liberated a number of people besides himself—and to a
word that kept forcing itself upon him: sui ... sui ... ?

The next morning Nikolsky was met at Kretinga by Uncle Kostya. They went straight to the stationmaster.

"A corpse? We had a general not long ago. You'll need a zinc coffin and special permission."

"Where can we find a zinc coffin?" asked Nikolsky. "Where did they find theirs?"

"I don't know," he said, and clearly did not want to make it his business to know. "You'll have to ask at headquarters."

Luckily there were two colonels on the bus to Palanga, and they proved sympathetic, especially the one from Moscow. "If *we* don't help each other here . . ." "We" clearly meant "we Russians," and "here" meant "here in Lithuania." The Muscovite was a political officer in the unit that had prepared the zinc coffin for the general, and he promised to do what he could

The countryside was gray and desolate, broken only by patches of dirty snow. Uncle Kostya droned on in a monotone, as if talking about events long past.

". . . and a nice little cottage. Nice and warm. Nice and clean. They're much better at that kind of thing than we are. The woman who comes to tidy up puts real elbow grease into it. The food is good too. Lots of dairy products. There's this white cheese—you'd swear it was made of sheep's milk, but no, it's ordinary cow's milk, just strained in a special way. Leopold Mikhailovich couldn't get enough of it. They've got smoked eel, the likes of which you haven't seen in years. Good sausage too.

"And you can't imagine how Danuta looked after us. The very sight of her made us feel good, pure. She was always ready to help. Always even-tempered—glowing somehow—even with two old geezers like us on her hands!

"Anyway, every morning Leopold Mikhailovich would write for a few hours. In the afternoon too sometimes. I even wondered if he wasn't overdoing it, but no, he was always cheerful and spry. When we went out for walks, I was careful to ask every once in a while whether it wasn't time to go back—he was still using his cane, after all—but no, he always wanted to move on, go here, go there. It was all so new. And the air! It's a special microclimate, they call it. Lots of iodine, lots of healthy pines, and the sea, of course. True, you couldn't depend on the weather, but we went out even in the rain. He liked that. And from the minute we got here he never once mentioned his troubles. He may still have thought about them, of course, but I know he slept soundly—he told me so. It's so hard to believe, Leonid Pavlovich. It happened so quickly."

He blew his nose, then forced himself to go on.

"We were resting after lunch. I'd just taken a nap and Leopold Mikhailovich was doing some writing. 'Tea?' I suggested. 'Good idea,' he said. Well, it turned out Danuta already had the water boiling, and we all sat around the table and Leopold Mikhailovich said, 'You've been working at your factory for thirty-five years now, isn't that so, Konstantin Vasilyevich? Well, tell me this: if somebody had told you thirty years ago that you could leave the factory but still get your pay—in other words, that you could do whatever you pleased—how long would you have stayed on?' Well, I laughed and said, 'A year or two at most. Nobody minds working until they're thirty-five or forty.' I was only joking really, but he took it all very seriously. 'You may be right. I can think of many people whose vital energy flagged at just that age.' Then he smiled and said, 'Thinking,' he said, 'talking, going for walks—people live their whole lives without knowing what wonderful things these are.' Then he leaned forward—know what I mean?—bent forward"—he swallowed hard and breathed deeply for a moment or two—"and well, I thought he'd dropped something. On the table, on the floor. But that was it. Can you believe it? That was it."

Nikolsky couldn't believe it, not even after seeing Danuta crying in the cottage or talking to the doctor ("What do you expect? An advanced case of sclerosis. Thrombosis of the cerebral artery. Death was instantaneous") or seeing the outline of the body under the sheet at the morgue the next day. Nikolsky did not uncover the body. The zinc coffin was ready and waiting, the train was due in soon, and he had a mound of paperwork to get through.

On the evening of Nikolsky's return there was a loud knock at the front door of the Refuge. Borya Khavkin went to open it. Hearing an angry exchange, Nikolsky immediately ran up. Vera was on his heels. It was the investigator.

". . . if you continue to hide his whereabouts!" he was shouting.

"Let me handle this, Borya," said Nikolsky, pushing him aside, "and take Vera with you."

As soon as they were gone, he pulled a sheaf of paper out of his breast pocket and handed the puzzled investigator a single sheet. "You can close the case now, chief," he said.

"I'll take this with me," he said hoarsely, after glancing at the paper. It was Leopold Mikhailovich's death certificate.

"Not so fast," said Nikolsky, snatching it out of his hand.

"You'll be hearing from us," said the investigator, but offered no resistance.

"Fine, fine," said Nikolsky, ushering him out of the door unceremoniously.

It snowed heavily the next morning, and snow fell on and off the whole day. The drifts along the Donskoy Monastery walls were so large that the hearse had trouble making its way to the crematorium and at one point had to be towed. Twilight came early, and by the time they had hoisted the coffin onto the iron bier in the crematorium courtyard, the ashen shadow of Leopold Mikhailovich's face was deepened by the shadow of the departing day. Vera kept brushing snowflakes from his eyebrows and eyelashes, but they remained in his hair and stubbly mustache.

All at once a heavyset woman pushed her way through the mourners, laid a small bouquet at the foot of the coffin, and began adjusting the lapels of the deceased.

"Make her go, Leonid," Vera said firmly.

"How dare you!" the woman said loudly and with great self-assurance. "I am his daughter. You were nothing to him. . . . Igor, where are you? Come and say goodbye to your grandfather!" She yanked the boy out from behind her, pulled off his hat, and wiped her eyes in one continuous motion.

"So you're hand in glove with our friend the investigator," said Vera. "Well, you're no more his daughter than . . ."

Just then Nikolsky seized the woman's wrist and, grinding her gold watch into her flesh, hissed at her, "Shoo! Scat!"

"This is an outrage!" she cried, but beat a hasty retreat. Borya Khavkin grabbed her bouquet and hurled it after her.

They were then told to move inside, where, while waiting their turn, they sat through a tribute to a man "who led an active, socially useful life even after going into well-deserved retirement and whom his fellow workers and the members of his Party organization would never forget," after which a piercing voice cried out in unfeigned agony, "Oh, Petya! Petenka! What will I do without you!"

Leopold Mikhailovich was next. They stood around the coffin in silence while Vera bent over to kiss him on the cheek and murmur her farewell. Nikolsky and Borya, who stood on either side of her, caught only "I promise . . . a true and faithful . . . you will be . . ." As she straightened her back, Nikolsky was again struck by the aura of triumph radiating from her.

"I hope you will all come to our . . . to my place," she said.

They were greeted at the Refuge by Varya, who had prepared the traditional Russian funeral feast, and they immediately fell to, surprised at how hungry they were.

Late that evening, after everyone had left, Vera told Nikolsky, "I don't . . . I can't keep it from you any longer. I'm pregnant. With his child. And I'm going to have it. He knew. He was so happy."

"I understand."

"There's much much more to it than meets the eye. He loved my mother. Now my child is his, and now he'll"—tears of joy ran down her face—"now he'll lie next to her in her grave. Isn't that proof that fate exists?"

"Yes. You're strong, a fine woman. That's what fate is."

"Yes. He made me strong. I was afraid of life, but no more. No more!"

VII

FINKELMEYER knew nothing of what had happened. Nikolsky had been to see him shortly before the telegram arrived, and was horrified by what he found: swollen eyelids, bloodshot eyes, the makings of a tic. Nikolsky was afraid that informing him of Leopold Mikhailovich's death would have dire consequences, and he postponed it first until after Palanga, then until after the funeral. In the end he lost his nerve altogether and decided to wait until the investigation died down, reasoning that once the pressure was off he could move in with Aaron and force him to eat at least one square meal a day and go to bed at a sensible hour.

Ever since the investigator started summoning him, Aaron led a strange life in which, even more than before, the division of life into periods dictated by physiology (from one intake of food to the next, one period of sleep to the next) and psychology (the desire to maintain communication with people, the desire for privacy) lost all meaning. Aaron had never more than merely resigned himself to the idea of eating and sleeping, and there were only two or three people he could talk to without feeling uncomfortable, but now that he was in total isolation—Nikolsky's apartment had none of the neighbors whose hovering presence at Leopold Mikhailovich's apartment he could never quite discount—he lived the life he had dreamed of, the life of an animal that has retreated to its lair, its den, to do whatever nature intended it to do, though rather than an animal, a mammal, he might have been called an anemone or some such underwater genus of the lower orders, assuming, of course, the genus in question had the ability to formulate thoughts, form visual, oral, tactile, gustatory, and olfactory images and put them into a flow, a torrent of syno/anto/homonyms and metaphorical leaps, a now rhythmic, now arrhythmic flow of precise, imprecise, appropriate, inappropriate, calm and tumultuous, liquid and solid, warm, hot, green, orange, blue, purple, kind, cruel, melodious, strident, foul, majestic words—yes, an organism of the lower orders which, though itself incapable of motion, lived in symbiosis with, say, a hermit crab and could at least manage to gain nourishment by waving its cilia.

Oddly enough, the role of hermit crab was played by the investigator. It was he who forced Aaron to leave his burrow, come up for air, which then heightened his hunger pangs, and if he happened to pass a grocery his cilia would grope in the direction of bread, sugar, and sausage. By the same token the investigator played a decisive role in the course of Finkelmeyer's poetic thought. For is not the hermit crab God to its parasite? Does it not therefore, this higher force, this mighty leader, provide food for the spirit as well as the body? And if for the past six months impression had become inseparable from word and if existence—"I think, therefore I am"— had come to mean artistic expression—"I write, therefore I am"— then was not Aaron wholly in the hands of the Crab? For what does Poetry express if not God?

The moment he came home from his first session with the investigator, he threw himself into a narrative poem consisting of dramatic scenes between two characters and peppered by the narrator's commentary—a commentary in verse, an integral part of the text—

on how they reacted to each other: their facial expressions, their gesticulation patterns, their standing ups and sitting downs. They did not reflect reality, nor were they a figment of his imagination. Dostoevsky speaks somewhere of a "fantastic realism," and of course there is *sur*realism, there was the then fashionable *réalisme sans rivages,* but Aaron had something else in mind: Goya's *Caprichos,* which he knew well from Leopold Mikhailovich's reproductions (he tended to think of literature in terms of painting, music in terms of poetry, and so on).

In any case, on and on he wrote, each visit to the Crab providing him with a new chapter, from clarion ode to balalaika ditty. The poem seemed to proceed by itself, without regard to the poet, though who is the Poet if not a mediator between Poetry and God? The poem needed material, and because the Crab had its own interests to look out for, the material it offered was not always suitable. So one day Aaron took it into his head to "direct" a dialogue, and lo and behold, the Crab swallowed the bait—God yielded to the Poet! All he had to do was give the line a tug and the secret world of the underwater kingdom opened up before him in all its length and breadth. And home he rushed to feed it to his Poem.

Thus the Poem grew and grew.

Things had gone so far that when the Crab called him in one day for an unscheduled meeting, he looked forward to the unusual! unprecedented! occasion as grist for the Poem.

"Thought you could take *me* for a ride, did you?" the Crab roared, bringing its right claw down on the desk. "Well, you've got another think coming, you bastard!" (It was the first time the investigator had used abusive language with him.) "We're going back to the beginning, back to bloody square one. I'll get the truth out of you if I have to shake it out, you son of a bitch, you fucking storyteller!"

Finkelmeyer was jubilant. What a finale! Or, rather, first-act finale.

"You know, maybe we should wait till tomorrow to start. It's the end of the first act and—"

"What-a-a-t?"

"It's the end of the working day, and you're tired, I'm tired. What do you say we start fresh tomorrow morning?"

The Crab glanced at its watch.

"Well, all right. But you'll be sorry. Because when I get you by the balls, I won't let go."

Aaron went home to his finale; the investigator set off for the Refuge. And that was the evening Nikolsky showed him Leopold Mikhailovich's death certificate. It was a black day for the Crab.

Finkelmeyer received no summons for either the next day or the days that followed. He was puzzled, of course, but did not trouble his head over it. Investigators had their reasons.

But contrary to everyone's hopes, the investigation had not died out; it had only—and only momentarily—died down. Even before Nikolsky managed to drop in on Aaron, he had a breathless phone call from Frida: the Master was trying to get hold of Aaron and she didn't know what to do "because Aaron's staying at your place now and you . . ."

"What's the problem, Frida? Just give the Master my number."

"But the things he said! That Aaron was in deep trouble and *he* might be in trouble too. Because of Aaron. And that he wanted Aaron to go and see him, Aaron and me both. I'm scared, Leonid Pavlovich, scared for Aaron and scared of the Master. I hate to ask you this, but do you think you could . . ."

"When does he want you there? Have you got the address?"

"Yes, I have, Leonid Pavlovich, and he said, 'Immediately, without delay,' but . . ."

The Master was sitting in a deep leather armchair, constantly twisting a blanket around himself though the room was not at all cold. He was surprised that Nikolsky had come in Aaron's stead, but it was soon clear that all he really cared about was letting off steam. Nikolsky and Frida (he patiently and with hidden irony, she terrified) sat through a long and bitter tirade, in which the Master accused "the boy" of completely misunderstanding life, of pathological immaturity and—yes! yes!—pretension, ostentation. Because ostentation was not only tooting one's own horn, showing off in public; it was also false modesty, self-abnegation as a way of setting oneself off from the common run of mankind. "Not that I think he did it consciously, no, and not that he's unique in this respect, but the fact remains that as a direct result of his attitude . . ."

He had gone on for quite some time when a majestic elderly woman entered the room. She threw Nikolsky and Frida a glacial glance and handed the Master some drops.

"The doctor said you were not to get upset."

"Yes, yes. *Merci.* I've nearly finished."

The woman withdrew. Whether it was the effect of her presence or the effect of the drops, the Master calmed down and came to the point at last.

A writer friend the Master trusted implicitly—enough to tell him about the gifted but unknown poet he'd taken under his wing—had stopped the Master on the street that morning and asked whether he'd heard the rumors about his protégé. No, he hadn't. Well, he didn't know much himself, but there was a scandal afoot and somebody was trying to implicate the Master in it. To settle old scores, by the looks of it.

"I've always had my share of enemies!" the Master said proudly.

The writer found out about the affair from a young editor friend who had recently gone out for a drink with a poet whose poems he had just published in his journal. The poet—Prebylov was his name—kept bragging about his first book, which was going to be longer than most and have twice the print run. The editor naturally asked him to what he owed the honor, and Prebylov must have been pretty drunk by the time because he started going on about a big case that the public prosecutor's office was putting together, a case with a bit of everything in it—foreign currency, black-marketeering, abstract art, plus a squirt of a Jewboy named Finkelmeyer whom Prebylov wanted to get even with for some reason or other. Things got pretty murky at this point—something about a Siberian poet who refused to pay a Russian more than he'd paid the Jew and a wild party where people said whatever came into their heads and jeered at Prebylov's patriotism. Anyway, Prebylov told the inspector from the public prosecutor's office all about it, and in the twinkling of an eye he had a call from some big shot in the Writers Union wanting to know who was behind the Jew poet.

"Well, I knew who *that* was! I wrote a novel for him once when I was down and out, and he's never forgiven me for it."

The Master's friend said yes, that made perfect sense, because apparently the Writers Union big shot showed no interest whatsoever in Finkelmeyer—Finkelmeyer wasn't a member of the Union, and the public prosecutor would take care of him—but he perked up when Prebylov mentioned the Master, and immediately offered to help him with his book and even put him up for an apartment.

"The bastards!" the Master commented with great gusto. "The

younger generation learns the ropes. Cynicism as a way of life." He then turned to Nikolsky and said, "You're a good friend of Aaron's, aren't you?"

Nikolsky didn't know what to say. If he told the Master that a whole group of them had been under investigation for weeks now, the Master would think he was liable to be summoned at any moment. If he told him that things had cooled off for the time being, he would have to break the news about Leopold Mikhailovich, which neither he nor Frida was in a state to swallow. So in his richest, most self-assured baritone he said that yes, there was a major case in the offing but that in the first place, it revolved around a set of artists whom he—Nikolsky—and Finkelmeyer knew only tangentially, and in the second place, it was basically over and done with.

The Master seemed to have regained his composure, and Nikolsky too felt better after formulating the situation as he had: who could believe the drunken ravings of a Prebylov, and wasn't the editor's information in fact outdated?

"It's all over," he said to Frida as they parted. "Everything will take care of itself."

"I don't know. I don't know," she sighed. "It's been so terrible." Then she handed him an envelope and said, "Could you give this to him the next time you see him? It came a week ago. From an army base."

After work the next day Nikolsky stopped off at his aunt's for tea before looking in on Aaron. He was absentmindedly glancing through the evening paper when a headline jumped out at him from the third page.

A CERTAIN FINKELMEYER

One fine day a certain Finkelmeyer proclaimed himself a poet. Now, everyone has a right to call himself what he will—the hero of Gogol's "Diary of a Madman" calls himself the Bey of Algiers—but no one had the right to make free with the norms of the collective and ignore his civic duties, one of the highest of which consists of performing a function useful to society. How does Finkelmeyer measure up in this respect?

In accordance with the most bourgeois conception of "the poet," he gave up his job. Not that he had ever been particularly productive: his coworkers had long since noticed the "elegiac languor" with which their "poetic" colleague carried out his day-to-day obligations (though he always jumped at the chance to go on a business trip—you don't need to work and you get a per diem to boot).

First our "poet" abandoned his job; then he abandoned his wife and two girls. What? you say. Abandoned his family? Yes. Oh, don't be surprised or indignant: that is the philistine way. A poet is supposed to live a "romantic life" free of children under foot and fumes of cabbage soup from the kitchen. True inspiration demands the bohemian life— all freedom, no responsibility.

How fitting that he should have found his element in the house of a teacher of Italian, where latter-day bohemians gathered regularly to drink vodka, make assignations, and—in an attempt to keep the "tone" up— discuss art (of the abstract variety, of course) and poetry (that is, the Finkelmeyer brand, which no one can understand).

And since there is no bohemian freedom without free love, one of Finkelmeyer's friends—a patent expert by profession but patently an expert in less savory matters as well—offered him the favors (doubtless out of respect for Finkelmeyer's poetic gift) of none other than his wife. Strange but true! When the police were called in to calm down a routine bacchanalia (which featured a wall-to-wall exhibition of obscene drawings), they had a hard time sorting out who was who: husband, wife, "poet," host (the man who had given the "poet" his room after he had abandoned his family). Alarmed by the visit, the "poet" moved into the patent expert's cooperative flat. Perhaps it came together with the wife.

All this would be simply distasteful were it not for the fact that Finkelmeyer has found patronage in high places in the person of a highly respected poet of the older generation, a man experienced enough to be able to put his eccentric young disciple on the true road, to impress upon him that each of us has a duty to serve the people: if you are a poet by vocation, you serve the people with your poetry, and if you are not (as Finkelmeyer very definitely is not) you serve the people to the best of whatever your abilities are. But no, this master poet was more concerned with discovering a "star" and playing the "grand old man." May other writers learn from his deplorable example.

It is our social duty to point a finger at all those who aspire to the "easy" life of the parasite. Our magnificent city must not be disgraced by even one of their kind, no matter how "poetic" a guise he chooses for himself.

Finkelmeyer the parasite will have his day in court.

—S. Bylov

S. Bylov? *Prebylov!* Nikolsky rushed to his flat. It was empty. Not until three in the morning was he able to ascertain that Aaron was in pretrial custody.

VIII

"SO THE INVESTIGATOR came . . ."

"That's right. He was sure we were hiding Leopold Mikhailovich."

"I see, I see. Yes, I see. . . ."

The lawyer had been driving Nikolsky wild with his "I see"s for a solid hour. The preoccupied tone in which he said them made it absolutely clear to Nikolsky that he didn't see a thing. And that silly little pipe he kept twisting and sucking and knocking against the desk and never lighting! The whole demeanor of the man rubbed him the wrong way: a man of his age shouldn't be running a comb through his hair every few minutes or snapping a pair of suspenders over a stomach they barely covered.

Nikolsky tried to make his answers as clear and concise as possible, but the lawyer, constantly rummaging through the papers on his desk or leafing through thick law books, barely listened. Every once in a while Nikolsky tested him by stopping short, but the lawyer always urged him on.

"Now tell me, the"—the lawyer gave him an ironic smile—"little lady of the big house—you know who I mean?—will she be taking the stand?"

"Under no circumstances! I categorically . . . It's out of the question. She's pregnant."

"I see, I see. And you're the father."

"No. Leopold Mikhailovich."

"Good Lord!' He frowned, looked down, and took a long suck

on his pipe. "And your . . . what shall I call her? . . . Your wife? Your friend's 'friend'?"

"What good would it do you?" Nikolsky exploded. "In the first place, she's in Lithuania. And then, she's had enough trouble as it is. Besides, it was a fictitious marriage—I told you that. We're divorced now."

"So you're divorced. I see, I see. Very interesting. A useful bit of news for a change."

He knocked his pipe against the desk, ran his comb through his hair, and glared over at a fuming Nikolsky.

"Now you listen to me, young man. I've had enough of your rage. Do you want me to help you or do you not? You have no time to find anyone else, and I don't imagine you would have much success either. I promised your late friend to do what I could, and—"

"Forgive me, I really didn't—"

"The only reason I bring it up is that we are in this together and need to trust each other."

"I understand. Thank you."

"All right. Now let's get down to business. The case could not have come at a worse time. We are at the crest of a campaign against parasites, spongers; furthermore trials against parasitism began so recently that there is not a great deal of precedent."

"But isn't the law simply the law?"

"Of course, of course. But let me show you what I mean. Parasite cases are theoretically administrative in nature, yet they tend to be treated as criminal; besides, they are so new as to be basically untested. We simply don't know where we stand. What *do* we know? We know that the investigator failed to make the speculation rap stick— the artists and the foreign currency and all that—and now his reputation is on the line. He has to find something, and your get-togethers are just the thing—a large number of people meeting privately to speak their minds, and none too careful about who is within earshot. Put yourself in the investigator's place."

The lawyer at last filled and lit his pipe.

"An unpleasant prospect," Nikolsky said sullenly.

"Well, it is what I do most of the time, young man," he said, pointing the mouthpiece of the pipe at Nikolsky's chest. "Let's do it together, shall we? He made a mess of the big one. Lack of evidence, lack of brains, interference at the top—who can tell? Have you noticed the invective against abstract art has been dying down lately? Anyway, suddenly—that famous 'suddenly'—everything changes. Do you see what I'm getting at?"

"I do. Leopold Mikhailovich dies."

"Precisely. So what do you do?—as the investigator, I mean."

"Set my sights elsewhere. Aaron, of course."

"See how quickly you fall into the role?" The lawyer laughed. "You—as yourself now—you show him the death certificate, and the very next day—imagine the night he must have had—the very next day he has a case. A parasite case to end all parasite cases. Why, the name itself—"

"The name?"

"Finkelmeyer! Fin-kel-meyer! It's got a real ring to it. And then there's the literary background. Which reminds me. Will your famous Master take the stand on behalf of the defendant?"

"Oh no," said Nikolsky, making a face. "It's not his way. Besides, he's on medication for his heart. And then, believe me, ironic statements on the fate of poetry won't get you very far."

"True, but a major literary figure will. If that 'Certain Finkelmeyer' article is any indication, the prosecution will challenge Finkelmeyer's right to be called a poet. What we need is a critic willing to go on about the social importance of poetry, its ability to instill the proper attitudes in people, and so on and so forth, because the prosecution will also want to show that Finkelmeyer was an antisocial element."

"Just a second," said Nikolsky, and he handed the lawyer a letter from his briefcase, the letter Frida had asked him to pass on to Aaron. Going through Aaron's papers for material likely to further his case, he had decided to open and skim it, and now he saw how it might be of use.

"I'll read it now, if I may."

Dear A,

I'm writing this for the third time, trying my best to purge it of emotion. Even the salutation has been a problem: Aaron is too official, Aroshka too familiar. I don't imagine you're much like the Aroshka I knew ten years ago.

I nearly began by saying, "I wonder if you remember who I am." But that would be a lie: I knew you wouldn't forget. I'm grateful you kept the promise you made and sent me your book. It *is* your book, isn't it? Your dedication says "Best wishes from the author," but the author's name is Danil Manakin. Why isn't your name on the title page? It is a little mysterious, you must admit.

By the way, when the library received a copy of *The Regiment's Flag* by A. Yefimov, I immediately ripped it to pieces. I didn't want anyone to talk about you, laugh about you. Nothing much has changed here.

To get back to *Good Fortune,* just think how much unexplored territory there must be—in the realm of poetry, I mean—if so marvelous a region is the poetry of a Manakin is still untapped. I've more or less taken up residence there. Who are these Tongors, anyway? What pure and beautiful people they must be! I wish I had been born a Tongor. I've actually been reborn as a result of their poetry. See what you've done?

I'm coming to Moscow. I've accumulated enough months to go to the moon, but Moscow it must be. You remember I vowed never to visit darling Papa at home in Leningrad, but now he's in Moscow giving a series of lectures—"The Class Approach to Literary History: From Plutarch to the Memoirs of Ilya Ehrenberg" or some such thing—and he's been bombarding me with letters that say, "To think that I shall die without seeing my beloved daughter." Well, I must be mellowing, because I've agreed to visit him.

By the time you read this, I'll be there. I am enclosing the address and telephone number of the relatives we'll be staying with. (I'd have much preferred a hotel.)

In any case, I'm looking forward to seeing you.

Olga Kareva

"Look at this," said Nikolsky, pointing to the sentence about Karev's lectures.

"So her father is *the* Karev! You don't know him, but he was a critic to be reckoned with in the twenties and thirties. And if he has not been heard of much since, well, which of the bright lights who survived the thirties has? No, Karev would be a real catch. What makes you think he'll bite?"

"He'll do anything his daughter asks."

"So Karev's in the bag, eh? Let me see now. What else do we need to go over?"

It was well after midnight by the time he was ready to let Nikol-sky go. Before leaving, however, Nikolsky tried to make up for his earlier attitude. "Remember when you said the name Finkelmeyer had a ring to it. Well, I didn't grasp what you meant at first. Now I see that you're right."

The lawyer maintained a tactful silence.

"My father once gave me a nasty slap when I was a little boy for calling a classmate of mine a 'kike.' He told me that during the pogroms my grandfather, who was a priest, gave sermons about loving the Jews, and hid Jews in his church."

"He may have hid me," said the lawyer with a smile. "My whole family was saved by a priest."

On the day before the trial the paper that had published "A Certain Finkelmeyer" printed a selection of letters to the editor under the headline "Make Our Capital Parasite-Free!" One or two were abstract homilies about the need to develop the proper collective values in the new generation, which would be the first to live under communism, and the concomitant need to oppose those elements which refused to contribute to society according to their abilities. A lawyer pointed out that the police were not so vigilant as they might be: why was it that in one region of the capital forty cases of parasitism had been reported and in a neighboring region only eight? Then there was a letter from a metalworker who had read the Finkelmeyer article. "I read poetry," the metalworker says, "I love poetry. But Finkelmeyer? My fellow workers have all completed secondary school or are working toward diplomas while on the job, and none of us has ever heard of him. We say, 'Try some manual labor if you want to know the true poetry of a workingman's existence.' " The final letter began, "I am a member of the intelligentsia," and came from a teacher who was particularly impressed with the legions of unsung engineers and scientists who had enabled the world to see the smile of cosmonaut Yury Gagarin. "To those who would dishonor the reputation of the Soviet intelligentsia let me say, in the words of the great Nekrasov:

> You may not be a poet, but
> A citizen you needs must be."

The following announcement, set off by a line of three asterisks, appeared below the letters: "The trial of Aaron Finkelmeyer will take place tomorrow at the Cultural Center of the Food Industry Workers. For further information, phone . . ."

IX

IT WAS nearly dark when Finkelmeyer jumped out of the police van after his guard. The van had stopped in the middle of a courtyard piled high with refuse: sticks of furniture, hastily daubed plywood from a dismantled exhibition, gauzy stage decorations. The guard, a pleasant round-faced officer, looked about uneasily. He had no idea where to go and no one to ask.

"Send the driver in," Finkelmeyer suggested. "He'll find out."

The officer perked up and ran over to the driver. The driver got out and tugged at each of the doors in turn. One finally gave, and he disappeared, to emerge a few minutes later with a fussy little man wearing a fur hat but no overcoat.

"Hello," he said, "I am the director of the center. You can't imagine how busy I am! This is a very . . . unusual assignment for us, and we're so understaffed we had nobody to meet you. But come in, come in! Follow me."

Finkelmeyer did as he was told, and the officer took up the rear. They climbed a narrow, poorly lit staircase, coming out through the wings onto a stage.

"You wouldn't happen to know where to put . . ." He looked over at Finkelmeyer, uncertain of what to call him: the prisoner? the defendant? the accused? . . . "him, would you? To the right of the judge or to the left?"

"Beats me," the officer said. "Why not ask the judge?"

"They're in conference."

"I'd say to the right," Finkelmeyer ventured. "What is justice, after all, if not *right*eousness." He laughed. The center director threw him a puzzled glance.

They stood waiting on the stage for nearly half an hour. Aaron was so hungry his head began to throb. The place was alive with stalwart young men sporting official armbands and Voluntary Militia badges. Finkelmeyer looked on, uncomfortable, as a few of them hustled past, dragging chairs and carrying a pitcher of water and the traditional red cloth for the tribunal. Through the drawn curtain separating them from the auditorium came the muted voices of what sounded like a throng—and all because of Aaron Finkelmeyer! Finkelmeyer, the center of attention, a tribute he did not deserve. All those people, all that fuss. If only they'd let him apologize and slip away quietly. Then the people out there could all go home and do what they felt like doing, forget about him. But much as he would have liked to cease to be or experience being, he was painfully aware of it, of being where he was and having to play out a role that tortured him with guilt, that was as thankless and shameless as it was inevitable. He had a lost look about him, as if he had bumped into somebody and meant to apologize but couldn't because the person had moved on, leaving him to brood on his own clumsiness. Seen from without, however, the lost look might be read as simple fear, all the more so as—unshaven, unfed, exhausted, suit wrinkled, shirt wilted, boots frayed—he was a sorry sight.

At last the center director ran up to them. "Time to go," he said to the officer nervously. "They're calling for him."

He was led into the auditorium through a side door near the stage and was walking past the first row when he heard a woman's voice sigh, "Oh, how could he?" The voice sounded familiar, and he raised his head to see Sveta, a girl who had worked in the ministry with him. He gave her a surprised smile and nodded, and she stared back at him, wide-eyed.

They told him to sit on a bench, a contemporary piece consisting of a heavy and heavily lacquered seat with thin metal tubes for legs. In front of the bench there were two small tables with similar legs—they must have come from the canteen—pushed together to form a barrier separating the accused from the rest of the world, the ordinary world. It didn't work very well, however, because Finkelmeyer, the policeman behind his back, the soldier next to him, and the lawyer were so close to the first row of chairs. Only the judges' chair, still empty but brightly lit, stood out from their vantage point on the stage.

Aaron twisted his head this way and that, trying to catch what his lawyer, who sat slightly in front of him and off to the side, was saying. He kept getting distracted. Look! Frida! And Father next to her. What had he come for? Hello! Hello! Really, Frida, won't you ever stop crying? And Lyonya! Legs crossed majestically, arm raised Roman fashion: *Ave, Lyonya! Ave, Caesar! Morituri te* . . . And Leopold Mikhailovich's neighbor. The old woman who . . . What in the world was *she* doing here?

As his eye roamed from row to row, he kept catching glances of people he had met somewhere, seen somewhere, known . . . but where? When? And what were they doing here? He had forgotten them, yet they seemed to remember him.

"I told you yesterday," his lawyer said with an ironic smile. "Your ministry colleagues account for ninety percent of the seats. The idea was to bring together a group of your peers."

"And I thought they'd be . . . well, just the public."

"I see. Well, there's no such thing as 'just' where the public's concerned. Your friends will have to stand outside and freeze."

At that moment a voice called out, "Everyone rise. Court is in session." As Finkelmeyer jumped to his feet, he saw the judge and standard jury of two people's jurors taking their place on the stage and realized he was on the judge's left hand. The judge was a woman, as was one of the jurors; both were middle-aged and gray and wore severe suits. The pleasant, simple face of the female juror was obscured by an unbecoming, disconcerting mask of self-importance. The male juror had the face of a born administrator. The pair of shapely legs encased in imitation nylon just above Finkelmeyer's shoulder belonged to a petite young court reporter, who immediately started taking down the proceedings.

" '. . . evidence in the case of Aaron-Chaim Mendelevich Finkelmeyer . . .' Is that name hyphenated? . . . No, no, no. You may remain seated."

"Yes. I have two names: Aaron and Chaim."

"Is that Aaron with two a's?"

"That's right. A-a-r-o-n."

"Thank you. '. . . date of birth, 1932; place of birth, Moscow; nationality, Jewish; Party affiliation, none; education, university degree; home address . . .' "

Finkelmeyer had to listen carefully in case he was asked to clarify any of the points. He found it extremely difficult to concentrate. He felt so out of place in front of the auditorium, against the stage, under the court reporter's legs—everywhere he looked he felt like looking away. He thought of solving the problem by looking down, but because avoiding the judge's gaze would be impolite and a lowered head might be taken as a sign of repentance, he jerked his head back in her direction and tried to appear as if he were paying attention.

Before long, however, he had reason to look and listen carefully: the judge started calling witnesses. First Frida, then Nikolsky, then the editor of the house that had published *Good Fortune* (she glared at him with hate in her eyes, and he felt a terrible pang of remorse), then Professor Karev. "Andrei Valerianovich Karev!" the judge called out, and an imposing epitome of the Party intelligentsia, 1920s-style, rose and came forward. Suddenly Aaron was worried. He peered out into the audience. Olga had to be there somewhere, but where? Where? Poor thing! Coming all that way, and for this! And who should jump into sight instead but—no, what a nightmare! Prebylov! Prebylov! What would he say?

"Oh, he'll find something, all right," the lawyer said unobtrusively. "They're all here for a reason. The gentleman approaching the stand, for example. Know who he is?"

Him? No, who is he, anyway? What did the judge say? Steinman! Steinman the critic? What in heaven's name . . .

"Yes, I do," Aaron replied in an agitated whisper. "He once read my poems, reviewed them, even suggested I should apply to the Literary Institute."

"I see, I see," the lawyer mumbled, shaking his head and scribbling *Steinman* in thick letters on his pad.

"Let me remind you that you are to speak nothing but the truth," the judge told the assembled witnesses in a studied voice, "and that witnesses may be called to account for refusing to testify or giving false testimony. The court now asks you to leave the courtroom."

The witnesses filed out of the side exit, Nikolsky taking Frida's arm, Steinman and Karev shaking hands and mumbling greetings.

People started shifting in their seats and coughing. It was some time before Aaron realized that his lawyer had risen to make an objection.

"Was that Manakin you said?" the judge asked, glancing down into her papers. "Yes, here it is. Danil Fedotych Manakin, correct? But he does not reside in Moscow."

"I consider his presence here to be of the utmost importance," the lawyer said. "He is one of the defense's main witnesses."

"What do you base your claim on?"

"Manakin is a poet and a member of the Writers Union. His testimony will throw light on the character of the defendant's literary activities, the main point at issue here."

"We know what point is at issue here," said the judge with an ironic smile. "What exactly do you propose?"

"I wish to have the current hearing postponed until such time as Danil Fedotych Manakin can take the stand as a witness."

A wave of indignation arose from the audience. The judge banged on the table with her fist and turn to Aaron.

The lawyer had told him the day before that although their request would be denied it had to be made for the record. But Aaron had not expected the din and the hundreds of eyes riveted upon him, and he had trouble standing when the judge asked him whether he agreed with the lawyer's request.

"Agree? Oh, yes, yes. Completely."

After a short consultation with the jurors the judge announced, "Given the fact that Danil Fedotych Manakin is not a resident of Moscow, he cannot provide us with any information on the defendant's daily activities."

"Right!" someone in the audience shouted.

"Moreover, we have enough writers and poets among the witnesses as it is. We therefore deny the defense's request. Have you anything to add?"

"Only that I hope this has been included in the record," the lawyer said with a certain lethargy. "And now a second point. My client's own statements and the statements of his relatives and others close to him make it clear that he led a solitary existence, often forgetting to eat—"

"Solitary existence!" a voice cried out. "What about those orgies? Don't you read the newspapers?"

A mild grumble ensued.

"If it please the court," the lawyer continued, raising his voice over the hum, "we must have at least a modicum of order."

"Order in the court! Order in the court!" the judge called out, rapping her knuckles on the table. "You may proceed."

"Before going any further, I wish to request that my client be given a thorough psychiatric examination."

"But he's had one!" she replied, barely able to conceal her glee. "We naturally foresaw . . ." she began, but immediately caught herself. The word "foresaw" implied that the court had formed an opinion in advance of the proceedings. "It naturally occurred to us that an expert opinion might be of use. You will find the report in the defendant's file."

"I was not informed of this," the lawyer responded with a slight, outwardly apologetic but actually ironic bow. "When did the examination take place?"

"Quite recently. Today, in fact."

"But the report——"

"The prisoner . . . the accused could have told you about it," the judge went on as if she had not heard him.

But the lawyer refused to yield. "The court has failed to apprise the defense of an important item in the defendant's file. I wish the record to show——"

"Very well, very well," the judge broke in. "Now that you know the examination took place, all you need is the results. I'll give you the report. You can glance through it on the spot if you like. It won't change anything. Let me read out the conclusion, only the conclusion: 'Aaron Finkelmeyer is not mentally ill, though he does display certain psychopathic symptoms: he is quite cut off from society, wrapped up in himself, skittish about contacts with the outside world, liable to unmotivated fluctuations in mood, and unrealistic in his assessment of his own personality. He is, however, fully competent to function and account for his actions—in other words, competent to work.' "

"Thank you," said the lawyer. The reporter leaned down from the dais with a few sheets of paper. Aaron took them from her and passed them on to the lawyer, who took them mechanically while continuing to speak: "... and was placed under police custody without cause, of which fact I feel bound to inform the court."

"Have you finished?"

"I have."

"Citizen Finkelmeyer, have you any comments concerning the composition of the tribunal? ... You accept it, then? Have you any other comments or objections? I want to make absolutely certain you are aware of your rights. You are free at any time to take active part in the proceedings."

The proceedings dragged on. When at last the judge asked him to rise, he felt the back of his neck start to throb, and for a time everything swam before his eyes. Even after he regained his equilibrium, however, he had the headache to contend with, and although, as usual, his hunger eventually subsided, he had great trouble breathing—he may have had a fever or caught cold—and putting his thoughts together. But whether he was in fact "unrealistic in his assessment of his own personality" or not, he had great trouble relating to the personality the judge was now reeling off from her notes. It belonged to a total stranger, a man who for the past six months had led an antisocial existence, sponging whenever possible, refusing to look for work, leaving a wife, two small children, and an elderly father without any means of support, indulging in well-documented bouts of debauchery—drinking, brawling, swapping bed partners and living quarters—the whole six-month period had been one long un-end-un-bro-un-be-liev-in-cre-di-ble-or-ga-sm-sm-sm-m-m-m!

"Do you understand why you have been summoned to appear before this court?"

"I do ... I mean ... I don't understand where you got ... where my where ... whereabouts ... account of?"

"That is the court's affair. Now answer my question. Do you understand what you are being accused of? You have been certified fully competent to work, yet you are unemployed. You are therefore leading an antisocial existence."

"I understand *what* I am being accused of. What I don't understand is *why*."

"Let us move on," the judge said in a soothing voice. "Would you tell the court whether you admit to having avoided socially useful work?"

"It depends on how you look at. True, I was not officially employed, but as for the social utility of—"

"Citizen . . . uh . . . Citizen Finkelmeyer! I am glad you admit to being unemployed, though of course you are surrounded here by your former colleagues, who know you resigned and failed to look for another position. Intelligent man that you are, you realize there is no point in wasting the court's time by trying to call black white. But what I wish to know is whether you confess your guilt as accused, not 'depending on how you look at it.' "

How simple it would have been to say, "I confess." It would have made everyone in the auditorium a lot happier and everything a lot easier for him. But the lawyer's shaking head reminded him they had agreed he would not confess, and Aaron forced himself to come out with: "No, I do not."

Why all the noise? Oh, his aching head!

"What did you do all those months you were not 'officially employed,' as you put it? What did you do with your time?"

"I . . . I spent it writing poetry. I mean, I worked on my poems . . . the whole time . . . is what I mean."

"Isn't what you *really* mean that you had the time of your life?" asked the judge with the trace of a smile.

As always, humor had a refreshing effect on Aaron. He immediately came to life, flashed a toothy grin at the judge, and said, "You might say that. Any poet will tell you there's no greater pleasure than working on a poem."

"Good for you!" the lawyer whispered, while the judge riffled through her papers. "But remember—as simple as possible, as simple as possible. Keep your audience in mind."

"Yes, thank you. I understand."

"It says here you're married," said a new voice. It belonged to the male juror. "So you're not divorced, right? And you leave your job and make the rounds of your friends' apartments, right? What's the matter? Your place too cramped for you?"

"No," said Aaron with a shrug.

The man gave a dignified nod and said, "No further questions."

"Has the defense any questions to put to his client?" asked the judge.

"Yes, I have," said the lawyer, standing. "Tell me, what is your connection with this book?" And holding up a small green volume, he read in a loud voice, *"The Regiment Flag* by A. Yefimov."

"I wrote it," Aaron said mechanically, knowing ahead of time what the lawyer would ask and what he was to answer. All his attempts to persuade the lawyer not to bring up the book had been in vain. "Yefimov is a name I used while I was in the army and wrote poetry for the army newspaper. I kept it when the poems appeared as a book."

"Did you sign a contract with the publishing house?"

"Yes, I did."

"Now let's look at another book," he said, emphasizing each word. "Danil Manakin, *Good Fortune.* Authorized translation from the Tongor. Tell us a little about this one too."

"It consists of poems published in various periodicals over the past few years. Published in Russian. I was the translator."

"What is an 'authorized translation'?"

"It means the author has approved it. There were certain . . . modifications involved."

"Thank you. I wish to submit both books as evidence."

Aaron took his seat, but the judge turned to him and said, "Now it is your turn to respond to the accusations made in the indictment, one by one. I want you to tell us why you reject the indictment, why you refuse to confess your guilt. Do you understand what is required of you?"

There was nothing for Aaron to do but to rise again, and because he detected a nervous catch in the judge's voice he hurried to reassure her by saying, "Understand? Oh, yes. Absolutely." The lawyer had advised him to write out the points he needed to make, and he had a list ready. "Let me see now. The reasons I feel I should not be considered a parasite are—"

"Just a moment," the judge interrupted. "What the court needs is facts. Facts, not what you 'feel.' We are the ones to decide whether or not you are to be considered a parasite. Be as specific as possible. Tell us why you left your work, how you managed to live, why you failed to look for employment. We have chosen to hold the trial in this hall to give your former colleagues a chance to hear what you have to say for yourself. May I ask you to explain to them, to the court, to everyone gathered here, why you acted as you did."

Turning back from the judge to his list, Aaron caught sight of his father cupping his hand to his ear, gazing at him with a sad smile, and nodding almost imperceptibly. Aaron sighed and felt a wave of indifference come over him. This time he spoke without stammering.

"I entered the work force as soon as I completed secondary school. I had no professional training and found employment at the post office. Before long I was called up for military service, and it was in the service that I wrote my first poems. My commanding officers needed verse commemorating various occasions for the army newspaper, and I was transferred to the newspaper staff. After my tour of duty was over, the poems were published in a separate volume, and I thought of entering the Literary Institute. The poems I submitted with my application differed from the ones I had written in the army; I considered them more . . . interesting. But I was rejected. I took a position at the Ministry of Fish Production in the Finance Department, enrolling simultaneously in a correspondence course given by the Institute of Ichthyology. After receiving a degree, I continued to work at the ministry, but switched to the Engineering Department, where I worked until the autumn of last year. I might add"—he looked up and then back down at his list—"I never had trouble with anyone at the ministry. Oh, and *The Regiment Flag* has been performed by the Red Flag Ensemble of Song and Dance, I mean, a musical setting of the poem . . ."

The more he talked the more his words made him sick. He boasted about what humiliated him—those awful military poems he had tried so hard to forget, for instance. But what positively nauseated him was having to talk about himself in such false and bloated terms, the goal of which was to lend credence to the claim that he had been a poet all his life. If he had been entrusted with those translations, it was only because he was recognized as such, and once they had appeared in book form he knew what he had to do: leave the ministry—for the time being! yes! only temporarily! of course!—he'd nearly forgotten the stress the lawyer had placed on that "temporarily."

". . . temporarily, while I still had the material resources to provide for my family and tide me over, an advance I had received to work on the book, *work* on the book. That's why it is wrong to claim I've been living on—what's it called?—unearned income, that's right, unearned income. No, I was writing the whole time, writing poetry, working, in other words. So no one can call me a parasite and claim I tried to shirk socially useful activity."

Suddenly Aaron stopped to think, and when he took up from where he had left off it came out all wrong. In fact, it scared the living daylights out of him.

"Though what does a poet do, actually? Is any poet's work socially useful? Poetry exists in and of itself, like air. Nobody asks whether air exists for the common good, yet we go on breathing it. Oh, it's good for us, all right, though, if I'm not mistaken, more than half is composed of nitrogen, which our lungs have no need for. In other words, oxygen is socially useful, nitrogen is not. Can a poet, a poet who writes *real* poetry, constantly worry about what is oxygen in his poetry and what is nitrogen? Shouldn't *society* determine what's *socially* useful?"

Out of the corner of his eye Aaron saw the lawyer making frantic signals to the effect of "Sit down! You must be out of your mind!" But by now he had the bit between his teeth and there was no stopping him.

"Everyone quotes Nekrasov's lines:

> You may not be a poet, but
> A citizen you needs must be,

and they're true, true enough. But what people fail to realize is that being a poet and being a good citizen are two separate things. Being a good citizen is, well, part of our day-to-day existence, while being a poet is something out of the ordinary, a category unto itself. Pushkin had something different to say on the subject, though unfortunately it's less well known. The passage in question goes something like this: 'Anyone who writes verse must first and foremost be a poet. If all you wish to do is expound on civic virtues, do so in prose.' The point may be argued, of course; it's not an absolute truth. But it certainly holds for most instances. Take these lines by Pushkin:

> The day's bright luminary is extinguished,
> A bluish mist hangs o'er the evening sea,
> I call upon my sail to flutter gently,
> Upon the sullen waves to roll for me.

Now what is 'socially useful' about a man standing on a deck writing poetry?"

"Citizen Finkelmeyer," the judge broke in, "may I remind you that—"

"Yes, yes! I'm almost through. What I've been trying to say is that while poetry as such is useless, society can make use of it. Pushkin again:

> You may not buy your inspiration,
> But you may sell your manuscript.

You see? The poet and society both profit. I've given it a lot of thought. It's very complicated, really. What else? . . ." He glanced down at his notes and began rushing through the rest of his points. "Anyway, I resigned temporarily and was never officially notified I needed to find other work. As far as the accusation of antisocial behavior is concerned, I did move away from my family for a while, but only to devote myself wholly to my work: creative work demands privacy. And that talk of drunken revelries and brawls—why, it's preposterous. I had friends in, true, but there's no law against that, is there? I just invited a few friends to . . ." He was about to say "to Leopold Mikhailovich's," but caught himself in time: the lawyer had strictly forbidden him to mention Leopold Mikhailovich or anything connected with the pictures for that matter (apparently whoever had turned Aaron in found it advantageous not to mention the affair, and if Aaron did there was no telling where it might lead. ". . . to my . . . uh . . . temporary residence, and we never spoke about anything . . . mm . . . untoward. But most important, I did not stop working and have no intention to do so. I therefore request that the court drop the charges of parasitism and antisocial behavior levied against me." He took his seat.

The auditorium began to buzz. The court reporter stood up and pointed to something in her notes; the judge responded, poking the sheet of paper with her pen. In the hiatus Aaron closed his eyes and saw a dark green field strewn with glittering, dilating red and yellow polka dots and a white irregular oval engraved with a matchstick-like 14, the number Aaron had just noticed on the armrest of the seat opposite him. Fourteen. A sonnet: a-b-b-a, a-b-b-a, c-d-c, c-d-c, though not necessarily; the tercets could go c-c-d, c-c-d, or even (which was the case with Pushkin's "Sonnet on the Sonnet," wasn't it?—the one that begins "Stern Dante never did despise the sonnet") c-c-d, e-e-d. Dante. Andante. Andante infernale. *Inferno, Purgatorio, Paradiso.* Why did he choose that order? Why hell first, then purgatory, and on up the mountain (Ararat) to paradise? For the elevation and purification of the soul? Oh, how naive the Middle Ages were! Purification through elevation! Things are different now. If Dante were alive today, he'd go the other way for purification. That's right! That's right! You had Vergil to lead you, and you . . . you can lead me. But down, down, so that I might be purified in accordance with my own times. And if it comes to that, the comedy will be far from divine. Quite the contrary. It will begin with paradise, move on to purgatory, and in conclusion, in *reclusion*—well, *Hell!* . . .

". . . two little girls, helpless little girls. How could you do such a thing?"

"Me? Sorry, I didn't quite catch what you were saying."

"You claim to need privacy to write your poems. But how could you abandon your family, your two little girls, for the sake of such . . . to write?" The woman juror was actually quite mild in her reproach.

Aaron stood up, straining to gather his thoughts.

"You didn't abandon your family," the lawyer prompted under his breath, staring into space.

"I didn't abandon my family," Aaron parroted. "I mean . . . I . . . I only left them. Temporarily." And sitting down, he sank back into Dante, andante . . .

"Frida Finkelmeyer to the stand!"

She was led in from the side, nervously chewing half her lower lip to keep it from trembling. It gave her round, chubby face a paralyzed look.

"Sign here to indicate you have been informed of your responsibilities according to the Criminal Code. . . . No, here. That's right. Has the defense any questions?"

"You are employed, are you not?" the lawyer asked, turning to Frida.

"Yes, I am," Frida said, nodding.

"Louder!" said the judge. "We need to hear you."

"Yes, I am. I'm a kindergarten teacher."

"Excellent," he said with the satisfaction of a doctor who has just learned that a patient is doing well. "And what are your main sources of income?"

"You mean money? . . . Well, there's Aaron's—I mean, my husband's—salary. Then mine. And Grandpa—he's got a small pension and he earns a little on the side, but don't misunderstand: he *wants* to work. We could do without it, but he *enjoys* working."

"Fine, fine. But to get back to your husband. He gave you all his salary while he was employed, is that correct? Does he contribute anything now?"

"Oh, of course!" she said at once. "He gives me—I mean, he contributes the amount we agreed on."

"You agreed on an amount, and he regularly contributes that amount," the lawyer repeated. "So you feel your husband has satisfied his financial obligations."

"Yes, I feel my husband has satisfied his obligations," she replied. Then, correcting herself like a good pupil, she added, "His financial obligations."

"What about his other obligations?" the judge asked.

There was a guffaw and a short flurry of whispers in the auditorium.

"I mean, are you satisfied with his behavior as a father, as a husband, as the head of the household?"

Frida, on the point of tears by now, lowered her eyes and said, barely audibly, "Yes, I . . . am."

"What makes you so satisfied?" a voice piped up unexpectedly. It belonged to the citizen prosecutor, a giant of a man sitting to the right of the judge. Aaron recognized him as another denizen of the ministry. "Your husband abandons his job, his family, abandons you; you don't know where he lives or who he lives with; and you tell us you're satisfied?"

"Objection!" the lawyer said firmly. "The question is inadmissible; it does not aim to elucidate the facts. Besides, I have further questions to put to the witness."

"You are very quick with your objections," the judge said just as firmly, "but you may proceed."

"So," the lawyer began, "you are satisfied with your husband on all counts, including—and I want to make this clear—your financial arrangements. Tell me, the money he gives you—do you know where it comes from?"

"Yes. From the poetry he translates. He told me *he* would hold out as long as *it* held out."

"Are you aware of any other sources of income your husband might have?"

"No, none."

"Tell me, does your husband drink?"

"Aaron? Drink?"

"I see. He doesn't, then. Has he any other passions, long-standing or recent? Cards? Horses? Anything that might cause him to lose large sums of money."

"No, no, nothing. Nothing like that," she said, very upset. "He's . . . how shall I put it? He's like a mole. He just sits there and writes. Nothing else."

"So you knew that he was writing poetry and that it meant the world to him. Tell me, did you think of divorcing him when he moved out?"

"Oh, no."

"Is it possible you spend more on your husband than he contributes to the family? Do you understand the question?"

"Yes, I understand. The money he gives me goes to the family, the girls. He takes practically nothing for himself. I even have to tell him when to buy clothes and things."

"And if he lived completely away from home, if he were deprived of an income, could you get along without him? You realize the court may well—"

"Strike the question!" shouted the judge. "I must—"

But the lawyer cut her off with a "Thank you. No further questions," and sat down.

"Has the citizen prosecutor any questions?" asked the judge, turning to the colossus at her right.

"The point I want you to clarify for us," said the colossus, rising slowly, "is the following: How do you feel about your husband abandoning his family and going off to live on his own? How does it strike you?"

A pall of silence fell over the courtroom. All eyes were on Frida. Her head was bent; her hands worked desperately to extract a handkerchief from her cardigan. It was as if *she* were now the accused, the perpetrator of some shameful act. The silence dragged on, unbearable. A cry of protest welled up in Aaron's throat like an abscess, but it was Frida who broke the silence—with a sob.

"What . . . what have we done wrong?" was all she could manage before bursting into tears.

"Give her some water!" the judge ordered. "You are excused. You may return for the rest of the proceedings once you get a grip on yourself. . . . New witness! Leonid Pavlovich Nikolsky."

Frida did not leave the courtroom, nor did she wait to be brought a glass of water. Her shoulders heaving, the tears running down her cheeks, she stumbled back to her seat near the lawyer, and because she held the handkerchief up to her face, Aaron was unable to comfort her with a glance, much less a word or caress.

Nikolsky was calm and businesslike. He signed what needed to be signed and asked whether he was limited to answering questions or had the right to make a statement based on his knowledge of the case. The judge, though far from overjoyed at the witness's initiative, told him to go ahead and make his statement.

"I have known Aaron Finkelmeyer for a year now," Nikolsky began in his richest baritone, a voice that proved as effective for depositions as for seductions. "We met quite by chance. He made a strange impression at first, but the better I got to know him the more clearly I saw that his . . . peculiarities stemmed from an extraordinary poetic gift. Let me state unequivocally that I am proud to be his friend. Aaron is a poet in the highest sense of the word. And poets are a special breed. One must love the poet in the poetry and remember that every work of real poetry conceals a unique personality."

"Enough declarations of love," said the judge. "Get to the point."

"But that is the point! As I see it, the court is examining Aaron Finkelmeyer's personality, his conduct. And I, as a close friend, know for a fact and declare openly, before everyone present, that for the past six months he has been intensely and intensively engaged in creative work. When a man has a passion, he devotes his whole life to it. Finkelmeyer didn't resign his position to sit around and do nothing; he resigned his position to do what he had to do. The quotation marks around the word *poet* in the newspaper article were completely out of place: Finkelmeyer *is* a poet, a true poet. The reason I let him use my flat was that he needed a quiet place to work. And until I could let him use mine, I found him someone else's. What can be more natural than to help a friend? I might add that I know the Finkelmeyers well and have observed Aaron in a number of situations. Never have I noticed the slightest degree of antisocial behavior in him. He is a modest man, modest to a fault, and he gets by on almost nothing. He has no interest in money, which partly explains why he left his job. He lives on what he earns, working all day and often into the night. Is that your definition of a parasite? No, I am convinced that after examining the evidence the court will have no choice but to absolve Aaron Finkelmeyer of all charges."

Although the burst of applause from the last rows of the balcony were cut short by a murmur of indignation, Nikolsky's diatribe had clearly made its mark. The judge waited for the auditorium to calm down, then gave the floor to the citizen prosecutor for questions.

"Where does your wife live?"

"My wife?" said Nikolsky, his legs apart like a boxer's. "What has 'my wife' got to do with the case?"

"We have reason to believe that your wife engaged in immoral acts with this 'modest man' you call your friend."

"Where do you get your information? The file? No. The article? No. Where do you get it, then?"

"Answer the question!" the judge ordered.

"All right, then. I have no wife."

The lawyer gleefully leaned back in his chair and drummed his fingers on the table while the prosecutor looked up at the judge in consternation.

"What do you mean?" she said, coming to the prosecutor's aid. "You're married, aren't you?"

"I was. I'm divorced. And to spare our most esteemed citizen prosecutor the questions, let me state at once that my former wife moved *out* before Aaron Finkelmeyer moved *in*."

"Stop trying to dodge the issue," the citizen prosecutor said threateningly. "Did the accused maintain an immoral relationship with your wife or did he not?"

"You ought to be ashamed of yourself!" Nikolsky fired back. "As if making her cry weren't bad enough." He nodded in Frida's direction.

"Answer the question!" said the judge. "And show a bit more respect. You could easily be held in contempt of court."

"All right, then. My answer is: I have no basis on which to formulate an answer. I know nothing about it."

"We have other evidence," said the judge.

"I repeat: I know nothing about it. And I have nothing further to say."

"Step down," snapped the judge. "But you can be sure we haven't finished with you."

"That's your problem," he said cuttingly and made a triumphal return to Frida's side.

The lawyer shook his head. "Easy, young man," he whispered. "Take it easy."

"All right, all right," Nikolsky whispered back and turned to Aaron. "How's it going?"

Aaron responded with an acrimonious smile and looked up at the dais, where his editor, a tense, pinched woman of about forty, was now standing. It was the first time he had seen her without a cigarette hanging from her lips. The lawyer questioned her with marked deliberateness, while she fired back her answers. How long had she known Finkelmeyer? She couldn't say, a few years, she didn't remember exactly. Didn't their acquaintance coincide with the first publication of the translations of Manakin's poems? She couldn't say, she was the editor of the book, the poems were first published elsewhere. But didn't you also work for the journal in which they were published and weren't you the one who encouraged Finkelmeyer to look for new poets in Siberia? Well, maybe, perhaps, something along those lines, though I don't remember when. Can't we establish the time by the publication dates of the poems in journal form? I suppose so, yes. By the way, was Finkelmeyer credited with the translation in the journal? I don't remember. Possibly, but I can't be certain. We don't always give the translator's name. I see, and what about the translator's fee? That's not my job. Ask bookkeeping. Then tell me this: Who signed the contract for the book? Manakin and Manakin only! But you knew at the time that Finkelmeyer had translated the poems, didn't you?

She now saw what he was driving at, and for the first time she stopped to think, think feverishly.

"Your questions refer to a period antecedent to the period under consideration by the court," the judge objected during the pause that ensued.

"My questions are directly relevant to the matter at hand," the lawyer responded sharply. "Are there any specific ones you wish struck from the record?"

"No, no. You may continue."

"Then let me repeat: Were you aware when you concluded the contract with Manakin that Finkelmeyer had translated his poems?"

"I . . . I don't know."

"But I assume you know the penalty for refusing to give testimony."

"The editorial process is a long and arduous one, and . . ." Suddenly she had an idea. "Officially the contract was with Manakin and the entire fee went to him. There is no *official* record of who translated the poems. We received a finished manuscript; we published it."

"I see!" the lawyer exclaimed ironically. "And Finkelmeyer never came to your office."

"People come to my office all the time."

"Did Finkelmeyer play a role in the preparation of the manuscript or did he not?"

"And if he did? You won't find a word about it anywhere. Anything he did was unofficial."

"Finkelmeyer claims he has been living on the money he received for the Manakin book. Did he receive money for translating it or did he not?"

"He did not."

The uproar in the auditorium quickly died down when the editor began to hedge: "What I mean is, not officially. I ordered that the full amount be paid to Manakin."

"May I remind you that your bookkeeping department transferred half of Manakin's fee to Finkelmeyer's savings account? You don't deny that, do you?"

"Of course not. There's a document to prove it."

"Precisely. But you deny that Manakin gave Finkelmeyer the money for his work on the book."

"How should I know what Manakin gave him the money for? Maybe he owed it to him or was making him a loan. It's none of my business—and certainly not the business of a publishing house."

"For the last time, let me ask you a simple, basic question, and let me request an equally simple, basic, yes-or-no answer: Did Finkelmeyer translate Manakin's book *Good Fortune* into Russian?"

The editor's eye began to twitch, and she pulled each of her fingers in turn.

"No," she whispered at last.

"Raisa Grigoryevna!" Aaron cried out so painfully that she shuddered.

"Very well," the lawyer said into the dead silence of the auditorium. "Then I am compelled to inform the court that Manakin is not the author of the book entitled *Good Fortune*. The author of the book is Aaron Finkelmeyer!"

"No! No!" she cried. "How can you say such a thing!" She threw up her hands as if to protect herself from the accusing finger he had pointed at her.

"I have no further questions," the lawyer said contemptuously.

The audience was puzzled, and when one of its number said aloud, "He's a clever one, that lawyer," public opinion decided that the accusation was a legal ruse and therefore beyond the ken of the common mortal. Aaron was disgusted, sick of the whole affair. It was one big lie from beginning to end. You tried to dam up time with lines and stanzas, to catch the gleam of a rainbow in printer's ink and put it between covers, and for that you pretended to be Manakin. Only Leopold Mikhailovich understood the truth, and when he came back they would go through the whole affair together and Leopold Mikhailovich would forgive him. . . .

All at once an image from one of Leopold Mikhailovich's reproductions loomed before him, a pretty, Carrara-marble face—white, matte, with blue, matte-blue eyes—moving closer and closer, bobbing up and down against a dark green background, coming to rest at last in the section set aside for witnesses.

"Olga! Olya! I knew you'd—"

"They wouldn't let me through," she said, smiling a timid smile.

"I had to wait for Father. They were afraid to stop me when I came in with him." She looked around, alarmed, than sank deeper in her chair, neck-deep in her green scarf as in a pool of dark water.

Professor Karev was by all indications distraught. He could not stop taking off and putting on his gold-rimmed pince-nez (which, like his speech, bore traces of the nineteenth century), slipping a hand in and out of his tightly buttoned jacket (a cross between a trench coat and a Tolstoyan blouse), leaning against the table and standing up straight. He was used to sermonizing *ex cathedra,* pouring forth incontrovertible truths, proclaiming objectivity, the laws of nature and society, a class-conscious approach to science, culture, and art. He never doubted the veracity of his words because they stemmed from a judicious combination of the Source and the latest Party directives. He was a fine orator in the old semiparliamentarian mold, and by twisting the dialectic this way and that he could come out unscathed from the most controversial discussions.

Yet now he was distraught. He was speaking from the stand rather than the lectern, and he had a distinct feeling that the law of the negation of negation was at work, transforming the incontrovertibility to which he was so accustomed into its opposite. On the one hand, a court by its very nature dealt with vexed questions, in other words, questions that might as well be answered in the positive as in the negative; on the other hand, this court was a people's court, in other words, a class-conscious court, and therefore obliged to uphold the interests of the working class and reject the slightest hint of ambiguity, that is, dualism.

As a matter of principle, therefore, the professor should have stood firmly behind the prosecution, which represented society as a whole, instead of the defense, which defended the interests of an individual. The professor had always stood up for the collective and only the collective. But in this instance there was a dialectical contradiction: Olga.

No sooner did the professor's thought turn to his daughter than all thoughts of society and objective laws vanished. And Olga had said, "You will take the stand as a witness for the defense. Go to the lawyer and ask him for the poems of Aaron Finkelmeyer. Finkel-meyer. Read them carefully. You're good with words. I want you to make it as clear as day that they were written by a professional poet—that's number one. And number two—that people need them, that they help people to work and live better, foster progress, or whatever they're saying these days. The lawyer will clue you in. If you refuse . . ." Her eyes flashed darkly.

"Of course, of course," he hastened to acquiesce. "What about your plans for the future?" If she could play on his paternal feelings, he could at least hint at his dream of many years: the prodigal daughter's return. "You do your part first. Then we'll see."

Only half an hour earlier the professor had learned that his fellow critic, Steinman, would take the stand as a witness for the prosecution. The news had completely unnerved him: Steinman represented the same general line of Marxism he himself was known for. Going on now about the aesthetic education of the masses, he lacked his usual confidence. The process was not always simple, he said, because morality, ethics, and aesthetics were secondary to material production, which was the very foundation of society, and as such—that is, as part of the superstructure—they had fallen behind. He gave examples of writers who, unlike the great proletarian poet Mayakovsky, had failed to apprehend that the pen was a bayonet, and reminded the court that even today—witness the exhibition of abstract art Comrade Khrushchev had recently seen fit to close—writers and artists all too often went astray.

As long as he kept to these well-trodden paths, the audience listened politely. But the moment he called upon them to exercise their literary sensibilities and sympathize with "those among us who seek their own approaches to art and literature," the general mood began to turn, and when he defended Finkelmeyer instead of condemning him it grew actively hostile. Experienced orator that he was, Karev sensed the change immediately, but was at a loss to win his audience back.

The judge took advantage of the situation to insert a question: Had he been a longtime admirer of Finkelmeyer's work?

"I read it for the first time yesterday," said the honest professor, trying to swallow his words. But they were met with laughter. "You don't understand. I wanted to be objective! I'm not personally acquainted with the poet!" The laughter only increased.

"Well, I hope you got more out of his poems than I did," said the juror. "Art belongs to the people, right? Can you guarantee that young people, working men and woman, will spend their free time reading that stuff? What good will it do them?"

Professor Karev tried to answer, but no one bothered to listen anymore.

"Has the defense any questions?" asked the judge.

"No questions," answered the lawyer, looking daggers at Nikolsky.

Meanwhile, Karev had started shambling in the direction of his daughter, but she shook her head furiously and he obediently found a seat off to the side.

Next came the first of the witnesses for the prosecution, the rather dapper specimen who had been Finkelmeyer's immediate superior at the ministry.

"Finkelmeyer's main character at work was his lack of initiative. You'd go up to him and say, 'Would you take care of such and such, Aaron Mendelevich?' and he'd ask you twenty times exactly what it was you had in mind before he'd go and do it. He always kept a low profile. Sometimes a whole week would go by before I realized he was off on one of his trips. When we read about his poetic ambitions, we wondered why he'd never volunteered for the ministry's in-house newspaper. But then, he always shied away from the collective. Which is why no one tried to dissuade him from resigning. I confess we are partly to blame for failing to take the necessary educational measures in time and realize that this may be seen as a blot on my department. However, I have met with our Party and union representatives and not only did we agree to condemn the defendant, we appointed a colleague to serve as citizen prosecutor." He nodded in the direction of the colossus on the right hand of the judge.

Good for you, boss! Aaron thought as he listened gleefully to the man's nimble reinterpretation of their relationship. In fact, the man had valued Finkelmeyer highly: Finkelmeyer never rocked the boat, never asked for a bonus or even a seat near the window or the radiator, and was ready to go off to Siberia in the depths of winter at a moment's notice. The only time there was any tension between them was when he forgot to bring the boss back some fish.

"Alexander Emmanuilovich Steinman!"

Steinman's large flabby body wobbled up to the stand, and he

began to speak even before completing the signing-in ritual. "Yes
... well ... you must (gurgle) understand ... I was ... thank you
... terribly surprised ... astonished really ... I mean, parasitism
and lit ... (cluck) literature! ... Now what are we to make of that?
... I want it to be perfectly clear ... I cannot limit my remarks to
my role as an expert witness ... no ... Ideology always comes
first!"

He turned to the judge for support, but all she did was wave him
on with a "You have our attention."

"Yes ... Well ... What has lit ... (cluck) literature to do with
all this, anyway? As the Russian people so wisely say, 'You don't
kill a wolf because it's gray; you kill it because it's gobbled a sheep.'
Bad lit ... (cluck) literature is not the real problem; the real problem is *anti*-literature. But I ... digress. What can I do for you?"

Again he turned to the judge, his curly head cocked like a poo-
dle's.

"Read this aloud," she said, taking a sheet of paper out of the
file and handing it to him, "and tell me what you know about it."

"We—the Writers Union—we're the ones who sent it to you," he
said with a flourish. " 'To the People's Court in response to your
...' And so on. ... 'It is our duty to inform you that Aaron-Chaim
Mendelevich Finkelmeyer is not a member of the Writers Union.
Furthermore, no member of the Writers Union has ever heard of
him, and we vigorously protest against his pitiful attempt to call
himself a poet. No one may usurp the lofty title of Soviet poet, no
one may use poetry to his own unworthy ends, ends incompatible
with the noble aims of Soviet lit ... (cluck) literature.' "

"You have just spoken of the 'lofty title of Soviet poet,' " said
the citizen prosecutor after Steinman had handed the paper back to
the judge. "Yet some of the witnesses we have heard today sing this
... this Finkelmeyer's praises. What do *you* make of it? Does he
write poetry in the manner in which you understand poetry?"

"Very well put!" said Steinman immediately. "Extremely well
put! Not poetry as such, outside time and space, but 'in the manner
in which we understand poetry.' Let me try and answer your question." He broke off, thought for a moment, and then launched into
a passionate tirade modulated only by the usual gurgles and clucks.

"May I begin with the words of a writer I had the privilege to know well, a writer famed for his stand against bourgeois—or Christian, if you will—humanism: Alexander (gurgle) Fadeev. The words I have in mind go more or less like this: The old humanism said, 'I don't care what you do as long as you are a decent human being.' Socialist humanism says, 'If you do nothing, if you don't work, we don't recognize what is human in you no matter how decent and intelligent you are.' I'm sure you all see how (gurgle) relevant these words are to the case before the court, the People's Court, today. But I wish to take them a bit further, go beyond their literal meaning. Bear with me, and you'll see how pregnant they are in this sense as well. Bourgeois lit . . . (cluck) literature says, 'I don't care what you write about as long as you are a decent writer.' Socialist Realism says, 'If you do nothing to depict our ideas and the greatness of our society, we refuse to recognize the writer in you no matter how refined your so-called creations are.'

"Why did the Writers Union choose me to come and speak here today? Because, believe it or not, I once read the work of the accused. Approximately ten years ago—and I remember it well, there are things one does not forget!—I was going through a pile of manuscripts submitted to the Lit . . . (cluck) Literary Institute by potential students when a group of poems caught my eye. Not that they were particularly good, you understand; in fact, they were weak, very weak. But, well, one forgives that sort of thing when the poet is young, a neophyte, and takes a stand on social issues. And these poems dealt with army life, the peaceful day-to-day existence of a typical battalion. Nice poems. Weak, naive, but nice. Anyway, I invited the young man in question to come and see me, and what did I find? Not only had he published his patriotic poems under a pseudonym, he'd saved his own name for some decadent, formalist claptrap. We rejected his application, of course, rejected it out of hand. And that young man was none other than . . ." He swiveled his paunch to face the judge, pointed dramatically at Aaron, and declared, "Aaron Finkelmeyer!"

Stunned by the cruel revelation, the audience turned in the aggregate to gape at Aaron, and Aaron, who had heard little of the diatribe but had caught his name, hurriedly pulled himself to his feet, stretched his neck up to the judge, and was about to ask her to repeat the questions when she waved him back into his seat and he realized he had added yet another blunder to his list.

Steinman was evidently quite thrown by Aaron's leap, but after lowering his eyes and concentrating for a moment he took up from where he had left off with renewed vigor.

"I admit to wondering at the time if we hadn't been too hard on him. Didn't Aristotle say that a young man's heart tends to dim his mind? Youth must have its (gurgle) fling and all that. But no! No! We were right to act as we did, right to shut the gates of lit ... (cluck) literature on him. And now what has he done? Turned away at the main entrance, he has come sneaking round to the back!"

He was so taken with the image that he paused, thereby allowing the lawyer to jump in with a "May I?"

The judge threw a questioning glance at the citizen prosecutor, who raised first his eyebrows, then his hands, as if to say, "What more can he ask? It's an open-and-shut case."

"I take it you are a member of the Writers Union," the lawyer said to Steinman.

"Of course," Steinman replied modestly.

"First you testify that no one in the Writers Union has ever heard of Finkelmeyer; then you testify that you have known him for ten years. Are we to conclude that the document you have just read aloud does not correspond to the truth?"

Before Steinman could recover, the auditorium exploded. Steinman was in luck: people were tired and irritable, they had been brought to the trial straight from work, and the lawyer's attempts to retard the natural course of events had got their hackles up.

"Cut the nit-picking and get on with it!" "Who chose that smart aleck anyway? Kick him out!" "What do you mean? He can say whatever he likes!" "Like hell he can!" "What a bunch of windbags." "Hey, quit the shilly-shallying up there! Read out the sentence! It's getting late!" "They just want to show they earn their keep!"

The judge let them go on for a while and then called the court to order.

Steinman suddenly came alive. "Perhaps the statement should have been worded a bit differently," he said to the lawyer with a smile. "Something along the lines of: 'Furthermore, no member of the Writers Union has ever heard of a *poet* by the name of Finkelmeyer.' Because he's no poet. He may write, but there's no such poet."

"No such poet," the lawyer repeated. "With your permission I shall return to that statement."

"By all means! By all means!"

"But now may I ask you why you were so certain you had done the right thing when you rejected him. Wouldn't it have made more sense to admit him and give your colleagues a chance to set him on the right path? Isn't it your fault he went astray?"

Again the auditorium began to rumble, but this time in favor of the lawyer. Steinman was not one to arouse sympathy for long.

"No (gurgle, gurgle, gurgle), no! How can you (cluck) say such a thing? No one's at fault, no one's to blame but himself. He didn't need the institute. Plenty of young poets work hard, work in factories, and write poetry with no (gurgle) professional training whatever." He was off and running again. "And as I'm sure you are aware, amateur literary and art groups are enjoying an unprecedented surge of popularity. Community courses, community theaters, community orchestras are springing up all over the country. In Moscow alone there are more than ten active societies for poetry lovers. Why not ask Finkelmeyer if he belongs to one of them?"

"The accused will answer the question," the judge ordered. "Repeat it, please."

"Are you a member of a poetry society?" asked Steinman, not quite looking him in the eye.

"No, I'm not," Aaron replied, his forehead wrinkling in an attempt to recall something the question had brought back to him. "Tell me, aren't you the one who did the survey of last year's poetry for *Friendship?* Yes. . . . Well, you quoted some lines of mine, quoted them as an example of what poetry should be. Lines I wrote. Or translated, if you prefer."

"No, no! Impossible!" he said, giving the judge a pleading glance. He looked like a ball that had just had the air kicked out of it.

"And you still maintain there is no such poet?" the lawyer intervened. "Why should we accept you as an objective judge? Professor Karev here, who is not personally acquainted with Finkelmeyer, has just testified that the poems he read are of the highest professional caliber. You are aware of Professor Karev's stature, I take it?"

But Professor Karev's stature was rather less than imposing as he huddled in his seat under the collective gaze of the auditorium, and Steinman realized he had a last chance.

"Professor Karev!" he called out reproachfully. "What am I to make of this? You (gurgle), a respected Party activist (cluck) ... How can you have allowed them to delude you? And so soon after the plenum on problems of ideology and aesthetics, the meetings with Nikita Sergeevich. Can we really be so far apart?"

"After everything I have heard," the professor began in a feeble voice and rising, beard first, "after everything I have heard, I am afraid I must admit . . . to having been deluded . . . to having . . ." He sank back into his seat.

Silence.

"Coward!"

The audience looked around with a start. Aaron, horrified, stared straight at Olga. He saw a crimson spot on her cheek, a chiseled profile, narrowed eyes.

"Who said that?" blared the judge. "Whoever said it will leave the courtroom at once!"

"No, no," the professor moaned. "She's ill . . . My daughter . . ." He burst into convulsive sobs.

Two voluntary militiamen rushed up to him and ushered him out solicitously. Aaron glanced over at Olga; her eyes were fixed on her father's bent back, and as she turned her head to watch him go, Aaron could see only a high cheekbone, the gentle slope leading from chin to earlobe, and, through the curls, the back of a slender neck.

The next expert witness was Sergei Prebylov, but the questions the judge asked him had nothing to do with his field of expertise. He was soon deep into a description of what his friends and he—he offered the court their names if the court so desired, but the judge told him it would not be necessary—"anyway, what me and my friends saw at this, well, orgy's really the only word for it, and you can bet your life we felt completely out of place. Why, the people there, Finkelmeyer and his friends, they insulted us right and left."

"Can you be more specific about what went on?"

"Well, it was in a large house owned by this one woman, and I'll leave it to the appropriate agency to look into how she came by the house and what kind of life she leads, but anyway, her drunken 'friends' brought her to the brink of a breakdown and then beat her, but before you know it she was back drinking vodka with them and laughing—you can see they do it all the time—and then they begged me to read my poems, but you can bet your life" (an expression he favored to excess) "that when they heard me sing the joys of honest labor they started insulting us again, and we wouldn't stand for it, so we left."

"Finkelmeyer was present, you say?" asked the citizen prosecutor.

"He's their guiding light."

"And the witness Nikolsky?"

"He's the . . . 'lover' of the woman I told you about—and the one who beat her!"

"Why you little . . ." Nikolsky muttered from his seat.

"Very interesting," said the citizen prosecutor. "Finkelmeyer is married but lives with Nikolsky's wife, so Nikolsky takes a mistress. Is that it?"

"I call upon witness Nikolsky to stand and comment on Prebylov's observations," said the judge.

"They're a pack of lies!"

"Lies? Lies?" Prebylov screamed. "You *beat* her!"

"Lies from beginning to end. No, sorry, he *did* read us some of his abominable, illiterate poems. By the way, *he* was the only person drunk, and he was *sozzled,* which may account for his totally fanciful interpretation of—"

"Silence!" the judge called out. "Finkelmeyer! Did you take part in the 'activities' the witness Prebylov described?"

"I did," said Finkelmeyer abstractedly.

The auditorium exploded.

"In other words, you saw Nikolsky beating his mistress," the citizen prosecutor said.

"He didn't beat her, actually," said Finkelmeyer, as if talking to a friend. "He just gave her a few slaps to—"

The rest of his sentence was drowned in laughter—the judge was laughing, the jurors were laughing, most of the auditorium was laughing. "I don't believe it!" "He's nuts, that's all!" "Looks like he wants to drag his pal down with him."

Aaron was past caring. He no longer had the strength or the desire, no longer had the *capacity* to think, feel, comprehend. Even the nausea that had invaded his innards, the ache that had racked his brain, now seemed somehow abstract.

After the auditorium had calmed down, the lawyer rose and turned to Prebylov.

"Can you tell me how many times you visited the house in question?"

"Oh . . . not too many."

"Can you be concrete? Five, ten, a hundred . . ."

"It's hard to say."

". . . or only once?"

"Well, and if it was only once. The things I've heard—"

"Only once, eh? I ask the court to take note of that fact. And when was that once?"

"How should I know?"

"You know very well. Do you refuse to answer?"

"I don't remember!"

"May I point out to the judge that if called upon to do so the defense will have no trouble proving that Prebylov met Finkelmeyer and Nikolsky only once and nearly a year ago, at which time Finkelmeyer was still employed by the ministry and would still be employed by the ministry for another six months. In other words, Prebylov's testimony has nothing to do with the case at hand."

"It seems to me you have used this argument before during 'the case at hand.' "

"You are unfortunately"—and here the lawyer made a malicious pause—"correct."

"Nastasya Fyodorovna Zavyalova to the stand!"

The old woman from Leopold Mikhailovich's communal apartment bustled up to the dais, all zeal and fear.

"Do you know the accused, Aaron Finkelmeyer?"

"Who, him? 'Course I do. Never knew his name, but I know everything else about him. He lived right next door to me!"

"I want you to tell the court how long he lived there, what he did, whether he went to work, whether he had any people in, how they spent their time. . . . Don't be afraid, now."

"Well, I'll begin at the beginning, all right? The real tenant, he hasn't lived there since the summer. And before that he had this woman come. Said she helped him with the cooking and the housework and things. Now I'm not saying there was any hanky-panky going on—he was too old for that—but she did spend an awful lot of time there. So did whatever-you-said-his-name-was. They had it all worked out. He'd tap at the window, and the other one'd run out and open the door for him. So as not to bother us, he said. As if we didn't hear the door slamming all the time. Anyway, the two of them, they kept coming to see him, and then others started coming, whole streams of them, day in and day out. Who knows what went on in there! But we mind our own business. Anyway, like I said, last summer he moved out, and those two, the woman and what's-his-name over there, they came and took his things away. So I asked them, I said, 'Who are you, anyway?' And she says, 'His niece.' His niece! They even took the kitchen table away! Anyway, for a month or two the place is empty, and then *he* moves in. And never goes out. I get to wondering: maybe he's hiding, you know? So I go to the authorities, and they come and ask him for his papers. But he wriggles out of it. They ask him where he works. He wriggles out again. They'll look into it, they say, nice and polite, and meanwhile he goes on living there like before. Oh, and every once in a while the other one comes back. Afraid of losing his Moscow residence permit, I bet. Then the window-tapping and door-slamming starts up again. Only much worse. So back I go to the authorities and I say, 'Look, there's something fishy going on.' And they say, 'You let us know the minute something happens.' So the next time, I call them and they come and you wouldn't believe what we saw! The room filled with these naked women and men! Pictures of naked men and women all over the room! I was ashamed to open my eyes. Anyway, they ask for everybody's papers, and just then one of them comes back from the corner with some bottles of vodka. I ask you now. Ogling naked ladies and swilling vodka—what kind of life is that? Anyway, they're making to leave, so I go up to the blonde who comes to spend the night with what's-his-name over there and I say to her, I say, 'You ought to be ashamed to yourself!' I say. 'You still married to your husband and all.' And you can be sure I didn't get a peep out of her. Whoosh! and off she went. Her kind wouldn't give the time of day to people like me. Anyway, that's it, comrades."

Zavyalova was the last witness, and there were no further questions. The judge turned to the lawyer and asked whether he was satisfied that Zavyalova's testimony was relevant to the case, and the lawyer answered that it "related to the *time* during which the incidents took place though not to the *essence* of the incidents." Whereupon the judge told Zavyalova to step down.

But the witness was in no hurry. "Could I ask a question?" she asked the judge.

"Go ahead."

"It's about the room. You see, Vova, my grandson, he's back from the army and he wants to get married, but where can I put him? I told the authorities, I said, 'Give me *his* room for Vova. When *he* moved in, Vitya—that's my son—was still living with his wife, and now Vitya's divorced and living with me again, and when Vova and his new wife move in—'cause where else can they go?— that's four of us in a room of twenty square meters.' And then I had this idea, you see. I told the authorities, I said, 'You tell me what to say to the judge,' I said, 'and then tell the judges to do what they can for me.' "

"But the court doesn't handle such matters. Go to your local housing office. We don't even know whose room you're talking about."

"Leopold Mikhailovich's. I know I used to give him a hard time, but he was a quiet man, and anyways, the authorities told me you might give me his room now that he's dead if I went to court and said what I—"

The chair overturned with a crash, setting the table and the officer in motion, and as the table fell and Aaron's back arched and his arms flew up, he cried out hoarsely, "Whowasityousaid . . . who . . . who's dead?"

Nikolsky jumped up, but the officer pushed him back with his elbow and fell chest-first on Aaron, whose only thought was to rush up to the dais, grab the old woman, and shake her, shake it out of her, the truth, who had died, no, it's a lie, she was lying, like everyone, everybody here, and what for, what's he to you, where is he, where is he, Leopold! He screamed, he whispered, the saliva dribbling down his chin. Oh, why am I so inept, such a weakling? Why didn't they tell me? Why didn't they tell me? Why? . . . He fell back in his seat.

While they picked up the table and put it back in place, he tried to think things through. Nothing fit. He saw Leopold Mikhailovich fingering his mustache, looking old, yes, very old, and then dead, his eyes closed, yet smiling, smiling and pointing, but at whom? At Nikolsky? Lyonya, did you know? Is it true?

Nikolsky looked down. Nikolsky looked up. Nikolsky whispered loudly, There was no time to tell you, Aaron. So it's true? Nikolsky nodded. But when? Nikolsky leaned forward. A-week a-go, a-week a-go, andante infernale. Down comes the barrier. White stripe and black. White stripe and black. Life is a zebra. White stripe and black. Life's a child's underpants, tattered and stained. Life . . .

Aaron had sunk so low in his chair that he could rest his head on his arms, which lay crossed on the table. At least he still had shoulders, elbows, and hands to make a cradle for his head, to shelter it right, left, and center and banish all sights and sounds. Weeping in his darkness, he felt almost whole again, even during the citizen prosecutor's summation, even during the lawyer's summation. When he heard a voice saying loudly, "Have you anything to add?" he simple twisted his head in one direction and the other and they let him alone. But then the officer self-consciously helped him up by the elbow and the judge read out the sentence in stentorian tones.

". . . in other words, has been unemployed and involved in suspicious activities for more than six months. He has abandoned his wife, two young children, and aged father. When the authorities made inquiries at his new place of residence, he moved to yet another. He has no residence permit for either. During the period in question he continually flouted the norms of society, giving and attending loud parties and drinking bouts and participating in immoral acts (cohabitation with a friend's wife, possession of pornographic pictures, brawling, libel). He failed to respond to a police warning charging him with parasitism and acknowledges that he has not been employed for an extended period of time, which fact has been confirmed by witnesses. Witnesses Steinman and Karev have disproved his argument that he is a poet and does not therefore need to work.

"The trial took place in the presence of a number of his former colleagues. Furthermore, the reaction of the readers of the daily press to his case were uniformly negative.

"After careful examination of the preliminary evidence and its corroboration by the witnesses and after the summations of the prosecution and the defense, the court finds the conduct of the accused punishable under the statute 'Improved Methods for Dealing with Individuals Avoiding Socially Useful Work and Leading Parasitic Lives.' The court therefore decrees that Aaron-Chaim Mendelevich Finkelmeyer, born in Moscow in 1932, be sentenced to four years of exile and compulsory labor."

A monstrous clap of thunder broke apart the swoon that stuffed my head; like one awakened by violent hands, I leaped up with a start. They waved and cheered and applauded wildly, and in the whirlpool of faces and features—flash! Nikolsky's fury—flash! Frida's swollen eyelids.

And having risen, rested and renewed, I studied out the landmarks of the gloom to find my bearings there as best I could. A little old man wandered through the crowd, which was now dispersing. He had a smile on his round, childlike face, and his fingers danced over his beard. He might have been pretending to be a goat, a mischievous goat—*Here comes the goat. Watch out for its horns. Butt, goat, butt! Maa! Maa!*—except that what he sang, and much louder than usual, was *Shema Yisrael Adonai Elohenu Adonai echad. Baruch Shem kvodo malchuto leolam voad.* Hear, O Israel; the Lord our God, the Lord is One. Praised be His Name whose glorious kingdom is forever and forever.

And I found I stood on the very brink of the valley called the Dolorous Abyss, the desolate chasm where rolls the thunder of Hell's eternal cry. The same dark stairs that had brought Aaron up to the courtroom took him back down to the courtyard. The officer, an old friend by now, climbed along behind. And up ahead, listing this way and that, landing to landing, constantly turning to catch one more glimpse of him, Olga Kareva ran down the stairs.

Oh, come with me to settlements forsaken,

Promise you'll write and tell me where you are—I'll find out anyway—and let me come and settle nearby, in your village, all right? Answer me!

Oh, come with me through sleep's eternal realm,

I won't make any claims on you—I promise!—but I've nothing left, have pity on me, I'm so alone, you know everything there is to know about me. Why don't you say something?

> Oh, come with me to long lost generations,
> My inspiration—truth and truth alone.

What's four years, after all? I'd have left anyway, I've written to you about it, you're the one who made me want to come here. Let me go with you. Let me go with you!

> I was created by the highest master,
> By knowledge all-consuming and first love,

Say something! You must let me come, you *must,* you must want me near you, you remember, you haven't forgotten. Say something!

> As old as this creation, as long-lasting,

Answer me, why don't you answer me? I hate the lives people cling to, I have no desire to go on living, only you, you, you can bring me back. And maybe . . .

> And as that ever-lasting one above.

But you'll have pity on me! You think you're all alone, abandoned, but you don't understand, you don't want to understand, I'm dead, a drop of life, is that too much to ask? A single drop, a single word? Aaron, darling . . .

> Abandon hope all ye who enter here!

"Out of the way, young woman! Go back inside! What are you doing here, anyway? How did you get here?'

The officer took Aaron over to the van, and the two of them climbed in. It was dark and freezing. Aaron began to shiver. He appeared to have fallen into a trance and did not come to until the van lurched forward. As they drove up to the gate, the driver gave a few furious honks. The voices of an agitated crowd pierced the van's thin metal frame. The van made slow progress, then stopped entirely. All at once a siren blared, and Aaron instinctively peered through the barred window into a pair of blinding headlights and the bloody blink of a directional signal. The crowd pushed and jostled its way into a semicircle of light just beyond which the front of a truck seemed suspended. The people were staring down at the snow-covered street. Aaron pulled himself up by the bars to have a look for himself, again more or less instinctively, but suddenly let out a shriek, recoiled from the window, and lunged at the door.

There on the snow lay a dark, amorphous little heap with head off to the side, the familiar features showing through a tangle of long hair.

The officer pounded frantically at Aaron's hands, but Aaron went on screaming and grabbing at the door. Finally the officer let out a curse and gave him a clout in the solar plexus.

Aaron crumbled to the floor.

X

Finkelmeyer to Nikolsky:

I will write whenever I can. I do not always have the time and place for it. By the time I finish this letter, we'll probably have crossed the Urals. We're not too far off now. To be more exact, I am lying on an iron bed in Room 101, a basement cell with old-fashioned vaults, thick, fortresslike walls, and thirteen beds set into the cement floor. The door is made of iron, as are the bars on the window (three vertical, three horizontal) and the barbed wire encircling the courtyard. The bucket in the corner is made of aluminum; it was originally meant for cow's milk, but now collects human urine and stinks accordingly. This is my fifth stop (not counting the prison hospital, where I spent three weeks just after the trial). Each one is entirely different and entirely the same—like life. I've learned a great deal lately, the main thing being that, oddly enough and with a few exceptions, I get on quite well with my colleagues. I have qualities they admire. For example, I have the makings of a first-class cardplayer: I almost never lose, or rather I lose only enough to keep animosity at bay. Even more important, *The Count of Monte Cristo* and *Ivanhoe*—the plots of which have been deeply ingrained in my memory since childhood—have made me the bard of these doughty Russian warriors. Art is highly appreciated here. The only area in which I have failed is varnish drinking, and the men are annoyed that I cannot therefore share their drunken revels. Their speech is a combination of the obscene and the scatalogical that tends to favor interjections over conjunctions. The result is a colorful and pithy means of communication. I am amazed at how superfluous most of our vocabulary is. The "great, free Russian language" we learned about in school is, from my new perspective, needlessly great and therefore largely free of day-to-day utility. But as Prebylov would say, it's not for the likes of me to pass judgment on things Russian.

Looks like we're moving tomorrow. North. There's a lot of winter ahead of us.

Yesterday we arrived in Salekhard after four days of nonstop tobacco-, sweat-, and urine-stench. We were driven from the station to the town across the frozen Ob in the midst of a raging blizzard. Salekhard, which lies squarely on the dotted line of the Arctic Circle, is not my final destination. I will be traveling some five hundred kilometers to the northeast, into the tundra.

I am lying on a wooden plank bed. I will soon be served dinner by a very sweet fourteen-year-old girl who during her short but action-packed life has accumulated more than twenty breaking-and-entering convictions. She seems to like me; at least we always smile at each other.

I've just come back from the post office. (I'll probably get into trouble for having gone, but nothing serious. After all, no one can possibly escape.) You'll never guess who I saw there! Remember Galochka, the waitress at the hotel in Zaalaisk? She says she's sure you remember her. Well, there she was. I don't know who she's here with—a sailor or a vagabond or a criminal in exile—she didn't go into her private life. But she was very curious about Danuta, especially about whether her marriage to you was real or not. You should have seen how happy she looked when I told her it wasn't. So the two of you had a little fling, eh? She sends love and kisses.

Until I have a permanent address there's no point in closing with the traditional "Drop me a line."

Nikolsky to Finkelmeyer:

I received your telegram. So you've finally arrived. I went straight to the atlas to see where they put you. The Taz, eh? I'll stick to the Inzer!

I've wired you fifty rubles. I decided against a larger sum because it might get stolen or you might give it away. Let me know when you start running low and I'll send you some more.

The lawyer has begun his siege. He's a real find, that man—all spunk and grit. (You probably don't realize you inherited him from Leopold Mikhailovich.) He's put together the brief for his appeal, and if nothing comes of it he's ready to go higher. He also took on the publishing house and actually got them to put in writing that "Finkelmeyer prepared the translation of Manakin's verse on the basis of a personal agreement" or some such blather. And when he told the Master what had happened, the Master hit the roof and raised an unprecedented hue and cry—first in the office of his arch enemy, then in a letter to the presidium of the Writers Union—tearing Manakin to pieces and praising you to the skies. He's also written a letter to accompany the brief— another of the lawyer's ideas. But the main card the lawyer has up his sleeve is a plan to call a mistrial: he hopes to prove the trial invalid by arguing that the evidence gathered by the police and the testimony given by the witnesses are inapplicable to the statute on parasitism. He gives himself a fifty-fifty chance.

Danuta has phoned several times from Palanga. She's working temporarily as a nurse's aid. She won't believe a word I say and has asked for your address. I sent it to her yesterday as soon as your telegram arrived.

Finkelmeyer to Nikolsky:

As I write I can see teams of reindeer running past the window. Then a tractor chugs slowly by. The blizzard has died down a bit for the first time in days. We live on the brink of geography, as my new friend, a Seventh-Day Adventist, puts it. He's asked me to move in with him, but for the time being I'll stay in the common quarters—first, an old sleeping car, now a two-room *izba*-like hut perched on a small hill.

There are seven of us. For some reason we live all piled together in one room. Besides our beds it has a rickety table laden with dirty dishes and a Russian stove strewn with—and surrounded by ropes hung with— trousers, boots, padded jackets, socks, and underwear. The indistinct but distinctly unpleasant odor emanating from all this is somewhat tempered by the two easily recognizable odors: cheap tobacco and cheap cologne. Cologne is a necessity here; it is drunk by the caseload. People can hardly wait for the ice to melt, because then boats bring in vodka and pure alcohol and the good life starts again.

But they manage to entertain themselves even now. There's a clubhouse where they can play records in the evening; there are huts where women sell themselves for vodka; there are songs to sing and cards to play and feuds to settle. Plenty of local color, in a word.

I take part too, after a fashion. The songs they get the biggest kick out of are the "thieves' songs," and believe it or not I can't stop churning them out. When I first got here, people called me the "goner" and more or less wrote me off, but now that I'm composing songs for them they call me "our Jewboy" and couldn't be more respectful. Some members of my work team who had gone to trade with the local Nanaets people brought me back an enormous fish today. When I offered to pay for it, they called me every name in the book. You can't imagine how touched I was. I'm about to write them a new song.

Nikolsky to Finkelmeyer:

It took a whole month for your Salekhard letter to reach me! Let's agree to write without waiting for a response.

I have nothing new to report as far as your case is concerned. The lawyer says it's too early to expect results.

I do have some news about myself, though. I've left my job. Fortunately, the decision was mine (though the possibility of a forced resignation hung over my head from the day my superiors learned that an investigator was on my tail); unfortunately, I was to blame. Oh, women! They'll be the death of me. A few years ago I had an affair with the boss's secretary, and I'm glad to report she was better in bed than she is at the typewriter. But she got married, and I bowed out. Then not too long ago she had a sudden yen for the old days. Right at work! Well, the boss was away and had thoughtfully left his couch behind. We were hardly out of our clothes when someone started pounding on the door. Even now I can't decide whether it was a put-up job. You should have seen the relief on my boss's face when I told him, the lily-livered bastard!

Spring is here in all its glory. I can't imagine what you're going through. Has the long night come to an end? What kind of socially useful work have they given you to do? I could ask you endless questions, but I hope your next letter will anticipate them all and fill me in on the details of your existence.

Nikolsky to Finkelmeyer:

I wrote you a real letter three days ago. I'm scribbling this note at the post office to let you know I've just sent off a large envelope registered. It contains a manuscript by Leopold Mikhailovich, something he worked on in Palanga. It was found on his desk open to the last page. His pen was still lying on it. The handwriting was very clear, so Vera had no trouble typing it up. I wanted you to have a copy now. I hope it doesn't get lost en route. Let me know when it comes.

ART UNFIXED

My first thought was to call these jottings "Before the Silence" or "Notes of a Silent Man," but both are too pretentious and focus on my person and why I feel the need to write. "Art Unfixed" expresses the essence of what I wish to say.

Yet before I begin, I must explain why I am now undertaking something I have avoided all my life. For much of the last few years I lectured on the history of art. My audiences were varied, though they consisted primarily of young people. I never wrote out lectures in advance; indeed, I came to think of speaking extempore as a principle. I am a great admirer of "thoughts unexpressed," and if, as Tyutchev said, "a thought expressed is a lie," then a thought written before it is expressed orally is a double lie.

I recently learned that my lectures had been written down. At V.'s instigation I read the transcripts and began to comment upon them, aspiring thereby to demolish the fine edifice of my own lies; in fact, all I managed to do was construct new and newly mendacious edifices. I have decided to close the circle with a device I am the first to condemn: a conclusion that will not only negate everything contained in the lectures but also refute their very essence as fixed and *eo ipso* tainted. Then there will be nothing left, and I shall fall silent.

None of this would have materialized had it not been for V.'s transcripts on the one hand and years of discussions about art with my dear friend the poet A.F. on the other. I might add that the personality, life, and work of A.F. epitomize the point I wish to make and express it with infinitely greater eloquence than the words that follow.

I

God created the world in two days. He spent less time on man. Man was child's play for Him, and when a child plays—babbles, sings, draws—it enjoys the moment of creation and then forgets its story, song, or drawing; they disappear, marvelous yet ephemeral.

God created man and immediately forgot the work of His hands.

Life is a beautiful, self-creating improvisation that does not admire the work of its hands. It is content to ignore the past and love what is, without knowing the future. So when life enters into us, as in a moment of love, we give ourselves wholly to its inspired game and think neither of the past nor of the future.

Oh, the selfless oblivion of art! Art is beautiful insofar as it avoids the deadly stamp of fixity.

Oh, the childlike innocence of art! Art is beautiful insofar as it avoids the deadly stamp of self-consciousness.

Oh, the mysterious link between the creator and his art! Art is beautiful insofar as it avoids the deadly stamp of notoriety.

2

But we must be careful to distinguish between "creation" and "art."

Creation pursues only itself. Its goal is to be, to exist, to find an emotion in the formative act.

Art pursues a result, something set, something permanent. Its goal is to fix, to transmit, to evoke an emotion after creation has taken place. The answer to the sacred question "What is art?" is therefore "The conservation of emotion." What could be more repugnant? Yet I can find no other.

Everything changes, and nothing changes more rapidly than feelings. But the basic emotions, the joys and sorrows, have remained constant for centuries.

Everything changes, and few things change more rapidly than art. Hence joys and sorrows cannot remain constant for the artist:

the artist may not repeat what has come before; he must be more subtle, more sophisticated, contribute something of his own.

The academies where art and music, literature, and theater are taught train the artist in the technique of fixing emotion, and once he has completed his novitiate he does his best to overcome the influence of the technique he has been trained in and find a new one to substitute for it. He may also have colleagues who are content merely to imitate, to fix an emotion they have not themselves experienced, as accomplished courtesans imitate love.

3

Art's vainglorious attempt to capture the moment *(Verweile doch, du bist so schön!)* appears today as an attempt to deceive nature. But nature will have its revenge. Art has reached an impasse; nature is laughing. Life is triumphant; art is suffocating.

How did this come about?

By way of response let me give a brief summary of certain ideas that made their way into my lectures in the form of introductions to, commentaries on, or digressions from the exposition of various styles, schools, and masters.

When man discovered that creation offered a simple outlet for the emotions, he discovered art. It was a charming, naive beginning. Emotion, its expression in the act of creation, and the pleasure it provided were as inextricably combined as the Divine Trinity.

But once the fruit from the beautiful Tree of Art had been plucked, the serpent began to gloat. For no sooner did the first consumer of art appear than readily recognizable signs or conventions emerged to help transmit the emotions of the creator to the consumer, to help the latter "read" the former. Hence the question *how* arose beside the original *what*. Moreover, the more art the consumer demanded, the less the artist could live without him. As professionalism gained ground, the artist experienced the creative process with less intensity; inspiration, intuition, and chance retreated into the background. As external pressures grew, art acquired an educational and cultural mission; society began exploiting the creative work of the individual. As technology developed, a veritable orgy of reproduction took hold; the private emotions of the artist were multiplied millions of times and made to compete with those of other artists on the open—and soon glutted—market. Why? Why not remain in obscurity?

4

Something has been happening to people lately. They say it has to do with the bomb. Be that as it may, people are less concerned with material things than they used to be, less interested in seeking material surrogates for the soul and immortality, and thus more likely to appreciate life, life as such; they have begun to see that the goal and higher meaning of life is emotion, emotion in all its variety—in love, in work, in contemplation. The desire to "originate," "increase," "acquire," "accumulate," and "surpass" is giving way in all spheres of life, and when people are willing to exchange the dead immortality of a museum canvas for the bliss of a fleeting moment, the consequences for art are bound to be far-reaching.

If art is to remain vibrant, it must return to its primordial, truly harmonious form: emotion, emotion in and for the creative process, with and for the creator, at and for the moment of creation. Art arising when the artist's emotion arises and vanishing when it vanishes, art freed from pandering to outsiders—only such art represents a goal to which the creative spirit can aspire. There will be no art for art's sake, just as there is no love for love's sake; art, like love, is a property of every living thing; it is true self-expression, pure emotion.

Intimate art—how beautiful!

Creative people everywhere are beginning to realize that an art which maintains its intimacy also maintains its purity, gives pure pleasure. A new kind of artist is beginning to appear, an artist who consciously maintains his anonymity. Artists of this sort may be looked down upon by some; they may be called dilettantes or amateurs. But they look down on professionals; they call them pimps living off the objects of their emotions.

The fine young artist T., who has done more than a thousand sketches of two naked figures, is wiser than many of the most venerable artists I have known. Every time he comes to a blank sheet, he delights in a new line, a new color. Why then come *back* to it? Why even keep it? The only sketch that moves T. is the one about to be born.

Disposable art—how beautiful!

In this respect the verbal arts require special attention. Color, movement, and sound (the basic elements in painting, the dance, and music respectively) determine nothing concrete, that is, they *fix* nothing; the word (the corresponding element in poetry) fixes meaning. But the essence of the earliest poetry was improvisation, and my friend A.F. sees his deliverance therein: improvisation is a way out of the deadlock in which poetry now finds itself and to which he himself was in danger of succumbing. A.F. (I keep referring to A.F. because he gave me numerous insights into the art of the word and has approached the bounds of the possible in his verse)—A.F. points out that improvisation increases the fluidity of words, expands the perimeter of meaning; intonation, tempo, and dynamics (in silent reading as well as in performance) can vary with the mood of the reader, who leaves out certain words or leaves space for others, thus giving rise to infinite possibilities for variation, and just as words can disappear in a torrent of emotions, so pauses of varying length and intensity can acquire a meaning of their own. Indeed, the ideal of poetry is the absence of words, the ideal of music the absence of sound, the ideal of painting the virgin canvas. Now I too am approaching silence.

What makes art beautiful is what leads to its demise. With every moment of life we advance towards death, which process lends life a certain zest, does it not? Only living art is vital, and the only living art is an art unfixed, born to die.

5

I collected pictures for decades, saving what is currently denied the right to exist. I do not regret what I did: I was merely following one side of my dual human nature. Neither do I regret what I did not do: I had no desire to be a slave to the art that was and still is.

Shall we ever find it in us to forswear that kind of art?

I was unable to do so; many are unable to do so. We are like those who seek spiritual tranquillity by making a joyful noise unto a Lord outside themselves and are told, "Do not pray to such a God, for he is not. There is another God, but He is within you, and only silent communion with Him who is your own spirit can give you true peace."

They will find it difficult to grasp the meaning of these words and even more difficult to forswear the prayers to which they are accustomed. Yet some will be able to do so. My dear A.F. has done so; others will follow. And soon they will wonder how they could have prayed as they prayed before.

But now—silence.

Finkelmeyer to Nikolsky:

A letter from you at last! For some reason the money preceded it. Thank you! I used it to buy a few warm things. It's been a hard winter. Apparently the air here has thirty percent less oxygen than in temperate zones. Coughs drag on; scratches take weeks to heal and are always full of pus. But spring has come, and my cough is subsiding.

From now on I'm going to try and live within my means, the fifty rubles I earn a month. Until recently I've been moving boxes, hacking at the permafrost, and extracting bricks from ice, but things have taken a turn for the better. My Seventh-Day Adventist friend has found me a job as a night watchman down at the pier. Working by night and sleeping by day is welcome because it means less contact with my hutmates. I still can't see my way clear to accept the kind man's invitation to move in with him. He regards me as a representative of the Chosen People and feels a responsibility to watch over me. He can't imagine I find his solicitude and religious ramblings hard to bear.

But I won't go on about personal problems. After all, what am I supposed to be doing here if not overcoming my parasitic, antisocial tendencies through good hard work? I can't say I've been particularly successful yet, but I'm doing my best.

For example, I have given careful study to the list of civic obligations for our region. (It comes on stationery decorated by a team of reindeer superimposed upon the northern lights.) It tells me that by the end of the year we will have increased the head of reindeer in our herd to fifty thousand and lowered the incidence of sterility in the doe population to such an extent that we can expect seventy-four out of a hundred to bring forth young! Moreover, the local female blue foxes have pledged to produce 5.5 baby foxes per litter, and the local teachers have pledged to raise the literacy level of at least one hundred semiliterates by one full year of school. As for me and my stalwart colleagues of the river navigation fleet, we have pledged to fulfill our plan for the year by the twenty-fifth of September!

Given such bright prospects for the next few months and the nightly prospect of curling up on the pier with any number of Eskimo dogs to keep my legs warm, I have all but forgotten the possibility of a retrial. I am ready to stay here as long as society deems it useful. Yes, I have never come so close to being like everyone else; in fact—and who could ask for a more beautiful mission on earth?—I'm beginning to merge with my environs. So please thank the lawyer for what he's done, but tell him not to be disappointed if nothing comes of it.

One more favor. Give the following message to Frida (I'd write her a letter, but I can't make her see the simplest things): I've decided we can't go on living together. I'm sure she'll do a fine job of bringing up the girls and taking care of Father. I'm the problem. Besides, I don't want to think about the future now. All I see is darkness. Put it in a way she'll understand. You're good at that sort of thing. Sorry.

Danuta to Finkelmeyer:

Much has happened since I left Moscow. I have been sad in the way Russians call *toska*. I feel it—the sorrow, the boredom, the longing— every day. I was happy to come to Lithuania with good friends, but now Leopold Mikhailovich has died and you are in the North. I cannot stay here when I know that you will be in the North for four years. I will come and be with you. I know the North. I can do many things there. It is hard for you, but I am used to it. I will do nothing to bother you. I will only help.

I promised Leonid Pavlovich not to leave until we hear if there will be a retrial. That is, until the summer is over. But the summer is not too hard. Just the flies. I know you want to be alone. Even when I am there you can still be alone. But in the North it is bad to be all alone. And when your sentence is over, I will go back to Lithuania. I will never bother you.

Finkelmeyer to Nikolsky:

I cried like a baby all the way through Leopold Mikhailovich's manuscript. Only now have I begun to accept the fact that he is no longer with us. For a long time it seemed like a hoax. When people told me he was alive, he was dead, so when they told me he was dead, I decided he was alive. In jail, perhaps, or in exile, like me. I kept listening to the stories of the new arrivals, hoping to catch his name. But now I feel an emptiness inside, the same emptiness I see all around me. Reading the manuscript, I had the feeling that everything was fading, disappearing, like a print being developed in reverse.

It must have started earlier, though. After recovering from my illness, I began looking at things differently. My consciousness used to be somewhat of a meat grinder, reducing everything that came its way to a mince of words and verses. Now nothing touches me. I am calm. I don't let words take over. I write nothing but letters and thieves' songs, forms that fit clear-cut molds. There won't be a third part to my dramatic poem; there won't be anything anymore.

Now I see it was all lies. The worst kind of immortality. I stopped at nothing when my writing was at stake. It all began with those first publications. I'll never forgive myself for setting foot on that slippery, slimy road. Life has rewarded me accordingly. I've turned into the most ordinary of men, thank God, and left behind the morass I was living in. For the first time in my life I feel light and airy inside, and when I read Leopold Mikhailovich's manuscript I experienced a relief that I'm sure will never leave me. Day and night I whisper "Thank you, thank you, thank you" to him.

Forgive me for writing so much about this.

It is summer. The Samoyeds have let the reindeer loose in the tundra, but they'll be back once the first snow falls.

Nikolsky to Finkelmeyer:

CONGRATULATIONS COURT'S DECISION REPEALED CASE CLOSED DOCUMENTS IN PREPARATION DETAILS FOLLOW NIKOLSKY

Nikolsky to Finkelmeyer:

Light the fires! Roll the drums! I don't know about you, but I'm going to get rip-roaring drunk when you come home. Not that I'm sober very often as it is. There's too much going on. I won't go into my personal life except to say that after I left my old job, I bummed around for a few weeks and then started a new one. I don't imagine I'll last long there either—the work is boring and the pay miserable.

Greetings from Mikhail Leopoldovich. That's right: Vera's son by Leopold Mikhailovich. He's all of a month old and Vera's pride and joy. Remember her friend Zhenya? Well, she's running the show like the head nurse at a maternity ward. Roly-polies are either rattlebrains or sweethearts, don't you think?

Now about your case. The lawyer is a genius. It may have looked as though they'd backed him into a corner by the end of the trial, but in fact he'd *decided* to pull back the better to come out punching in the next round. As I think I told you, his first move was to get the Master's hackles up and bring out the troublemaker in him. The Master implicated everybody he could: his old enemy and Prebylov and Manakin in the Writers Union plus half the publishing house. The lawyer's strategy was to make things so hot for the big shots that they themselves would beat a retreat. And that's exactly what happened. They blamed it all on Manakin. The publishers suddenly discovered (not without the lawyer's assistance) that (and I quote) "Manakin failed to provide us with the original, that is, the Tongor manuscript" and called upon him to produce it. When Manakin failed to respond, they made inquiries at the District Committee where he is in charge of Tongor culture, and before long the machine started working in reverse and exonerated you completely. You will enter Moscow on a white charger, the dragon at your feet.

Picture my room. It's nine or so. I've just finished supper. I'm raising my glass (and not for the first time) to the triumph of justice when all at once the doorbell rings. I open the door to find—Comrade Manakin in person! Well, well, to what do I owe the pleasure? I ask, pouring him some Stolichnaya and waiting for him to stay Stop. He doesn't, the son of a bitch, so all I've got is a drop left for a toast. Anyway, there he sits, looking around inquisitively, and then I realize what's wrong: he's surprised to find such a bigwig (I told him I was high up in the ministry, remember?) living in such a pigsty (I haven't been looking after myself lately). Well, I make up for it by giving him some sausage to eat, and he gobbles it down with nary a chew. And even then I might have felt sorry for him if he hadn't begun pouring out his soul.

"Aronmendelch" may have gone heavy on the pantheism, he said, but he gave Manakin his fair share; Prebylov was all Tongor pride in honest labor, but he gave Manakin next to nothing. And when the letters started coming in from Moscow—Moscow was dissatisfied with Manakin!—the District Committee decided not to wait for a decision from the top and pow! socked him with (1) incompetence (read: he'd made a mess of his "cultural mission"), (2) amoral behavior (read: he comes to work drunk all the time), and (3) deceiving the Party leadership about his literary activities (read: we don't want to be implicated in the scandal). So goodbye Party sinecure, goodbye Party card, goodbye Writers Union!

Anyway, here he is in Moscow to plead his case, and no one will even see him. And then you know what happened? He burst into tears!

The only way I could get him to stop was to open a bottle of three-star Armenian cognac I had stowed away for a special occasion. Well, he tossed a glass of it off in one go and calmed down enough to say, "Put in a good word, Comrade Nikossky! You told me to write the book. Now I cannot be a writer. Now I cannot be an official. Now I cannot be a hunter—my eye is weak, my hand shakes, I am fat, I can hardly walk." Then he launched into a string of curses that made my hair stand on end. And all aimed at Aronmendelch. Well, I really gave it to him. "You fucking bastard, you! It's time you knew that while you were living the life of a prince you sent Aronmendelch to four years of exile in the North. Aaron is my closest friend, and if you say one more word against him I'll knock your block off. And while we're at it, only a blockhead like you could think I had anything to do with a ministry and was anything but a filthy clerk in a stinking office!"

You should have seen his face! He put on his coat and hat like a sleepwalker, and when I shoved him into the elevator, he just stood there. I had to yell at him several times before he pushed the button. The moment he disappeared, I polished off the cognac.

Now a few words about Frida. I went to see her as soon as I heard the news. Well, she had her cry, of course, but then she had some news for me. Remember telling me about a boy from her street who'd ended up at the orphanage with her? Nonka Maizelis was his name. Well, she kept in touch with him—you apparently knew about it—and when she told him about your exile he rushed to Moscow from the gasline he was laying somewhere in Belorussia (he's an engineer) and offered to help. She told him she could get by on what you'd left her, but he still slipped her a little bundle. Why not?

Anyway, he started visiting her regularly, and I don't suppose I need to spell it out for you. Before long they were wallowing in true confessions: he hadn't married and couldn't forget their childhood infatuation; she'd never been happy without him. Then you wrote and said you didn't think you and Frida should go on living together. To cut a long story short, the lovebirds resolved to keep their distance until you returned, and suddenly here you are practically on your way! Frida is all plans. Nonka has a nice little nest egg and an astronomical salary, and—Frida made a special point of this—the girls are wild about him.

So that's how things stand, and if you ask me they couldn't be better. Frida cries and says she'll always love you as a brother and then laughs and says, "And I thought I loved Nonka as a brother! Women don't know their own minds."

What about men, Aaron? We'll have to talk that one over when you're back.

Finkelmeyer to Danuta:

I've sent in all the paperwork. I'll take the first plane out when it comes back. But I won't leave this place the way I came seven months ago. First of all, I look different: I'm going gray, I'm even skinnier than I was, and I've lost two front teeth. But I'm different inside too: my character and my view of life have changed. Things I used to ignore are important to me now, and things I pondered for hours on end don't concern me in the slightest. It's hard to explain, but the man you knew is no more. Or almost. We always felt it would be wrong for us to stay together, though we never quite put it into words. Now I wonder. I'm a different man, Danuta; maybe we do belong together. In one of your letters you said, "I know you want to be alone." But I don't. Not anymore. I want something different.

So if you have no objections, this is what I'll do: after two or three days in Moscow, just enough to see the girls and a few friends, I'll come and stay with you in Palanga. I'm not required to start work for a month, and Lyonya will lend me enough to live on, so I can unwind for a while and think over the future with you. We could go back to Moscow, or we could stay in Lithuania. I'm a pretty good bookkeeper; I can find work anywhere—in an office or factory, even on a collective farm. I'd be perfectly happy to live in the country if it made you happy. It's up to you. In the meantime I'll just hope and wait.

XI

IN THE early twilight of the Arctic September, when village life comes to a standstill, a stranger appeared at the post office and knocked on the locked door.

"We're closed!" came a woman's voice from inside.

"Open! Open!" the stranger shouted back. "I come from Moscow!"

The door finally opened, and the stranger pushed two voluminous suitcases into the room.

"Hey!" the woman shouted, trying to stop him.

But the stranger bent down, unzipped one of the suitcases, and pulled out a box of chocolates.

"From Moscow," he said. "For you."

Dumbfounded, the woman took the gift.

Then the stranger bent over again, took something else out of the suitcase, and stuck it under his arm.

"I have many gifts," he said with a drunken giggle. "I will leave my things here. I have come to see a friend. Come from Moscow."

"Well, I suppose it's all right. I'll be on duty at the telegraph until eight. Who is it you're looking for?"

The stranger pulled a soiled scrap of paper out of his pocket.

"Oh, him. See that *izba* over there on the hill? The one with the four windows and the light on?"

She locked the door after him and watched him through the window.

Instead of going to the *izba,* he headed in the direction of some Samoyed tents he had noticed on his way from the airstrip. He chose the one made of the finest skins and stood outside it, making a high-pitched "Ee-yoo" noise until a flap opened and a man came out. The man stood there, silent and motionless except for a jaw moving up and down.

"You chew tobacco?" the stranger asked. He took a deep breath and let it out with a snort and a giggle. "You drink perfume, cologne? No good." He thrust his right hand under his left arm and produced a small flat bottle of cognac. "I have liquor. Much liquor. From Moscow."

The Samoyed nearly fell as he reached for the bottle, but the stranger whisked it out of his range.

"You Yakut?" asked the Samoyed.

"Yes, Yakut, Yakut. You want liquor? I have more. In the post office. I need reindeer."

The Samoyed turned and entered the tent, an invitation for the stranger to continue their conversation in warmer surroundings.

Half an hour later the stranger left the tent and teetered back to the village.

"Why didn't you see your friend?" the woman at the post office asked.

"I have much time," said the man, laughing and picking up his suitcases.

"You're not one of them, are you? You're not a Samoyed."

"No," he said jovially. "Yakut, Yakut."

When he returned to the tent with the suitcases, there were two powerful reindeer standing there. He inspected the reindeer with the eye of an expert. He was satisfied. Then he and the Samoyed repacked the contents of the suitcases into two bundles, leaving out three large dark-brown bottles. The Samoyed tugged at the corks and stuck his index finger down the necks of all three bottles, each time holding the finger up to his eyes, then carefully licking it clean. He too was satisfied.

They went into the tent and sat down. The guest had brought in some smoked sausage, and the host ordered his wife to bring in some fish. They ate and drank in silence. Then the stranger put on the fur jacket his host had given him.

"You big there," said the Samoyed, pointing to his guest's stomach.

The stranger frowned, and his drunken mien lost its joviality for a moment.

"You heavy. Reindeer ride slow."

"I must take the plane tomorrow," the stranger said to the Samoyed suspiciously. "Tomorrow morning."

"Dark soon. Road not see. Reindeer ride slow-slow."

They went outside. The Samoyed skillfully flung the bundles over the back of one of the reindeer and saddled the other as close to the withers as possible. The heavy stranger mounted clumsily, but straightened up as soon as he was in the saddle. He coaxed the animal into a walk, then slid off.

"The reindeer is good. He did not lie down" he said. "Show the way."

The Samoyed turned, stretched out an arm, and said, "Ice." That was the north, the ocean. Then he turned in the opposite direction, stretched out the other arm, and said, "Water."

"The river," said the stranger.

"River," the Samoyed repeated, and then said, "Water, road," indicating that the water should be on the man's left. "Water near road." He turned again and pointed to the sky. "Weather bad."

The stranger took the reins without a word and set off for the village. The Samoyed watched him go and disappeared into the tent.

The village was in total darkness by then. There were no streetlights, only a bulb here and there—at the warehouses, the general store, the post office. The stranger did not pass a soul. He circled the hill, looking for a post to hitch the reindeer to. He felt no need to hide them. He scrambled up the hill and, after leaning against the back wall of the *izba* to wait for his blood to stop pounding, peered through a window. But the incline was so steep that if he stood outside the square of light streaming from the window all he could see was a white ceiling and bare light bulb. He went over to the corner of the *izba*, grabbed hold of a log that stuck out from the others, inserted a foot between two of the lower logs, hoisted his heavy torso up to window level, and slid back to the ledge with his free hand. Thus pressed cruciform against the wall, he could look straight into the room.

Four men were sitting around an up-ended box playing cards; two more were asleep, one fully dressed and clearly drunk, the other in his underwear, tattoos shining.

The stranger slipped to the ground unnoticed and went back to the reindeer. He loosened the harness to get at one of the bundles and pulled out two flasks, which he concealed under the fur jacket the Samoyed had given him. Then he scrambled up the hill again.

The knock interrupted the players' concentration.

"Shut the fucking door, for Christ's sake!" one of them shouted.

The stranger squinted at each one in turn and said nothing.

"What do you want, walrus face?"

"He wants us to give it to him."

"Fuck that! They stink to high heaven, those Samoyeds!"

"How do you know he's a Samoyed?"

"Look at his fucking jacket."

"Well, fat ass, you gonna tell us what you want?"

He went up to them and held out the scrap of paper with a frown. "I am looking for him."

They put their heads together and sounded out the name.

"What do you want him for?"

He did not answer. He knew what he would say when the time came, but for the time being he said nothing.

One of them set fire to the paper with his cigarette. "Hey, walrus face! You don't tell us what you want him for, we don't tell you where he is. And you don't leave here with your pants on, get it?"

"Liquor." He had said the magic word. The men were all ears. "Four glasses. One comes with me, shows me where he is; three stay here. When I come back, I will give you four glasses. Good Moscow liquor."

"You wouldn't lie to us, would you, you bastard?" But the desire to believe him was stronger than the desire to jump him.

"You three stay! You"—he poked the one who struck him as the most harmless—"come with me."

"Sh-i-i-t!" the chosen man said as he stood.

"Go on, get a move on," the others said, pushing him out after the stranger, "and don't come back without the booze!"

They went down the hill in the direction of the river. After they had walked along the bank for a while, the guide turned and pointed to a shack on the pier. "Look. There he is."

Just to make sure, the stranger moved closer. The river or, rather, a broad baylike expanse of water, stretched before them into invisibility. In a square of light hanging in the darkness as in a void the stranger saw two men talking intensely across a table.

"Satisfied? He's on night duty."

"All night?"

"He's the watchman on the pier, shithead! You think he's out there for his health?"

They headed back to the hill. The stranger calmed down the guide by taking the two flasks out from under his jacket.

"Ninety-proof?" asked the guide, unable to believe his luck.

"Ninety-proof. Drink."

He took a swig, groaned a rapturous groan, rushed up the hill, and disappeared in the flash of light between the opening and closing of the door.

The stranger unhitched his reindeer and hurried back to the river with them. The wind was strong. The wind was cold. Wind from the north. Bad weather, the Samoyed said. But wind is good. Wind hides sound, sound of reindeer, all sound. Wind, winter. Beasts, hunting. Money, liquor. A woman cooking.

There they were. One was reading from a book. He was young, he had long hair, his lips were moving. The stranger's blood began to pound again. Blood must not pound; blood must flow. Slowly. He waited until his blood flowed slowly again. Only then did he

notice a low brick structure near the riverbank. He laughed with
joy when he reached it: he could easily see the two men from there,
and the wall hid him and protected him from the wind. He brought
the reindeer down under the eaves, one on each side of himself.
Now it was time to rest. Rest eyes. Rest hands. Soon he would act,
act fast. Now he rested. But first he would drink. He removed a
flask from the pack. He drank and drank and drank. He was too
tired to stop. He hid the flask under his jacket. He looked at his
watch. Half past ten.

He would wait. He was good at waiting. He could wait like a
tree. Better. The tree did not know it was waiting. He knew. He
was like a beast. The beast knows. The hunter knows. The beast
knows well. The hunter knows better. Eh-ta-ha, to-yo-ho! He is
better than the beast. The beast does not know everything. He knows
everything. He knows liquor, he knows money. Money is good.
Furs are better. He knows more than others know. He knows the
taiga. He knows Moscow. The taiga gives furs. Stupid taiga. Moscow takes furs and gives liquor. Much liquor, few furs. Stupid Moscow. He knows better. He knows the plane. Not the plane he took
here. People saw him. Dangerous. Good reindeer. Nice reindeer.
The reindeer will take him to the next airport.

He would wait. He was good at waiting. Eleven. He could wait
one more round of the clock. He could not wait longer. The plane
would not wait. But he was good at waiting.

He took another swig from the flask. The wind had begun to
howl. It blew an empty can along the rocks; it blew water in from
the ocean. The bay growled. Waves beat against the piles; nearly
invisible boats and motor launches bobbed on clanking chains. The
wind grew stronger, the waves more daring until one washed across
the pier itself, and another, and another, casting a powerful, insis-
tent, admonitory spell.

The shack door opened. The wind practically tore it off its hinges.
A shadow flashed across the light. It was a man running along the
slippery planks, clumsily waving his arms to keep his balance. Closer
and closer he came, until he was bending over the side, tugging on
a chain, arching over the dark waters.

He was good at waiting and had waited well. He felt the cold
rifle against his hand. The bullet did not have far to go. Fly bullet,
fly. The bullet knows.

Flash! Clutching the chain, bony knees buckling, the man on the pier plunged headlong into the cold Stygian deep and by the time he surfaced, his fingers had released his light underwater body from the now useless chain. He floated quickly out of sight.

Soon the reindeer were racing through the tundra.

"Aion neprigen! O-o-o! A!" the stranger shouted, laughing. *"Aion neprigen!* Tongor!"

The reindeer galloped through the tundra. The man had forgotten the words of the Samoyed: "Reindeer ride slow-slow." The man was in a hurry, he was happy, he was drunk. Good fortune had come to the Tongor. It was taking him away from the tundra, taking him south to the plane that would come in the morning and take him to another plane that would take him to a helicopter that would take him to the taiga! Then he would be a true Tongor again. *Aion neprigen!* O-o-o! A! *Aion neprigen!* Tongor!

The reindeer flew through the tundra as if they feared the wind and wanted to escape it. But what they really feared was the man. The reindeer he was riding had never carried such a heavy load, and the man kept sliding to one side, making the animal stretch its neck painfully to the other.

He slid to one side whenever he took a swig from his flask. He still had a good supply, both under his jacket and in the pack. He had sold all his furs in Moscow, sold them for liquor. Moscow was clever. But he knew more. He had fooled Moscow. He took liquor, not money. Stupid Moscow. Run fast, reindeer! Stupid tundra. Stupid river. Hey! Hee! Stupid wind. Run fast, reindeer! Run faster than the stupid wind!

But the reindeer carrying him stumbled to a halt and lay down, and the other one stood close by, bending its neck over it. The Samoyed was a bad man. He had sold him a bad reindeer. The man took the rifle out of his pack. The wind blew straight in his face. He had trouble breathing, seeing. He held the rifle close to the reindeer's snout and fired.

Then he mounted the other reindeer. He left his pack on the frozen ground next to the reindeer that had carried him before—he took only his rifle, which he slung over his back, and the two remaining bottles of liquor, which he tucked into his jacket—and off they went. He knew he should not stop, but soon he needed a drink. The plane would take him away in the morning. The road knew where to stop. The road knew where the plane was. The big plane would wait for him. It was standing and waiting for him. Waiting to take him home.

Aion neprigen! The sun is out! Sun and snow. Hunting. Furs. Liquor. A woman cooking.

The Tongor goes to sleep. The Tongor has come home. *Aion neprigen.*

For some time the man sat propped against the heaving reindeer, his legs spread wide. But the wind was of hurricane velocity, and the animal could not remain on the ground for long. It stood. The man fell back. The animal set off, as before, in the direction of the wind, but quickly descended the slope to the river, which curved to the east there and thus afforded it shelter.

The first snow swept across the tundra that day. It soon covered the little mound the animal had left behind. It raged on through the night, the first long night of an early winter.

EPILOGUE

THOUGH DRESSED in the height of foreign fashion (down to the Sabena bag hanging from his shoulder), the lanky young man did not particularly stand out in the Moscow crowd. True, there were many foreign tourists now, but there were even more young Muscovites who managed to put together the outfits, grow the hair, and ape the Euro-American way of walking and even looking you in the eye. Not that Mother Russia (who is inclined to ignore certain things or not take them far enough) doesn't keep her hold on some, especially the young ladies. Still, there was something definitely non-native about the tall young man with the delicate brown eyes and luxuriant black curls. Why, for example, did he seem so unfamiliar with the city, carefully reading the names of the streets and the numbers of the houses? If he was a foreigner, though, what was he doing so far from Gorky Street? And how was it that when asking his way he didn't act like a representative of civilization among the barbarians? How was it that he had no trouble with Russian, indeed, that he spoke it with no trace of an accent?

"Who are you looking for?" the woman sitting next to the elevator challenged when he slowed his pace after entering the building.

"Nikolsky. Leonid Pavlovich Nikolsky. He lives in flat fifty-nine, I believe."

"Eighth floor," she said, and true to her profession she couldn't help muttering, "He *believes!* If you've got a reason to see somebody, you should *know.*"

"Thank you very much," the young man said with such sincerity that the woman glared back as if to say, Awfully polite, these longhairs. You never know what they're *really* thinking.

It was a lazy summer Saturday, and the doorbell got Nikolsky off the sofa. He trudged to the door wondering not very enthusiastically who it could be.

Nikolsky had turned into a heavy drinker. He had been going through a particularly bad patch lately, and when the bell rang he was musing whether his next spree would take him back to a sober-ing-up station or on to a mental institution. And suddenly there was that boy at the door.

"Hello. I'm terribly sorry to bother you, but you wouldn't be Leonid Pavlovich Nikolsky, would you?"

"Yes, yes. Come in," said Nikolsky in a hoarse whisper. "And you are . . ."

"Don't I look like him?"

"Wait! Give me a minute to . . . What's your name?"

"My name is Alexander Burkov, but Burkov is my *father's* name, the name of my mother's husband, if you see what I mean."

The boy was quite at ease by now, which Nikolsky could not say of himself. In fact, he felt premature senility setting in.

"This is all so sudden. Look, let's sit down and take things in order. First, what do you want me to call you? Sasha?"

"Alex is what I'm used to, actually."

"Alex? Has a nice ring to it, though I can't say I've heard it used in Russian before."

"No. It's the influence of—what do you call it?—the decadent West."

He had an infectious laugh. This Alex was a nice kid.

"Actually, though, I've come to see you about something that may change my life," he said, suddenly dead serious. "What I mean is . . . can you tell me anything about Aaron Finkelmeyer?"

"I see, Alex, I see. And why should I?"

"Well, I think . . . I think I'm his son."

Nikolsky stood up, walked over to the window, and glanced down at the idiotic crowds milling in the street. All at once he banged the back of his hand on the windowsill and, gasping in pain, went back to the sofa.

"Aaron? Your father?" he repeated, rubbing his eyes with his fists in the hope of clearing his brain. "But how . . . No, we can discuss that later. . . . Where did you . . . No. Just tell me what you want to know, how much you know now."

"I know nothing, Leonid Pavlovich," Alex said softly. "I don't even know . . . whether he's alive."

If only he were. If only he could hand him over. He would have given his life to sit them down next to each other, here on this damned sofa.

"And he didn't know you existed."

"You say, 'He *didn't* know.' Does that mean . . ."

"Yes, Alex. Your father is dead. How old are you?"

"Nineteen," he answered mechanically, and Aaron Finkelmeyer flashed in the sad, fathomless depths of his eyes.

"Your father has been dead for eight years."

Nikolsky paused to give the boy time to accept the idea. To try and accept it himself. Eight years. Eight years. It was easy to calculate, because Vera's little devil Mishka was eight years old. His father too had been dead for eight years. Mishka had never known his father; Alex had never known his. Aaron had has so much in common with Leopold Mikhailovich, and now this as well. It was enough to make you believe in desti . . . in predestination.

"What can you tell me about him?"

"Everything," Nikolsky sighed, "and nothing."

"Well then . . ."

"Yes, of course. I'll tell you everything. But first I wonder if you wouldn't tell me . . . It's not just idle curiosity . . ."

"You want to know a little about *me* first, is that it? Who I am, how I found you."

He had a terrific smile, that kid.

"Well, not only did I never know my father, I never knew my mother."

"What?"

"At least that was no mystery," he said with a sad smile. "You see, my mother died in childbirth. Well, not exactly. They were living in the tropics, my mother and father, and—" He stopped short, disgusted with himself, and continued as if he were reading from a document. "My late mother, whose husband was a Soviet diplomat and trade representative by the name of Andrei Burkov, died of blood poisoning several days after my birth. Medical attention was hard to come by, as they were living in the tropics at the time."

"Why didn't they send her home to give birth?"

"It was spring there—autumn here—and there'd been torrential rains. All communications had been cut off."

"Cut off for weeks, months?"

"Apparently my mother had been concealing her pregnancy. I didn't know a thing until recently, when my father . . . You see, I still call him 'father'!"

"That's all right, Alex. Don't be embarrassed."

"Anyway, he told me my mother very much wanted to have me. She apparently loved my father, my real father, very much, and didn't realize she was pregnant until after she'd joined my father, my stepfather, abroad."

"Of course, of course!" Nikolsky cried, grabbing Alex by the arm. "Emma! That's was her name, wasn't it?"

"That's right! You mean you knew her?" Alex cried, grabbing Nikolsky, and they shouted back and forth, shaking each other.

"No, but he told me about her."

"So he remembered her?"

"She was his first . . . his first love."

"He didn't abandon her then?"

"How can you think such a thing? There was never a more romantic . . ."

"So they loved each other, and I . . ."

"Go on with your story, Alex. I'll tell you all about them later."

"My story," he said, calming down somewhat. "I hardly know what to say. My stepfather remarried. A woman he'd loved before he married my mother. It took three years to arrange. . . . I don't like talking about it."

"It's nothing, Alex. It happens all the time. You're young, that's all."

"Maybe," he said with Aaron's sad smile. "In any case, I've spent most of my life in our, you know, little 'workers' colonies' abroad, but I came here to finish school under the guidance of my father's relatives. From the start I had a feeling that something was wrong, but it took some time before I discovered what it was: my appearance! I didn't look a thing like my 'father,' and both he and my mother had light hair." He laughed again.

"I see. A Jewish look—is that what they saw in you?" Nikolsky asked with a frown.

"Yes, yes. Have I really got it? You know my father. Do I look like him?"

"We'll talk about that later. You're not through with your story yet."

"Okay. I finished school and entered the university, and then one day who should show up but dear step-papa. Well, he takes me out to dinner at the National—"

"The National!"

"Is something wrong?"

"No, no. Go on."

"And suddenly I'm Oliver Twist. You do know *Oliver Twist,* don't you?" And so saying, he removed a chain from his neck.

Nikolsky had noticed the chain and assumed it was for a cross, crosses being the rage at the time. But Alex handed him a medallion. "Be careful. It's . . ."

Nikolsky had an idea what it was. The face looking out at him from the medallion was a young, naive Aaron, a face at once unfamiliar and—now that he had Alex in front of him—very much alive. The photograph was encircled by a lock of shiny black hair.

"Mother told him everything and gave him this before she died. She wanted me to have it. Romantic, isn't it?"

"Watch your tongue there, young man," said Nikolsky gently.

"Sorry. Well, that's about it. . . . Oh, except for this." He pulled a little notebook out of his pocket, extracted a yellowed piece of newsprint from it, and handed Nikolsky "A Certain Finkelmeyer."

"Where did you find that?"

"My stepfather cut it out of the paper. He happened to be in Moscow at the time, recognized the name, and wondered whether the man wasn't the certain Finkelmeyer who had fathered his son."

Yes, he definitely had Aaron's propensity to laugh when he was down.

"It was the article that led me to you, actually," Alex said, immediately serious again.

"But how?"

"My stepfather looked into the matter before our dinner at the National, and the public prosecutor's office showed him the file. Your name figured as the prime witness for the defense."

"Why do you think your stepfather let you in on all this?"

Alex laughed again. "He's a good man, for one thing. But he's also the father of two little boys by my stepmother, and, well, I think he'd have an easier time of it if I weren't around."

"You mean—the look?"

"That too, perhaps. What do you think?"

"You never know."

"The funny thing is, I've already decided to—" He broke off.

"You've decided to . . ."

His face clouded over, and he asked Nikolsky as he would ask a boy his own age, "Promise you won't tell?"

"Tell what?"

"I have a . . . girl friend. Her name is Sandy. She's an American. A year ago I made up mind not to stay here. You can take it any way you like, but I don't feel at home here, and I know I never will. Besides, I have no one to keep me here, and Sandy's promised to get me out. She'll come on an exchange and we'll . . . we'll get married." He watched for Nikolsky's reaction as he laughed.

"You may have no one here, but you do have people abroad. And you can handle the whole thing a lot more easily through them."

"What do you mean?" Alex cried.

"Aaron, your father, was married. He had two daughters. They're a few years younger than you and your only blood relations. After Aaron died, their mother remarried and just last year the whole family—their name is Maizelis—emigrated to Israel."

Nikolsky paused. Alex said nothing.

"I promise to tell you everything from the beginning, and I start from the end."

"Then please tell me something else out of turn. Was my father's death connected with the trial?"

"It was."

"And one last thing, if it isn't too much to ask. The article makes a mockery of my father. Was he or was he not a poet?"

For a while Alex must have thought that the question had gone unheard, but Nikolsky had heard it, and the effort his eventual response cost him revealed how world-weary, life-weary he had become.

"See that bookshelf? See that row of volumes bound in blue? Those are your father's collected works. In typescript. There is no other edition." He paused. "Look, here's what I propose. I'll go out and do some shopping—I've got nothing to eat here and, more important, nothing to drink, God knows I need a drink—and meanwhile you can get to know your father through his poems. I won't be long."

Eight years, he thought as he closed the door behind him. Eight years had passed since the events he was now called upon to recall and recount. He'd gone downhill fast: here he was, just over forty, and he had all the signs of middle age. It wasn't only the alcohol either. He changed jobs too often, leaving on his own or being asked—sometimes politely, sometimes not—to leave; Victor had recently got him set up as an electrician at the taxi garage—a position that required no education whatever. He had stopped looking at women, or rather he tried not to look at them, and he was so unsure of himself that they didn't seem to notice him anymore. As for his friends, the few he had left, they pitied more than loved him; moreover, he accepted their pity, because he knew it was sincere, and sincerity was a virtue he did not meet with often.

Eight years. Uncle Lyonya had all but stopped going to visit Vera and Mishka, because Borya Khavkin was jealous of him, the idiot. Or maybe because the wonderful little Refuge had been torn down, may it rest in peace. Or because they had made their own refuge without it. Yes, *you* were the one who was jealous. Vera and Borya had lost something and then found something together, whereas he'd lost everything and found nothing. He'd lost Danuta. He had rushed down to comfort her, console her, as soon as they heard about Aaron, and—how could he have done it! how depraved, degenerate could he be!—he went berserk for a minute, a single minute, and everything fell to pieces. The next morning, half drunk, he wept at her feet, and she told him she didn't know, with time perhaps; she would always have considered him a friend; now he would have to leave; she never wanted to see him again.

He began to think about Aaron. Then Alex. Then himself again. He could really grow to like Alex, he thought, but Alex would soon be leaving. Everyone seemed to leave him, he thought. Aaron and Leopold Mikhailovich and the Master—who had died in the interim and been buried with great pomp—or Vera and Boris, Frida and her Nonka.

Well, he was on his way as well. Like the millions and millions who drowned their lives in alcohol. Everyone leaves as best he knows how, but the result is the same. No matter how the cost of vodka varies, the empty bottle is always worth twelve kopecks.

He tried to look at himself from the outside. At first it seemed

nothing but a cheap symbol to him, and then he thought, no, it is
perfectly normal:

while he was waiting his turn for vodka in a crowded basement
Alex was alone in his eighth-floor flat
reading Finkelmeyer's poems.

1971–75
Moscow